Daughters of Seferina

Lois Jean Thomas

This book is a work of fiction. Names, characters, places, and incidents are the product of the author's imagination or are used fictitiously. Any resemblance between events, locales, or persons, living or dead, is co-incidental.

Cover art by C. Zane Shetler

ISBN: 978-0-9910749-07
LCCN: 2013921697

This book is dedicated
to my friend Mary Ruth Fox,
who has been present with this story
since its inception.
Thank you for sharing the journey.

Contents

Acknowledgements

I can't begin to say how much I appreciate my husband Allen Thomas for his work in formatting this manuscript. Without your dedication and patience, Allen, this book would have never taken form.

I also owe much gratitude to my son C. Zane Shetler for creating the beautiful cover art. You're the best, Zane! I'm looking forward to sharing projects with you in the future.

The members of my writers groups, Marnie, Sue, Judy, Richard, Ann, Isabel, Elaine, April, and Bob, deserve credit for their help in making this a better story. Thank you all for bearing with me!

Part I

SISSY

Chapter 1

Cecily's fingers paused on the keyboard as the yellow banner flashed in the corner of her computer screen. The tiny print said, "Your 4:00 PM appointment has arrived." She glanced at her watch and saw that it was only 3:55.

I still have time to finish this, she thought. Her fingers flew rapidly over the keys, typing the last few sentences of the progress note on her previous client. Her shoulders ached with tension.

The ringing telephone interrupted her train of thought. A glance at her Caller ID told her the call came from Meredith's extension at the reception desk. She sighed wearily. Meredith tended to be obsessive about her job, and if the therapists didn't respond immediately to her computer alert, she'd feel the need to back up her electronic communication with a phone call.

Cecily picked up the receiver. "Yes, Meredith?" she said, trying not to sound irritable.

"Dr. Hartman-Gray, your intake appointment's ready," the receptionist announced in her shrill soprano voice. "He's here with his mother. She's got three other little ones with her. Poor thing has her hands full."

"Okay, Meredith, thanks for the heads up," Cecily said. "I'll be out in a minute."

As she hung up the phone, Cecily wondered for the hundredth time why South Bend Community Mental Health Center failed to hire a receptionist with a pleasant voice. She also wondered when Meredith would learn that not all the psychotherapists at the center could rightfully be called *doctor.* She, Cecily Hartman-Gray, was not a doctor; she was a Clinical Social Worker licensed in the state of Indiana.

She picked up a stack of papers faxed to the center from a near-by elementary School. She'd read the documents earlier in the day, but felt compelled to glance through them one more time. The first-grade teacher was concerned about the behavior of a six-year-old boy in her classroom, and had made a referral for a family assessment.

Cecily reached into her bottom desk drawer for her handbag, pulled out her makeup case, and checked her lipstick in a small mirror. She noticed the dark circles under her eyes.

God, I wish I could sleep, she thought. *I'd give anything for a good night's sleep.*

She ran her fingers through her shoulder-length auburn hair, fluffing it back from her face. Standing up, she straightened the slim, knee-length skirt of her gray business suit. As she walked toward her office door, a wave of weakness passed over her, and she leaned against the door jamb for support.

"Okay, Cecily," she murmured to herself. "You can get through this." She forced the tired lines of her face into a cheery smile and walked briskly down the hall toward the center's waiting room.

A minute later, she stood at the door as the family of five filed past into her office. "Please have a seat wherever you feel comfortable," she said.

She glanced again at the information sheet in her hand, double-checking names and ages. The form indicated that the mother, Michelle Wilson, was twenty-six years old, a year younger than Cecily. But Cecily thought Michelle looked at least forty.

The haggard woman was wearing sweatpants and an oversized tee-shirt, her straggly hair pulled into a ponytail. She carried seven-month-old Kayla in one arm, and a filthy diaper bag was slung over the other shoulder. Runny-nosed two-year-old Brittany toddled after her mother, followed by sad-faced seven-year-old Ashley. Six-year-old Tyler lagged sullenly behind the rest of the family.

Michelle glanced timidly around Cecily's immaculate office. Cecily prided herself in creating a soothing environment for her clients. The office was decorated in shades of soft blues and greens. A shimmering sun-catcher mobile hung in the window, and potted plants of various sizes sat on tables and shelves. Water in a small fountain trickled over a pile of stones, creating a mesmerizing sound.

Michelle seated herself on one end of the sofa, and Ashley sat on the other end. Little Brittany snuggled up to her older sister and popped a thumb into her mouth. Tyler sat on the edge of one of the large chairs and stared openmouthed at the fountain on the table opposite him.

"I'm glad you came," Cecily said, catching all the family members in the beam of her forced smile. She hoped she sounded convincing. "It looks like we have some important work to do together." She then focused her attention on Michelle and began reviewing with her the documents faxed from Tyler's school.

Little Brittany wriggled off the sofa and headed across the room toward shelves filled with toys and games. Ashley reached out and grabbed her little sister's shirt. "No, Brittany!" she whispered.

"She's okay," Cecily reassured Ashley. "Let her explore the toys." Ashley released her hold on the shirt, but kept an anxious eye on her sister while she rummaged through the playthings.

For several moments, Cecily sat transfixed, watching Ashley watch Brittany. Then she startled, realizing the interview had come to a halt. She glanced down at the papers in her hand, then looked up to meet Michelle's hopeful gaze.

I can't do this! The thought screamed through Cecily's mind, accompanied by a stabbing pain in her right temple. She winced and reached up to touch her head, and then caught herself. *Of course you can do it. You have to do it.* She took a deep breath and returned her attention to Michelle.

"So, Michelle, this is what the school has to report. How do things look from your point of view?"

Michelle's haggard face contorted with pain, and tears streamed from her eyes. Ashley scooted over on the sofa, and taking a tissue from the box Cecily offered, she pressed it into her mother's hand. Then she took Kayla from Michelle's arms and expertly cuddled the baby on her lap, as if she were accustomed to the task.

Brittany toddled back to the sofa with a stuffed rabbit in her arms and climbed back up to her seat beside her big sister. Ashley shifted Kayla's weight to her right arm and drew Brittany into the protective circle of her left arm.

As Cecily gazed at the trio of ragged little girls on the sofa, the pain in her chest was so unbearable, she could scarcely breathe. She forced her attention back to their mother.

"I can see you're very sad about this," she soothed the weeping woman.

Michelle began pouring out the details of her unhappy life, her tears flowing freely. Cecily willed herself to listen, murmuring words of sympathy, and she began drawing Tyler into the conversation as well. But her attention kept slipping back to the riveting scene on the other end of the sofa.

Cecily knew the scene was stirring up feelings from the deepest recesses of her memory. Her professional training had prepared her for this. She recalled the words of one of her graduate school professors.

"Just remember," old Anna Branson had said, looking sternly over the top of her bifocals at the class of budding mental health professionals. "Your unconscious mind is just as unconscious as anyone else's unconscious mind. Therapists aren't immune to having their own issues triggered."

This is a normal reaction, Cecily coached herself. *Focus! Focus! You can get through this.*

She could hear herself continuing the conversation with Michelle, her voice sounding surreal in her own ears. But each time she glanced over at the little girls on the sofa, the knot of pain in her chest grew tighter.

She willed herself not to look in their direction. She knew this was professionally inappropriate. She needed to draw Ashley into the therapeutic process, as the girl deserved to have her perspective acknowledged.

But Cecily was afraid to speak to the child. She couldn't bear to know the unspoken feelings harbored in the little girl's heart. Ashley reached up to brush the limp, untrimmed bangs from her face, and the gesture touched Cecily so deeply, tears welled in her eyes.

Get a grip, Cecily, she scolded herself. *You can't be falling apart like this!*

She didn't know how she managed to do it, but she made it through the haphazard interview. As Michelle stood up to leave, she beamed through her tears and gratefully clutched Cecily's extended hand. Cecily watched the family trail out of her office, wishing she had the confidence in herself that Michelle had in her.

She sat down at her desk and stared at the notes on her pad of paper, unable to comprehend what she'd written. She turned to her computer and brought up the assessment form on Tyler Wilson. When she began completing the section entitled, "Presenting Problem," her usually fluent writing came out nonsensical. She could not erase the picture of Ashley and her two little sisters from her inner vision, and she was too exhausted to ward off the flood of dark memories that had been lurking in the recesses of her mind.

All Cecily wanted to do was lay her head on her desk and weep.

Five-year-old Sissy Dickerson sits on a rumpled bed pushed up against one wall of the tiny bedroom. Four-year-old Starly sits on the frayed, dirty carpet, holding a half-dressed doll. Baby Shaney lies on the bed beside Sissy, sleeping on her tummy.

Sissy shivers at the sounds of violence in the kitchen.

"Take it easy there, Seffie," Jimmy pleads in his high-pitched whine. "Just calm down now."

Sissy hears another crash, and Mommy Seffie's voice explodes into a string of profanities.

Starly hurls the doll across the room and throws herself on the floor. She kicks her legs and pounds her fists, screaming hysterically. Baby Shaney wakes up, rolls over, and joins Starly in a chorus of wailing.

"Be quiet, Starly!" Sissy whispers. "You have to be quiet, or Mommy Seffie might come in here."

Starly's cries drown out Sissy's words. She gets up on her hands and knees and bangs her head on the bedroom wall.

Sissy scrambles down and wraps her arms around Starly's middle. Using all the strength in her little body, she heaves her struggling sister onto the bed, and then climbs up after her. She sits with her back against the wall and pulls Starly close to her, holding one hand over her sister's mouth to muffle her cries.

She spots Shaney's baby bottle in the folds of the covers, dripping milk from the nipple onto the filthy bedclothes. She shoves the nipple into Shaney's mouth. The baby sniffles several time, then begins to

suck. Sissy rocks Starly gently and sings the lullaby Mommy Eileen al-
ways sang to her.

"Hush little baby, don't say a word . . ."

Starly's screams subside to sobs. Sissy releases her hand from her
sister's mouth and begins to stroke Starly's head. One of Starly's long
braids has come undone, and her hair is tangled and matted.

"Sissy's gonna buy you a mockingbird . . ."

The front door slams, the impact reverberating throughout the mo-
bile home. Then all is quiet. A moment later, Jimmy opens the bedroom
door and anxiously peers in. His fat face relaxes at the sight of the trio
of little girls huddled together on the bed.

"Good girl, Sissy," he says.

Cecily stared at the computer screen, trying in vain to complete the
assessment form. She typed a sentence, then deleted it and started
over again.

"Give it a rest, Cecily! My God, you don't have to be perfect all the
time!"

Cecily startled at the sound of the voice. She looked up to see her
coworker Amanda standing in her doorway, looking as unprofessional
as ever. She wondered how her fellow therapist managed to avoid a
citation for violating the agency's dress code.

Amanda was wearing a short denim skirt that showed way too much
leg, especially on a girl as plump as she was. Her black top was embel-
lished with colorful beads in the shape of a butterfly, and her footwear
was nothing more than glorified flip-flops. It looked like she'd given up
on her hair for the day. She'd pulled it back into a ponytail, and the various layers stuck out at odd angles.

"Your paperwork can wait until tomorrow, Cecily," Amanda scolded.
"Just go home on time for a change. You make the rest of us therapists
look bad, you know."

Cecily forced a tired smile. "I won't be long," she said. "I just want
to finish this section, and then I'll go."

As Amanda's flip-flopping footsteps echoed down the hallway, Cecily
focused her attention back onto her computer screen. But a moment

later, she smelled the musky scent of a man's cologne. Without look-ing up, she knew Dr. Evan Carter was standing in her doorway.

Evan Carter did the psychological testing for the clinical team Cecily belonged to. He was approaching forty, and was so erotically hand-some that he made the women around him feel inadequate. Currently divorced, he had the reputation of being the office Lothario, and he didn't hesitate to use his sexy good looks to his advantage.

Cecily had been the recipient of his artfully subtle advances from time to time. While she felt flattered by the fact that Evan was attract-ed to her, being near him made her uneasy.

"Such a dedicated worker," Evan said theatrically in his smooth bari-tone voice.

As Cecily glanced up, she was struck by the impression that he'd just stepped out of the pages of a men's fashion magazine. He was leaning against her door jamb, hands in his pants pockets, tie loosened, and shirt collar open. His stylishly cut black hair, tinged with gray at the temples, was slightly tousled. His dark eyes looked at her with both amusement and unveiled admiration.

Cecily averted her gaze. "I'm just trying to get as much of this as-sessment done as I can. I have a full schedule tomorrow. I don't like getting behind with my paperwork."

"Cecily, you push yourself too hard," Evan said with genuine concern in his voice. "You've looked dead tired all day. If you keep this up, you'll burn yourself out in another couple of years. I'd hate to see that happen."

Evan's words struck a nerve, and tears sprang into Cecily's eyes.

"Hey there, young lady, what's wrong?" Evan stepped uninvited into her office and seated himself on the sofa, leaning toward her in a pos-ture of attentiveness. "Something's been going on with you. You ha-ven't been yourself recently. Is administration giving you a hard time?"

Cecily shook her head.

"Or is it a personal problem?"

Cecily felt a tear escape and slide down her cheek. She reached up to brush it away, and Evan caught her hand in his as she lowered it to her lap.

"Talk to me, Cecily," he urged.

Cecily panicked as she felt her defenses begin to crumble. Part of her wanted to move over to the sofa and sob in Evan's arms like a distraught child. But a small voice of reason told her this was not the time to let her guard down.

"I just did a difficult assessment," she said. "For some reason, it got to me."

"I know these clients can bring you down." Evan's other hand covered hers in a tender gesture. "You really need to make a point of taking care of yourself. I don't think you've been doing that."

Cecily found herself squeezing Evan's hand ever so slightly. But a sudden thought jolted her mind and rescued her from the brink of complete vulnerability.

"Oh my God!" she exclaimed, pulling her hand free. "I almost forgot. I'm supposed to be at my parents' house at six."

Evan looked startled at her sudden change in demeanor.

"My husband works late on Wednesdays," she explained. "He teaches an evening class at Notre Dame. I always have dinner with my parents on Wednesday. I need to get out of here."

She logged off her computer, and while it was shutting down, she gathered the papers from her desk top and shoved them in a drawer.

"Are we the last ones in the building?" Evan asked.

"I think so," Cecily said, feeling embarrassed, as if she'd been caught in an after-hours tryst.

Evan stood beside her as she nervously entered her code in the security box by the back exit. He held the door for her as they quickly left the building to avoid triggering the alarm.

"Remember, Cecily, I'm here for you," he said as they stepped out into the warm May evening. "Let me know if you need to talk. I'm available anytime. You can even call me at home if you need to."

"Thanks, Evan." It frightened Cecily to realize that she appreciated his offer.

Chapter 2

It took Cecily only twelve minutes to drive from the community mental health center to her parents' home on the southwest side of the city, scarcely enough time to clear job worries from her mind and shift into the mode of Leonard and Eileen Hartman's beloved daughter. But as she pulled into her parents' driveway, the sight of their beautifully restored Victorian house lifted her spirits. She loved visiting the home in which she'd spent most of her childhood years.

"Cecily, you look exhausted," Leonard Hartman said as the family sat down to dinner. "Have you been working too hard again?"

"I always work hard," Cecily answered, smiling bleakly. "It's part of being a professional person."

"You're losing weight again, aren't you, dear?" Eileen reproached, scrutinizing her daughter's appearance. "Your face looks thin."

"Cecily, there's no need for you to be overdoing it like this," Leonard continued. "Stephen makes enough money at Layman Labs to support both of you in fine style. You're running yourself ragged for a few thousand dollars a year. It's not worth it. Why don't you take it easy for awhile?"

"Look, Dad," Cecily said, a hint of irritation in her voice. "I'm not working because I need to. I'm working because I want to. Right now, I'm doing exactly what I want to do with my life." She immediately regretted her tone of voice when she saw the pained expressions on her parents' faces.

Leonard opened his mouth to press his point, but closed it again when his wife shot him one of her *that's enough* looks. Then Eileen steered the conversation to the innocuous topic of her work as an office volunteer at the First United Methodist Church.

"Reverend Thompson will be starting a new sermon series next month," she said. "It sounds interesting. I typed the announcement for the church newsletter this morning."

Cecily smiled fondly at the parents whom she knew loved her more than life itself, and whom she loved dearly in return.

Leonard and Eileen could not be called a handsome couple, but what they lacked in physical beauty, they made up for in style. Cecily's father was a short, stocky, ruddy-faced man in his late sixties, but his carefully combed snow-white hair, his expensive tailored suits, and his confident manner gave him an air of dignity.

Four years ago, Leonard Hartman had retired from his position of vice-president of a large corporation in South Bend. His extraverted personality and his ability to communicate with people had contributed to his career success. His sonorous bass voice was warm, but commanding. Having belonged to the Toastmasters club for years, he was well known for his spellbinding motivational speeches, and was still called upon to speak to church and civic groups.

Two years older and several inches taller than her husband, Eileen Hartman was a fine-boned woman with a thin, nervous, but kindly face. If she hadn't tended to her appearance so meticulously, she could have been described as homely, with her long nose and receding chin. But Eileen did her full routine of styling her hair and applying makeup every day of her life. Cecily had never seen her mother appear anything less than impeccably groomed.

Eileen had started a career in banking in her early twenties. By the time she was thirty-five, she'd worked her way up to the position of loan officer at First National Bank. But when Cecily had come into the Hartmans' lives, Eileen had happily called a halt to her career in order to devote her time to raising their only child.

When Cecily had left home to attend college eight years ago, Eileen had attempted to fill the hole in her heart by focusing on the renovation of their Victorian house. After his retirement, Leonard had taken up the hobby of landscaping, and the Hartman home was now a wonder to behold.

If the Hartmans had been able to produce a biological child, it wouldn't have been half as beautiful as their beloved Cecily. Their adopted daughter was of medium height and slender build, with thick auburn hair, bright blue eyes, and a flawless fair complexion. Eileen's most cherished possession was her collection of photo albums filled with pictures of Cecily at various ages, dressed in one adorable outfit after another.

Leonard and Eileen had met when they were both living in Elkhart, Indiana, and they'd married when they were in their early thirties. They'd spent six agonizing years trying to conceive a child. When they realized having a biological child was not a possibility, they focused their attention on adoption.

However, the Hartmans were disappointed to discover that adoption agencies were hesitant to place newborn infants with couples approaching forty. Undaunted, they turned to the local welfare department and became licensed foster parents, in the hopes of adopting a child through that system.

Again, they suffered disappointment. It seemed as soon as they became attached to the little ones placed in their care, the children would be snatched away to be reunited with their biological parents. Leonard and Eileen could take no more heartbreak. They informed the welfare department they would only accept foster children who were available for adoption.

Three years went by with no contact from the welfare department, and the Hartmans began to reconcile themselves to life without a child.

Then came that unforgettable day in September.

Now, almost twenty-four years later, as Eileen gazed at Cecily's weary face across the dinner table, she was struck by the fact that her daughter's sad blue eyes hadn't changed a bit since that day.

It was a rainy Wednesday afternoon. Leonard was at the office, and Eileen had just come home from her work at the bank. She'd stopped by the drugstore to buy hair conditioner, and had then picked up Leonard's suits from the cleaners. Juggling the suits, the bag from the store, and an umbrella, she stood on the front steps of their home in the pouring rain, fumbling with her keys.

Then she heard the phone ringing. Suddenly, she was filled with an unexplainable sense of urgency. She draped the suits over the stair railing, found the right key, unlocked the door, and rushed soaking wet to the phone in the kitchen. She picked it up on the fourth ring.

"Hello," she said breathlessly.

"Oh," said the frantic voice on the other end of the line. "I was afraid you weren't home. I've been calling all day, and either no one's at home or they don't have any room. Thank God you're home!"

"Who is this?" Eileen asked, bewildered.

"I'm sorry," the caller said. "This is Mindy Barnes from Elkhart County Child Protective Services. This has been the day from hell, and I think I'm on the verge of losing my mind. Bear with me, okay?"

"Sure," Eileen said, curious about Mindy's mission.

"I've got a little three-year-old here in need of an emergency foster care placement," Mindy explained. "The police brought her in this morning. Like I said, I've been calling all day and can't find anyone who can take her. I know we haven't used you for several years, but your foster care license is still active. Would you be willing to take her? At least for a few days?"

Eileen stood frozen, gripping the telephone receiver. A thousand questions raced through her mind, but she couldn't find the words to ask them. Somehow, it seemed like destiny was hanging on this moment.

Finally she said, "We've told your department we'll only take children who are available for adoption. Is this little girl free for adoption?"

"To be honest with you, no, she's not," Mindy said nervously. "But I think there's a ninety-nine percent chance that she will be in the very near future. Her mother was arrested this morning for dealing drugs, and she'll probably be doing some time in prison. She's got a long police record, and she's very young, only nineteen. Our department has received all kinds of calls on her. This little girl has already spent eighteen months in foster care, and her mother just got her back six months ago. The mother also has a two-year-old who's been in foster care since infancy. You can see this gal doesn't have a very good track record. I think I can safely say she's going to lose this child permanently this time. The chances of this little girl being free for adoption are very, very high."

"What's she like?" Eileen asked. "Does she have any particular problems?"

"She seems healthy," Mindy responded, clearly trying to make a sale. "She may be a little slow. She doesn't seem to talk. But that's not unusual in cases like this where the child has been through so much. They *usually catch up quickly when they're placed in a better environment."*

Mindy paused for a moment, and when Eileen didn't respond, she continued. "She's really cute! She's got the most beautiful big blue eyes you've ever seen. Do you think you could take her? At least for a few days, until we find another placement for her?"

I need to call Leonard first, Eileen thought. But she was shocked when she heard herself say, "Okay, I think we can give it a try."

Mindy gave an audible sigh of relief. "Bless you, Mrs. Hartman, you just made my day! You live on Gaylord Drive, right? I know where that is. I can have her over there in twenty minutes."

After hanging up the phone with Mindy, Eileen called Leonard's office and had him paged out of a meeting.

"Honey," she exclaimed, "they're bringing us a child! They're bringing us a little girl!"

"What are you talking about?" Leonard asked. "Who's bringing what, when?"

"The welfare department. They're bringing us a three-year-old."

"I thought we told them we weren't going to . . ."

"I've got to go now," Eileen interrupted. "I've got to get ready. They'll be here in a few minutes. I'll call you later."

When Eileen heard the doorbell ring exactly eighteen minutes later, she was in one of the upstairs bedrooms, frantically going through a box of clothing left from previous foster children. With her heart pounding, she rushed downstairs to answer the door.

The rain had stopped. Mindy, a chubby girl in blue jeans, stood on the steps holding Leonard's rumpled suits in their plastic bags. "You must've dropped these," she said, holding them out for Eileen to take.

"Come in," Eileen said as she hung the suits on the coat tree in the entry way. Then she saw the tiny child half-hidden behind one of Mindy's legs.

Mindy gently guided the little girl forward. "Sissy, this is Mrs. Hartman," she said.

The child stepped through the doorway. Eileen squatted down to greet her on her eye level. She found herself gazing into the most dazzling pair of eyes she'd ever seen, large, almond-shaped blue eyes in a sad, pinched, grimy little face.

"Oh," she said as her heart leaped in her chest.

Her gaze took in the rest of the child's appearance. The little girl's strawberry-blonde hair was sticky and matted. She was wearing a stained tee-shirt and a disposable diaper. Her skinny little legs were dotted with flea bites, and her tiny, sockless feet swam in filthy sneakers several sizes too large.

"I changed her diaper and cleaned her up a little at the office," Mindy said. "She was pretty nasty looking. She could use a good scrubbing. As you can see, she's not potty trained. Sorry about that."

"What's her name?" Eileen asked, her gaze once again riveted on the child's eyes.

"Sissy," Mindy replied. "Sissy Dickerson. Her mother is Seferina Dickerson, from Nappanee."

"Sissy? Is that her nickname?"

Mindy grimaced. "No, unfortunately, that's her real name. That Seffie, she's a case. Somebody in the office told me she didn't have a name picked out before her baby was born, and she just started calling her Sissy. When they left the hospital, the baby still didn't have a name. So Sissy is the name that ended up on the birth certificate. Poor little kid!"

"Sissy," Eileen said. "Sissy is short for Cecily. We'll give her a proper name. We'll call her Cecily." She stretched out her hand. "Come here, Cecily."

The little girl slipped a dirty thumb into her mouth, shyly lowered her head, and walked obediently to Eileen. Eileen gathered the child in her arms, then stood up, holding her close. Little Cecily, light as a feather, lay limply across Eileen's shoulder.

A deep sense of calm swept through Eileen's body. *This is just where she belongs,* she thought.

"Thank you!" she said to Mindy.

"Well, thank you," Mindy said, surprised by Eileen's response. "I apologize. I didn't bring any of her stuff. The few things Seffie got around for her were so nasty, we had to throw them out. Do you have any clothes that might fit her? If not, let us know, and we'll help you *out."*

"We'll manage," Eileen said as she caressed Cecily's tiny back.

"I've gotta run now," Mindy said, heading out the door. "I'll bring papers around for you to sign in the next couple of days. Thanks so much for helping us out in a pinch. I know it was really short notice, but things happen that way around our office. I'm just glad I caught you at home."

"So am I," Eileen murmured.

Holding Cecily in one arm, Eileen dialed Leonard's office. "Our daughter is here," she announced to her husband. "Her name is Cecily. Come home early if you can."

Eileen smiled to herself as she remembered the blissful days, weeks, and months that followed Cecily's arrival in their home. Under the Hartmans' loving care, little Cecily had quickly blossomed. In her mind's eye, Eileen could still see that wonderful spirit unfolding from a shriveled bud into a magnificent flower. What a joy Cecily had been! What fulfillment she had brought to their middle-aged lives!

Eileen forced her mind to stop on the pleasant thoughts. Tonight, she would refuse to think about the troublesome years that had followed. She had enough to do, handling the problems of the here and now. She sensed a dark uneasiness in her daughter, and it frightened her.

"That was a wonderful dinner, Mom," Cecily said in an attempt at lightheartedness. "You've outdone yourself again. I've got to get your recipe for the Chicken Cordon Bleu."

"Do get a good night's rest," Eileen urged as she kissed her daughter goodbye at the front door.

Chapter 3

Thursday morning, at 1:43 AM, Stephen Gray awoke from a sound sleep. The air conditioner had been running all night, and the bedroom was chilly. Shivering, he groggily rolled over to reach for the warmth of his wife's body. When he encountered emptiness on the other side of the king-sized bed, he was instantly wide awake. She was gone again.

"Cecily?" he called.

There was no answer. Stephen sat up and reached for his glasses on the bedside stand, then peered around the dark room. The glow from Cecily's computer screen was not visible, so he knew his wife was not engaged in her usual pastime of working when she couldn't sleep. He switched on the lamp beside the bed. Cecily was nowhere in the room.

Stephen thumped his pillow in helpless frustration. *This is happening way too often,* he thought. *Damn it, this is getting out of hand.*

He slipped on a robe and tied it around his ample middle. Then he padded across the cold hardwood bedroom floor, into the hallway, then into one room of the house after another, hoping to discover his wife engaged in some late night activity geared toward relieving her unrelenting insomnia.

But Cecily was not soaking in a warm bath scented with drops of lavender oil. She was not in the kitchen sipping a cup of chamomile tea, nor was she curled up under an afghan on the living room sofa reading one of her favorite romance novels.

"Cecily?" Stephen called again, his voice filled with fear. "Honey, where are you?" But except for the hum of the air conditioner, the house remained ominously silent.

Stephen hesitated in the hallway, overwhelmed with helplessness and uncertainty, feelings alien to his take-charge personality. His wife had been distant and withdrawn the past few months, not her usual sweet, affectionate self. *What was she up to? What on earth was going on?*

He wondered whether he should pick up the telephone and call someone. Who would he call? Mr. and Mrs. Hartman? The police?

Then the air conditioner kicked off, and he heard what he'd been listening for, evidence that Cecily was still in the house. Muffled sobs came from the family room in the basement.

Without turning on the light, Stephen slipped quietly down the basement stairs, as the sobs became increasingly audible. The faint light of a street lamp drifted through the basement window, and when he reached the bottom of the stairs, he could see the outline of his wife's thin body huddled in the corner of the sofa.

She sat with her knees pulled up to her chest, her face buried in her hands. She appeared motionless, except for the slight heaving of her shoulders as she sobbed. The sight of his wife in this condition terrified Stephen, and his fear erupted in a harsh tone of voice.

"What the hell are you doing, Cecily?"

Cecily startled and gave a little yelp. Removing her hands from her face, she wrapped her arms around her folded legs and pressed her forehead against her knees. Stephen could barely hear her desperate whisper: "Don't be mad at me. I didn't know you were up. I'm sorry. I'm sorry."

Little Sissy closes her eyes and wills sleep to come, but it doesn't work. Even though it's very late, she can hear traffic driving in and out of the mobile home park, with the loud grumbling of old mufflers and the blaring of radios tuned to country music stations.

The bedroom is cold. Starly has pulled the covers off Sissy again, and she's sprawled out across the twin bed the two girls share, sleeping heavily. Her arm is flung across Sissy's chest, and Sissy feels like she can't breathe. She slides out from under Starly's arm, sits up and attempts to rearrange the errant limb across Starly's body. Without waking, Starly flings her arm back over onto the bed, in the process swatting Sissy in the nose. It hurts so bad Sissy's eyes well with tears.

She gives up on sleep. Holding her stinging nose, she scoots off the bed and tiptoes out of the bedroom, down the hall, and into the living room. She climbs onto the couch and sits on her knees so she can look out the window, her chin resting on her arms folded across the top of the couch's sagging back.

She sees a cluster of people milling around in the neighbor's yard. Their lit cigarettes, like Fourth of July sparklers, make glowing arcs in the night sky as they gesture with their hands. The faint buzz of conversation is punctuated by bursts of raucous laughter. A car slows down and stops, and one of the men in the yard goes over to talk with the person in the passenger seat. As Sissy watches, her insides feel hollow and lonely.

Suddenly, she hears footsteps coming down the hallway. She holds perfectly still, scarcely breathing, bracing herself for trouble. She doesn't need to turn her head to see who it is. She knows. The footsteps aren't slow enough or heavy enough to be Jimmy's.

The footsteps move past her through the living room and into the kitchen. Out of the corner of her eye, Sissy sees a shadowy form standing at the refrigerator. The door creaks open, and the refrigerator light briefly illuminates Mommy Seffie, wearing an old tee shirt and panties, helping herself to a can of beer.

Sissy remains motionless, watching Seffie's movements in her peripheral vision. Seffie walks back into the living room, where Sissy can no longer see her. She hears her mother plop herself down in the ragged, creaking recliner.

"Can't sleep worth shit in this dang blasted trailer," Seffie mutters. "That damn Jimmy snores like a fuckin' hog." Sissy hears the click of a cigarette lighter, and the flame creates a small burst of light in the dark room. She knows she's been detected.

"What the hell are you doin' up, Sissy?" Seffie scolds. "You know you ain't supposed to be out here. Get your skinny little ass back to bed!"

Without a word, Sissy scrambles off the couch and scampers through the living room toward the hallway. Seffie swats her bottom as she runs past the recliner.

Regretting his harsh tone, Stephen moved cautiously toward the sofa. "I'm not mad at you, honey," he said, softening his voice. "I'm just worried about you."

He sat down beside his wife and placed an arm around her shoulders. Her body was cold, and he realized she was wearing only a flimsy nightgown.

Cecily didn't move. She didn't lean into her husband's arms for security, like she usually did when she felt the need for comfort. She didn't recoil from him, either. It felt to Stephen like she was indifferent to his presence.

"I'm just worried about you, honey," he repeated.

Cecily lifted her head from her knees and slowly eased her feet to the floor. Stephen watched her force the transformation from a pitiful weeping child into a grown woman in charge of herself.

"There's nothing to worry about, Stephen."

"Then explain to me what's going on." Stephen's voice rose again. "Why have you been acting so strange recently? Why haven't you been sleeping? And why the hell are you sitting here in the cold basement in the middle of the night?"

"You don't need to be a jerk about this, Stephen," Cecily retorted. "I was just a little upset, and I didn't want to disturb you. This really isn't any of your business."

Stephen knew he was on the brink of blowing up, and he forced himself to remain silent. He recalled the accusations of his previous wife, who'd characterized his analytical responses to her personal problems as insensitive, and who'd experienced his occasional flares of temper as emotionally abusive. *Was he falling back into old patterns with his current wife? Was Cecily pulling away from him? Was she thinking about leaving him?*

He racked his brain to recall the advice from the self-help books he'd devoured in his effort to make his second marriage successful. *Communicate, communicate,* he thought. *Calmly. I'm not going to blow up again. I'm staying calm.*

"Cecily," he said in a gentle tone. "It scares me to death to see you like this. You've been different recently. You've gotten so quiet, and you seem distant. You don't seem happy. Is it me? Is it something I've done? Is something wrong with our marriage?"

He suddenly wondered what his wife saw in him, a balding, paunchy scientist ten years her senior. With her stunning good looks, she could have had any man she wanted. Maybe there was someone else. The thought wrenched his insides.

"No, Stephen," Cecily said wearily. "It's not anything about you or our marriage. You haven't done anything wrong. I'm just going through something. I'll snap out of it soon. Just let me be, and don't worry about me."

In spite of his resolve, Stephen exploded again. "Cecily, for Christ's sake, how can I not worry? Day after day, I watch my wife sink deeper into some kind of black hole, and I'm not supposed to worry! I love you, Cecily, and God knows that losing you would kill me. Talk to me, tell me what's going on!"

"Stephen, don't!" Cecily held up a hand in protest. "I don't want to get into this."

"Look, if you can't talk to me, find someone you can talk to. Cecily, you're a therapist. How would you deal with a client who was acting like this? Huddled up crying in a cold basement in the middle of the night? Take some of your own medicine. Talk to someone!"

"Stephen, let it go!" Cecily scooted to the edge of her seat, ready to get up.

But Stephen was on a roll he couldn't stop. "How much sleep have you gotten this week, Cecily? It seems like every damn night when I wake up, you're not in bed. What am I supposed to think about that? Don't you like sleeping with me anymore?"

Cecily's body sagged, and she leaned back against the sofa again. "Please, Stephen, don't take this so personally. I told you this isn't about you. It's work, okay? Sometimes I get overwhelmed with work."

"Damn that job!" Stephen thundered. "If it affects you this way, then quit. Quit right now! Call in tomorrow and tell them you're resigning!"

"I can't do that."

"Cecily, you've got to do something. Either quit that job or . . . just do something! I just can't stand here watching that job drive you to the brink of insanity. I can't take it anymore!"

"Is that a threat, Stephen?" Cecily's voice was cold as ice. "Are you going to walk out on me like you did the previous Mrs. Gray?"

Cecily's words stabbed Stephen in the gut, and he almost doubled over with the pain. His first inclination was to storm up the stairs, slam the front door, and roar away into the night in his BMW. Taking a deep breath, he checked his anger.

"No, honey, it's not a threat," he said calmly. "I'm not leaving you, not now, not ever. Let's go to bed. See if you can get a little bit of sleep, then call in sick tomorrow morning. You can take it easy tomorrow and get some rest."

He reached out his hand to help Cecily to her feet, and then followed her up the stairs. When they were back in bed, he pulled her close, tenderly caressing her back. It seemed like ages since they'd been intimate.

"Honey, I love you, I love you so much!" he whispered. But Cecily didn't respond, and her body remained cold and unyielding in his arms.

Stephen released his embrace and rolled onto his side. *What did you expect after being such a jerk?* he chided himself.

The next morning, Cecily opened her eyes to find daylight streaming through the window and Stephen standing in front of the dresser mirror, straightening his tie. She rolled over and peered at her alarm clock. It was almost 7:00 AM.

"Oh, my God!" she exclaimed. "I'm going to be late!"

"Don't get up," Stephen said cheerfully. "Remember, you're staying home today. I turned your alarm off so you could get a little extra snooze time. I'll call your office, if you want."

Cecily was stunned when she realized she'd actually slept, almost four hours by her calculation, more than she'd slept in one stretch in weeks. Stephen came over and sat down on her side of the bed. Brushing her hair out of her face, he kissed her forehead. Cecily knew he was trying to make up for the argument in the basement just hours earlier.

"You're not going to work today, sweetie," he said. "You're going to rest. Want me to call in for you?"

"No," Cecily said. "I'll do it."

Stephen took her hand. "I'm sorry about last night. I was a jerk. But I want you to know I'm trying, I'm really trying." He kissed her forehead again. "Just rest today. Promise me. No housework. And make sure you eat something. Don't worry about dinner. I'll bring home carry-out."

After her husband left for work, Cecily sat up and reached for the phone on her bedside stand. In spite of the sleep she'd gotten, she felt dizzy and exhausted. Her head throbbed, and every joint in her body ached.

She dialed her work number and left a voicemail message for Meredith, glad she didn't have to deal with the receptionist's nosey questions. Listening to her own shaking voice, she knew no one would question whether she was well enough to come to work.

She lay down in bed again, but darkness crept into her mind, threatening to engulf her in despair. She knew she had to get up to escape it.

Wrapping the bed comforter around her, she padded to the living room to rest on the sofa. She picked up a magazine, but couldn't concentrate on reading, so she turned on the TV. Then she remembered she'd promised Stephen to eat, so she went to the kitchen, where she fixed a cup of tea and ate a muffin and an orange.

Throughout the interminably long day, Cecily moved listlessly from one room of the house to another, trying in vain to settle into a state of relaxation. Her body was dead tired, but wracked with tension. Anxious thoughts raced through her mind, circling around and coming back again.

Around 4:00 PM, she decided to take a bath. No sooner had she lowered herself into the sweet-smelling bubbles than she heard the front door opening and Stephen calling her name.

"I'm in here," she called out, trying to sound cheerful.

Stephen appeared in the doorway of the bathroom, an eager smile on his face. "I knocked off work early today. We need a relaxing evening at home together. Did you have a good day? Want me to wash your back?"

As he knelt down beside the tub, he exclaimed, "God, you're beautiful, Cecily!"

Sissy sits in the stained blue bathtub, her legs encircling Starly, who is sitting in front of her. Uncle Augustus kneels beside the tub. "You girls are so damn cute!" he says. "You're gonna be super hot chicks some day!" He makes a funny clicking sound with his mouth.

Sissy wrinkles her forehead. She doesn't know what Uncle Augie is talking about.

Uncle Augie takes an old plastic tumbler, dips it in the water, and pours its contents over Starly's head. Starly screams. Uncle Augie pours shampoo into his hand and begins to lather up Starly's scalp, pulling the suds through the long hair trailing down her back.

"My eyes hurt, my eyes hurt," Starly wails.

Uncle Augie fills the cup with water several more times, rinsing the shampoo from her hair. Then he picks up the bar of soup, rubbing it around in his wet hands until they're covered with bubbles. He begins to wash the front of Starly's body, and she shrieks louder than ever.

Sissy can't see what Uncle Augie is doing, but she's afraid. She decides to tell him she's big enough to wash herself.

Jimmy pokes his big head through the bathroom door. "What's going on in here?" he growls. "Augie, you better not be messin' with my girls."

"I'm not doin' nothin'," Uncle Augie protests. "I'm just givin' these kids a good scrub down. They're filthy little brats."

"Get out of here, you son-of-a-bitch!" Jimmy thunders.

"Hey, I was just tryin' to help out," Uncle Augie says. He gets up, wipes his wet hands on his pants, and swears under his breath as he leaves the bathroom.

Stephen dipped his fingers into the bubbles. Cecily recoiled when he ran his wet hand down her back.

"Don't!" she said before she could stop herself.

Stung by her reaction, Stephen stood up and backed away from the tub. "So now I can't even touch you." His voice was filled with a mixture of pain and sarcasm. "You said it was work that was getting you down. This has nothing to do with work. This is something different. You haven't told me the whole truth."

Feeling utterly vulnerable, Cecily slid down into the tub, covering her body with bubbles, closing her eyes to escape Stephen's intense gaze.

"It's just memories," she murmured. "Work makes me remember things."

"You mean to tell me you're letting what happened in the past get you down?" Stephen demanded to know. "That stuff's all over and done with, Cecily. You need to stop dwelling on those things. You've got a great life now. You need to focus on the present."

Behind her closed eyes, Cecily slipped into a dark tunnel where she zoomed far away from her husband's intolerant reasoning. "Whatever, Stephen," she said.

Later that evening when her husband tried to apologize once again for his insensitivity, Cecily said, "Stephen, I'm done talking."

Chapter 4

"Are you feeling better this morning, Cecily?" Frank McArthur asked as the team members assembled in the conference room for the Friday morning staff meeting.

Frank, a kindly teddy bear of a man, supervised the clinical team to which Cecily belonged. Everyone was present that morning: the therapists, Paul, Scott, Amanda, Kathy, Doug, Lila, and Jeff, team psychiatrist Dr. Cruz, and testing psychologist Dr. Evan Carter.

"I'm okay," Cecily lied. She wanted Frank to get off the topic of yesterday's absence. She didn't feel up to being in the spotlight.

"Well, we're all glad you're back," Frank said. He moved on to address team business, peering at the computer printouts on the table in front of him. "Our stats were exceptionally good last week. You've all been working hard, and I appreciate that. And it looks like everyone's keeping up with their paperwork. I don't see any overdue documents listed. Oh, wait a second here." He scrutinized the printout. "It looks like you have an incomplete assessment, Cecily."

Cecily felt shame burning her neck and spreading up to her face. Never before had she been called out in a staff meeting for being negligent with her work. "I'm really sorry, Frank," she said. "I'll get it done today."

Amanda snickered. "I can't believe it! Cecily's the one lagging behind this time! She's usually the Goody Two-Shoes of the team."

Cecily stared down at her own copy of the printouts, her documented error taunting her, flashing at her in neon lights. She felt too humiliated to raise her head and face everyone. The other team members sat in silent reproach of Amanda's comment.

"Well, I'm just saying . . . ." Amanda's tone was defensive.

Evan interrupted her. "Knock it off, Amanda."

Frank took charge, bringing the topic to a close. "I'm sure you'll get it done, Cecily. I'm not worried about it. You know how to manage your workload."

When the hour-long meeting was over, Cecily bolted from the conference room instead of pausing to chat with her teammates. As she hurried down the hall to her office, she heard footsteps running up behind her.

Amanda caught up with her and grabbed her arm. "Hey, I just wanted to apologize for what I said in the meeting. I didn't mean anything against you."

Cecily pulled her arm free. "Amanda, please leave me alone." She was surprised to hear the uncharacteristic hostility in her voice. "I've got a lot on my mind, and the last thing I need is to be hassled by you."

She left the dumbfounded Amanda standing in the hallway while she entered her office and closed the door, hoping to prevent any other intrusions by coworkers.

She didn't even open her door during her lunch break. But halfway through the hour, her solitude was interrupted by a few taps on her closed door.

"Yes?" she called out, irritated.

The door cracked open, and Evan peered in. "Are you hiding out in here?"

"Yes. I'm finishing up my delinquent assessment."

Once again, Evan stepped into her office uninvited and seated himself on her sofa. "Having a rough day, Cecily? I was worried about you when I heard you called in sick yesterday."

He paused, as if waiting for her to explain her absence. When she didn't respond, he continued. "I hope you didn't let what happened in the staff meeting upset you. All of us are late with documents once in awhile. Sometimes, it can't be helped. Amanda's just envious of you."

Cecily stared at him in disbelief. "Why in the world would she envy me?"

"Why wouldn't she?" Evan said. "You're everything she isn't. You're a bright young clinician and an exemplary employee, with a promising career ahead of you. Amanda doesn't aim very high. She just gets by. You excel, Cecily."

Something broke inside Cecily, and tears slid down her face. Evan discreetly reached over and closed her office door.

"Evan, I don't excel," she protested. "I don't excel at all. I feel like a failure. My life's falling apart. I can't sleep. I can barely eat. I've got my parents worried about me. My husband's unhappy with me. And now my work is slipping."

"Here's a reality check, Cecily," Evan said. "One late assessment doesn't mean your work is going down the tubes. And how could your husband be unhappy with you? As pretty and sweet as you are, how could anyone be unhappy with you?"

"My husband's unhappy with me because I've been upset. He doesn't like that. He thinks I have no reason to be upset."

Evan grimaced. "Not a very sensitive guy, is he?"

"Stephen's a good husband," Cecily said defensively. "He's just a rational-minded scientist, that's all. He gets impatient with people when he thinks they're being too emotional."

"That's not fair to you, is it?"

Cecily shifted in her chair, uncomfortable with Evan's scrutiny of her personal life. "I don't know how you do it, Evan," she said, laughing nervously. "You read me too well. It scares me."

Evan chuckled. "I'm a clinician. That's what I do."

Cecily felt the warmth of Evan's demeanor melting the icy wall she'd built around her. She glanced at him, and then averted her gaze when she saw the kindness in his eyes.

"So what is it that you're so upset about?" he asked.

Cecily exhaled forcefully. "Wow, Evan, if I understood that myself, I wouldn't be falling apart like I am. It's hard to explain."

"Give it a try."

"Not now," she said, pulling her guard around her again. "I have a client in ten minutes. I've got to get myself together."

Evan sat with his elbows on his knees, contemplating his folded hands. Then he asked, "Do you have any open slots this afternoon?"

"My four o'clock canceled."

"Good. I have a cancellation at three. I have a four o'clock coming in, but I'll have Meredith call them and tell them to come an hour early. You and I will have an appointment at four. You're going to talk to me then. No excuses. Okay?"

He stood up to leave. "I'll be back then, and you'd better be here. No skipping out on me."

After Cecily's last client left her office several minutes before 4:00 PM, she left her door slightly ajar, anticipating Evan's arrival. She felt a twinge of guilt about having agreed to this meeting. She had plenty of documentation to complete, and she told herself she should be using the free hour to catch up on her work. She certainly didn't want to re-peat the experience of having her negligence pointed out in a staff meeting.

Furthermore, she knew she was arranging a private meeting with a man who was sexually attracted to her. And she had to admit to herself that she found Dr. Evan Carter far from unappealing. But her despera-tion to unburden herself to a sympathetic listener outweighed her res-ervations.

Several minutes later, Evan appeared in her doorway, smiling. "Ready?" he asked.

"I'm ready," Cecily said. "Come on in."

Evan took off his jacket and tossed it over the back of a chair, loos-ened his tie, then seated himself on one end of the sofa. Cecily logged off her computer, and then moved from her desk chair to the other end of the sofa. They both sat sideways, facing each other.

"So, talk to me," Evan said.

"Evan, why are you doing this?" Cecily blurted out. "Why are you so interested in what's going on with me?"

Evan chuckled. "You're afraid I'm putting the moves on you, aren't you? Well, if you were available, I'd develop feelings for you in a split-second. But you're not, so I won't. I don't put my heart through un-necessary pain, and I know how to keep my drives in check."

Cecily felt her insides quivering in response to Evan's disclosure, but she forced her voice to remain dispassionate. "So answer my question."

Evan looked thoughtful. "I suppose I'm doing this because I sense that whatever you're going through, you're going through it alone. I think you need someone to care about you right now."

He grinned. "And maybe I need to care about somebody. Most of the time, I'm just a self-centered jerk. Caring about you makes me a little better than that."

The tightly clenched knot in Cecily's abdomen began to soften, and she suddenly felt very relaxed in Evan's presence. She let her pumps slide off her feet, and then folded her legs delicately to one side.

"So talk to me," Evan repeated. "What's bothering you?"

"I . . . I don't know how to start," Cecily stammered.

"Anywhere. Start anywhere."

"Well . . . I'm adopted." As soon as the words escaped her mouth, she felt stupid. *Why did you say that?* she chided herself. *Being adopted isn't the problem.*

Evan looked surprised. "Really? I had no idea. I just assumed you were the biological child of upper middle-class parents who doted on you and raised you really well."

Cecily smiled. "You're partly right. Everything you thought is true, except for the biological part. My parents are well-to-do, well-educated people, and they're absolutely the best parents in the world. But they aren't biologically mine."

Interest flickered in Evan's eyes. "Were you adopted at birth? Did your parents pay big bucks for you? They should have, because they got quite a prize."

Cecily looked down, embarrassed. "Please stop saying things like that, Evan. It makes me nervous."

"Sorry," he said. "I don't mean to make you uncomfortable. So what's the story about your adoption?"

"I was placed in my parents' home as a foster child when I was three years old," she said. "They adopted me when I was seven."

"And the part that bothers you?"

Cecily buried her face in her hands. "Memories. I've been bombarded by memories, memories of things that haven't bothered me for years. And now they're haunting me. Every day, something new pops up."

She looked up at Evan with imploring eyes. "I feel like I'm losing my mind. I'm so emotional. It doesn't take anything to set me off on a crying jag."

"Well, my friend," Evan said. "As a therapist, you know this is a normal psychological process. Memories come up like this when it's time to deal with them. This must be your time."

Cecily nodded mutely.

"What is it that you're remembering?"

"Things that happened at my biological mother's house."

Evan furrowed his brow. "You're remembering things that happened before age three?"

"No, no," Cecily said. "I don't have memories of being that young. My very earliest memories are of being with my adoptive parents, the Hartmans. They're all good memories. I know the story of how I came to their home as a foster child, because my mother told it to me. But I don't remember the event."

Evan squinted and scratched his head. "Well, now you've got me totally confused."

"Sorry," Cecily said. "It's complicated. After I stayed with the Hartmans for awhile, I had to go back to my biological mother's home. Twice, it happened twice. I stayed with her when I was five, then I went back to my foster home. I had to go back to her again when I was six-and-a-half. When I was seven, I went back to the Hartmans permanently, and they adopted me."

Evan nodded. "Okay, I get it now. The memories of staying with your biological mother, that's what's eating away at you."

"Yes," Cecily said. "That's it."

"What was your biological mother like, Cecily?"

Cecily felt her body go weak, and suddenly she was almost too exhausted to talk. "Her name was Seffie," she said slowly. "Her last name must've been Dickerson, because that's what I went by when I stayed with her. I was Sissy Dickerson when I started kindergarten. It didn't seem right to me, because in my heart I truly believed I was Cecily Hartman. I thought everyone was mistaken, that they had me mixed up with some other little girl."

She closed her eyes as she collected her thoughts, resting her head against the back of the sofa. "Seffie was very young when I stayed with her, pretty much a kid herself. My adoptive mother told me she was only sixteen when I was born.

"How would I describe her? I guess you could say she was tough, or rough, maybe both. She was poor and uneducated and kind of wild. She had a temper, and she had quite a mouth on her. Hardly a sentence came out of her mouth without a curse word in it. My adoptive parents would've never thought of talking like that, and I wasn't used to it."

She smiled. "But you know, I always thought Seffie was kind of pretty. She had that going for her. But she didn't keep herself up. I'd even say she wasn't all that clean."

"Wow, Cecily!" Evan shook his head in disbelief. "That totally blows my mind. I absolutely can't fathom you coming from someone like that! You're the exact opposite of everything she was."

Cecily shrugged. "It must've been the Hartmans' influence on me."

"It's got to be more than that," Evan mused. "What about your biological father? Do you know anything about him?"

"Nothing at all," Cecily said. "Not a clue."

"That's interesting. Maybe you inherited an outstanding endowment from his side. But I'm getting you off track. Tell me more about your memories of Seffie."

"She was with a man named Jimmy. He was a really big guy, heavyset. I know for sure he wasn't my biological father. One time I called him Daddy, and Seffie made a point of telling me he wasn't my father. She insisted that I call him Jimmy.

"I was scared to death of Seffie, but not Jimmy. He was a lot more easy-going than Seffie. It seemed like he spent half his time trying to calm her down. Jimmy actually took care of us girls more than Seffie did."

Evan looked puzzled. "Girls?"

"Yes," Cecily said, "I had sisters." Tears sprung to her eyes, and she almost doubled over from the pain in her abdomen. She sat with her head bowed for a few moments.

Evan reached over and touched her knee. "This is the heart of it, isn't it, kiddo? It's something about these sisters that's causing you all this pain."

"I guess so." Cecily rocked back and forth to soothe herself. "I didn't realize how much it hurt until I said out loud that I had sisters. My heart feels like it's torn to pieces."

She glanced up at Evan, and the compassion in his eyes invited her to continue.

"The first time I went to Seffie's house, she had a baby girl named Shaney, just a few months old, I think. Seffie and Jimmy told me she was my baby sister. Soon after I moved in, another little girl joined the family. Her name was Starly, and they said she was my sister, too.

"Starly was just a year younger than me. I was five, and she was four. She was a wild little kid, always screaming and crying and throwing fits. She drove Seffie crazy. I felt bad about that. I loved Starly, and I tried hard to be extra nice to her because Seffie was so mean to her.

"Starly wasn't there all the time. She'd come and go a lot. I didn't know why. I thought maybe it was because Seffie got tired of her and sent her away. I have no idea where she went. Back to a foster home, I suppose. Starly had the longest hair I'd ever seen. When she'd come to stay with us, it would be fixed up so nice in two long blond braids. Seffie would never do anything with it, and after a day or so, Starly's hair would be an awful mess."

Cecily stopped, and a tear slid down her cheek.

"What's happening?" Evan asked. "Are you remembering something?"

She nodded. "I remember trying to fix Starly's hair when her braids came undone. I'd try to get her to sit still so I could braid it back up. But I never could figure out how to do it."

"You tried to take care of those little sisters," Evan observed. "Seffie wasn't taking care of them, so you thought you had to. At five years old, you tried to be the mom."

She nodded again, burying her face in her hands.

"You're missing those sisters, aren't you?"

Cecily stood up, took a tissue from the box on her desk, and wiped her eyes. "Terribly," she said. "Evan, I miss them terribly. I have no idea where they are, or if they're okay. It tears me up inside."

She sat back down on the sofa. "It's so weird. I hadn't thought much about any of them for years, Seffie, Jimmy, Starly, or Shaney. And now, I'm falling apart over them. Can I tell you something, Evan?"

"Of course."

"Two days ago, I did an assessment with a family that had three little girls. The oldest was taking care of the two little ones because the mother was distracted with her own problems. When I saw that, it totally unnerved me. I was so shook up I barely got through the session.

"I couldn't sleep that night. I tried not to wake Stephen when I got out of bed, but he got up later and found me crying. Then he got upset because I was so upset, and it all went downhill from there. And that's why I didn't come to work yesterday. I was a total mess."

"So that's how this all came down," Evan reflected. "You're dealing with all these intense emotions, and you've been trying to hide them from everybody, people at work, your husband, probably your parents."

"That's right."

"You and I both know, Cecily, that what you're going through is normal. Normal, but very painful."

"Yes," Cecily said. "And confusing. You know, when I was a little girl with the Hartmans, I was in a child's Utopia. I had everything I wanted, and I had my mother's constant attention. She took me everywhere she went. I was showered with love by both of my parents. I felt totally safe, totally secure. And then came the day when I was put in some social worker's car and driven to a filthy, run-down mobile home where I met my loud-mouth tramp of a biological mother. It was like all the lights in the universe went out. My world turned horrible and dark and scary."

"My God, Cecily! That must've been awful! Did they place you in Seffie's home that abruptly?"

"No, I had one or two weekend visits first, to get to know her. Then they left me with her fulltime." Cecily hung her head, sighing deeply. "I was devastated. I remember being unable to say a single word. I must've been totally mute for a couple of weeks. But somehow I got used to it. I adapted. I had to."

Then she looked up, smiling. "But I loved my sisters! I was an only child at the Hartmans, and having siblings was something new for me.

My sisters and I went through so much together, like little soldiers in the trenches. When I learned I was going back to the Hartmans, I was so excited. But in a way, I went with a heavy heart, because I had to leave my sisters. Starly and Shaney vanished from my life. And I missed Jimmy, and even though I hated Seffie, I missed her a little bit.

"The second time I went to Seffie's, Starly wasn't there. This time, Shaney was two, and Seffie had another baby girl named Stella. Even though I was heartbroken to leave my foster parents, I was delighted to see Shaney again. I kept waiting for Starly to show up, but she never came. Finally, I asked Seffie where she was."

Six-year-old Sissy sits on the floor in front of the couch, playing with the Candyland game she brought with her from Mommy Eileen's house. Her opponent is an imaginary Starly. The yellow marker belongs to Starly, and the blue one belongs to Sissy.

"Okay, Starly, it's your turn," Sissy murmurs. She picks up a card, then moves Starly's yellow marker forward several spaces. "Okay, now it's my turn." She picks up another card, and then moves the blue marker.

Seffie sits in the ragged recliner, watching "The Price is Right" on TV. She's smoking a cigarette and drinking Mountain Dew from a can. She mutters a string of profane comments about the stupidity of the show's contestants.

Sissy finally musters the nerve to ask the question that has been playing on her mind for weeks. She gets up from her game, walks over to the recliner, and lays her hand on Seffie's arm.

"Where's Starly?" she asks. "Why doesn't she stay with us anymore?"

"She ain't part of this family no more," Seffie snaps. "So don't be talkin' about her."

"Why isn't she part of this family?" Sissy asks, knowing she's pushing her luck.

Seffie stubs out her cigarette in an overflowing ashtray. "Because she's a brat, that's why. I can't take the way that little weirdo acts, throwin' her fits all the time. She just got on my last nerve."

She fixes Sissy with a sinister gaze. "Now I said don't be talkin' about Starly. From now on, your sisters are gonna be just Shaney and Stella."

Sissy turns away from Seffie and walks down the hallway to her bedroom. She lies down on the narrow bed she used to share with Starly, her heart drowning in sorrow.

"Did Seffie answer your question?" Evan asked. "Did she tell you what happened to Starly?"

"Sort of," Cecily replied. "She insinuated that Starly got sent away because of her behavior. That confused me. I wondered if the Hartmans had sent me away because of the way I acted, but I really didn't think that was true. I wondered if Seffie would send me away if I misbehaved, and I thought about trying that tactic as a way of getting away from her. But I was afraid of where she'd send me, maybe some place worse than her house. It never occurred to me that if she hadn't wanted me, I would've gone straight back to the Hartmans."

Suddenly, she felt too tired to talk any longer. As she gazed wearily at her friend, the understanding in his eyes comforted her. She felt like she'd released a tremendous burden that had been weighing down on her, and her body felt exhausted, yet light as air. She wished she could collapse on her office sofa and sleep for hours.

She startled when she heard a knock on her door. Glancing at the clock on her wall, she saw that it was after 5:00 PM. When she jumped up to answer the door, she found Frank McArthur standing there.

"Sorry to disturb you, Cecily," he said. "I was just checking to see if you were still here. I'm getting ready to go, and I wanted to make sure everyone was out of the building before I set the alarm."

He shot a curious glance at Evan, who was still seated on the sofa. "I'll let you guys set the alarm when you're ready to leave. You're the last ones here."

Evan got up and reached for his jacket. "We were just getting ready to go," he said.

Neither Cecily nor Evan spoke as they left the building. Evan walked her to her car and opened the door for her.

"Evan, I'm so grateful for what you did for me," Cecily said before she slid into the driver's seat. "You have no idea how much it helped. Now I owe you a favor."

"You don't owe me anything." Evan said. "It was my pleasure. Have a great weekend, and get some rest."

Cecily slept soundly that night, dreaming vividly. She woke up when Stephen got out of bed the next morning, then rolled over and went back to sleep. Stephen decided not to wake her, and she slept until almost noon.

The two of them went out to dinner that evening. Cecily felt quiet and relaxed, deeply absorbed in thoughts about her conversation with Evan.

"It seems like you're feeling better," Stephen observed.

"Yes," Cecily said. "I think a good night's sleep did wonders for me."

"How are you doing with those bothersome memories?"

"I'm dealing with them," Cecily replied.

I'm doing what you asked me to do, she thought. *I'm talking with someone.* But she decided it would be best not to speak that thought aloud.

Chapter 5

Early Monday morning, Evan poked his head into Cecily's office. "You look like you're feeling better," he said. "How was your weekend?"

"I had a great weekend," she responded. "And I am feeling better. I actually got some sleep, and that makes a world of difference. I feel like I'm getting a grip on things again. Talking with you last Friday helped me get so much off my mind. Thanks again for what you did for me."

Evan smiled. "It was my privilege. Any time you need to talk, I'm here."

Cecily turned her attention to her computer, checking her schedule of clients. She felt more energized than she had for weeks, ready to take on whatever the day brought her.

Evan lingered a moment, then turned to walk away. "See you later," he said.

"Wait a second, Evan," Cecily said. "I want to tell you something. I had a weird dream Friday night, the most surreal dream I've ever had, and I don't know what to make of it. But it put an idea in my head about something I've never considered, not even remotely."

"Wow!" Evan said. "Now you've got me hooked. Want to tell me about it over lunch?"

"That would be nice. Unless you have something else you need to do. I don't mean to impose on your personal time."

"Don't be silly. You're not imposing. What do you plan to do for lunch?"

"I brought something from home."

"Good. I'll get a sandwich and join you here."

"So tell me about your surreal dream," Evan said as he unwrapped his sandwich.

Cecily carefully peeled the foil off her container of yogurt. "It was about my biological mother. I've never dreamed about her before. I was sleeping soundly, having all kinds of nonsensical dreams. Then

Seffie's face popped up, very vivid, very lifelike. I could see all the details about her I remembered from my childhood. She had the same straggly brown hair hanging in her face. Her skin had a grimy look about it. But she had the most beautiful blue eyes."

"Like yours?" Evan asked.

Cecily paused to consider the idea. "Maybe so. I've never thought about that. But anyway, in the dream Seffie looked worried. She was talking to me, and it seemed like she was trying to get an urgent message across. But her speech was muffled, and I couldn't make out what she was saying. I tried hard, but I couldn't get it, and then her face faded away.

"Then I woke up, and for the first time in my life, I had a loving feeling toward Seffie. For a few minutes, I missed her and longed for her. I felt sad because I hadn't been able to understand her in the dream. I really wanted to know what she was trying to tell me."

"That's very strange," Evan said. "But awesome. It almost sounds like you had a supernatural experience."

"You mean like a vision?"

"I don't know. Maybe."

"Seriously?"

"I can't say. I'm not an expert on those things."

Cecily looked at Evan intently. "What could this mean, Evan? Why would I have a dream like this after all these years? Do you think in real life Seffie wants to tell me something?"

He shrugged. "I surely don't know. But it does seem like the dream is important."

"I know it's important, Evan. When I woke up, it felt like something significant had happened to me. Maybe even life-changing."

The two of them ate in silence for several minutes. Then Evan said, "You told me this morning the dream put an idea in your head."

Cecily nodded, stirring her spoon around and around in her container of yogurt. Then she spoke hesitantly.

"Evan?"

"Yes Cecily?"

"What do you think of the idea of me trying to find Seffie and my sisters? Adopted people look up their biological families all the time, don't they?"

"Some do, some don't," Evan said. "It's really an individual choice. But if that's what you want to do, go for it."

"But I'm not sure it's a good idea."

"Why not?"

"Because I'm pretty sure it would devastate my parents, and that's the last thing in the world I want to do to them. I owe my mom and dad everything. Who knows what I would've been without them? They saved me from the terrible life I would've had with Seffie. In my heart, they're my real parents."

Sighing, she set her unfinished yogurt on the coffee table. "But what about this dream I had? I can't just blow it off. What if Seffie wants me to find her? What if that's what she was trying to tell me?"

Evan listened thoughtfully, chin resting in his hand. "I know this is a dilemma for you, Cecily," he said. "A huge dilemma. I wish I could tell you what to do, but I can't. I've got only one piece of advice. Don't make a decision right now. Think about it for a while, and see what else comes up. Maybe later, you'll have a better sense of direction."

Tuesday morning, Stephen awoke to the sound of his wife crying in her sleep. "No," she sobbed. "No! Don't go!"

He shook her gently. "Wake up, honey," he said. "You're having a bad dream."

Cecily sat bolt upright in bed, looking frightened and disoriented.

"What's going on?" Stephen asked.

She exhaled deeply. "Whew! That was pretty crazy!" She sat in a daze for a few minutes, then got up and began getting ready for work.

Mid-morning, Cecily stopped by Evan's office. He looked up from his work and smiled at her. "Hi there, kiddo. How's it going?"

"Oh, my God, Evan!" she exclaimed. "I had another weird dream!"

"Wanna tell me about it over lunch?" he asked. Then he glanced out the window. "It's so nice outside. How about if we take a noontime stroll along the river? It's a shame to waste such a beautiful day cooped up inside. We can talk while we walk."

"Sounds lovely," Cecily said.

"I dreamt about Seffie again," Cecily confided to Evan as they left the building and made their way toward the river that ran behind the center. "I was a little girl, and she and I were together in a room. She was staring at me, like she was trying to figure me out. She seemed interested in me, and I liked that.

"I started walking across the room toward her, but then some policemen came bursting through the door. They put handcuffs on her and started dragging her away.

"I screamed, 'Don't go!' Seffie started crying. She mouthed the words, 'I'm sorry!' And then I woke up."

Evan placed his hand on Cecily's back to guide her down a flight of steps. "Did this happen to you in real life? Did you watch Seffie being taken away by the police?"

Cecily tried to ignore the electric shiver triggered by her companion's touch. "No, I don't think so," she said. "I wouldn't doubt that Seffie was in trouble with the law at different times, but I don't remember watching her being arrested."

The two of them turned onto a paved path running beside the river. Cecily walked with her head down, staring mindlessly at the trail in front of her.

"Hey," Evan said. "We're out here on a nature walk on one of the most beautiful days of the year. You look like you're on a path of doom. Lift your head, look around."

"Oh," Cecily said, feeling stung by her friend's reproach. "I guess I've been too preoccupied to notice anything going on around me lately."

"Of course," Evan said. "I didn't mean to scold you."

As they walked on, Cecily tried to enjoy her surroundings, but the ducks gliding across the rippling water and the squirrels scampering up and down the tree trunks failed to provide her with any pleasure. After a few minutes, Evan broke the silence between them.

"Do you remember what Seffie did to get you taken away from her?"

"I've never really known the reason for being removed from her home," Cecily mused. "I can guess, though. I remember her leaving a lot. She'd get upset with us girls, and would take off and leave us alone for awhile. Both times when someone came to take us away, we were alone in the house."

A wave of weariness passed through her body. "I'm tired, Evan. I don't feel like walking any farther."

Evan gestured toward an empty park bench. "Want to sit for a few minutes?"

"Yes," Cecily said. She sank down onto the bench and closed her eyes, remembering.

Four-year-old Starly, ever the ringleader, jumps up and down on the ragged couch. "Giddy up, giddy up, giddy up," she chants to the rhythm of her bouncing. Then she jumps to the floor, shouting, "Whoa!" Giggling, she climbs back on the couch to repeat the pattern. "Giddy up, giddy up, giddy up, whoa!"

Five-year-old Sissy catches the spirit and follows suit. Together, the girls bounce and chant, "Giddy up, giddy up, giddy up!" Then they land with a resounding, "Whoa", shaking the floor of the mobile home.

The next time around, Sissy adds her own twist to the chant, borrowed from a song she heard on the radio. "Giddy up a-oom-papa-oom-papa-mow-mow." Starly finds this hilarious, and doubles over with laughter.

"Knock it off!" Seffie yells. "You kids are gettin' on my nerves."

Starly and Sissy are too caught up in their fun to pay attention. Together they bounce on the couch, twirling in circles while they sing at the top of their lungs. "Giddy up a-oom-papa-oom-papa-mow-mow."

Nine-month-old Shaney grabs on to the edge of the couch and pulls herself up to a standing position. She chortles with delight at her sisters' antics, and smacks the couch with her chubby little hand.

"I'm warnin' ya," Seffie yells again. "You guys better knock it off!"

One of Sissy's flying feet catches baby Shaney on the side of the head. Shaney falls to the floor, wailing.

"That's it, I'm outta here!" Seffie hollers as she leaps out of the recliner. "I can't take any more of this bullshit. If I don't get outta here, I'm gonna beat you kids to death!"

Cecily lifted her eyes and looked at Evan sitting on the other end of the bench. Then she spoke, slowly and thoughtfully.

"Evan, you told me to see what else came up before making a decision about my biological mother. I know it hasn't been that long, but I've decided what I want to do. I'm going to look for Seffie and my sisters. The second dream convinced me. It seems like Seffie's trying to connect with me. Maybe I'm being crazy and superstitious, but I've got to do this."

She gazed at Evan imploringly, waiting for confirmation for her decision. "If I don't, these memories and dreams are going to drive me insane. My mind isn't going to let me rest until I do this."

"Go for it, then," Evan said. "I'm behind you, and I'll help you any way I can. How do you plan to start?"

"Well, I suppose the first thing I need to do is tell my parents. I don't want to disrespect them by going behind their backs. It'll be really hard. I'll have dinner with them again tomorrow night, and I'll figure out a way to bring it up."

"You'll do fine," Evan said. "You always do." He glanced at his watch, and then stood up. "I could stay out here with you forever, but we've got to get going. It's five minutes to one."

He reached for Cecily's hand to help her to her feet, and didn't release it until they'd taken several steps down the path. Cecily felt a twinge of sadness when her confidante's comforting hand separated from hers.

Chapter 6

"So, Mom and Dad, what's new in your lives?" Cecily asked as she sat down to dinner with her parents Wednesday evening.

She hated herself for what she was doing, laying the groundwork for the news she was about to break. She wanted to show her parents that she cared about them before telling them something that would turn their world upside down.

Leonard and Eileen exchanged glances, surprised but pleased by their daughter's question. "You go first," Eileen said to her husband.

"Well, I don't suppose I have too much going on," Leonard said. "I was at Lowe's this afternoon. I've got my eye on a Japanese maple tree they have in the garden center. I'm thinking about putting it out back by the patio. I guess that's all it takes to get an old man excited."

"I've decided to become a volunteer at Memorial Hospital," Eileen said, her eyes sparkling. "I went through orientation yesterday. I'll be starting in the gift shop next Tuesday."

Both of Cecily's parents were beaming, clearly enjoying her attention. Knowing what was to come, she felt like a horrible daughter.

"How about you, honey?" Eileen asked. "What's new in your life? I'm sure you have more going on than we do."

This is it, Cecily told herself. *This is your opening. Take it.*

"Uh . . . ." The words stuck in her throat.

"Yes dear?" Eileen said.

"I . . . I . . . ." Cecily could feel her face turning red. Her parents' smiles had been replaced by expressions of concern, and she lowered her eyes to escape their worried gazes.

Leonard cleared his throat. "Cecily, is there a problem you need to tell us about?"

"I . . . I guess maybe there is." *Just say it,* she told herself. *Get it over with, and then try to do some damage control.*

She took a deep breath. "Mom and Dad, I've decided to look for my biological family. My mother and sisters, I mean."

Cecily watched her parents' faces go slack, and both looked like they aged ten years before her eyes. She'd never before seen her self-possessed father with his mouth hanging open in disbelief. Her mother looked mortally stricken. She desperately wanted to take her words back.

The stunned silence that fell over the three of them seemed to go on forever. "Why, sweetie?" Eileen finally asked, choking on her words.

"I've been having dreams . . . and memories . . . and it just seems like something I need to do . . . ." Cecily knew her explanation sounded weak. How could she explain the yearning in her heart to the people who'd given her everything, who'd given so much that any lack should be unthinkable?

Leonard spoke, his voice filled with pain. "Is it something we did, or didn't do? I know we weren't the perfect parents for you."

Tears poured from Cecily's eyes. "Oh, but you were, you still are! You're the best parents in the world! This doesn't have anything to do with you. I just didn't want to do something behind your backs. Please don't take it like I don't love you."

"I just don't understand," Eileen said with a hint of anger in her voice. "Your biological mother almost ruined your life. We did everything we could to fix things for you. We fought to keep you as our daughter, while she didn't seem to care. I just don't understand why you'd want to go back to her now."

Eileen picks up the receiver of the ringing telephone. "This is Mindy Barnes from Child Protective Services," the voice on the other end says.

"Oh, hello, Mindy," Eileen says. "It's been a long time since I've heard from you."

"Mrs. Hartman," Mindy says, "I'd like to stop by your house sometime within the next couple of days. I've got a little business to take care of with you."

"We're pretty busy. Can't we just do this over the phone?"

"I'd rather do it face-to-face."

Cold fingers of dread grip Eileen's abdomen. "Okay," she says, feeling slightly nauseas.

When Mindy arrives the next evening, little Cecily accompanies her father when he goes to answer the door. She skips along at his side, wearing a pink sundress, her strawberry blonde hair tied up in two pony-tails.

Mindy asks Cecily to play in the next room while she talks with Leonard and Eileen in private. "You folks have done a wonderful job with Sissy," she says. "She looks great."

"We call her Cecily," Eileen says, somewhat sharply.

"Well, her legal name is still Sissy," Mindy responds, her voice tone matching Eileen's.

"So what's your business with us, Mindy?" Leonard asks.

"I'm sure you're suspecting that I don't have good news," Mindy says. "Mr. and Mrs. Hartman, Sissy's mother, Seferina Dickerson, is ready to have her daughter returned to her care. She's done well enough with her case plan, and we have no choice but to give her child back to her."

Leonard and Eileen stare at Mindy in disbelief.

"I'm not saying I fully agree with this decision," Mindy says. "But the woman does have her legal rights. And I have a court order stating that I need to return Sissy to her care." She offers Leonard and Eileen a packet of papers to inspect.

Eileen holds up a hand in protest, refusing the documents. Over-whelming rage surges through her body. "How can you do this? You talk about the mother's rights. What about the child's rights? Cecily's bonded to us now. She has no memory of Seferina Dickerson!" She spat out the despised name. "We're the only parents Cecily knows!"

"Do we have any rights in this matter?" Leonard asks.

"No, you don't." Mindy is clearly impatient with the way Leonard and Eileen are responding to her news.

Eileen's rage melts into grief. She begins to weep, deep gut-wrenching sobs. "You can't take my baby! She's my child now."

"I think you need to leave." Leonard's voice is firm. "You've upset my wife enough for one day." He stands up and ushers Mindy to the front door.

After Mindy leaves, Eileen rushes to the bathroom and vomits her dinner. That night in bed, Leonard holds her close. "We'll get through this," he says.

Eileen is outraged by her husband's attempt to comfort her. "No, we won't! If we lose Cecily, I'll never get over it!"

She gets out of bed and spends the night roaming the house, feeling sicker than she's felt in her entire life, every cell of her body devastated by grief. She stops weeping only long enough to vomit, and then she weeps again.

Cecily stared at her mother, the pain in her heart so intense she could hardly bear it. "I won't do it, then," she said. "I can't do this to you. The two of you are too important to me. I'm so sorry for bringing this up, for hurting you like this. I wasn't thinking. I was being selfish."

Leonard tried to steer the conversation in a lighter direction, but none of them found much to say for the remainder of the meal.

Cecily didn't sleep much that night. She told herself she didn't mind another night of insomnia. At least she wouldn't dream about Seffie.

She went to work the next morning in a dark mood. *This is a day to keep my door closed,* she told herself. She didn't want to see any of her coworkers, not even Evan. She especially didn't want to see Evan, the co-conspirator of the idea that had inflicted so much pain on her parents.

But to her dismay, she ran into him in the reception office when she was photocopying documents.

"How's it going?" he asked.

"I'm calling it off," she said, avoiding eye-contact with him. Gathering her documents, she hurried out of the office.

Evan followed, catching up with her in the hallway. "Calling what off?"

"You know what I'm talking about," she snapped. "My search for my biological mother. I brought it up with my parents last night. The whole thing backfired, and I'm feeling pretty crappy right now."

"I'm so sorry," Evan said.

"Whatever." Cecily waved her hand dismissively and walked on.

"Are you mad at me?" Evan called after her.

Cecily didn't respond, and continued toward her office.

She heard Meredith say, "What's up with her?"

"She's having a bad day," Evan said.

By the time she got back to her office, Cecily felt remorseful. She realized she'd taken her frustration out on a person who'd been nothing but kind to her. She sat down at her computer and accessed her intra-office email.

Dear Evan, she wrote. *I apologize profusely for how I treated you just a few minutes ago. I'm very confused and frustrated right now, but you aren't to blame. I made my own decision, and it backfired on me. You've been a good friend to me, and I appreciate that. Hopefully, I can get back to my life the way it used to be, that is, if my parents ever forgive me. I'll just have to keep those memories in check. And I really hope I won't have any more dreams."*

When she checked her email later in the day, she smiled at Evan's response.

Hey, kiddo, I appreciate your apology. You have every right to be confused and frustrated, considering all that's going on in your life. What kind of friend would I be if I couldn't withstand a few storms in our relationship? If you do have more dreams, remember that I'm still here to listen.

Thanks, Cecily typed, then clicked on *send.*

Midway through a therapy session the next day, Cecily saw the red light on her phone flicker on, signaling that Meredith had just put a caller through to her voicemail. After the session, she listened to the message, and was astounded when she heard her mother's voice. Eileen had never called her at work before.

"Cecily, honey." Eileen's voice was shaking. "I just wanted to call you to tell you I love you, and that I'm sorry for what I said to you Wednesday night. I was the one who was being selfish. I just couldn't bear the thought of sharing you with another mother. Yesterday, I had a good talk with Reverend Thompson. He helped me understand why it might be important to you to find your birth mother. I'd like to help you in any way that I can. Let me take you out to breakfast tomorrow morning, just you and me, and we'll have a nice long chat. I love you, honey."

Cecily stared at the phone in disbelief. Then she turned to her computer. *You won't believe what just happened,* she emailed Evan. *Just when I think I'm going in one direction, my life does a big U-turn and takes me back the other way!*

At her next trip to the reception office, Cecily saw a gigantic bouquet of assorted flowers sitting on Meredith's desk.

"Those are beautiful!" she exclaimed.

"They're for you," Meredith said, pushing the vase in her direction. She watched as Cecily opened the accompanying card. "Are they from a secret admirer?"

"No." Cecily chuckled. "They're from my parents."

To our beautiful daughter, the card read. *No matter where life takes you, you'll always be in our hearts."* It was signed, *Leonard and Eileen Hartman.*

"My mother invited me to go out to breakfast tomorrow morning," Cecily told Stephen that evening.

"Okay," he said from behind his newspaper. "Any special reason?"

"No," Cecily lied. "She's probably just lonely and wants to chat."

I'll need to tell him sooner or later, she thought. *But not just yet.*

Chapter 7

"It might actually do me some good to talk about this," Eileen confessed to her daughter as they waited for their breakfast orders to arrive. "I've kept a lot of feelings bottled up."

"Then why haven't we talked before?" Cecily asked. "Why the silence all these years?"

Eileen delicately folded creases in her napkin while she considered what she wanted to say. "Honey, do you remember the first time you came back to us, after staying with your birth mother for awhile? You'd just turned six. For the first couple of weeks, you were so quiet it scared me.

"I kept asking you questions: 'What was it like at Seffie's house?' or 'How do you feel about living with us again?' You'd never answer me. You'd act like you hadn't heard a word I said.

"Finally, your father took me aside and said, 'Eileen, just leave her be. She'll talk to you when she's ready.' So I took his advice and stopped asking questions. But you know what, honey? You never did talk to me about your other home. You just fell back into the routine of life with us. After awhile, it seemed like you'd never left."

She emptied a packet of sweetener into her coffee and stirred it slowly. "What was it like, honey?"

Cecily set her cup back in its saucer and sighed deeply. "What can I say, Mom? It wasn't good. Most of the time, I was scared, scared of Seffie, scared about things that happened in her home. She had a bad temper. She was unpredictable, and I never knew what to expect. Her house was nasty. Compared to her place, your home seemed like a mansion to me." She chuckled. "Believe me Mom, I was glad to come back to you!"

Eileen reached over the table and patted Cecily's hand. "And of course, we welcomed you back with open arms," she said. "When the social worker asked me if we'd be willing to take you back, I said yes before I could even draw a breath. There was no question in my mind, and I knew your father felt the same."

"I'm sure glad you said yes," Cecily murmured.

"Honey, do you remember what I said to you when you were leaving for Seffie's house the second time?"

Cecily furrowed her brow, shaking her head.

"I said, 'Don't worry, you'll come back to us soon.' I knew I had no right to tell you that. But I felt fully confident in saying it. Child Protective Services had told your father and me that this was Seffie's last chance with you. I knew that before too long, things would fall apart at her house again. And I was right."

Cecily lowered her eyes. "Mom, do you know why I was taken away from Seffie?"

"Well, the first time you came to us, it was because she'd been arrested on drug charges. The other two times were because of neglect. That's what the court papers said. The social worker told me Seffie had left you alone, without any adult supervision."

"That's what I suspected," Cecily said. "I remember Seffie leaving the house when she'd get mad. It's like she never thought about us kids needing someone to watch us. She'd just be thinking about getting away."

Eileen shook her head in disbelief. "I can't imagine a mother thinking like that."

"I don't think she was anywhere near ready to handle the responsibility of a child," Cecily said. "Let alone three. And later, four."

"What?" Eileen exclaimed. "I had no idea Seffie had four children. I was only aware of two, you and a girl a year younger than you."

"You must be talking about Starly." Cecily smiled fondly at the thought of her little sister. "How did you know about Starly?"

"The day the social worker first brought you to our home, she mentioned that your birth mother had another daughter, a two-year-old. After you left and then came back to us, I'd sometimes overhear you talk about Starly while you played with your baby-dolls. I found this very curious, as you hadn't done that before you stayed at Seffie's.

"So one day I asked, 'Who's Starly?' You said, 'My friend,' then went right on playing. I wondered if Starly might've been the little sister the social worker had referred to.

"Shortly after that, I was asked to attend a meeting with a Marshall County Child Protective Services worker in Plymouth. An Amish woman was sitting in the waiting room, and she had an appointment with the same social worker I was there to see. She had a little blue-eyed, blonde-haired girl with her who looked to be about four or five years old. The child was adorable, with her hair done up in long braids. She was wearing an Amish dress, and she looked like a child from the *Little House on the Prairie* show.

"I commented on how cute she was. The Amish woman told me the little girl was her foster child, and that she and her husband were hoping to adopt her. She said they had a family of boys, and that they'd be so pleased if they could keep this little girl.

"Right then and there, I had a strong suspicion she was Seffie's other child. Some of her features reminded me of you, especially her eyes. The little girl clung to her foster mother, but she was very restless, constantly squirming, climbing onto her mother's lap and then sliding off again half a minute later."

Cecily laughed. "That was Starly, for sure! You described her perfectly! Except I never saw her dressed in Amish clothing. She always wore the same kind of clothing I wore when we were at Seffie's."

"The foster mother called her Annie," Eileen continued. "'Now Annie,' she'd say. 'Try to see if you can sit still for a minute.' Sometimes she'd scold her in the Pennsylvania Dutch language."

"Yes," Cecily said, "that had to be my sister. But this is the first time I had any inkling that Starly had been living in an Amish home. That's incredible! It just blows my mind! I guess that explains her long braids. I was always fascinated by Starly's braids."

"If I remember correctly," Eileen said, "when the social worker mentioned Seffie's other daughter, she said the child had been in her foster home since infancy. That means Starly would've known only the Amish way of life, up until she went to Seffie's house."

"Wow!" Cecily exclaimed. "Unbelievable! Did the Amish lady tell you anything else?"

"No, she didn't. I wanted to ask more questions, but she was called in to meet with the social worker before I had the chance."

The waitress served their breakfast orders, and the two women ate in silence, mulling over the information they'd just exchanged.

Then Eileen said, "Tell me about your other sisters."

Cecily put down her fork and pushed aside her half-empty plate. "When I first arrived at Seffie's house, the only other child was a baby girl named Shaney. She was very tiny, just a few months old, I think. She was the cutest thing I'd ever seen, and I liked to pretend she was my baby-doll. Starly came a little later. She'd stay just a few days, and then she'd leave again. When I went to Seffie's house the second time, Starly wasn't there anymore. But Shaney was there, and Seffie had another baby girl named Stella."

"I can't believe this, honey," Eileen said. "In all the years that have passed since then, you've never once spoken to me about any of those little girls."

She sighed deeply and closed her eyes for a moment before speaking again. "Now, honey, I need to ask you a question, and I don't want you to think I'm being unkind or critical. Why are you feeling the need to see your biological mother again? It's important for me to understand."

Cecily drew a deep breath. "That's a tough question, Mom. I've been having a hard time figuring that out myself. This might seem strange to you, but in a way, I feel like I let Seffie down. I never loved her, you know. You were the only mother I loved."

Eileen smiled, tears welling in her eyes.

"I feel guilty about not loving her," Cecily continued. "I think Seffie knew I didn't want to be with her. She and I never connected when I was living there. I felt differently about my sisters. I loved them dearly. But not Seffie."

She shook her head, biting her lip. "She wanted to be my mother, and I didn't want anything to do with her. I feel like I abandoned her."

"But you know it was the other way around, don't you?" Eileen said. "It was Seffie who abandoned you."

"I know that," Cecily said. "But I still feel the need to find her, to give her another chance, I guess. I want her to know I'm okay, and that I don't have any hard feelings toward her. And I need to know that she's okay. I'm afraid she may not be. The way her life was going, it's possible she might not be doing so well right now."

"I understand, honey. What you're feeling makes sense to me."

Cecily sighed with relief. "Thanks, Mom. I can't believe how wonderful you're being about this."

Eileen smiled sheepishly. "I don't know about being wonderful. I just want you to be happy." Then she looked at Cecily quizzically. "How can I help you?"

"What do you mean?" Cecily asked.

"How can I help you find your birth mother?"

Cecily leaned back in the booth, her brow furrowed in thought, one hand twisting a lock of hair. "I guess I don't know, Mom. I actually have no idea how to start this search. Do you think I can get any information from Child Protective Services records?"

"That information would be confidential," Eileen said. "I don't believe they'd release any documents."

"Then just tell me anything else you know about my birth mother."

"Well, her last name was Dickerson. Her first name was actually Seferina."

"Seferina Dickerson." Cecily tried out the sound of the name. "I always knew her as Seffie. Seffie's short for Seferina. That makes sense."

"When you first came to our home, Seffie was living in the same county we were living in. We lived in Elkhart, and she was in Nappanee. Do you remember our house in Elkhart? We lived there until we adopted you, then we moved here to South Bend."

Cecily nodded. "Of course I do."

"When Child Protective Services placed you in our home," Eileen continued, "the social worker told me Seffie had just been arrested. She was expected to be incarcerated for a period of time. I suspect when she got out of jail, she moved to Marshall County, because when you were placed back into her custody, you went to Marshall County. Some small town, I believe."

"Marshall County," Cecily mused. "When I was that age, I had no idea what county we were in. All I knew was that I was a long way from your house."

She stared down at the table, deep in thought. "When I was in Seffie's home, she was living with a man named Jimmy. I don't know whether she was married to him. If she was, she probably changed her last name."

"As far as I know," Eileen replied, "Seffie's last name remained Dickerson. That's the name that was always in the court documents."

"Do you know the last name of the family Starly lived with?"

"No, honey, I'm sorry, I don't remember a name at all. Wait a minute, let me think."

Eileen removed her glasses and rubbed the bridge of her nose, trying to concentrate. "I believe the social worker addressed the Amish lady by the name of Martha. Maybe it was Miriam, something along those lines. I'm pretty sure it started with an 'M'. I remember thinking the social worker was being disrespectful to address her by her first name."

Cecily's heart pounded with excitement. She was getting clues, the first leads toward her destination. "Do you know where the Amish lady lived? Was she from Elkhart County, too?"

"Let me think," Eileen said. "I remember the social worker asking her whether she'd hired a driver to bring her to the office. The lady said she'd come by horse and buggy, because it wasn't too far of a drive from their house to Plymouth. And I recall having seen a horse and buggy tied up in the parking lot. That unusual sight had caught my attention. So I don't think your sister's adoptive family could've lived in Elkhart County. It had to be some place in Marshall County. Not in Plymouth, but some place nearby."

As Cecily drove home from the restaurant, she mulled over the bits of information her mother had given her. *I've got so much to tell Evan,* she thought.

When she walked into the house, she found a note from Stephen on the kitchen table informing her he'd gone golfing. Unencumbered by her husband's presence, Cecily headed to her computer, accessed her work email, and began typing a message to Evan.

The breakfast meeting with my mother went splendidly. She's over the shock of my announcement, and she's being amazingly supportive and helpful. She was able to give me my first clues about my birth family. My biological mother's full name is Seferina Dickerson, and the last my adoptive mother knew, she was living in Marshall County. My sister Starly may have been adopted by an Amish family, and they probably live in Marshall County, too. See you on Monday!

As Cecily clicked on *send*, she felt a pang of guilt. Her relationship with Evan had now crept into her home life. Here she was, emailing him in secrecy while her husband was away from home.

I should probably put a little space between Evan and me, she thought.

That evening, Cecily and Stephen sat on their deck sipping wine coolers, looking out over their backyard.

"We have a pretty nice place here, don't we, Cessy?" Stephen observed.

Cecily cringed at the sound of Stephen's pet name for her. It sounded too much like Sissy, and it felt like he was invading her private world. But she tried to hide her discomfort. "Yes, we do have a nice place."

"Cessy, what do you think about sharing this place with a kid? Can you picture a swing-set out there in the yard? Maybe a kiddy pool and a sandbox?"

When Cecily didn't respond to her husband's subtle suggestions, he went straight to the point. "I think it's time to stop taking your birth-control pills."

"Huh?" Cecily said, startled.

"Well, don't act so surprised. We've had this conversation before. In fact, you brought it up the last time."

"Sorry. You just caught me off guard."

Stephen looked at her pointedly. "You're really not into this idea, are you?" His voice sounded accusing.

"I'm thinking about it, Stephen," Cecily said, trying to repair the damaged moment. Inwardly, she panicked. *Oh my God, this isn't the time! I can't have a baby now, not in the middle of all I've got going on.*

Chapter 8

As it turned out, Cecily had no difficulty maintaining distance from Evan that week. Her work days were hectic, and she didn't even have time to leave her office for lunch. She ate at her desk, grabbing a few bites between returning phone calls and completing documentation.

So there were no opportunities for long conversations with Evan, and she was relieved. She was glad her busy work schedule diverted her attention from her personal concerns. Her thoughts about finding Seffie and her sisters continued to play in the recesses of her mind, but she had no time to delve into them or to formulate plans.

On Thursday morning, she checked her overflowing inbox for new email messages and found one from Evan.

So you're avoiding me now, huh? he wrote. Cecily knew he was joking, because he'd inserted a smiley face at that point in the message. *Seriously, I know it's been crazy around here, and you're probably breaking your neck to keep up. I wanted to let you know that after I received your email Monday morning, I did some internet research on your behalf. If you have a few minutes after work, stop by my office.*

Cecily stared at the message, flabbergasted. *I can't believe he went to all that trouble for me. What a sweetheart!* She couldn't wait to hear what he had to tell her.

"Come on in, Cecily," Evan said as she stood at his office door. His voice sounded surprisingly serious.

Cecily seated herself on an upholstered chair. Evan remained seated at his desk, but swiveled his chair around to face her. His grim expression frightened her, and a sense of foreboding clutched her stomach.

"So what do you have to tell me, Evan?" she asked.

Evan gazed at her with unsmiling eyes. "Cecily, I don't know how to make this easy for you, so I'll just cut to the chase. Your mother is dead."

For a second, Cecily thought Evan was referring to Eileen Hartman, and her heart fell to the floor. The next second, she realized if it was her adoptive mother who'd died, Evan wouldn't be the one delivering the news. Reality crashed into her awareness. Evan was referring to Seferina Dickerson. His research had led him to the information that her biological mother was dead.

She stared at him in disbelief. "Are you sure?"

"As sure as I can be," he said. He picked up a sheet of paper from his desk and read the contents to her.

"Seferina Dickerson. Date of birth: February 21, 1965. Place of birth: Plymouth, Indiana. Children: Sissy Dickerson, born July 17, 1981, paternity unknown; Starly Dickerson, born August 29, 1982, father Gregory Smith; Shaney McDaniel, born August 11, 1986, father James McDaniel; Stella McDaniel, born November 20, 1987, father James McDaniel."

Evan glanced up at Cecily, and then continued to read. "Date of death: April 16, 1991."

"No. That can't be." Cecily closed her eyes and shook her head, trying to ward off the unbearable news. Evan waited in silence until she opened her eyes again.

"How . . . how did you get this information?" she stammered.

"I compiled it from several different websites," Evan explained. "It occurred to me that before you began searching for your mother, you needed to know whether she's still living. I suspected that, given the lifestyle Seffie had going, the odds of her dying young were greater than average. And I was right. Unfortunately, I was right."

Cecily slumped forward, burying her face in her hands. "Why did I even start this?" she said to herself more than to Evan. "I just keep running into problems and stirring up pain."

"I'm so sorry," Evan murmured.

She raised her head. "I'd been fantasizing about finding Seffie as a mature person, not so young and wild. I pictured us having a heart-to-heart conversation. I wanted to tell her that I don't hate her, and that even though I loved a different mother, she meant something to me. Now I'll never have the chance, Evan. I'll never have the chance."

With that, she began to sob uncontrollably. Evan stood up, and taking her by the hand, he led her to the sofa where he folded her in his

arms. The minutes passed while she wept like a broken-hearted child.
He held her patiently, stroking her hair and her back.

When Cecily finally regained her composure, Evan kissed her forehead and released his embrace. She pulled herself back and reached
for a box of tissues to wipe her nose and smudged makeup.

"I feel like a fool," she said. "I was putting so much stock in those
dreams, thinking they meant Seffie was communicating with me, telling
me to look for her. How stupid was that? She couldn't have wanted to
me to find her. She's been dead for seventeen years."

"How do you know she wasn't trying to communicate with you?"
Evan asked.

Cecily stared at him, incredulous. "You mean from the other side?"

"I don't know. Maybe. Who knows how to explain the experiences
you've had?"

"They probably didn't mean anything," she said bitterly. For a few
moments, she fixed a mindless gaze on a set of bookshelves across the
room. Then she said, "Well, I guess this was all for nothing. It's the second time my plans have crashed. That means it's time to let go of this
crazy idea. "

"Why would you give up now?" Evan chided. "You still have your sisters. There's more we need to discuss about my research, but not now.
You need to go home and deal with the news you've just heard. We'll
talk later."

Cecily stood up to leave. "Thanks again, Evan," she said. "I can't believe how good you are to me."

He walked her to the door, and then wrapped his arms around her
for a final hug, pressing his cheek against hers. Cecily surrendered to
the tenderness of his embrace, wishing she could stay in the circle of his
comforting arms forever.

"Where on earth have you been?" Stephen demanded to know
when Cecily walked through the front door. "You're forty-five minutes
late!" He scrutinized her face, suspicion in his eyes. "What's going on?
You've been crying."

Her husband's harshly voiced concern threatened to overwhelm

Cecily's fragile emotional state. Frantically, she searched her mind for an explanation that would keep him at bay.

"I just had some bad news," she said. "I'm still shook up, and I can't talk right now. Let me get myself together, and then we can discuss it over dinner."

While Stephen put the finishing touches on the meal he'd prepared, Cecily washed her face, brushed her hair, and changed into comfortable clothing.

"So what happened?" Stephen asked as he watched his wife toy with her food.

Cecily took a deep breath. "You remember when I told you I was bothered by memories?"

"Yes." Stephen's voice sounded guarded.

"I also had some dreams along the same line."

"What about?"

"My birth mother."

Stephen looked perplexed. "Okay . . ."

"You remember when I was crying, and you told me to talk with someone?"

"I'm not sure I remember telling you that, but okay."

"Well, I've been talking to someone."

Stephen put down his fork and stared at his wife. "Who?"

"One of my coworkers, Evan Carter."

"You mean the psychologist?"

"Yes."

"Why him?"

"I don't know. It just happened. One day he noticed I was upset, and he asked me about it. "

"So I take it you've talked with him more than once about this stuff?"

"Yes, we've had a few conversations about it."

"Isn't he that guy who's always coming on to women in the office?"

"That's what some people say about him."

"I'm not comfortable with the idea of you talking to him."

Anger rumbled in the pit of Cecily's stomach, threatening to erupt in an ugly explosion. "Look Stephen," she said sharply. "I really don't care whether or not you're comfortable with this. I needed someone to talk to. You weren't there for me, but Evan was. And he's been very help-ful. Now if you want to know what happened today, you need to stop interrogating me."

Stephen sat back in his chair and folded his arms across his chest. "Go ahead and talk. I'm listening."

Cecily spoke tentatively, eying her husband warily. "In the course of my conversations with Evan, I made the decision to look for my birth mother and sisters."

"What the hell?" Stephen looked ready to bolt out of his chair.

"What do you mean, what the hell?" Cecily retorted.

"I mean, why would you want to do something like that?"

"Maybe because I have sentimental feelings. But of course you think that's ridiculous."

"So you're making me out to be an insensitive jerk. Is that all you think of me?"

Cecily pushed her chair back and stood up. "Okay, I'm done talking."

"Wait!" Stephen demanded. "I have the right to know what's going on. In case you haven't noticed, I'm the guy you've been married to for the past four years!"

Cecily sighed and sat down again. "Okay, I'm going to make this short. I told my parents about my decision to find my birth family. They were upset at first, but now they're being really nice about it. When I went out to breakfast with my mother last Saturday, we had a long talk about my birth family. She gave me a few pieces of information, which I passed on to Evan. He took it upon himself to do some research. Hon-estly, I had no idea what he was up to. Today, he emailed me and asked me to stop by his office after work because he had some information for me. His news is what shook me up so badly. He told me my birth mother is dead."

Stephen's features had hardened into a rigid mask, and Cecily couldn't tell what emotions lurked behind it. "So that's what you were crying about?" he asked.

"Yes."

"But you haven't seen her for . . . for twenty years or more! How could this be so upsetting to you?"

Cecily shook her head in disbelief. "I give up, Stephen. I give up."

But Stephen plunged ahead. "So when were you planning on telling me all this? First, you tell that guy at work, who I'm pretty sure has ulterior motives for talking with you. Then you tell your parents. But you didn't bother to tell me until I pulled it out of you."

"In case you haven't figured this out," Cecily snapped, "you aren't exactly an easy person to talk to, Stephen. If I happen to act like a human woman with emotions, you make me feel like an idiot. You're not going to like this, but I'm going to say it anyway. Evan's easy to talk to. He doesn't make me feel stupid. He understands everything I tell him."

The dinner plates clattered as Stephen abruptly pushed away from the table. Cecily grabbed her water glass to keep it from toppling over.

"I bet he does!" he muttered as he stalked out of the room.

Utterly exhausted, Cecily cleared the table and piled the dirty dishes in the sink. Then she went to her bedroom, closed the door, and curled up on the bed. She stared out the window, watching the evening light fading into darkness, her mind so weary she couldn't put a coherent thought together.

Around ten o'clock, Stephen tapped on the door, then opened it a crack. "Can I come in?"

"If you want to." Cecily's voice was flat.

Stephen entered the room and sat down on the other side of the bed. "I'm not even going to bother apologizing for being a jerk," he said, "because I know you don't want to hear it. But I've been sitting in the living room all evening, trying to figure out what I want to say to you."

He exhaled deeply, running his hand over the top of his head. "I just don't understand you right now, Cecily. Maybe Evan does, and he's the better man for it. But I'll be honest and admit that I don't. You're not the woman I married four years ago. Back then, you seemed satisfied with your life. Your parents had given you everything you wanted. And quite frankly, I don't think I've done too shabby by you myself."

"I know," Cecily murmured. "I'm not complaining. Have you ever heard me complain?"

Ignoring her question, Stephen continued. "You're someone most other women would envy. You've got your looks and your career and, believe it or not, a husband who adores you. So I can't figure out why you're so down in the dumps about stuff that happened decades ago."

Cecily shrugged. "Sorry, I can't explain it."

"Maybe I should understand," Stephen said, softening his voice. "But I don't. So you know what I've decided?"

"What?"

"I've decided to stay out of this, because every time I get involved, I screw up and get you upset. So talk to whoever you need to talk to. Talk to Evan if you need to. But promise me one thing, Cecily."

She sighed wearily. "What, Stephen?"

"Just be careful with Evan. Promise me you'll be careful. I couldn't take it if anything happened."

"Don't worry about it. Nothing's going to happen."

"Do you want me to come to bed now?"

"No."

"Should I go to the guest room?"

"Yes, please. I need to be alone tonight."

Stephen leaned over and kissed her forehead. "I really am sorry," he said as he left the room.

After the argument with her husband, Cecily was prepared for another night of insomnia. She pulled the covers tightly around her, comforting herself with the memory of Evan's embrace.

But she slept and she dreamed, not of Seffie, but of Evan. She and Evan soared through the stars in the night sky, flying effortlessly, sometimes hand-in-hand, sometimes wrapped in an intimate embrace.

And Evan's dream touch melted the aching tension in her body. She was surprised when she awoke the next morning feeling refreshed.

Chapter 9

The team members milled around the snack table in the conference room, helping themselves to coffee and pastries before the start of the Friday morning staff meeting. Cecily had just filled a cup with coffee when she felt a light touch on the small of her back. She turned and found Evan at her side.

"How are you feeling this morning?" He flashed his dazzling smile. "I was worried about you last night."

Cecily smiled back. "I'm feeling fine."

The encounter was only momentary, but as the two of them parted ways to sit on opposite sides of the conference table, Cecily felt a twinge of pain at the loss of her friend's nearness.

Later that morning, she stopped by her supervisor's office to get his signature on a form. As Frank handed the signed document back to her, he asked, "Cecily, is Evan bothering you?"

She felt her face redden. "No, not at all. If you've seen Evan and me together, it's because we're working on a project."

"That's fine," Frank said. "It's none of my business. I'm aware of the fact that Evan tends to cross the line with women. I thought if he was creating a problem for you, I'd have a talk with him."

Once again, Cecily worked through her lunch hour, tackling the ever-present backlog of documentation. Suddenly, she heard a voice from her doorway. She glanced up to find her most irritating coworker standing there.

"Where's Evan?" Amanda asked, smirking.

"How should I know?" Cecily turned her eyes back to her computer screen, hoping Amanda would go away.

"So the two of you aren't having lunch together?"

"Does it look like it?" Cecily responded sarcastically.

After Amanda walked away, Cecily panicked. *People are starting to talk about Evan and me. Two people in one day have insinuated that something's going on between us.*

Later in the day, she received an email from Evan. *When do you want to finish our conversation about my research?*

The message unleashed a flood of conflicting emotions in her. She typed, *How about if I stop by your office after work?* Then she deleted the sentence. As much as she wanted to hear what Evan had to say, her good judgment brought her eagerness into submission.

She knew it wouldn't be wise to go home late again that evening, as she didn't want any more conflict with her husband. She didn't want to feed any rumors among her coworkers by lingering in Evan's office at the end of the day. But her biggest reason for avoiding contact with Evan was a personal one. She couldn't deny the fact that physical desire for him was welling up inside her. It needed to simmer down before she spent time alone with him again.

So she typed, *How about lunch on Monday?* She hesitated, and then clicked on *send.*

That evening, Cecily and Stephen shared a carryout pizza while they watched TV in the living room. Then Stephen announced he was going to the bedroom to work on his computer. Cecily followed him and lounged on the bed, reading a novel. She was pleased the two of them were getting along well enough to be together in the same room, but relieved that her husband wasn't pressuring her for intimacy. They slept in the same bed that night, back to back.

On Saturday afternoon, Cecily sat beside her mother while Eileen tended the cash box at her church rummage sale. After having heard the news of her birth mother's death, Cecily felt the need to be near her adoptive mother, to absorb the comfort of Eileen's nurturing presence.

For several hours, the two of them kept busy with customers, Eileen taking the money while Cecily bagged the purchases. Cecily knew she needed to share the news of Seffie's death with her mother. Eileen had committed her support to the search for her biological family, and was eager for updates.

When the rummage sale traffic died down, Cecily seized the opportunity to talk. "Mom, I have something to tell you."

A flicker of fear passed through Eileen's eyes, quickly replaced by a gentle smile. "What is it, dear?"

"I thought I should tell you what I found out two days ago. My biological mother, Seferina Dickerson, is dead."

Eileen startled, bringing a trembling hand to her mouth, and Cecily was once again sorry to deliver news that shocked her elderly mother.

"A friend of mine did some internet research for me," she explained, "and I learned that Seffie died seventeen years ago. Obviously, my search for her is over. I'm really sorry I put you through this."

Still stunned, Eileen stared at her daughter. Cecily realized how fragile her mother had become. She put her arm around Eileen's thin frame and laid her head on her shoulder.

Then Eileen spoke. "Honey, I'll admit there was a day when I would've been relieved to hear this news, because it would've meant your birth mother couldn't cause any more problems for us. But now, I can't feel anything but sadness. Searching for her was important to you, and for that reason, it was important to me."

Cecily wondered how she'd ever cope if this mother of hers should pass away. At the moment, she couldn't imagine surviving it.

"What about your sisters?" Eileen asked. "Are you still going to look for your sisters?"

Cecily kissed her mother's cheek. "I haven't thought much about it since I heard the news of Seffie's death. But, yes, I'm still going to look for them."

"They're talking about us," Cecily fretted when Evan stepped into her office for their Monday lunch date. "I think there's a rumor going around."

Evan shot her a wicked grin as he took off his jacket and slung it over the back of a chair. "Let them talk, kiddo," he said, seating himself on the sofa. "I'm used to people talking about me. It doesn't bother me. If they enjoy it, let them talk."

He posed a striking figure, leaning back in a relaxed posture, one ankle crossed over the other knee, one arm stretched over the back of the sofa. Utterly at ease with himself, he looked devastatingly handsome.

Cecily suppressed an urge to abandon her seat on her desk chair and jump on the sofa to snuggle with Evan. She wanted to run her fingers along his chiseled features and through his thick black hair. She imagined herself loosening his tie and undoing his shirt buttons. Then, in her fantasy, she nuzzled her face against his muscular neck and slid her hand inside his shirt, caressing his chest and taut abdomen.

Shocked by her erotic reverie, she looked away from her companion. *Stop it, Cecily,* she scolded herself.

"What's on your mind, kiddo?" Evan asked, flashing his charming smile.

"I'm just waiting to hear about your research," Cecily lied.

Evan shifted his position and leaned forward, elbows on his knees, ready for business.

"So are you still interested in finding your sisters?"

"Yes, I am."

"Well, I'm pretty sure it won't be too difficult to find Shaney and Stella. According to my research, they live in the small town of Belmont, which is just north of Plymouth. They're not that far from here. Neither one of them shows a name change, so they've probably never married. And it appears they share an address with their father, James McDaniel."

"Wow!" Cecily said, her mind spinning with the implications of Evan's information. "That means Shaney and Stella were never adopted. They stayed with Jimmy!"

Somehow, the idea pleased her. An image of Jimmy's kindly face drifted through her inner vision.

Jimmy's huge body spills over the sides of the kitchen chair as he sits at the table with his buddy from the trailer park. An open can of Coke sits beside the baby bottle in front of him. He cradles baby Stella in one fat arm as he keeps an eye on little Shaney, who is toddling around the kitchen rifling through the cupboards.

Sissy sits on the living room floor with a coloring book and a box of crayons. From time to time, she looks up from her coloring to see what's going on, but she knows things will be okay. Jimmy's in charge.

Jimmy's friend pulls a six-pack from a grocery bag. "Wanna beer, Jim?" he asks.

"No, Butch, I'm stickin' to my Coke here," Jimmy says. "I'm a family man now."

"These kids all yours?" Butch asks.

"Yup." Jimmy grins proudly. "This'n here's my baby Stella, named after her gramma. That'n over there's Shaney. That'n there in the other room is Sissy. She ain't really mine, but I claim 'er. She's a good little girl, real nice to have around."

"Didn't ya used to have another one runnin' around here? A little girl with long blonde hair?"

Sissy puts down her crayon and watches Jimmy intently, waiting for his reply.

The proud gleam leaves Jimmy's eyes, and his fat face goes slack. "Yup," he says in a heavy voice. "Seffie had another one she used to call Starly, just a year younger than Sissy over there. Seffie couldn't handle 'er so she gave 'er up. Starly was a purty little thing, she was. I just thought it was a damn shame the way things turned out."

"Bummer!" Butch says. He rips a beer out of the six-pack and pops it open.

"Keep it to one or two, there, Butch," Jimmy cautions. "Cain't have nobody gettin' stupid around these kids."

"So Jimmy's still living, then," Cecily murmured, more to herself than to Evan. Her eyes welled with tears.

"It appears he is," Evan said.

"What about Starly? What did you find on Starly?"

"Nothing. Not a damn thing. Nothing at all on Starly Dickerson."

Cecily stared at Evan, bewildered. "Why not?"

"If Starly was indeed adopted," he explained, "she would've had a name change."

"Of course," Cecily said. "She's probably Annie now."

"And we don't know what her new last name is. We suspect she's Annie, but Annie who?"

Cecily clenched her jaw in determination. "I'm not doing this without Starly. Maybe Seffie could let her go without a second thought, but I can't. I'm finding Starly first, no matter how hard it is."

"Okay," Evan said. "What do we have to go on?"

"We think she was adopted by an Amish family who lives in Marshall County. She'd be twenty-six now. That's all I have." Cecily studied her carefully manicured fingernails, pondering the situation. "So what do you know about the Amish, Evan?"

"Very little," Evan responded. "I'm not from around here. I never laid eyes on an Amish person before I moved out here a few years ago."

"Where are you from?" Cecily asked. She suddenly realized she knew very little about Evan Carter.

"Colorado. I was born and raised in Colorado." Evan looked preoccupied for a moment before focusing back to the subject at hand.

"What do you know about the Amish?" he asked.

"Probably not much more than you do," Cecily admitted. "But I think my father's familiar with them. He grew up in LaGrange County, and there's a big Amish settlement there. And I'm sure there's information on the internet."

"Do you want me to do some research about the Amish?" Evan offered.

"No," Cecily said. "Let me do it."

That evening, Cecily sat at her computer for several hours, reading through articles about the Amish religion and culture. Then she encountered a short passage that sparked an idea in her mind: *The Amish church has no formal national head office. Each Amish congregation is independent. The Bishop provides spiritual leadership for the congregation. He preaches and performs baptisms, marriages and funerals.*

"The bishop!" Cecily exclaimed. "The bishop would know all the families in his congregation. If I could find an Amish bishop in Marshall County, I might get somewhere."

Just then, Stephen walked into the bedroom. "Did you say something to me?"

"No," Cecily said. "I was talking to myself."

"What are you doing?"

"Some online research."

"About what?"

"The Amish."

"Why?"

"Just curious."

"Okay." Stephen picked up the book he was looking for and left the room.

Chapter 10

When Cecily arrived at her parents' house for dinner on Wednesday, her father greeted her at the door with a warm hug. "I'm sorry to hear about your birth mother's death," he said. "I'm sure that was difficult news to hear."

"Thanks, Dad." Cecily linked her arm through his and accompanied him to the dining room, where her mother was putting dinner on the table.

Eileen served a green salad followed by salmon fillets, wild rice, and baby peas. She insisted on serving a formal meal of at least three courses when Cecily came to eat with them.

"Dad, would you have time for a chat this evening?" Cecily asked as they finished their chocolate cake and coffee.

Leonard and Eileen exchanged questioning glances. Eileen nodded at her husband, as if to give him the *go ahead* signal.

"Sure," Leonard said. "I have plenty of time. All the time in the world for you, sweetheart."

"I'll clear the table," Eileen said. "Why don't the two of you go to the study?"

Cecily followed her father to the room that had been dear to her heart since childhood. Leonard sat at his desk, and Cecily took a seat in the massive leather recliner. She thought of the countless times she'd sat in that chair as a little girl. Back then, its huge size had dwarfed her. As a child, Cecily had thought her father's special room with its over-flowing bookshelves was aptly named. She imagined he was always studying some mysterious body of knowledge unfathomable to her young mind.

Leonard's study had never been off-limits to Cecily, as she'd viewed the room with awe and had never misbehaved in it. She'd climb onto the recliner and, with all seriousness, raise some childish academic question to her father, who seemingly knew all things. Leonard never failed to treat Cecily's questions respectfully, and would expound on them at her level of understanding. She'd listen intently for a few minutes, then would slide off the chair and run off to play.

As she sat in the recliner enjoying her fond memories, Cecily knew her aging father was remembering the same. Leonard had swiveled around in his chair to face her, wearing the same kind, patient smile he'd worn years ago.

"Dad," she asked, "did Mom tell you I plan to look for my sisters?"

"Yes, she did. It sounds like you're preparing for quite an adventure."

Cecily breathed a sigh of relief and leaned back in her chair. She sensed that, like her mother, her father had made peace with the idea that she was searching for her biological family.

"Did Mom tell you that we think one of my sisters was adopted by an Amish family in Marshall County?" she asked.

"Yes, she did."

"Well, I've been thinking about how I might start looking for her. I did some internet research about the Amish. From what I came up with, I'm guessing the best source of information about the families in the Amish community would be an Amish bishop. It seems like he would know all the families in his congregation, and what's happened in their lives over the years."

"Good thinking," Leonard said. "I believe you're on the right track."

"So how would I go about finding an Amish bishop? According to the information I found on the internet, there isn't any national organization associated with the Amish church. And they don't have phones, so there wouldn't be churches or bishops listed in the phone book. Am I right about that?"

"You're correct. The Amish have no phones, no computers, no electronic devices of any kind. Your only way of communicating with them would be face-to-face or through letters."

"So how would I locate a bishop?" Cecily persisted. "Would I just walk up to an Amish person and ask them for the name of their bishop? And where would I find an Amish person? There aren't any around here."

"No, there aren't. But there are quite a few in Elkhart and Marshall Counties. Of course, the biggest population in this area is in LaGrange County."

"So I might have to go to one of those counties," Cecily mused. "But I'd feel pretty weird walking up to an Amish person and asking them about their bishop."

"The Amish are, for the most part, friendly people of a gentle nature," Leonard said. "If you approach them in a respectful manner, they'd probably be willing to provide you with whatever information they have. You could strike up a friendly conversation and then lead up to your questions."

"Where would I do that, Dad?"

"How about some place where a lot of Amish people conduct business? Unfortunately, I'm not aware of any such place in Marshall County. In Elkhart County, there's Amish Acres in Nappanee. You'd find Amish people employed in restaurants and shops there. The Essen Haus in Middlebury is another place."

Leonard stopped to think for a moment. "Have you ever been to Shipshewana in LaGrange County? You'd find unlimited opportunities to talk with Amish people in that town. Have you and Stephen ever been to the flea market in Shipshewana?"

"No, we haven't. What's it like?"

"It's an enormous flea market, with hundreds of vendors. You'd find everything from food to clothing to house-wares to tools. You name it, it's there. You'd find quite a number of Amish vendors there, and the rest of the town is filled with tourist shops that employ Amish people. A trip to Shipshewana can be a whole day's adventure."

Her father's suggestion struck a chord with Cecily. "I'll plan on going there, Dad. Is the flea market open every day?"

"No," Leonard replied, "to the best of my knowledge, it's open only on Tuesdays and Wednesdays. So if you want to visit the flea market, you'll have to take a day off work."

A plan began formulating in Cecily's mind. Tomorrow, she'd ask Frank if she could take the following Wednesday off, and she'd go to Shipshewana. There was no need to wait. Nothing would stop her now. Even if the thought of it daunted her, she was going to venture into the world of the Amish to find her sister. She'd ask all the questions she needed to ask until she found Starly.

When Cecily arrived at work the next morning, she went straight to her supervisor's office. "I know this is short notice," she said, "but I'd really like to take a vacation day next Wednesday."

"Is this absolutely necessary?" Frank asked. "You're schedule is already full that day."

"It's important to me," Cecily said. "Extremely important."

Frank thought for a moment, and then shrugged. "Okay, Cecily, go ahead. Tell Meredith right away so she can reschedule your clients."

"Thanks so much, Frank," Cecily said. "I really appreciate it." After informing Meredith of the change in her schedule, she went to her office, turned on her computer, and typed an email message to Evan.

You won't believe what I'm doing next Wednesday! I'm taking the day off, and I'm going to Shipshewana. I plan on talking to Amish people to get information about a bishop in Marshall County. I'm thinking an Amish bishop would know what's going on in the lives of the families in his community, and maybe he'll know something about Starly's adoption.

Later in the day, she received a reply: *Go for it, kiddo. I'm proud of you. You're unstoppable!*

"We haven't done anything fun in a long time," Stephen said at the end of a mundane weekend at home. "Why don't we plan something for next weekend? We could call friends and go out for dinner. Or we could invite them over here for a barbeque. Or we could go to Chicago for the weekend. We haven't done that for awhile. Anything you want, it's up to you. It seems like our life is getting a little boring, don't you think?"

Cecily knew that several months earlier, she would have eagerly assented to any of the suggestions Stephen had just offered. But that evening, nothing appealed to her. She didn't want any form of excitement to distract her from her mission of finding her sisters. She wanted to say to Stephen, *I don't know about yours, but my life definitely isn't boring.*

She looked at the man she'd been married to for four years, who now seemed like a stranger to her, someone toward whom she felt rather indifferent. She thought about the day she'd met him, almost five-and-a-half years ago, at a friend's New Years Eve party. At that point, she was ready to start graduate school, and was brimming with excitement about the career possibilities open to her.

Stephen, thirty-two at the time, had just landed a lucrative job at Layman Laboratories. The future had looked promising for both of them, and it had seemed natural for two upcoming professionals to join forces and create a life together.

She hadn't considered Stephen to be handsome in a classical sense, but he was a pleasant-looking, clean-cut man. Her parents had heartily approved of him, despite the fact that he'd been married before. Leonard had been impressed with Stephen's career success at such a young age, and was relieved to know his future son-in-law could support his daughter in the style to which she'd become accustomed.

Now Cecily faced a thirty-seven-year-old balding husband who looked slouchy in his khaki trousers and polo shirt. He'd become quite paunchy, and she suspected he'd put on twenty-five pounds since the day they married.

What does this man have to do with me? she wondered. She couldn't help but compare him to Evan, who, although a few years older than Stephen, was handsome and physically fit, always looking like a million bucks in anything he wore.

At that moment, she felt like the victim of some huge cosmic mistake. Surely Evan was her true life partner, the one she confided in, the one whose company she enjoyed, the one to whom she felt overwhelmingly attracted. And here she was, stuck with someone she didn't even know anymore.

She knew there was no good way to explain her lack of interest in the activities Stephen had suggested. So she said, "That all sounds like fun, but maybe later. I've got a lot going on right now."

She braced herself for his sarcasm, but all he said was, "Okay."

Suddenly, it occurred to her that she hadn't told Stephen about her plans to visit Shipshewana. "Oh, by the way," she said. "I'm taking a day off work on Wednesday."

"Why?" he asked.

"I'm going to Shipshewana to visit the flea market."

"That sounds interesting. Want me to take the day off and go with you?"

Cecily cringed. "No, I need to go alone."

She saw a flicker of pain in her husband's eyes. "Does this have something to do with your search for your sisters?" he asked.

"Yes, it does."

He shrugged. "Do what you need to do, then."

Tuesday afternoon, Cecily received an email message from Evan: *Have a good trip tomorrow, kiddo! Drive safely, then come back and tell me all about it.*

Wednesday morning, Cecily woke up early. The moment she re-membered her plans for the day, she jumped out of bed to get ready for her outing.

Stephen watched her rifle through her closet for something to wear. "This is a big day for you," he said.

"Yes." Cecily felt guilty about not saying more, but she wanted no questions intruding into the bubble of solitude surrounding her mission.

She finally selected a pair of white slacks, a brightly patterned top, and sandals sturdy enough for hours of walking. Grabbing her handbag and a pair of sunglasses, she headed toward the door, then turned back and dutifully kissed her sleepy husband goodbye.

The day was perfect for her trip, the sky cloudless, the air crisp and cool. It seemed as if the universe had bathed her mission in an aura of magic. She felt an inexplicable conviction that this day marked a turn-ing point in her life, and unspeakable joy welled inside her.

It was a forty-five mile drive to her destination. An hour after setting out, she pulled into the town of Shipshewana and located a parking lot.

She decided to take in the shops in town before heading toward the flea market. She wandered through immaculate little stores overflowing with Amish baked goods, old-fashioned candy, quilts, and antiques. But she found herself more interested in the Amish sales clerks than she was in their merchandize. She wanted to strike up conversations with them, but the shops were filled with customers, and the clerks were too busy to say more than, "Thank you, have a nice day."

As Cecily strolled along the sidewalk between the shops, she realized she was surrounded by Amish people. *Maybe Starly is here,* she thought. *I might see my own sister on the street and not even know her.*

When she passed a young couple with small children in tow, she wondered whether Starly was now a wife and mother. She had difficulty imagining her as anyone but a tiny four-year-old with big blue eyes and long blonde braids.

Cecily kept waiting for her opening, for some serendipitous event to unfold which would allow her to strike up a conversation with an Amish person. But she passed several hours in town, and no such opportunity arose.

The magical aura surrounding her mission began to dissipate, disappointment and frustration creeping into its place. Disheartened, she decided to move on to the flea market, where she wandered up and down the endless rows of vendors' booths. Before long, she lost interest in what she was looking at, and contemplated going home.

Then a display of figurines caught her eye, Amish men and women dressed in their traditional garb. On impulse, she bought a pair, thinking she'd give them to Evan as a souvenir from her trip. But as the vendor wrapped the figurines in tissue paper and put them in a bag, she told herself that presenting Evan with a gift might be inappropriate.

Absorbed in her guilty thoughts, she almost missed the opportunity she'd been waiting for. She'd come upon an area where people were resting at picnic tables and on benches, enjoying the food they'd purchased from vendors.

Eager to get off her tired feet, Cecily looked around for a place to sit. She spotted an empty space on one end of a bench occupied by three young Amish women. One of them had a small boy who appeared to be about two years old. He wore tiny blue denim trousers and a pale green shirt. He kept toddling off, and his mother repeatedly jumped up to fetch him, scolding him in the Pennsylvania Dutch language.

The young women were chatting with each other, and Cecily could hear English phrases interspersed with their Pennsylvania Dutch. Suddenly, hope stirred in her heart again. *This is your chance,* she coached herself. *Take it!*

Given the fact that all the other seats were filled, it seemed like an entirely natural act for her to lay claim to the empty space on the bench next to the women. A moment after she sat down, the little boy toddled away from his mother and stood in front of her, staring.

Cecily thought her appearance must have seemed odd to the child, as his Amish mother and her companions were all wearing long dresses, black bonnets, black stockings, and heavy shoes. She suddenly felt garish in her brightly colored blouse and large dangling earrings. She glanced down at her painted toenails peeking out from her sandals, and imagined the child found her to be ridiculous.

But she smiled warmly at the little boy and said, "Hello there!" He grinned shyly, then ducked his head and scampered back to his mother, who lifted him onto her lap. Cecily glanced at her, and the two women exchanged smiles.

"He's very cute." Cecily said. "What's his name?"

"Isaac," his mother responded proudly.

Isaac slid off his mother's lap and walked over to stand in front of Cecily again. "Hello, Isaac," she said, extending her hand.

Isaac put his tiny hand in hers, and she shook it gently. "Please to meet you, Isaac."

The little boy burst into giggles and ran to his mother again. The three Amish women laughed at his antics, and Cecily laughed along with them.

She knew this was her moment to seize. "I'm Cecily," she said. "I'm from South Bend. I've heard so many nice things about Shipshewana, so I decided to come spend the day here."

The women seemed surprised at her personal introduction. In spite of her embarrassment, Cecily pressed on. "What are your names?"

The women glanced at each other, and then Isaac's mother said, "I'm Rebecca." She gestured toward each of her companions. "This is Elizabeth and this is Grace. They're sisters."

"Where are you ladies from?"

Again, the women exchanged puzzled glances before Rebecca responded. "We're all from around here. I live on a farm with my husband. Elizabeth and Grace aren't married, and they live with their parents."

Cecily took a deep breath. "Do you know anyone who lives in Marshall County? I'm looking for an Amish girl from Marshall County that I knew many years ago."

The three women consulted with each other in Pennsylvania Dutch, and then Rebecca said, "I'm sorry, we don't know anyone from Marshall County. Grace and Elizabeth say their uncle used to live there, but he moved away."

Undaunted, Cecily continued. "Do you by any chance know anything about an Amish bishop in Marshall County?"

"No I don't," Rebecca said. Elizabeth and Grace both shook their heads.

Cecily's obvious disappointment brought sympathetic expressions to the faces of the Amish women. "What's the name of the friend you're looking for?" Rebecca asked.

"Her name is Annie," Cecily said. "I don't know her last name."

The women looked at each other and chuckled, and Rebecca said, "Many Amish women are named Annie."

Suddenly, shy Elizabeth tugged on Rebecca's sleeve and whispered something in her ear. Then Rebecca turned toward Cecily and smiled. "Elizabeth has an idea that might be of help to you. She said our bishop knows many people all over northern Indiana, and he might know the name of a bishop in Marshall County."

Cecily's heart began to pound, and she could barely contain her excitement. "How could I contact your bishop?"

Elizabeth whispered something to Rebecca again. "Do you have pencil and paper?" Rebecca asked Cecily.

"Yes, I do." Cecily took a small notebook and an ink pen from her bag and handed them to Rebecca. Rebecca gave them to Elizabeth, who bent over the paper, concentrating on her writing. Her companions peered over her shoulders, offering suggestions.

Finally, Grace handed the notebook back to Cecily. On it was written *Ezra Miller,* followed by a LaGrange County mailing address.

"We hope this address is correct," Rebecca said. "We're quite sure it is."

"Thank you, thank you!" Cecily breathed. "You ladies have been so helpful to me." She carefully tucked the bishop's name and address into her bag, as if she was handling pure gold.

Chapter 11

Thursday morning, Cecily stood in the doorway of Evan's office, smiling broadly. "I've got something for you," she said, placing a gift bag on his desk.

Evan looked up from his work. "What are you up to, kiddo?" He pulled the bundle of tissue paper from the bag and unwrapped the figures of the Amish man and woman. Laughing, he set them on his desk. "So here's proof you went to Shipshewana yesterday."

Cecily nodded. "You told me you haven't seen many Amish people. Now you won't forget what they look like."

Evan laughed again. "No, I won't. Thanks, kiddo. I'll keep them right here on my desk in front of me."

Cecily picked up the figure of the woman, turning it over in her hands. "Do you suppose my sister looks like this?"

"That's hard to imagine, isn't it?" Evan said.

She set the figure back on the desk. "Guess what else I got in Shipshewana!" She pulled a piece of paper from her handbag and handed it to him.

Evan stared at the paper, and then looked up at her, wide-eyed. "A bishop? A Marshall County bishop?"

"No," Cecily said. "A LaGrange County bishop. But supposedly he knows a lot of people in this part of the state. Hopefully, he knows a bishop in Marshall County."

"Awesome! That's absolutely awesome!" Evan jumped up and hugged her tightly. "Cecily, you're awesome!"

That evening, Cecily composed a letter on her computer.

July 9

Dear Bishop Miller,

Your name was given to me by some kind ladies I met in Shipshewana. I was inquiring about the name of an Amish bishop in Marshall County. The ladies told me you might be able to help.

If you could provide me with the name and address of a bishop in Marshall County, I would be most grateful. I'm looking for a loved one I haven't seen in many years, and I believe she lives in Marshall County. I'm hoping the bishop can help me find her.
Sincerely,
Cecily Hartman-Gray

Cecily mailed her letter the following morning. After several days, she began fretting about the lack of response, even though she knew it was far too early to hear from Bishop Miller.

Nine days later, on a Saturday afternoon, Stephen tossed a handful of mail on the dining-room table. He picked up an envelope and looked at it curiously.

"Do you know an Ezra Miller from LaGrange, Indiana?" he asked Cecily, who was in the kitchen loading the dishwasher.

Cecily jumped as if she'd been shot, then flew into the dining room and snatched the letter from Stephen's hand.

"Whoa, there!" he said. "What's all this about?"

"This is very important!" Cecily clutched the letter to her heart.

"Something to do with your sisters?"

"Yes."

She tore open the letter and perused its contents, written in the shaky handwriting of an elderly man.

Dear Mrs. Hartman-Gray,

I am responding to your request for the name of an Amish bishop in Marshall County. To the best of my knowledge, there is only one bishop in that county, Levi Schlabach. I have inquired on your behalf, and have been told that his mailing address is 31320 County Road 9, Bremen, Indiana.

May God bless you as you search for your loved one.
Sincerely,
Ezra P. Miller

Cecily sank onto a chair at the table and buried her face in her folded arms, her body trembling, her heart pounding. Stephen caressed her back for a few moments, and then walked away.

After she'd regained her composure, Cecily went straight to her computer to draft another letter. She sat there an hour, writing, deleting, and writing again, until she was satisfied with her composition.

July 18
Dear Bishop Schlabach,

Your name was given to me by Bishop Ezra Miller of LaGrange, Indiana. I'm writing about something that is very important to me.

I have reason to believe that I have a biological sister who was raised in an Amish foster home somewhere near Plymouth. I believe that when she was five or six years old, she was adopted by her foster parents. Unfortunately, I don't know the last name of the family, although I've been told her adoptive mother's name might be Martha. I've also been told the family had a number of sons.

My sister's birth name was Starly Dickerson, but I believe her adoptive family called her Annie. As a child, she had blue eyes and blonde hair. She would be twenty-six years old now.

I would be so grateful for any information you could give me. My heart longs to see my sister again.
Sincerely,
Cecily Hartman-Gray

Cecily folded the letter and placed it in an envelope addressed to Bishop Schlabach, but she didn't seal it. She wanted to get Evan's opinion before mailing it.

On Monday morning, she typed a brief email message to Evan. *Can we do lunch today? I have something to show you.*

Evan wrote back, *Sorry, I can't today. I have a conference call at noon. But I can tomorrow.*

Tomorrow's fine, Cecily replied. She felt miffed at being put off by her friend, but told herself she was being childish.

Evan seemed distracted when Cecily joined him in his office for lunch the next day, and the change in his demeanor unnerved her. She told him about the letter from Bishop Miller, hoping her enthusiasm would be contagious. But his only response was a forced smile.

Undaunted, she handed him the letter she'd written to Bishop Schlabach. "I want you to see what I wrote before I send it. Tell me if you have any suggestions."

Evan perused the letter while Cecily anxiously watched for his reaction. But his face remained somber. "No, I don't have any suggestions. I think what you wrote is perfect."

"Evan, is something wrong?" Cecily blurted out. "Are you upset with me? Are you getting tired of listening to me talk about this stuff?"

"Oh no, not at all." Evan folded the letter and handed it back to her. "I never get tired of listening to you. I enjoy every minute we spend together."

"Then what is it? Something's wrong."

Evan sighed. "Cecily, I need to talk with you about something before Frank announces it at our staff meeting. You and I have gotten close, and I don't want you to be caught off guard when the news gets out."

Cecily stared at him, seized by a sense of foreboding. "What news, Evan?"

He hung his head, avoiding her gaze. "I'm leaving here, kiddo. I got a job offer. You know that conference call I was on yesterday? That was to finish negotiating the contract. Now it's a done deal."

Cecily sat in a daze, unable to comprehend what her friend had just told her. Evan raised his eyes and gazed at her sadly. A wave of intense pain lingered in the air between them.

"Where are you going?" she asked plaintively.

"Back to Colorado," Evan said. "My former employer offered me a position that involves a significant promotion. I'd been thinking about moving back home, anyway. My father's having health problems, and my parents need my help. A week from Friday will be my last day here."

Stunned, Cecily slumped in her chair, the energy draining from her body.

"I feel like I'm abandoning you, kiddo." Evan slid closer to her on the sofa and took her hand. "The timing of this stinks, but there's not much I can do about it. I really wish I could be here to see how things turn out for you and your sisters."

Tears spilled from Cecily's eyes. "So do I," she whispered.

"Wanna come with me?"

"Huh?" His words jolted her, and she wasn't sure what he was suggesting.

"Just kidding." Evan chuckled. "But not entirely. I'm half-serious, even though I know it isn't fair to ask you that question. But the first thing that came to my mind after I accepted the job was that I would be leaving you. And that thought made me very sad."

Cecily's dazed mind reeled with possibilities. What would it be like to pack up her life and leave for Colorado with Evan in ten days? To clear her things out of the house and tell Stephen the marriage was over? To say a hurried good-bye to her parents and promise to fly back to see them at Christmas? To abandon the search for her sisters?

"In fact," Evan continued, "the thought of leaving you hurt a lot. And I knew I needed to ask you a question. I know full well you can't leave this area right now. You're in the middle of one of the most important projects of your life, finding your sisters. And you've got your parents here. But you know what? If I thought there was half a chance that you and I could be together, I wouldn't leave. I'd stay here with you. I'd call Colorado and tell them the deal's off."

His eyes reflected the intensity of his feelings, and Cecily's breaking heart wanted to cry out, "Don't go, Evan. Stay here with me." But all that came out of her mouth was, "I . . . I don't know what to say."

"Sorry, kiddo, I had no right to ask that. I can't ask you to turn your life upside down for me."

Abruptly, he stood up, walked over to the CD player on his desk and put in a disc. The sweet, haunting strains of soft music filled the room. Then he extended his hand. "Dance with me, beautiful lady."

Ever so gently, he pulled Cecily to her feet, and she glided into his arms. "I'll think of you every time I listen to this music," he whispered in her ear.

At first, they danced in formal ballroom position, their movements perfectly synchronized, as if they'd danced together a thousand times before. Then he drew her closer. She wrapped her arms around his waist, laying her head against his shoulder.

Her body ached with desire. She wanted to melt into Evan, to merge with him. The thought of parting with him seemed unbearable.

Then a bold idea entered her mind. *I'm not letting Evan Carter go without kissing him. Just one kiss. I may regret it later, but I'll regret it more if I don't. Just one kiss.* She lifted her head, knowing his lips would find hers, and as they swayed to the music, Evan kissed her deeply, passionately.

She moaned softly, sweet ecstasy dancing in every cell of her body. For the moment, their two souls became one, and something unfinished inside her felt complete.

The ending of the song disrupted their sublime reverie. Evan released his embrace, and the slight space between them felt excruciating to Cecily.

He took her face in his hands. "I love you," he said. "I love you in a way I didn't know was possible. But I have to go, and you need to stay."

He stepped back, turning away from her. "God, I wish it could be different. Life is so cruel."

Cecily didn't know how she made it through the rest of the week. She mailed her letter to Bishop Schlabach the next morning. Then she mustered every ounce of her will to go about the business of her daily life.

But the tenderness of Evan's words, and the memory of his body pressed against hers stayed with her every moment of every day. She felt something like a gaping wound in her solar plexus, as if the cord maintaining their deep connection had been ripped away. The pain was searing.

Chapter 12

As Frank went over team business during Friday morning's staff meeting, Cecily knew the dreaded announcement of Evan's resignation was soon to come.

She hadn't spoken to Evan since their heart-wrenching encounter three days earlier. Now he was sitting diagonally across the table from her. When she glanced at him, she saw he was looking at her with sadness in his eyes. She averted her gaze, knowing that if she maintained eye contact with him, she'd weep right there in front of the entire team.

Frank cleared his throat. "Now I have some sad news to announce. Some of you may already know this."

He means me, of course, Cecily thought, lowering her head and pretending to study the computer printouts in front of her.

"I regret to tell you," Frank continued, "that Dr. Evan Carter is resigning from our team. His last day at the center will be a week from today."

He paused, allowing the bewildered team members to absorb the news. Then he said, "Evan, I'll let you tell us about your future plans."

Evan glanced around at his coworkers, catching them all in the beam of his smile. "I've been offered a position with my former employer in Colorado. It will involve some new responsibilities, and I'll be supervising a team of psychologists. More importantly, it's time for me to move back home. My parents are getting older, and my father just had open-heart surgery."

"Well," Frank said, "we'll certainly miss you, Evan."

The rest of the team chimed in, wishing Evan well, asking questions about his new job. Cecily forced herself to smile and murmur, "We'll miss you, Evan," so as not to stand out. She desperately wanted the meeting to be over.

For the next week, Cecily plodded mechanically through her days. The searing pain in her abdomen had been replaced by a heavy cloud that enshrouded her body and mind.

At work, she willed her way through uninspired sessions with clients and forced herself to complete paperwork. She avoided communicating with Evan, except to utter a faint "hi" on the rare occasions when she passed him in the hallway. There were no emails.

At home, she went about the motions of life with Stephen, holding the necessary superficial conversations. In the dullness of her mind, she occasionally asked herself if she should feel guilty about kissing Evan. She found no strength to muster anxiety or remorse about the matter.

Once a day, when she checked her mailbox, a spark of excitement flickered in her mind, only to be extinguished when she failed to find a letter from Bishop Schlabach among the bills and junk mail.

Cecily sat through the following Friday's staff meeting in a daze, as the team discussed matters related to the last few clients Evan had tested. Somewhere in her cloudy mind, it registered that she and Evan would need to say their final goodbyes that day.

Shortly after 5:00 PM, she looked up to find Evan standing in her office doorway. They gazed wordlessly at each other, agonizing desire hanging in the air between them.

Then Evan spoke, his voice husky. "I can't kiss you again, Cecily, even though I desperately want to. If I did, I wouldn't be able to leave. I can't even touch you, because if I did, I'd want to hold you and never let you go."

Cecily bit her trembling lip, trying to hold back tears.

"I just came to say goodbye," he continued, "and to wish you all the luck in the world in searching for your sisters. I feel like such a heel, running out on you when you need my support the most. The timing of this stinks, for sure."

Cecily felt the shroud of dull heaviness transmute into throbbing pain. Tears poured from her eyes.

"Thank you," she said, her voice breaking. "I can't begin to tell you how grateful I am for what you've done for me. You're the first person who's really understood what I went through as a child."

She watched a tear slide down Evan's cheek. He brushed it away with an embarrassed chuckle. "It was my pleasure," he said.

Then he looked down at the floor. "Cecily, I hope you never think I got close to you just to mess with you. If I hurt you in any way, I apologize a thousand times. I know I've played around with a lot of women, women I didn't have any feelings for."

He took a step toward her, and then stopped himself. "But Cecily, I feel something for you I've never felt for another woman. I guess I was lying when I told you I could keep my feelings in check. It wasn't intentional. I really meant what I said at the time."

He grinned at her. "But you managed to wiggle your way past my defenses. I care a lot about you, Cecily, and in fact, I think I've fallen in love with you. And I suppose that's one reason I really need to leave. Because I care enough about you not to complicate your life. Even though he's not always what you want him to be, you've got a pretty good thing going with Mr. Gray."

Cecily fought the urge to rush into Evan's arms for a final lingering embrace. Holding back was agonizing, but she forced herself to remain seated.

"Well," Evan said coyly, "I've bared my soul here. It's your turn, Cecily. Say something to me."

Cecily opened her mouth, expecting to stammer awkwardly. But she was surprised to hear words flow eloquently from some part of her being she was scarcely aware of. "I love you, too, Evan," she heard herself say. "I have feelings for you that I've never felt for anyone else. I suppose that's a terrible thing for me to say when I'm married to another man, but it's true. You and I fit perfectly together. We're in tune with each other in ways I don't even understand."

"I know," Evan said. "We've got amazing chemistry. It feels like we've known each other forever."

Cecily nodded, smiling through her tears. "But I have so much going on right now, and my emotions are all jumbled up. It would be way too easy to make a decision that felt right now, that would be totally wrong later on. I know I can't leave now. I can't stop my search for my sisters. And one thing I'll never do is move far away from my parents. Never. I'll stay close to them until they die. That's what I owe them."

"I understand that," Evan said. "You always try to do the right thing, Cecily, and I love that about you. If you'd be willing to dump your responsibilities to come with me . . . well, I'd be a little worried."

"I try to be responsible," Cecily said, "and I have to try with my marriage. It's hard to tell where Stephen and I stand. We're struggling right now. But I'm not sure I've been entirely fair to him recently."

"Maybe our time isn't now," Evan said softly. "Maybe later in this life. Maybe in the next life, who knows? I'm not going to ask you to stay in touch with me. I won't put that on you. But if anything ever changes for you, look me up. You're getting pretty good at hunting people down these days."

Cecily laughed. "Okay, I will."

"Just remember, kiddo, you're always here." Evan tapped his chest. "Right here in my heart."

He blew her a kiss, then turned abruptly and walked away, his footsteps echoing down the hallway. The back door opened and then slammed shut, and Cecily shuddered at the finality of the sound. She sat motionless at her desk, listening as Evan started his car and pulled out of the parking lot.

When she arrived home, she hoped her husband wouldn't sense her tangle of emotions and begin asking questions. But Stephen had apparently grown accustomed to the distance between them, and he occupied himself with his own interests that evening.

As they were getting into bed that night, Cecily said, "Stephen, I need to get away tomorrow. I need time to sort some things out. I'm going to drive up to St. Joseph in the morning to visit Lake Michigan."

"Whatever you need to do," Stephen said. He gave her a quick kiss, and then turned away from her onto his side.

When Cecily peered out her bedroom window early the next morning, she was disappointed to see dark, low-hanging clouds spitting out a drizzling rain. For a moment, she thought about canceling her traveling plans, but immediately dismissed the thought. *It'll probably clear up,* she told herself.

While her husband continued to sleep, she pulled on jeans and walking shoes. She cracked the window open to check the temperature, and was shocked by a blast of unseasonably chilly air. So she grabbed a jacket from her closet and tiptoed out of the bedroom.

As she drove north toward Michigan, the rain increased, beating hard against her windshield. "Yikes!" she said aloud. "Maybe I should turn around and go home."

But she felt no inclination to turn back. The inclement weather seemed to be in tune with her state of mind, and the pouring rain felt cleansing, like everything in the universe that had been bottled up was now releasing.

By the time she reached her destination an hour later, the rain had stopped. It was still chilly and overcast, but now and then the sun peeked through the banks of heavy clouds. Cecily drove through St. Joseph's quaint downtown area, remembering her family's summer trips to the tourist town during her childhood. Her parents had enjoyed bringing her there to take in the festivals, visit the children's museum, and spend time on the ever popular Silver Beach.

But that morning, the town seemed quiet and sleepy. As Cecily turned west toward Silver Beach, she was pleased to see there were no swimmers in sight, as it was still early in the day and far too chilly for anyone to enter the water.

But as she parked her car, she spotted several people walking their dogs on the pier. She wanted to be alone. On impulse, she turned left and drove along the lake until she arrived at the more secluded Lion's Park Beach. There, she was pleased to find total solitude.

When she climbed out of her car, the chilly lakeside wind whipped at her clothing and played havoc with her hair, so she zipped up her jacket and tied the hood securely in place. The rain began again, spitting intermittently.

She made her way toward the rugged south end of the beach, where huge boulders were piled close to the shoreline. The wind blew the waves high, and they crashed against the rocks. Carefully, she climbed down the rocks toward the water. Midway down, she found a rock suitable for sitting.

The cold dampness seeped through her jeans, but she sat unmoving for half an hour, listening to the sound of the waves thundering around her. The unrelenting roar soothed her ruffled feelings and swept the dark confusion from her mind.

"My life's a mess," she whispered to the lake. "What do you have to say to me?"

The waves rose high, then fell with a resounding crash against the rocks below her. She imagined she heard words in the rhythm of the water's rise and fall: "All is well . . . all is well . . . all is well . . . ."

"What will I do without Evan?" she whispered. "How will I ever get over him?"

"All is well . . . all is well . . . ," said the lake.

"What if I never find Starly?"

"All is well . . . all is well . . . ."

"What if I find Shaney and Stella, and they aren't happy to see me?"

"All is well . . . all is well . . . ."

"What if nothing comes of this whole thing I've started? What if I've stirred up my life for no reason at all?"

"All is well . . . all is well . . . ."

The lake's soothing compassion caressed Cecily's sorrowful heart, and love for the lake welled inside her. She wanted to be closer to it. So she gingerly climbed down more rocks until she reached the sandy stretch at the water's edge. Unmindful of being cold, damp, and dirty, she seated herself cross-legged on the sand just out of reach of the waves slapping the shore.

She ran her fingers through the wet sand, tracing designs, then smoothing them away. Without thinking, she wrote the name *Evan*. As she gazed down at her creation, she suddenly felt the full pain of her loss. She began to weep, her body wracked with wrenching sobs.

She had no tissues to wipe her nose, so she got on her knees and moved closer to the water. Cupping her hands in the water, she rinsed her face, her tears now one with the lake.

She looked at the letters she'd traced in the sand. Then she dipped her cupped hands into the lake again, and poured the water over the name of the man she'd grown to love. She repeated this action until the letters were completely obliterated.

She smoothed the sand, and then traced the name *Seffie*. Suddenly, the wind picked up and a gigantic wave crashed farther onto the shore, soaking her before she had a chance to jump back. Shocked and exhilarated by her icy bath, she laughed aloud. When she looked down at the sand, it was smooth as satin. The wave had erased Seffie's name in an instant.

There, Cecily thought, *I've released my pain to the lake.* She felt cleaner, lighter.

Suddenly, she realized how cold and wet she was. It was time to go. She turned and walked several steps back toward the rocks, then hesitated before stooping to write in the sand again. With great care, she traced the names *Starly*, *Shaney*, and *Stella*.

It remains to be seen, she thought, *whether these names will be washed away from me or whether they will be preserved in my life.* At that moment, she felt sad, but serene, knowing she could accept any outcome.

It was past noon when Cecily arrived back in South Bend. The warm sun had driven away the chilly rain. As she drove up the street toward her house, she could see Stephen sitting on the backyard patio, reading a book.

She turned into the driveway and pulled the car into the garage. But instead of going into the house, she followed a sudden impulse to walk through the back door of the garage leading to the patio.

Stephen looked up from his book, surprised. Cecily had no idea why she was walking toward her husband. All she knew was that the wall around her heart that had served as a barricade between them had been washed away by the waves.

Stephen stood up, chuckling at her dirty and disheveled appearance. "Come here, Cessy," he said, holding out his arms. He brushed the sand off her face and then kissed her tenderly.

That night, Cecily dreamed about her birth mother again. Seferina's figure rose up before her, tall and regal, emanating a soft glow. Her face was peaceful, her features relaxed, her hair flowing. And she smiled sweetly at her beloved eldest daughter.

Part II

STARLY

Chapter 1

Annie Kauffman exhaled deeply as she lowered her tired body into the bathtub. She'd worked hard that day, weeding the garden and giving the house a good Saturday cleaning. The warm water felt soothing to her aching muscles.

The light through the single window in the bathroom was growing dim, and the gas lamp overhead bathed the room in a soft glow. Annie leaned back in the tub, then scooped up a handful of water and trickled it over her breasts, enlarged and tender with her pregnancy. Caressing the curve of her belly, she smiled at the thought of the lovemaking that had planted the growing baby in her womb.

"Hello, little one," she whispered.

Annie could never get enough of Luke's lovemaking, and she seemed to need it even more when she was pregnant. She knew her desire made Luke happy. When she'd reached hungrily for him last night, he'd laughed and said, "If you keep this up, you'll have twice as many babies as your mother had."

She lathered her washcloth with soap and slowly began scrubbing her body. She was in no hurry to get out of the tub. This was the only break she'd had from the children all day.

But her reverie was broken when she heard little Sarah wailing from the living room. "Are you almost done, Annie?" Luke called through the closed bathroom door. "The children need you out here."

Sighing, Annie hoisted herself out of the tub, the bathwater running off her body in rivulets. Her diminutive form was exquisitely proportioned, except for the melon-sized bulge in her mid-section.

She grabbed a thick white towel that smelled fresh from the clothesline, and as she dried her body, she gazed at her reflection in the bathroom mirror. Her face was deeply tanned, but her shoulders and arms, always shielded from the sun by her long-sleeved dresses, were snowy white.

Annie imagined what her entire body would look like if it was all as tan as her face. She wondered what it would be like to lounge in the sun in a swimsuit like the English women did. She loosened her platinum blonde hair from the confines of its bun and fluffed it with her fingers, allowing it to hang softly around her face. Turning this way and that, she tossed her hair, posing seductively like the women on the covers of magazines in the supermarket. Puckering her lips, she blew a kiss to her reflection.

Annie was well aware that with her blonde hair, delicate features, and sky-blue eyes, she was considered to be one of the prettiest young women in her church district. Even after giving birth to two children, she hadn't become heavy like many other Amish women she knew.

As she contemplated her reflection in the mirror, Annie wondered for the millionth time what it would be like to be English. She imagined herself wearing short skirts to show off her nice legs and low-cut tops that showed just a hint of her breasts. She told herself that if she applied red lipstick and enough makeup to render her blue eyes sultry, she'd be pretty enough to be on television or in the movies.

Sarah let out another tortured squeal. "Daniel, stop bothering your sister," Luke commanded.

Annie finished toweling off her body and slipped her white cotton nightgown over her head. When she stepped out of the bathroom, she found Luke standing in the kitchen, holding sniffling two-year-old Sarah in one arm while trying to restrain squirming five-year-old Daniel with the other hand. Daniel broke loose and began running laps around the large wooden table.

Unable to be stern with her son, Annie chuckled at his antics. She chased him around the table, laughing and calling, "Do you have the devil in you, little boy?"

Daniel giggled hysterically as he tried to evade his mother's grasp. "I've got the devil," he chanted. "Devil, devil, devil!"

Little Sarah decided she was done crying. She wriggled out of her father's arms and pranced in joyful circles around the kitchen.

Luke shot Annie a disapproving look. "See what you've done to the children? It's not proper to teach them to speak of the devil in a light-hearted manner. Now you've got them riled up, and they won't be able to fall asleep. They'll be grouchy when we try to wake them in the morning. Don't forget, we need to start out early for the preaching service at your parents' house. I need to help your father arrange the benches and set up tables for the noon meal."

"Alright, then," Annie sighed, her spirits dampened by her husband's scolding. "Come, children, let's go upstairs and put on your night-clothes. Then Papa and I will help you say your prayers."

The next morning, Annie took out the dark blue Sunday dress her mother had just finished sewing for her, designed to accommodate her expanding girth. She sighed as she pulled on the drab garment, wishing her mother would have chosen a brighter color.

As she was winding her long hair into a bun, Luke came in from the barn. She could hear him washing up in the bathroom. He walked into the bedroom just as she was placing her white net covering on her head.

He came up behind her, his face appearing above hers in the mirror. "Your new dress brings out the blue in your eyes," he said.

Gazing at both of their reflections, Annie asked, "Luke, do you think I'd look nice in red?"

"What a question!" Luke chuckled. "Who's ever seen an Amish girl in red? But I imagine you'd look pretty in red, just as you look pretty in everything you wear." He winked at Annie in the mirror. "To me, my wife is always beautiful."

Annie turned and wrapped her arms around her husband's middle, squeezing hard. "That makes me so happy," she chortled.

Luke pried her arms from his body and began removing his soiled work shirt. "But Annie, you're too vain. It bothers me that you dwell on such things."

It was only three miles from Luke and Annie's farm to the home of Annie's parents, Jonas and Martha Bontrager. Annie was glad it was her parents' turn to host the preaching service. She felt more comfortable in her mother's kitchen, in the house in which she'd been raised. It seemed like in the kitchens of other church women, she'd always em-barrass herself when she tried to help with the noon meal. Inevitably, she'd break a plate, or spill a pitcher of lemonade, or drop and ruin an entire pie.

After Luke hoisted Annie and the two children into the buggy, he climbed into the driver's seat and took the reins. Lulled by the steady rhythm of the horses' prancing feet, little Sarah fell asleep on Annie's lap before they'd traveled a quarter of a mile down the road.

Sitting on the buggy seat between his parents, Daniel began making clicking sounds with his mouth, imitating the clip-clop of the horses' hooves on the pavement. Without thinking, Annie joined in Daniel's noisemaking, clicking her own tongue.

Luke cleared his throat. When Annie glanced over at him, he shot her a reproachful look. "Annie, you need to remember that you're the parent, not the child."

Stung by her husband's disapproval, Annie turned her head to gaze out the buggy window, hiding the tears in her eyes. She loved her husband dearly, but when he scolded her, she felt like running away from him.

Daniel seemed to sense his mother's distress. He stopped his sound effects and leaned against Annie, wrapping his little arm around her swollen abdomen.

"Mama," he asked, "why is your belly so fat? Did you eat too much breakfast?"

Annie smiled at her son's question, her melancholy mood dissipating. "No, Daniel, I didn't eat too much breakfast. Mama's belly is fat because she has a baby in there."

"A baby!" Daniel chortled. "How did it get in there?"

Before Annie could speak, Luke took both reins in one hand and reached over Daniel to place his other hand on her shoulder.

"God put the baby in your mama's belly, son," he said. "Now let's stop these silly questions. Scoot over here and sit on your papa's lap so you can help drive the horses."

The church service seemed interminably long to Annie that morning. First, she had to endure the droning hymns sung from the Amish hymnal. At times, her lively soprano voice would soar above the others, but then she'd grow tired of the song and stop singing. Luke would glance at her and frown, so she'd sigh and start singing again.

Then Bishop Schlabach stood up in front of the congregation and delivered a sermon on the sin of pride. It seemed to Annie he issued the same grim warnings every time he spoke.

Although the windows were open in her parents' living room, the number of people squeezed into the small space made the room unbearably stuffy. The wooden bench felt hard as a rock under her bottom, and she shifted uncomfortably from side to side. She looked at Fanny May Yoder's wide bottom seated comfortably on the bench in front of her, and wondered how she managed to sit so still.

Sarah slept soundly in the crook of her father's arm, and Daniel had lain down on the bench to rest his head on Annie's lap. Annie glanced down and saw that her son's eyes were closed. His index finger was shoved up his nostril, and it looked as if he'd fallen asleep in the act of picking his nose.

Annie couldn't stop herself from giggling at the comical sight. Embarrassed, she tried to turn her laugh into a cough. Then she coughed a few more times to convince any doubters that she truly had a tickle in her throat. Fanny May glanced over her shoulder, peering disapprovingly over the top of her wire-rimmed glasses.

Angered by the judgmental look, Annie felt a sudden urge to poke her finger in the middle of Fanny May's back to make her jump. A stray wisp of hair curled on the back of Fanny May's fat neck, and Annie felt like giving it a yank. She clenched her hands into fists to stop her impulses.

Luke seemed to sense her agitation, and laid a hand over one of hers. Annie desperately wished Bishop Schlabach would end his sermon so they could stand up and sing again. She didn't think she could sit on that hard bench one more minute.

Jonas and Martha Bontrager and their six sons, Eli, Jonathan, Levi, Aaron, Reuben and Joel, gather for family worship, a solemn evening ritual of scripture reading and prayer. They've brought in kitchen chairs to add to the meager living room furniture, so there is enough seating for everyone.

Martha attempts to contain squirming five-year-old Annie on her lap. Annie slides off. Martha scoops her up and sits her firmly down again.

Jonas hands the worn Bible to his eldest son, sixteen-year-old Eli, and asks him to read the scripture passage. It seems to Annie that Eli is taking forever. She slides off Martha's lap again, crawls around behind her chair, and sits on the floor playing with her mother's apron strings. Martha decides to leave Annie be, as long as she remains quiet.

But Annie quickly becomes bored with the apron strings. She scrambles off the floor and tugs at her mother's sleeve. "Are we almost done?" she whispers loudly.

Martha puts her finger to her lips. "Sh-h-h."

Annie wraps both arms around her mother's arm and leans against her shoulder for a few moments. Suddenly, she lets go and darts across the room to where her brother Eli sits ponderously reading scripture verses. Before anyone can stop her, she slides her little hands under the big book and deftly slams it shut. Eli stares openmouthed at his little sister.

"Annie!" Martha scolds as she jumps up to gather her errant daughter in her arms.

"Annie, you must sit still on your mother's lap until our family worship is over," Jonas commands. "You must not interrupt scripture reading again!"

Annie sits obediently, but she crosses her arms in a huff, her lower lip thrust out in an exaggerated pout. "We don't have to do this at Seffie's house," she announces haughtily.

Eight-year-old Joel contorts his face into an expression of disdain. "Yah! She just wants to be English!"

Chapter 2

Annie stood in the doorway of her mother's kitchen, watching the other church women put the final touches on the food for the potluck meal. Their husbands stood around the yard in clusters, visiting while waiting for the home-cooked feast to be served.

Several of the women had begun carrying food out to the serving tables: platters of fried chicken and ham, bowls of baked beans, mashed potatoes, cabbage slaw, and garden vegetables, baskets of homemade bread, chocolate cake and angel food cake, and all sorts of fruit pies and cream pies.

Annie walked over to the window to see what her children were doing. Daniel was running around the yard with other little boys his age, while Sarah entertained herself in the same sandbox Annie had played in as a child. She saw Luke standing with Moses Graber where the horses and buggies were tied, admiring Moses' new buggy horse.

Then she saw the Amstutz brothers, Olan and Ivan, standing near the end of the serving table where the desserts were being placed. They hadn't been present for the preaching service, but they evidently couldn't pass up the delectable spread that followed.

Every time Annie saw Olan Amstutz, she felt stirred up inside. She didn't know whether Olan excited or frightened her. He was a long, lean fellow, with dark, hooded, unsmiling eyes and a large hooked nose in a narrow face, a combination of features which rendered his appearance somewhat sinister.

Whenever Annie was around Olan, she couldn't help but stare at him. He'd meet her gaze with his lascivious dark eyes, and ever so subtly, he'd flick the tip of his tongue around his lips. And Annie would know Olan was remembering the same thing she remembered.

When Annie was barely fifteen, she had blossomed into such a pretty young woman, the Amish boys from miles around flocked to the Bontrager home, looking for opportunities to court Jonas and Martha's only daughter. And Annie had been chomping at the bit, eager to start her running around years. She enjoyed the attention from all the boys, but the one she was drawn to like a magnet was Olan Amstutz.

Olan, three years her senior, had developed a reputation for being reckless and headstrong, a youth who lived his running around years with great gusto. There were rumors that he'd bought a car that he kept hidden in the woods. He supposedly took it out on Saturday nights and drove it around with a load of English girls. The devout men and women in the church clucked their tongues over the wayward ways of Willard and Sadie Amstutz's eldest son.

Olan had pursued Annie relentlessly, with his less-daring younger brother Ivan always at his heels.

At first, Jonas and Martha had trusted Annie with a bit of freedom, in the same way they'd trusted their six sons when they'd entered adolescence. After all, Amish youth were expected to run around for a time, sowing their wild oats before joining the church. If Annie wanted to socialize with a group of young people on a Saturday night, her parents allowed her to go.

Olan Amstutz tended to lurk around the edges of such social events, and every time he had the opportunity, he'd have his hands on Annie. She'd giggle at his touch, batting her eyes, egging him on, and his hands would roam to places they shouldn't have gone.

One Saturday evening, Olan drove to the Bontrager home in his father's buggy to pick up Annie for their first real date. Although leery of Olan's intentions, Jonas and Martha could find no reason to deny Annie the privilege allowed any other Amish girl her age.

Sixteen-year-old Annie scrambles into the buggy, her heart pounding with excitement. This is her first time alone with Olan, without being in the confines of a group setting. But then she glances over her shoulder and sees Ivan in the back seat.

"Where are we going tonight?" she asks Olan.

Olan's mouth stretches into a sinister grin. "It's a surprise."

He snaps the reins to get the horse moving, but after they travel half a mile, he abruptly pulls the buggy off to the side of the road next to a wooded area.

"Take the buggy into town and park it behind the drug store," he in-

structs Ivan. *"We'll meet you there with the car."*

The car! The word sends shivers of excitement through Annie's body. Olan steps around to her side of the buggy, grabs her by the waist, and swings her to the ground. *"Come with me,"* he says, his voice low and smooth.

He takes Annie's hand and leads her into the woods. They stumble through the brush, the briars catching on Annie's long dress and snagging her stockings. Suddenly, the woods open up into a clearing, where a car is parked beside an overgrown dirt road.

Olan pulls a ring of keys from his pocket, unlocks the door of the passenger seat, and gestures with a flourish. *"Get in, my dear."*

Annie has ridden in the van of her English neighbor Shirley Price, who takes the Bontrager family shopping if they need to go as far as Goshen or Shipshewana. But she has never been in a low-riding, bright red sports car. She can hardly contain her excitement.

Olan gets into the driver's seat and starts the car, revving up the engine. Before he pulls out onto the dirt road, he leans over and gives Annie a lingering kiss. Annie has never before been kissed by a boy. She likes the feel of Olan's lips pressed against hers, and the sweaty smell of his skin makes her feel stirred up and crazy inside. She decides that she likes kissing, and she wants Olan to kiss her again and again.

But Olan pulls away and reaches into the back seat. He tosses a plastic Wal-Mart bag into Annie's lap. *"We'll stop at a gas station, and you can change in the restroom,"* he says.

Annie opens the bag and pulls out a pair of blue jeans like the English girls wear. Then she pulls out a pink and white striped top. She looks at Olan questioningly.

He laughs at the perplexed look on her face. *"Whatsamatter? Never worn English clothes before? Well, there's always a first time for everything."*

Olan drives slowly down the dirt road, but as they pull out onto the highway, he picks up speed. The landscape through Annie's window zooms by much quicker than it does through a buggy window. Olan turns a knob on the dashboard, and loud, fast-beating music fills the car.

"Rock and roll," he says, grinning. *"How do you like it?"*

Annie smiles back at him. She taps her fingers on her knee, keeping time to the music.

They drive past a sign on the outskirts of town that says, "Welcome to Bremen." Olan pulls up at a gas station. "Take off your bonnet," he says irritably before they get out of the car. Annie obliges, tossing her black bonnet into the back seat with a flourish.

As they enter the convenience store, Annie stops to stare at her strange surroundings. Olan nudges her and points toward the ladies' room. Then, carrying a bag of his own, he disappears into the restroom marked "Men."

With her bag of English clothing in hand, Annie enters the restroom and locks herself in a stall. She takes off her dress, her slip, her black tennis shoes, and her black stockings. Then she pulls on the blue jeans. It's been many years since she's worn a garment with a zipper, not since she was a tiny child at Seffie's house. The jeans fit snuggly, and she thinks they might be a bit too small. She's never felt something fit this tight across her bottom.

She pulls the pink and white shirt over her head. It clings to her body. She looks down at her breasts, which poke out conspicuously through the knit fabric. She considers her bare feet, and decides to wear her shoes without stockings. Then she folds her dress, slip, and stockings and stuffs them into the Wal-Mart bag.

Tentatively, Annie emerges from the stall. She checks her appearance in the mirror above the sink and realizes she's still wearing her white net head covering, knocked askew during the process of pulling clothing over her head. She snatches it off and stuffs it into the bag along with the rest of her abandoned garments.

When she walks out of the restroom, Olan is waiting for her, wearing blue jeans and a green polo shirt. He grins widely at Annie's appearance, then turns her around so he can inspect her back side.

"Yowza!" he exclaims. "You've got quite a shape on you!"

When they walk out to the car, Ivan, also dressed in English clothing, is waiting in the back seat. Before he starts the engine, Olan reaches over and pulls a few pins out of Annie's bun. Her hair tumbles down around her shoulders. He fluffs it up with his fingers.

"There," he says. "You look sexy!"

No one has ever said that word to Annie. Her body trembles with excitement.

Olan pulls away from the gas station and turns onto a side street. Then he drives up and down the streets in the residential section of town where the English people live. The evening light is dimming, and the electric lights in the English houses shine through the windows with a yellow glow. Annie peers out the car window, wondering what mysterious things those English families do in their houses at night.

Olan turns back onto Main Street, and parks the car along the street. Then he ushers Annie and Ivan into a low-lit, sour-smelling bar, with which he appears to be quite familiar. They sit in a booth along the wall, Ivan on one side and Olan and Annie on the other. Olan presses his thigh against Annie's.

"We'll have three orders of cheeseburgers and fries," he says to the waitress, his voice cocky.

"What do you want to drink?" the waitress asks.

"I'll have a beer," Olan says.

The waitress looks at him suspiciously. "I need to see your ID."

"Sure." Olan reaches into his pocket and pulls out a plastic rectangle. The waitress looks at it and shrugs. "Okay." She looks at Ivan.

"I'll just have a Coke," Ivan says sheepishly.

Then she looks at Annie. "What do you want to drink, hon?"

Annie pauses, wondering whether she's allowed to drink what Olan ordered.

"I'm not bringing her a beer," the waitress says to Olan, as if reading Annie's mind. "There's no way this girl is twenty-one."

"She'll have a Coke, then," Olan says, smirking.

As the waitress turns her back and walks away, Olan tosses the plastic card on the table for Ivan and Annie to see. "Fake ID," he says. Then quick as a wink, the card is back in his pocket.

Annie is so busy staring around the room and watching the English men at the bar, she can't keep her attention on her food. Olan jabs her in the ribs with his elbow.

"Quit gawking and eat," he commands. "I'm paying good money for

that food." While they eat their burgers and fries, he orders himself a second beer.

After they finish their meal, Olan leads Ivan and Annie to the pool table in the corner of the bar. He stands behind Annie, his body pressed against hers, and puts his arms around her to show her how to hold the cue stick. Although they play game after game, Annie can't get over her clumsiness. But she admires how skillfully Olan plays, and she suspects he's come here to play pool many times before.

Olan has two more beers while they play, and the more he drinks, the bolder his hands become as they roam over Annie's body. Annie enjoys his touch. She's feeling more comfortable in her new environment, and she smiles and bats her eyes at several English men who challenge Olan to a game of pool.

Olan gives her a dirty look and squeezes her arm a little too tightly. "You're with me, so knock off the flirting with the English guys," he whispers in her ear.

Annie is getting sleepy. She tries to stifle a yawn, but can't. "Guess I'd better get you home," Olan says.

They drive back to the drug store, where Ivan gets into the buggy. Olan and Annie follow him in the car. "You'd better change your clothes," Olan says. "Your folks might still be up, and you don't want them seeing you like this."

Annie stares at Olan, openmouthed. She's never even thought of undressing in front of the opposite sex before.

"Go ahead," Olan urges. "I've got to watch the road. I won't look at you."

After they park the car in the woods, Annie climbs into the buggy, her dress in disarray. She straightens her clothing, then twists her hair back up into a bun. She sighs as she puts on her head covering and bonnet, the symbols of restriction she'd so happily shed a few hours ago.

When they arrive at the Bontrager farm, all the gas lights are out and the house is quiet.

"Your folks must be asleep," Olan says. "Let's go up to your room."

The three of them take off their shoes before entering the back door of the house. Then they tiptoe up the creaking staircase to Annie's bed-

room. The room is dark, with only a little moonlight coming through the window. Annie sits on the bed, wondering what's going to happen next.

The shadowy shapes of Olan and Ivan hesitate in front of her. Then Ivan goes to the chair in the corner of the room, as if to move himself out of the way of what is to come. Olan sits on the bed beside Annie and nuzzles her neck. Annie giggles.

"Sh-h-h . . ." Olan cautions. He pushes her down on the bed and kisses her roughly. Then he fumbles with the front of his pants, and before Annie knows what's happening, he pulls her skirt up and pushes himself inside her. She screams at the searing pain. Olan covers her mouth with his hand, and Annie bites hard.

"Damn it!" Olan yells, yanking his hand away. Then he checks his reaction. "I'm not going to hurt you," he whispers in her ear, his breath hot and reeking of alcohol. "Just relax, you'll like it. You know you've been wanting this all night."

Annie stops struggling and lays still, wondering what this new experience is all about. Just as she begins to feel some strange, pleasurable sensations, Olan groans, rolls over and lays beside her in the dark.

Suddenly they hear the sound of heavy footsteps on the stairs. Olan hurriedly fastens his trousers. Annie sits up and straightens her skirt.

The bedroom door opens, and Annie's father stands there, holding a flashlight. He shines the light around the room, checking every corner. "You boys go home," he says, his voice thick with anger. "Go on, get out of here. And in the future, stay away from my daughter, or you'll hear from me again."

Without looking back, Olan and Ivan clatter down the stairs and out the back door. Jonas points the flashlight at Annie, who sits on the bed, cowering in fear.

"Go to bed now, Annie," he commands.

He turns to leave, then hesitates. "And you make sure to keep away from those Amstutz boys. They're nothing but trouble. They don't know how to control their lower natures."

As her father's footsteps move down the stairs, Annie hears him mutter, "I wouldn't even trust those boys around my buggy horses."

After her night out with Olan, Annie's parents decided they needed to keep a closer watch on her. Martha had sat Annie down in her bedroom to explain the matter.

"I know Amish parents generally let their teenagers run for a few years before they join the church," she said. "It's good to let them sow their wild oats and get their foolish ways out of their system. But Annie, your nature is too unruly. I fear that if we let you go, you'll be unable to stop yourself from plunging headlong into trouble. Your father and I don't want you to do things that you'll regret later. So from now on, when you go to the young people's gatherings, your brother Joel will need to be there to keep an eye on you."

After her mother's pronouncement, Annie had flung herself on her bed and cried, and she pouted for a few days after that. But as much as she wanted to, she was never allowed to run with the Amstutz brothers again.

Other suitors came and went, young men whom Annie's parents approved of, quiet, steady boys who worked on their father's farms. But Annie found none of these young men appealing. Compared with the adventurous and daring Olan Amstutz, the run-of-the-mill Amish boy seemed stodgy and boring.

Then along came Luke Kauffman, a tall, handsome man who'd inherited a nice piece of property. Annie admired Luke's broad shoulders, the confidence in his stride, and the good-natured glint in his hazel eyes, and she was quite happy to fall in love with him.

Jonas and Martha believed Luke was steady enough to guide their daughter in the right direction, and they heartily approved of the match. But Jonas took Luke aside and spoke to him in confidence, asking him to wait until Annie was at least twenty before proposing marriage. "My daughter needs a few more years to mature before becoming a wife and mother," he told his future son-in-law.

Olan Amstutz was now twenty-nine and still single, although his younger brother Ivan had finally settled down and married last year. Olan had his own home, but he didn't have much land to farm. He was employed in a woodworking factory in Nappanee, and reportedly made a nice living in that occupation. People in the church still clucked their tongues and told stories about how Olan carried on with the English women who worked with him in the factory.

Annie suddenly realized she'd been staring out the window at Olan for three or four minutes. He'd moved closer to the serving table, and was inspecting the array of desserts. On impulse, Annie picked up a coconut cream pie and carried it out the door, knowing full well she would attract Olan's attention.

He looked up and saw her coming, his dark eyes fixed on her, and as she approached the table, he spoke to her in a low, seductive voice.

"Looks like you've got another bun in the oven, Annie. You and old Luke must be going at it like rabbits." He chuckled lasciviously.

Annie smiled coyly, then leaned over to place her pie in an empty spot on the other side of the table. Quick as a wink, Olan's big hand darted out and gave her bottom a hard squeeze.

Annie shot him a look of mock outrage, but as she turned to walk back to the house, she gave her bottom a decided wiggle.

Olan laughed heartily, and then turned back to Ivan. "I sure wouldn't mind having some of that again," Annie heard him say.

She'd taken only a few steps toward the house before she realized what a terrible thing she'd done. Her face burned with shame, and she prayed to God that no one had seen what had happened. What would Luke ever think if he knew she'd disrespected him in such a way?

As soon as Annie entered the kitchen, Martha was there waiting for her. Without a word, she took her daughter by the arm and escorted her to the bedroom she and Jonas shared. She sat Annie down on the quilt-covered bed, and then sat facing her.

"I saw what happened out there by the food table, Annie." Martha's face was stern.

Annie hung her head, shame burning her entire body.

"Annie, I know a mother shouldn't say such a thing," Martha continued, "but I sometimes think I love my adopted daughter more than the six boys I gave birth to. However, there are times when your behavior makes me ashamed of you. You must remember that you're a married woman and a mother. Your behavior out there by the food table was most unbecoming."

She sighed wearily. "I suspect that in the past, something happened between you and Olan Amstutz. I'm sure I wouldn't want to know about it, as it would be nothing but a burden on my heart."

Then she lifted Annie's chin, forcing her daughter to look her in the eye. "Now Annie, you must listen to me. You have no business going anywhere near Olan Amstutz. I know you're no longer a child, but I'm still going to exercise my authority as your mother and forbid you to have any contact with him. You must not even speak to Olan Amstutz, do you understand? Nothing good can come from it."

Sobbing, Annie threw herself into her mother's arms. Martha rocked her gently.

"Annie, Annie, Annie," she crooned. "What am I going to do with you? Just love you, I suppose. I know it's difficult for you to control your unruly nature. But you must try, Annie, you must try."

"I will, Mama. I'll try as hard as I can." Annie buried her face against her mother's plump shoulder, soaking the front of her dress with her tears.

Chapter 3

Martha Bontrager dried the last of the supper dishes and hung up her dish towel, then sank wearily into a chair at the kitchen table. As she rested her exhausted body, she gazed out the big window overlooking the front yard.

She never grew tired of that view. An enormous maple tree shaded the front of the house and kept the kitchen from getting too hot in the summer. A rope swing dangled from one sturdy horizontal branch, and the sandbox in which all seven of her children had played now provided hours of entertainment for her sixteen grandchildren. Colorful beds of geraniums, marigolds, and petunias bordered the walk from the driveway to the front steps. Several kittens from the barn cat's new litter scampered across the yard.

Martha always felt exhausted the day after having the preaching service at her house. At her age, it had become difficult to host large groups of people. The week before the service, she'd done some in-depth house-cleaning, which had nearly worn her out. And after the service, there were so many things to tidy up and put back in order.

All day long, she'd willed herself to keep going, forcing herself to complete her chores. The extra weight she'd accumulated over the years put a strain on her joints. Her hips and knees ached, and her swollen ankles made her heavy shoes uncomfortably tight.

She heard her husband come in the back door and take off his dirty boots in the breezeway. He'd just finished his evening chores in the barn. Jonas's short, wiry frame was stooped from years of laboring in the fields, and Martha knew his work was taking its toll on him.

He wasn't doing as much farming as he'd done in the past, because most of their land had been divided up among their five oldest sons. Their youngest, Joel, was working in town, but in a year or two, he'd take over the remaining parcel of land Jonas was still farming. Joel and his family would move into the big house, and Jonas and Martha would build a smaller home across the yard from them.

When they'd discussed the plan to build the small house for their retirement years, Jonas and Martha had disagreed. Martha thought they should build the home on Luke and Annie's property, so she could help Annie with her children and household chores. Jonas felt that being so close to Annie would keep Martha's mind in a state of turmoil.

"You've fretted over Annie for twenty-six years," Jonas had told her. "You've helped her enough. Now you need a daughter to help you in your old age." He'd pointed out that Joel's wife, Mary, was strong, even-tempered and competent with her chores. She would require no help, and she'd be able to cross the yard and tend to Martha's needs as well as those of her own household.

Jonas trudged through the kitchen and into the bathroom to wash up. As Martha gazed out the window, she spotted a buggy coming down the road. She hoped it would pass on by their house, as she felt too exhausted to entertain visitors.

But the horse turned into their driveway. "Jonas," Martha called. "We have a visitor." She strained to recognize the face of the bearded man driving the buggy. "Why, it's Bishop Schlabach! Jonas, the Bishop is paying us a visit."

Bishop Levi Schlabach stood in the Bontragers' front doorway, black hat in hand. He was a tall, lean man nearing seventy years of age, with a bushy gray beard and a face lined with wrinkles. His black trousers and plain black coat gave him an austere appearance, and he carried himself with the dignity befitting a leader of the church.

"Come on in, Bishop Schlabach," Martha said, suddenly energized by this special visitor. "Would you like to sit at the table and have a piece of pie with us? We have plenty left over from yesterday's potluck."

"Thank you, Martha. That sounds good." A smile broke the somber lines of the bishop's face.

Jonas came out of the bathroom and shook the Bishop's hand. "We're pleased to have you visit our home," he said.

The men sat down at the table, while Martha cut slices of pie and poured cups of coffee. While they ate, Jonas and the bishop chatted about the weather and their prediction for crops that year. Martha listened contentedly.

Then Bishop Schlabach laid down his fork and wiped his mouth with his napkin. "Jonas and Martha, I have a matter of importance to discuss with you."

Martha felt a surge of dark premonition pass through her body. She glanced at her husband.

"We're listening," Jonas said, his hands folded serenely on the table.

Bishop Schlabach reached into an inner pocket of his coat, pulled out an envelope, and laid it on the table. "Last week, I received an unusual letter in the mail, from a woman by the name of Cecily Hartman-Gray. She informed me she's looking for a long-lost sister whom she believes was adopted by an Amish family in our community."

In her mind's eye, Martha saw an unwelcome wave of change washing over her home and family, destroying life as she knew it. Her heart sank into a pool of desolation.

Bishop Schlabach handed her the letter. "I believe Mrs. Hartman-Gray is referring to your daughter Annie."

Martha read the letter's brief contents, and then passed it on to her husband, her face white with shock.

Jonas's face remained placid as he perused the letter, but a vein throbbing in his temple told Martha he was agitated by what he read.

The three of them sat in silence while Martha and Jonas attempted to digest the import of the letter. Then Martha spoke, her voice trembling.

"There's no doubt that Mrs. Hartman-Gray is describing our Annie. Twenty-six years old, blonde hair and blue eyes, named Starly at birth. That's our daughter. We never called Annie by the name her birth mother gave her. We didn't believe the odd name of Starly was fitting for someone in our community."

Jonas nodded in silent agreement.

"When Annie was a tiny child," Martha continued, "we were forced to allow her to spend time with her birth mother. It was the law, we were told, and even though it grieved our hearts to let her go, we had no choice. At that time, we learned that Annie had sisters."

She shook her head in disbelief. "I never imagined I'd see the day when our Annie's past would come to trouble us like this."

"I didn't think this news would be easily received," Bishop Schlabach said. "Mrs. Hartman-Gray's request is not a matter to be taken lightly. I wanted to discuss it with the two of you, rather than going straight to your daughter, even though Annie is an adult."

He hesitated, as if trying to phrase a distasteful opinion in a delicate way. "I'm aware that your daughter hasn't always been of a stable mind or a steady disposition. I didn't know how she'd respond to the news that her sister is searching for her. I'm not sure she'd be able to make a sound decision about this on her own."

Martha suddenly felt defensive, even though she was usually the first to acknowledge Annie's shortcomings.

"I made this a matter of prayer for several days," Bishop Schlabach continued, "and the Lord laid it on my heart to seek the advice of Annie's parents."

Jonas furrowed his brow. "I have grave concerns about this. If Annie should open her life to the influence of her English sister, it may lead her down a path she shouldn't follow. Annie is unable to withstand temptation the way other Christian women do. She's easily led astray."

"My thoughts were along the same lines," Bishop Schlabach said. "Perhaps it would be best if Annie never knows about the letter. Are we of one mind in thinking that we should let this matter drop?"

Jonas nodded solemnly, but Martha laid a hand on his arm. "Wait," she said.

Martha stands at her kitchen counter preparing yeast dough for cinnamon rolls. Five-year-old Annie scoots a kitchen chair up to the counter to see what her mother is doing.

Martha spreads melted butter over the flattened dough. "Let me help!" Annie demands.

Martha shows her how to sprinkle cinnamon and sugar over the melted butter. Then she begins rolling the dough into a long tube. Annie sticks her little hands between her mother's hands to get in on the rolling action.

"Mama," Annie asks suddenly, "when will I go see Sissy and Shaney again?"

"You won't be going to your sisters' house anymore," Martha tells her. "You'll be staying here with us."

"Oh." There's a hint of disappointment in Annie's voice.

"Do you miss your sisters, Annie?" Martha asks.

"Yes," Annie says. "I want to see Sissy and Shaney."

"Do you miss Seffie, then? Do you want to see Seffie again?"

"No!" Annie shouts. She jumps off the chair and runs around the kitchen table. "No, no, no!" She circles into the living room, then back into the kitchen and around the table again. "No, no, no!"

She begins giggling hysterically, and Martha senses her daughter's emotions are careening out of control. She wipes the flour off her hands, and then runs after Annie, catching her up in her arms. She sits down in the rocking chair in the living room, holding her tightly.

Annie continues to giggle, struggles to get free, and then begins to cry. Martha rocks her gently, crooning a hymn. Annie stops flailing and snuggles against her mother's breast.

Suddenly, she sits up straight. She puts her tiny hand, sticky from the cinnamon rolls, on Martha's cheek, turning her mother's face to look at her.

"Can Sissy and Shaney come live with us?" she asks.

Bishop Schlabach looked at Martha questioningly. "What are your thoughts, then?"

Martha felt a twinge of discomfort, knowing she was about to speak out in disagreement with the two most important men in her life, her husband and the leader of her church.

"I believe Annie has the right to make her own decision about the letter," she said. "Although we don't know how this will turn out, I believe that getting to know this long-lost sister might put to rest some uneasiness that has been stirring in Annie's soul. Maybe it will help calm her agitated spirit."

Tears welled in her eyes, and she reached up to dab them with her napkin. "I remember a day when Annie was a tiny child, grieving over her separation from her sisters. Who are we to hold her back?"

The two men listened intently, weighing her words carefully. "I believe there's truth in what you say, Martha," the bishop said. "You're Annie's mother, and you know her better than anyone else."

Martha looked at Jonas, who was stroking his beard, deep in thought. "I'll go along with your idea, Martha," he said, "but on one condition."

"What's that?" she asked.

"Before we give Annie the letter, we will write to Mrs. Hartman-Gray to let her know where we stand as Annie's parents. We must request that she be careful in how she influences our daughter."

"I agree with you, Jonas," Martha said. "Let's take some time to compose a thoughtful letter to Annie's sister."

Bishop Schlabach gestured to the letter lying on the table. "I'll leave this in your hands," he said. "I only advise you to make this a matter of prayer before you begin a course of action."

After the Bishop left, Jonas and Martha went into the living room for their scripture reading and prayer. There was a time when their evening worship involved a family of nine, but now there were just the two of them. After reading from the book of Psalms, Jonas closed the Bible and reached over to take his wife's hand.

"Dear Lord," he prayed aloud, "we thank you for the many blessings you continually bestow upon us. We're especially grateful for our six sons and our daughter. And now we raise to you our concerns about Annie. We face a matter that causes us a great deal of turmoil and confusion. We place this matter into your hands and ask that you provide us with the wisdom to do your will. Amen."

The next evening after they finished their supper, Martha cleared off the kitchen table while Jonas went to his desk to get a pen and a pad of paper.

"I'll let you do the writing," he said as he handed Martha the pen. With her husband's assistance, Martha composed a letter to their daughter's sister.

August 4

Dear Mrs. Hartman-Gray,

Yesterday evening, our bishop paid us a visit and brought us the letter you'd written him. Without a doubt, the sister you are searching for is our beloved daughter, Annie.

We know it's a blessing when long-lost family members reunite. We recall years ago when Annie spent time with her birth mother and sisters. While we were relieved when that confusing time was over and Annie came back to our family on a permanent basis, we knew she grieved being separated from her sisters. She continued to ask about you for months after her visits ended. We're sure she'd be thrilled to hear from you.

And yet, we must raise our concerns. You seem to be a reasonable person, and we hope you can understand. Before we inform Annie of your intent to find her, we must make a request of you.

We've done our best to raise our daughter in the Amish faith. Unfortunately, this has been difficult. While Annie is a loving and kind-hearted girl, she seems to have been born with an unruly spirit. She's prone to making foolish mistakes, and is easily misled.

We're quite sure that having contact with an English sister would stir thoughts in Annie's mind about wanting to be English. Annie is now a wife and mother. It would be most unfortunate for all concerned if her way of life were to be disrupted. We ask that you respect Annie's position as a member of the Amish church, and that you refrain from influencing her in the ways of the English.

With that in mind, we give you our blessing to write a personal letter to your sister. We would appreciate you sending the letter to our mailing address, and we will pass it along to her.

You probably called Annie by the name of Starly when she was a little girl. She's never been known by that name in our family and community. Annie's married name is Mrs. Luke Kauffman.

Sincerely,

Jonas and Martha Bontrager

Chapter 4

"Try to sit still for a minute, Sarah!" Annie scolded her two-year-old daughter. Sarah fussed and squirmed on the kitchen chair while her mother struggled in vain to secure her blonde baby hair into two tiny braids.

Annie finally decided the results were as good as they were going to get. She turned her attention to her son, who'd just finished his breakfast and was playing in the corner of the kitchen with his collection of farm animals.

"Let me see your face, Daniel."

Daniel looked up, and Annie saw a streak of grape jelly on one cheek. She lifted Sarah off the chair, and then got a washcloth from the bathroom to wipe Daniel's face.

"Grandma will be here in just a minute," she said. "Remember, you'll be spending the day at Grandma's house while Mama goes to a meeting."

"Will we have lunch at Grandma's?" Daniel asked.

"Yes," Annie said. "She'll fix you something special."

She looked out the window when she heard the clip-clop of horse's hooves on the driveway. "Here she is," she announced. "Let's not keep her waiting. Grandma will drop Mama off at her meeting, and then she'll take you back to her house."

Martha got out of the buggy to help Annie and the children settled in, then climbed back into the driver's seat. She was happy to have Daniel and Sarah for the day, even though they were a handful. Annie's children seemed to be more rambunctious than her other grandchildren, and they wore her out quickly.

Martha had been the one to arrange the day's activities. One of the church women, Emma Schrock, was holding a quilting bee in her home, and Martha wanted Annie to enjoy the event without having to cope with the demands of her children. She'd been pleased to notice that Annie was forming friendships with several of the other young wives in the congregation, and she wanted to encourage that trend.

A dozen women had gathered around the quilting frame at Emma's house to do the quilting on a project she'd pieced together. Emma was well known in the community for her expertise in quilt-making. She had a flare for design and color, and her finished products were breathtakingly beautiful. This particular quilt was destined to be auctioned off at the Mennonite Relief Sale in Goshen in several months, and the women were all proud to have a hand in completing the project. They expected the quilt to be sold for a considerable amount of money.

"Oh, this will be fun!" Annie exclaimed when she saw her friends Katie Swartzentruber and Leah Graber. As the women seated themselves around the quilt, she made sure to sit between the two of them.

Most of the women in attendance were older than Annie, in their fifties and sixties. Emma's widowed mother-in-law, Lydia Schrock, was eighty-eight and nearly blind. Unable to join in the quilting, she sat in a rocking chair in a corner of the room, enjoying the company of the younger women.

Annie watched in amazement as the other women rendered tiny, even running stitches without having to draw their needles and thread out of the fabric after every stitch. Her own process was much more laborious. When she'd tried to help her mother with quilting in the past, she'd struggled with the projects, and hadn't had the patience to sit for long.

But as she chatted with Leah and Katie, Annie was glad she'd come. Unencumbered by her children's needs, she felt young and free. She artfully teased her two friends, sending them into giggling fits. She turned her attention to the older women as well, making humorous comments that brought smiles to the faces of all. Even blind old Lydia Schrock chuckled as she rocked in her chair.

One of the ladies began singing a hymn, and the rest joined in. Annie had always been told she had a nice voice, and she began singing loudly, her needle and thread moving with gusto to the cadence of the song. Mesmerized by the rhythm of singing and stitching, she began swaying in her seat.

Katie nudged Annie's side, disrupting her blissful trance. "Annie, quiet down a bit."

Annie glanced up and saw that several of the women were looking at her curiously. Her face burned with embarrassment. As the singing continued, she kept her voice to a low hum.

Suddenly, she felt the sharp stab of her own needle in her finger. "Ouch!" she yelped. She popped her finger in her mouth to soothe the pain.

"Oh, no, there's blood on my quilt!" Emma Schrock cried. "I've got to get it out right away, before it sets and becomes a permanent stain."

All the ladies fussed and clucked as Emma hurried to the kitchen to get a wet rag. "Make it cold water," Ruth Stoltzfus called out. "That's the best for taking out bloodstains."

Red-faced with anxiety, Emma rushed back into the room with a cold wet rag. "This will never sell if it's stained," she fretted as she dabbed furiously at the droplets of blood. The other ladies hovered around Emma as she worked, hoping their collective handiwork hadn't been ruined.

Annie moved out of the way and stood against the wall, feeling ashamed and worthless. Finally Emma straightened up and said, "There! It's all out now. You could never tell anything happened."

"I'm so sorry!" Annie wailed. "I'd feel just terrible if I ruined your quilt!"

Emma smiled graciously. "It's okay Annie. Accidents will happen. Should I get you a band-aid for your finger?"

The ladies decided it was time to break for lunch. Emma had prepared ham sandwiches, and some of the women had brought salads and desserts. While the older ladies stayed in the kitchen to eat, Annie filled her plate and went outside to sit with Katie and Leah at the picnic table in the front yard.

Relieved that she hadn't ruined Emma's quilt, Annie quickly returned to a buoyant mood. She and her two friends giggled as they told stories about their husbands and gossiped about other people in the church.

After the three young women went inside and deposited their empty plates in the kitchen, they walked back into the living room where the older women had already taken seats around the quilt. They stopped short, perplexed, when they saw other women sitting in the seats they'd occupied before lunch.

"We decided to switch seats," Emma explained.

Katie's mother, Miriam Hershberger, was sitting where Annie had been sitting. Unaware that the young women had entered the room, she was busy ripping out the stitches Annie had put in before lunch.

"What are you doing?" Annie blurted out.

Miriam startled and looked up, her face stricken with embarrassment.

"Why are you taking out my stitches?" Annie demanded to know.

"Some of them were a little too big and too far apart," Miriam said. "I just thought I'd do this section over."

Annie struggled to contain a surge of anger. "What difference does it make?"

Emma Schrock jumped in to rescue the awkward moment, explaining how stitches on a high-priced quilt needed to be evenly spaced and very tiny. "I know you're new at quilting," she said to Annie. "With a little practice, you'll do fine."

Out of the corner of her eye, Annie could see Katie and Leah nudging each other and whispering. She turned to glare at them. Katie bit her lip to stifle nervous giggles, but Leah couldn't contain herself. She covered her mouth and rushed into the kitchen, her shoulders heaving with silent laughter.

Utterly humiliated, Annie rushed out the front door. Hesitating on the steps, she wondered what she should do next. She desperately wished she could run away and leave this awful experience behind her.

But she had no way to get anywhere, other than walking, and she knew she wouldn't make it very far because of her pregnancy. Besides, her mother would be coming to pick her up at three o'clock, and she'd be terribly worried if Annie wasn't there.

There was nothing to do but wait. So she walked back over to the picnic table, and sat in shame at the spot where, minutes earlier, she'd been having so much fun.

Half an hour later, Ruth Stoltzfus came out and sat down at the table with her.

"We all wish you'd come back inside, Annie," she said. "We miss your joyful spirit. Lydia Schrock is asking what happened to the fun-loving girl. It's not the same without you. None of us wants you to feel bad about what happened."

"Maybe I'll come in after a little while," Annie mumbled. "I'm feeling nauseated, and the fresh air helps."

Ruth stood up, laying a hand on Annie's shoulder. "Well, come in when you feel better."

Another thirty minutes passed before Katie Swartzentruber came out to sit with Annie. "My mother feels terrible about hurting your feelings," she said. "And Leah's in the bedroom crying because she thinks you're angry with her. She didn't mean to laugh at you. She was just caught off guard by what happened."

"You were laughing, too," Annie snapped.

Katie's face reddened. "I'm sorry about that, I really am. Please come back in, Annie. You're so much fun, and we miss you."

"I'll come in when I'm ready," Annie said curtly. Katie shrugged and walked back into the house.

When Martha arrived with the children an hour later, Annie was still sitting at the picnic table.

"Whatever's the matter, Annie?" she asked, dismayed by the distraught look on her daughter's face.

"I don't want to talk about it," Annie muttered as she climbed into the buggy. Ignoring the clamoring of her children for her attention, she turned her face to stare out the window.

Martha snapped the reigns to get the horse moving. "Annie, if something happened to upset you at Emma's house, I'll hear about it sooner or later. I'd rather hear it from you. Please tell me now, so I won't be fretting about what I don't know."

Annie turned around to face her mother, crossing her arms defiantly over her bulging abdomen. "I ruined everything!" she said.

Her pose reminded Martha of when her daughter was a misbehaving little girl. "I'm sure that's not true," she said, hoping Annie hadn't done something reprehensible.

"Oh, yes it is," Annie retorted. "First of all, I pricked my finger and got blood on Emma's quilt. All the women made a big fuss about it."

"Did Emma get the bloodstain out?" Martha asked.

"Yes, but I was so embarrassed."

"So there was no harm done. Is that all that happened?"

"No. I went outside to eat lunch with Katie and Leah, and when we went back inside, Miriam Hershberger was taking out the stitching I'd done. She said my stitches were too big. I got upset, and Katie and Leah laughed at me. It was horrible. I couldn't stay in there with all those women thinking I'm stupid, so I stayed outside for the rest of the afternoon."

Martha reached over and laid a comforting hand on Annie's arm. "I'm so sorry. I was hoping you'd have a good time."

Inwardly, she cringed at her daughter's display of emotional fragility. She thought about the letter that would inevitably arrive from Cecily Hartman-Gray. If Annie couldn't handle ordinary social events, how would she cope with something as shocking as hearing from a long-lost sister? She questioned her wisdom in opposing the bishop's suggestion that they ignore Mrs. Hartman-Gray's request.

Chapter 5

Three days later, Martha found a large manila envelope in her mailbox. It was rumpled from handling, and the return address, penned in black marker, was smudged. But there was no mistaking the sender: Cecily Hartman-Gray. The letter Martha had come to dread had finally arrived.

She carried the envelope into the house with the rest of the mail and laid it on the kitchen table. Unable to face the contents just yet, she focused her attention on supper preparations. She filled a bowl with potatoes from the pantry, picked up a paring knife, and began to peel.

But halfway through the second potato, she sighed and dropped it back into the bowl. Then she turned to the stack of mail on the table and ran the blade of her knife through one end of the manila envelope.

When she reached inside the envelope, she found two smaller envelopes, both sealed. One was labeled *Annie Kauffman,* and the other was addressed to *Jonas and Martha Bontrager.*

Martha fought the urge to tear open the letter addressed to her and Jonas, at the same time fearing what she would find. She decided it was best to postpone reading it until her husband was with her.

When Jonas came in from the fields for supper, Martha handed him the manila envelope. "What's this?" he asked.

She shook her head, biting her lip. Jonas pulled out the two smaller envelopes and stared at them with furrowed brow.

"I'll let you open it," he said, handing Martha the envelope addressed to the two of them.

With trembling hands, she tore open the letter and read its contents aloud.

August 8

Dear Mr. and Mrs. Bontrager,

Thank you so much for your letter. I can't begin to tell you how excited I am to find my little sister's family! When I began my search for

Starly, your daughter Annie, I had no idea what I would encounter.

Thank you for giving me your blessing to write to my sister. I respect your concerns about my influence on her. Please understand that I have no intention of disturbing her faith or her way of life.

I am so happy Starly was raised in a family who loves and cares for her. I have sad memories of her being mistreated by our birth mother. For some reason, Seffie couldn't handle Starly, and she ended up hurting her.

I've worried so much about my little sister. Hopefully, the loving care she received in your family made up for the abuse from our birth mother.

Anytime you have concerns about my relationship with your daughter, please let me know.

Sincerely,

Cecily Hartman-Gray

Jonas and Martha sat with bowed heads, digesting the weight of the words they'd just taken in.

"I'd like to think we made up for it." Martha choked on a sob. "I pray to God we haven't failed her."

Jonas nodded, placing his hand over Martha's. They sat in silence, each knowing the heaviness in the other's heart.

Then Jonas picked up the envelope addressed to their daughter. "I suppose we need to deliver this to Annie soon. Since we won't have a preaching service this week, let's pay her and Luke a visit on Sunday."

Sunday afternoon, Annie decided to lie down with Sarah for her nap, and ended up falling asleep. The next thing she knew, Luke was shaking her.

"Annie," he whispered, so as not to wake their sleeping daughter. "Your folks are here for a visit." He extended his hand to help her off the bed.

Groggily, Annie straightened her clothing and smoothed her hair, then went out to the living room to greet her parents, who were seated on the sofa.

"Mom and Dad, I'm surprised to see you!" she exclaimed. Then, puzzled by the somber expressions on their faces, she asked, "Is something wrong?"

"We need to talk with you and Luke," Jonas said.

"We should have this conversation in private," Martha added, mindful of Daniel's presence in the room.

"Daniel, why don't you go out to the barn and check on the new calf?" Luke suggested. Then he turned to his in-laws. "Sarah's sound asleep. I don't think she'll be waking up soon."

"Martha, I'll let you speak," Jonas said after Daniel had gone outside.

Martha looked down at her folded hands, trying to decide where to begin. "Several weeks ago, Bishop Schlabach paid us a visit," she said. "He brought a letter with him. Annie, the letter was from your older sister, Cecily Hartman-Gray."

"Huh?" Annie said, bewildered. "Cecily Hartman-Gray? I don't have a sister named Cecily." Suddenly, her face went pale with shock. "Sissy! You mean Sissy!"

Her body began to tremble uncontrollably. Luke moved his chair close to hers and put his arm around her. After a few moments, his comforting touch steadied her enough so she could speak again.

"I never dreamed I would hear from Sissy!" she whispered. "What did she want?"

Martha leaned forward on the sofa. "Annie, Cecily told the bishop she was looking to reunite with a sister adopted by an Amish family in Marshall County. From her description, the bishop thought she might be talking about you. He brought the letter to us, and we discussed the matter. Then your father and I wrote a letter back to Cecily."

She reached out to hand Annie the sealed envelope she'd been holding on her lap. "Several days ago, we received this letter addressed to you."

Annie turned the envelope over and over in her trembling hands. "Why did you wait so long to tell me about this?" she asked. "Why didn't you tell me right away?"

Martha and Jonas exchanged concerned glances, and then Jonas spoke. "We were worried about how this would affect you. We wanted to make sure that hearing from your sister wouldn't upset you too much."

They had no right to keep this from me, Annie thought. *They just won't stop treating me like a child.* But her overwhelming desire to know the contents of her sister's letter overrode her anger, and she tore open the envelope.

"Do you and Luke want to read the letter in private?" Martha asked, making a move to get up.

"No," Annie said, motioning her to stay. "You don't need to leave."

She unfolded the letter and read it silently.

August 8

Dear Starly,

I hardly know how to begin this letter. You can't imagine how thrilled I am to find you! I'm your older sister you used to know as 'Sissy.' When I started my search for you, I had no idea whether or not it would be successful. I don't know how you feel about hearing from me, but I hope you're as happy as I am to reconnect with a long-lost sister.

As I write this letter, I'm flooded with memories of us as little girls at our birth mother's house. Some of the things that happened are painful to remember, but the memories of us playing together are so happy. The two of us were quite a pair! I remember how close we were when I was five and you were four. It was so hard to adjust to not having you in my life.

I hope we can get to know each other again as grownup sisters. I know this letter is taking you by surprise, and maybe you'll need some time to think about what you want to do.

Your parents have already informed me that you are a wife and mother. I hope you will write back soon and tell me more about your life. I'm also married, but I don't have children. I'll tell you more after I hear from you.

Your sister,

Cecily Hartman-Gray (Sissy)

Annie looked up, a dazed expression on her face. Her parents and husband gazed at her expectantly. The room was so still, Annie could hear Luke breathing next to her.

"Do you want to tell us what's in the letter?" Luke finally asked.

"I can't," Annie said. "Not right now."

"That's okay," Martha reassured her. "What do you plan to do?"

"I'm going to write a letter back to my sister," Annie said indignantly, as if any other response would be unthinkable.

The family sat in an awkward silence while Annie withdrew into a world of her own.

Then Jonas said, "Martha, we need to go. It's almost time for the evening milking."

"How are you feeling, Annie?" Luke asked after Jonas and Martha had gone. "Is there something I can do for you?"

"I think I need to lie down again," Annie whispered. "I'm really tired all of a sudden."

"Of course," Luke said as he helped her to her feet. "This letter came as quite a shock, didn't it? Don't worry about anything. I'll look after the children the rest of the day."

Martha slept fitfully that night, as she couldn't get Annie off her mind. She worried that her high-strung daughter might still be agitated by the jolting news she'd received earlier that day. Although she would never voice such a thought, that night Martha wished she had a telephone in her home like the English people did, so she could call to check on Annie.

The next morning while she was fixing breakfast for Jonas, Martha answered a knock on the front door and found her son-in-law standing there, looking decidedly haggard.

"I'm sorry to bother you," Luke said, "but I need your help. Annie didn't sleep at all last night. The letter from her sister really upset her. She spent the night pacing the floor, crying. She wouldn't even talk to me."

He ran his hand through his rumpled hair. "I'm really worried about her. I wouldn't want anything to happen to her or the baby. I'm wondering if she can stay with you for the day while I get some work done in the fields."

"Of course, of course," Martha said. As exhausted as she was, she was glad for the opportunity to keep an eye on her daughter.

"Thank you so much," Luke said, his voice catching. "I think this is a time when Annie needs her mother more than anyone else. She and the children are in the buggy. Is it okay if I leave Sarah here, too? I'll take Daniel with me."

"Of course," Martha repeated. She followed Luke out the door and down the driveway. He reached into the buggy and lifted out Sarah, who was still sleeping soundly.

Then Annie slowly climbed out, pale-faced and unkempt. Instinctively, Martha held out her arms, and Annie collapsed into them, sobbing like a frightened child.

"There, there," Martha murmured as she stroked her daughter's back. "Come on inside, and I'll put you to bed. You need to rest. You need to sleep."

Chapter 6

Martha led her weeping daughter up the stairs to her childhood room and helped her into bed. Little Sarah, who'd woken up the minute Luke brought her into the house, cried to stay with her mother, but Martha picked up the fussy two-year-old and carried her downstairs. She sat Sarah down on the living room floor and opened the wooden toy chest Jonas had built for their grandchildren.

"Oh, look!" Sarah chortled. She began rummaging through the toys, and Martha set about her task of cleaning up the kitchen. But before long, Sarah was crying for her mother again, and Martha realized she needed to give her granddaughter undivided attention in order to keep her in good spirits. She stood Sarah on a chair at the kitchen sink, allowing her to splash her little hands in the dishwater.

Just when Martha was ready to put Sarah down for an afternoon nap, Annie came down the stairs, looking disheveled and sleepy-eyed. She went straight to the sofa and lay down again. Even though the August day was hot, she pulled the crocheted afghan from the back of the sofa and huddled under it. Martha knew her daughter was seeking security.

Little Sarah climbed onto the sofa, snuggled against her mother, and was sound asleep within a minute.

"Are you hungry, Annie?" Martha asked. "What would you like me to fix you? I have some fried chicken and potato salad in the refrigerator."

Annie made a face. "I'm not that hungry. I just want soup. Tomato soup."

Martha smiled, knowing Annie was requesting her favorite childhood meal. "It's a little warm for soup, don't you think?"

"I don't care!" Annie's voice sounded petulant.

Sighing, Martha opened the door of her pantry, where she kept rows of fruits and vegetables in quart jars. She selected one of the few remaining jars of tomato soup she'd canned last summer. While the soup was heating, she grilled a cheese sandwich made with thick slabs of homemade bread. Sweat trickled down the sides of her plump face, and she wondered how she'd find the strength to make it through the day.

"Your lunch is ready," she called. Annie eased her body away from her sleeping child and shuffled to the table. Thoroughly exhausted and emotionally drained, Martha sat down on a kitchen chair to keep her daughter company.

Annie took a few bites of the soup, then laid her spoon down and looked at Martha imploringly. "Mama," she said in a childlike voice, "tell me how I came to live with you."

Martha had attempted to tell this story many times earlier in her daughter's life, but Annie had always been too restless to listen. She'd ask a question pertaining to her adoption, but couldn't focus her attention long enough to hear a complete answer. Martha had decided to wait for the day when Annie would be interested in hearing the entire story.

"You came to us when you were two months old," she began. "A social worker from the welfare department, Mindy Barnes, brought you to our home."

"Why?" Annie asked. "Why to your home?"

"Because your father and I were licensed foster parents," Martha explained. "Before you, we kept many foster children. We never took any more after you came. You were our last one."

Annie grinned. "I know, I was such a naughty child, you had your hands full with me."

Inwardly, Martha agreed with Annie's statement, but she didn't want to hurt her daughter by voicing such a thought. "Your father and I were getting older, and we decided it was time to stop being foster parents," she said. "We felt our family was complete, with our six boys and one little girl."

Wearily, she leaned her elbow on the table, chin resting in her hand, her mind traveling back to the day when little Annie came into her life. "You were so tiny. At two months, you weighed only seven pounds. Mindy Barnes told me your birth mother had left you in the care of her father. The neighbors heard you crying for hours on end, and someone finally called the police. The police found your grandfather passed out from drinking. They took you into protective custody."

Annie shuddered, but said nothing.

"When Mindy placed you in my arms," Martha continued, "I could see you weren't well-nourished. You were crying and flailing your little arms." She held up her index finger. "They were hardly bigger than this. When I started cleaning you up, I discovered your little bottom was bright red from diaper rash. You screamed in pain while I washed you and put ointment on you.

"The first night at our house, you cried all night long. I stayed up with you, feeding you, walking the floor with you, rocking you, singing to you. Your pitiful wails just broke my heart. I did everything I could to console you, and at times the tears ran down my own face. I couldn't imagine how a little one could be so neglected and left in such a pitiful state.

"Finally, around five in the morning, just before Jonas got up to do the chores, you wore yourself out and settled down to sleep. I was holding you in the rocking chair, and you were lying on my shoulder with your little head nestled against my neck. It was still dark outside, and the house was quiet. It felt like there was no one else in the world, just you and me. I was praying, and I could sense the Lord was speaking to me, telling me that He'd put this child into my hands for safe-keeping."

She wiped a tear off her cheek. "I knew from the depths of my being that it was my job to take care of you. And then I felt a wave of such sweet love surrounding the two of us. It felt like you were part of me, and from that moment on, you were my child. I promised the Lord I'd do my best to love and protect you."

Annie reached for her mother's hand, and the two women sat with tears streaming down their faces. Then Annie wiped her face with her napkin, and her mood seemed to lighten.

"Was I okay, then?" she asked. "Did I get better?"

"Oh, yes!" Martha said. "You came along just fine. For the first couple of months, the women in the church helped me. They brought in meals and did some of the laundry so I could devote my time to you.

You ate well and started sleeping better. You were always tiny, but you filled out nicely. You were a beautiful baby."

Annie cocked her head, batting her eyes and smiling coyly, but her expression quickly changed to one of concern. "What happened to my birth mother after I was taken away?"

"I don't know," Martha said. "We didn't hear much of anything about that part of your family. Mindy Barnes would pay us a visit every couple of months to check on how you were doing. After a year or so, we assumed you were going to stay with us permanently. But when you were four, everything changed."

The painful memories added to Martha's exhaustion, and she suddenly felt completely drained. She wished she could stretch out on her bed for a nap, but she doubted she'd have the energy to get up and walk to the bedroom.

Perk up, Martha, she scolded herself. *Your daughter needs you.*

"Is that when my visits with Seffie started?" Annie asked.

Martha sighed deeply. "Yes, that's when the visits started. Those were difficult times for our family. We'd had no idea this was coming. We were planning on adopting you. We were just waiting for your birth mother's parental rights to be terminated."

"What do you mean by terminated?"

"Termination of parental rights means the birth parent is no longer the child's legal parent," Martha explained. "They're no longer allowed any contact with the child, and it means the child is free to be adopted by someone else. It involves signing a legal document. Sometimes parents terminate their rights voluntarily, and sometimes a judge orders their rights to be terminated."

"So since you did adopt me," Annie mused, "my birth mother's rights must've been terminated."

"Yes," Martha said. "That happened when you were five, and we adopted you soon afterward. But we had to go through so much to get to that point. One day when you were four, Mindy told us that your mother, Seferina Dickerson, was ready to take care of you again. She'd met the welfare department's standards, and by law, they had to give you back to her."

Annie sat motionless, eyes closed, listening intently.

Martha continued. "They started you out with short visits and grad-ually increased them, until you were staying at Seffie's house about half a week at a time. Do you remember?"

Annie nodded her head, shuddering. "I remember, but I try not to. I don't like to think about that."

"I understand," Martha said. "Those visits were awfully hard on you. Poor thing, you were so confused. I'd have to change you from your Amish dress to your English clothing before you'd leave our house. Here at home, you spoke Pennsylvania Dutch, but at your birth mother's house, you spoke English. Even your name changed. We'd always called you Annie, but you went by Starly at your birth mother's house. Half of the week, you were a little Amish girl named Annie Bontrager, and the other half of the week you were an English child named Starly Dickerson.

"I could see this was a terrible thing for you to go through. I wanted so badly to protect you, but I was powerless to do anything about it. When you'd come home from your birth mother's house, you'd cry and throw tantrums and cling to me. You'd scream, 'You don't love me an-ymore.'"

"I remember saying that," Annie said. "I didn't really mean it."

"Perhaps you did," Martha replied. "I was the only mother you'd known, and no matter how I tried to explain it, you thought it was my decision to send you off to a stranger's house every week. You were so young, and I couldn't make you understand that I wasn't your real mother."

Martha's eyes brimmed with tears again, and she stopped to wipe them with the corner of her apron. "I'm so sorry, Annie. I can't tell you how much it hurt my heart to know that you felt rejected by me. I felt like I wasn't keeping my commitment to protect you. But truly, there was nothing I could've done to stop what was happening."

Annie reached over to hold her mother's hand again. "It's okay, Mama. Maybe I didn't understand then, but I understand now." She looked thoughtful. "So why did the visits stop?"

"I think Seferina Dickerson got in trouble with the law somehow," Martha said. "All of her children were taken away from her for a little while. And her parental rights with you were terminated."

"Did she do it voluntarily, or did the judge order it?"

Martha sensed it was important to phrase her response carefully. "Yes, she terminated her rights voluntarily, but the welfare department put pressure on her to do it."

"Why?" Annie asked, undisguised pain in her voice.

Martha sent up a silent prayer, asking for help in speaking the right words. "Seferina Dickerson didn't seem to know how to be a mother to you. It's probably because the two of you hadn't bonded when you were a baby. She didn't handle you very well, and the welfare department suspected she was abusing you. I suspected that, too, because of the way you behaved when you came back home." She gazed quizzically at her daughter. "Do you remember anything?"

Annie lowered her head, staring at her uneaten bowl of soup. "Yes," she said.

"Hold still, Starly," Sissy says. The two girls are standing in the trailer's filthy bathroom. Five-year-old Sissy measures almost a head taller than four-year-old Starly, and Starly can barely see her reflection in the mirror. Sissy bites her lip, concentrating hard as she attempts to twist Starly's long locks into a braid.

Starly stands on tiptoe, peering into the mirror to inspect Sissy's handiwork. "That's not the way my mom does it!" she announces indignantly.

Suddenly, Seffie appears in the bathroom doorway, her eyes blazing with anger. "That fat Amish bitch ain't your mother!" she yells. "Don't you ever forget that!"

"Yes she is!" Starly screams at the top of her lungs.

Seffie grabs Starly by one arm and yanks her out into the hallway. Starly's world begins to spin violently, and then breaks into jagged pieces as Seffie strikes her hard on her bottom, again and again. Then she lets go of Starly's arm and gives her a shove that makes her fall to her knees.

"Go to your room!" she orders.

Crying hysterically, Starly scrambles up and runs to the bedroom she shares with Sissy. She flings herself onto the narrow bed and buries her face in the sour-smelling pillow.

Sissy quietly follows her sister to the bedroom. "Sissy, you don't need to take care of that crybaby," Seffie mutters.

Sissy acts like she didn't hear what her mother said. She lies down on the bed next to Starly and begins patting her sister's back.

The rhythmic pat, pat, pat of the tiny warm hand soothes Starly's agitation, and she stops crying. The hand lies still for a moment.

"Don't stop!" Starly commands, her voice muffled by the pillow.

"What are you remembering, Annie?" Martha asked.

"I remember Sissy taking care of me after Seffie hurt me," Annie murmured.

Martha took a deep breath, unsure whether she wanted to hear the response to the question she was about to ask. "How did Seffie hurt you, Annie?"

Annie grimaced and shook her head. "Let's not talk about that." She picked up her spoon and took a bite of her soup. It had grown cold, so she shoved the bowl away from her.

"Did Seffie terminate her rights on the other girls?" she asked. "Or was it just me? Was I the only one she couldn't handle? Was I the only one she didn't want?"

Help me, Lord, Martha prayed silently. Aloud, she said, "Annie, I honestly don't know what happened with the other girls. But we know her rights to Sissy had to be terminated at some point, because she's been adopted, too."

"But she would've wanted Sissy," Annie protested. "She liked Sissy. Sissy was always good. It was me she didn't like." She looked imploringly at Martha. "Mama, why am I always the one nobody can handle? I make problems everywhere I go. Am I that bad?"

"Now Annie," Martha said firmly. "Let's not go down that line of thinking. You know you've always been loved and wanted in this family. You may be high-spirited, but you're not bad."

Just then, sleepy-eyed little Sarah toddled into the kitchen. She climbed onto Annie's lap and demanded to be fed bites of the cold soup. The presence of her child seemed to lighten Annie's mood, and she giggled at Sarah's silly behavior.

As she watched her two-year-old granddaughter, Martha suddenly remembered another toddler who'd once been placed in her care.

"Annie," she said, "I misspoke when I said you were the last foster child we took in. When you were six, we took in a little girl who stayed with us for just a week."

"You did?" Annie asked. "Who was it?"

"Don't you remember? It was your baby sister Shaney. She was Sarah's age at the time."

Annie's eyes grew wide. "Oh, yes, I do remember!"

On a warm September afternoon, Mindy Barnes parks her car in the Bontragers' driveway. Six-year-old Annie looks up from her play in the sandbox. When she recognizes the visitor, she scrambles up, brushes the sand from her dress, and runs to the car.

"I'm not going with you," she says haughtily. "My mom says I don't have to visit Seffie anymore."

Mindy laughs. "I'm not taking you anywhere, Starly. You're going to stay right here. But I brought someone else for your mom to take care of."

She opens the back door of her car and lifts a little girl out of the car seat, a toddler with frightened blue eyes and a mass of blonde ringlets.

"Who's that?" Starly demands to know.

"Don't you recognize her?" Mindy asks. "This is your sister Shaney."

"No, it isn't!" Annie says. "Shaney isn't that big. She's just a baby."

Mindy laughs again. "Shaney has grown, Starly, just like you've grown."

"Oh!" Annie says, rolling her eyes and clapping her hand to her forehead. Then she turns and runs into the house ahead of Mindy, her bare feet flying.

"Mama, Mama!" she calls. "Shaney's here!"

Mindy sits at the kitchen table talking with Martha. Little Shaney sits on her lap sucking two fingers, her big blue eyes wide with fear. Starly plants herself in front of Mindy, hands on her hips.

"So when are you bringing Sissy?" she asks.

"Whatever happened to Shaney?" Annie's eyes held a faraway look. "Why didn't she stay with us?"

"The welfare department put her in her father's care," Martha explained.

Annie wrinkled her forehead, thinking hard. "Jimmy? Was her father Jimmy?"

"I believe so," Martha responded.

Just then, they heard a tap on the front door. Before Martha could get up, the door opened and Luke called out, "It's just me."

"Daddy!" Sarah chortled, sliding off Annie's lap and running to the door. Luke scooped his daughter up in one arm.

Annie got up and rushed to greet her husband, wrapping her arms tightly around his waist. Luke encircled her with his other arm.

Martha was struck by the childlike nature of Annie's posture with her husband. She wondered if Luke sometimes felt like he was raising three children.

That night, as Annie slept soundly with her head on Luke's chest, she dreamed she was a tiny child nestled in Martha's arms, her head resting against her mother's soft bosom. Martha was rocking her, crooning an Amish hymn. But when Annie lifted her head to gaze into her beloved mother's face, she was startled to see it wasn't Martha's. Straggly hair framed the gaunt, unwashed features, and tears streamed from large blue eyes.

"I'm so sorry, baby," Seffie whispered. "So sorry. So sorry."

Chapter 7

When Annie awoke the next morning, Luke was already out of bed, getting dressed for his day's work in the fields. Annie stretched, feeling contented and well-rested.

"I had a strange dream last night," she said.

Luke sat down on the edge of the bed to lace up his boots. "What was it about?"

"My birth mother."

He shot her a quizzical look. "Why would you dream about her? You barely knew her."

Luke's cool response served to deflate Annie's good mood, and she decided not to say anything more about the dream. Luke leaned over and kissed her forehead.

"It's time to get up, Annie. Sarah's awake. She'll be getting into mischief if you're not up to watch her."

Annie sighed and threw back the covers. Luke held out his hand to help her to a sitting position.

While Sarah napped that afternoon, Annie sat at the kitchen table to compose a letter to her sister. Panic welled inside her as she stared at the blank sheet of paper in front of her. *I don't know what to say. Should I call her Cecily or Sissy? What should I tell her about myself?* She chewed nervously on the end of her pencil until she finally mustered the courage to write.

August 18
Dear Cecily (Sissy),

I was so surprised when I received your letter. I don't think I've ever been that surprised in my entire life! Of course I was happy, too. We've been apart for so many years, and I can hardly believe you actually found me. Reading your letter brought back many memories, things I hadn't thought about in years.

You asked me to tell you something about myself. You already know

I was adopted by Amish parents, Jonas and Martha Bontrager. I came to them when I was a baby, and lived with them until I got married six years ago. So they're the only family I've ever known, except for the short time I stayed with you at Seffie's house.

God has blessed me with a good life. My parents are Christian people, and I love them very much. I have six older brothers, but I'm the only girl in the family. My husband Luke is a wonderful man who provides well for me and treats me kindly. We have two children. Daniel is five, and Sarah is two. We are expecting our third child in two and a half months.

We live on a farm. Luke raises corn and wheat and beef cattle. I stay busy every day taking care of my children, working in my vegetable garden, and doing chores in the house.

I would be very happy to see you. Please write again and tell me more about you.
Your sister,
Annie (Starly)
P.S. I feel funny calling myself Starly. I've never gone by that name except at Seffie's house. But you can call me Starly if you want to.

Annie checked the letter for errors, and then carefully copied it in ink on another piece of paper. When Luke came into the house later that afternoon, she handed it to him.

"Read this and tell me what you think," she said. "Is it okay? Should I write anything else?" She hoped he'd be pleased with the part where she'd said nice things about him.

Luke read the letter silently. Annie watched his face for any expression of approval, but he remained dispassionate.

"Well?" she asked.

"It's okay." Luke handed the letter back to her.

"You don't think it's good!"

"The letter's fine." He ran a hand through his hair. "It's just that. . ."

"What?"

Luke stood up and began pacing the floor. "Annie, are you sure you want to do this? Two days ago, your sister's letter upset you so badly it left you shaking like a leaf. You cried all night and couldn't sleep. I don't want you to keep getting worked up about your sister. We have a family to take care of. We have our hands full. We don't need anything else piled on us."

He stopped and turned to face her. "Annie, it's hard for you to keep up with your responsibilities as it is. I can't have you falling apart all the time."

Annie stared at her husband, tears welling in her eyes. "I'm just a problem for you, Luke. I'm nothing but a problem."

"That's not what I'm saying, Annie. But I do need more help from you. I know you're slowing down because of your pregnancy, and I'm trying to be understanding. But if this business with your sister keeps upsetting you, I won't be able to handle everything."

"You should've picked a better wife then, Luke Kauffman!" Annie screamed before breaking down in sobs. "Why don't I just leave? I'm a burden to you. You'd do fine taking care of the children if I was out of the way!"

"Annie, don't twist my words like that! You know you aren't a burden." But Luke ended up speaking to his wife's back as she rushed off to their bedroom to cry in solitude.

When she was safely alone behind her closed bedroom door, Annie opened her top dresser drawer, where she'd hidden Sissy's letter under a stack of undergarments.

She sat on the bed to read the letter again, her tears running like a river as she absorbed her sister's kind words. *Sissy wants me,* she thought. *Sissy has always wanted me. She doesn't judge me. She loves me the way I am.*

Annie's mind trailed off into a fantasy world in which she and Sissy met for the first time in their adult lives. Sissy understood her perfectly, just like she did when they were little girls. She and Sissy felt so close to each other, they decide they couldn't be apart. Then Sissy invited her to move into her home.

Shocked by the direction her imagination had taken her, Annie suddenly felt ashamed. *I've got to get supper started,* she thought as she stuffed the letter back into her drawer.

The next morning, after Luke had left for the fields, Annie carried the letter she'd written to Sissy down the long lane to the mailbox. Daniel and Sarah walked with her, and she chatted with them lightheartedly. She decided it was best not to talk with Luke about her correspondence with her sister.

Three days later, Annie loaded the children in the buggy, along with a bushel basket filled with green beans from her garden, and drove to her mother's home. She and Martha had planned to spend the day cleaning and canning the beans.

Throughout the morning, they sat in the shade of the maple tree in the front yard, snapping the ends off the beans while Daniel and Sarah played nearby. Martha noticed her daughter was uncharacteristically quiet.

"What about my father?" Annie asked suddenly.

"What do you mean?" Martha asked. "Your father's out working in the barn. He'll be in for lunch."

"No, I mean my birth father. Jimmy wasn't my birth father, was he? It never seemed like he was."

Caught off guard by her daughter's question, Martha put aside her bowl of beans and sat for a moment to collect her thoughts. It had been years since she'd given any thought to Annie's brief encounter with her biological father. "No," she said, "Jimmy wasn't your father. Your birth father was a young man by the name of Gregory Smith. You saw him one time when you were five. Don't you remember?"

Annie wrinkled her forehead, trying to recall an event from years ago. "Vaguely," she said.

The English driver, Shirley Price, drops Martha and Annie off by the front door of the building where the visit is to take place. Martha barely notices the nervous young man standing by the door, smoking a cigarette. He's a wiry, pint-size fellow who appears to be in his early twenties. His platinum blonde hair is almost hidden by the baseball cap he's wearing.

Martha takes a seat in the waiting room, but Annie is too agitated to sit. "Why did we come here?" she asks her mother.

"I already told you, Annie," Martha says patiently. "You know how Seffie is your birth mother?"

"She's not my birth mother," Annie hisses.

Martha ignores her daughter's denial of an unpalatable truth. "Well, you have a birth father, too. You're going to meet him today. He wants to get to know you."

"Do I have to go stay with him?"

"No, you're just going to visit him."

"I don't want to!"

"Now Annie, you need to be nice," Martha scolds. "I expect you to act like a big girl."

The visit supervisor opens the door of the waiting room. "Hello, Mrs. Bontrager," she says. "Starly's father is here. She can come on back now."

She bends down to make eye contact with Annie. "Do you want to come with me, Starly? I have lots of fun toys in my room."

Annie's eyes grow large with fear. "No!" she shouts. She runs to Martha, jumps on her lap, and buries her face in Martha's breast.

The supervisor looks helpless. "How about if you come back with her, Mrs. Bontrager? It'll be okay for the first visit, but after that, she'll need to spend time with her father on her own."

Martha stands up to follow the supervisor. It seems Annie has suddenly grown eight arms and legs, each wrapped tightly around her mother like an octopus. Martha carries her into the visit room.

The blonde-haired man who was smoking by the front door is sitting on a sofa. Still holding Annie, Martha sits down on a chair. The supervisor makes introductions.

"Mrs. Bontrager, this is Gregory Smith, Starly's biological father. Greg, this is Starly's foster mother, Martha Bontrager."

Gregory Smith's nervousness appears to verge on terror. He clearly doesn't know what to do next. Annie is still hiding her face, but she sneaks a quick peek at the strange young man they're calling her father.

"How's it goin', Starly?" Gregory says to her.

Annie buries her face again, making babyish squeals and grunts.

"Annie," Martha scolds. "You need to act like a big girl."

Gregory looks helplessly at the visit supervisor. "What am I supposed to do?" he asks.

"Why don't you set up the dollhouse?" the supervisor suggests. "Maybe she'll get interested in what you're doing."

Gregory crosses the room and picks up the dollhouse and a box of dolls and furniture. He sets them down in the middle of the floor. With awkward, shaking hands, he arranges furniture in the different rooms of the house. Annie turns halfway around on her mother's lap so she can see what Gregory is doing.

"Would you like to go play with him?" Martha coaxes. "See those nice little dolls? Wouldn't you like to play with those?"

Annie slides off Martha's lap. "Good girl," Martha says. "You can do it!"

Annie walks over to where Gregory is sitting cross-legged on the floor. As he watches her approach, a half-smile lights up his thin face. Annie stands in front of the doll house for a few moments.

Martha continues her encouragement. "Why don't you sit down and play with him?"

Suddenly, Annie kicks the dollhouse as hard as she can, and dolls and furniture go flying. "You're not my dad!" she screams at Gregory. "My dad is Jonas!" She runs back to Martha and jumps on her lap, burying her face once again.

"Annie, Annie!" Martha scolds. "That was naughty!"

Annie's shell-shocked father gets up off the floor. "This is bullshit," he says to the visit supervisor. "If this is what it's going to be like, then I'm done. This kid's fuckin' crazy! You can tell Mindy Barnes I'll go ahead and sign off on her goddamn paper." He walks out of the room without looking back.

"I don't think we'll schedule another visit," the supervisor says to Martha. "If Gregory changes his mind, I'll let you know."

As Martha carries the fretful Annie out of the building, Gregory Smith is squatting down by the front door, sucking on a cigarette as if his life depends on it. He averts his eyes as they pass him.

"You're not my dad!" Annie screams one more time, as if he hadn't already gotten the point.

"Whatever happened to Gregory Smith?" Annie's voice was wistful.

"He signed off on his parental rights," Martha said. "He gave his consent for you be adopted."

"He didn't want me, either."

"Now Annie, don't make this into another story about rejection," Martha scolded. "If you recall the story correctly, you'll remember it was you that didn't want him. You rejected him totally and completely, and the poor fellow didn't have the confidence to try to win you over. He was scarcely more than a child, Annie, only twenty-one, younger than you are now."

Annie hung her head, absent-mindedly snapping the beans in the bowl on her lap. Martha knew her daughter had withdrawn into her own world.

Just then, Daniel came running up to them, his eyes dancing with excitement. "Mama, Mama, come see what I found!" When Annie didn't respond, he patted her arm to get her attention, but she continued to stare listlessly at her bowl of beans.

Daniel shook her arm vigorously. "Mama, Mama, come see!"

Annie lifted her head and glared at her son. "Stop it, Daniel!" she snapped. "Go play! I'm busy now!"

Martha saw a flash of pain in her grandson's eyes before he turned and walked away.

"Annie," she said in a firm voice. "I know you're distracted by the letter your sister sent you. I know you're troubled by memories from the past. But you're a grown woman, and you have responsibilities. You can't neglect your children because of this."

Annie's eyes took on a veiled look, and Martha knew her daughter had completely shut her out.

She sounds just like Luke, Annie thought. *Three days ago, my mother understood me. She was on my side. Now she feels the same way Luke feels. I just can't be who they want me to be. They'd be better off without me.*

Sissy, Sissy. She repeated her sister's name over and over in her mind to soothe her distress. *Sissy wants me. Sissy can't wait to see me.*

Chapter 8

The next four days, Annie moved listlessly through her chores, enveloped in a fog of gloom. All she wanted to do was lie down and sleep, yet when she did go to bed at night, she felt restless.

"You look tired, Annie," Luke said one evening at supper. "Why don't you go sit in the living room? I'll clean up the kitchen."

"I'm okay." Annie got up to clear the table. She didn't want to give Luke another reason to criticize her.

But when she found a letter in the mailbox the next afternoon, her excitement pumped her full of energy. She rushed back to the house, dropped the rest of the mail on the table, and tore open the envelope.

August 25
Dear Starly,

I was so excited when I received your letter! Finding you is like a dream come true! I'm so thrilled to have a sister in my life again.

I promised I'd tell you more about myself. I was adopted by Leonard and Eileen Hartman when I was seven. I came to their home as a foster child when I was three. My father is a retired business executive. My mother stayed home to raise me.

I'm their only child, and people say I was spoiled. I probably was, as they treated me so well. Like you, I was fortunate to be raised by loving parents. I'm sure both of us had better lives than we would've had if we'd been raised by our birth mother.

My parents helped me through college and graduate school, and now I have a career as a therapist in a mental health center. I love my job, even though it wears me out.

I married my husband, Stephen Gray, four years ago. We don't have children yet, but we're talking about it. I'm a little scared about being a mother. When that time comes, I might rely on you for advice.

When I had to leave my adoptive parents to live with our birth mother, my whole world collapsed. But a wonderful thing waiting for me at Seffie's house was a beautiful baby girl named Shaney. I'd never had a sibling before, and I adored my little sister. I pretended she was my own baby.

And then one day, you came along, a sister close to my age, someone I could talk to and play with. You were so much fun and so full of life! The silly things you did kept me laughing. Do you remember our little giggling fits? They used to drive Seffie crazy! Even though I was so sad to be away from my adoptive parents, you, Starly, brightened up my world. Your name fit you—you were like a twinkling star.

The first day you came to Seffie's house, I was mesmerized by you. I thought you were the cutest little girl I'd ever seen. You were like a walking, talking doll. I had strawberry blonde hair then, but your hair was lighter than mine, almost white. I envied your long braids. I'd never seen anything like them. You were so tiny, and I was much taller than you. But your personality was larger than life.

I can't help but wonder what you look like now. I'm sure you're still beautiful.

So tell me more about you! What do you enjoy doing in your spare time? Do you have hobbies? What is your favorite color, your favorite food, your favorite music? Tell me anything else you can think of. I'm interested in finding out what we have in common.

Write back soon! I can't wait to hear from you. And of course I can't wait to meet you. I'm trying to make contact with Shaney and Stella. My dream is that all four of us will be able to meet together the first time.

Love Always,

Sissy

As Annie stared at the letter, her thoughts raced wildly, and a mixture of emotions competed to shape her perspective on her relationship with her sister.

Sissy has rich parents. She probably grew up in a fancy home. She has a college education and a career. She might think I'm not very smart.

Well, at least I know something about being a mother, and she doesn't.

Sissy thought I was special when we were little girls. I meant a lot to her then, and I mean a lot to her now. She thinks I'm beautiful. I hope she won't be disappointed when she sees me.

Who's Stella? She must be another one of Seffie's children. I didn't know about her.

Sissy loves me always! And I'll love her forever!

Annie laughed aloud, clutching the letter to her heart.

"What is it, Mama?" Daniel asked. "Why are you so happy?"

"Mama got such a nice letter from her sister!" she exclaimed.

As the day passed, Annie's excitement began to fade as she contemplated the need to tell Luke about the letter. But before she could come up with a plan, Daniel introduced the topic at the supper table.

"Mama was so-o-o happy today," he announced, proud to be the bearer of important news. "She got a nice letter from her sister."

Luke shot Annie a dark look. "So you sent her the letter you wrote?"

I don't have anything to hide, Annie told herself. *I've done nothing wrong.* Aloud, she said, "Yes, I sent the letter."

"You didn't tell me that."

"Well, I'm sorry! Do I need to tell you every move I make?"

Daniel glanced from one parent to the other, trying to make sense of the tension between them. Annie checked herself and changed her tone. "Would you like to read Sissy's letter after supper?"

"Sure." Luke's voice was flat, and he continued eating without looking up.

When Annie handed him the letter later that evening, he read it silently. Then he handed it back to her, a troubled expression on his face. "Why does she call you Starly?"

"I told her she could call me that. Remember? She knew me as Starly when we were little girls."

"I know that. But you're not Starly now."

Disappointed once again by her husband's reaction, Annie refolded the letter and tucked it back into the envelope. As she got up to put it away, Luke asked, "Who are Shaney and Stella?"

"Shaney's our little sister," Annie said. "She was a baby when I lived with Seffie. I don't know who Stella is, but I assume she's another one of our sisters. Maybe she was born after I left Seffie's house. I'll have to ask Sissy about her."

"So you're going to keep writing to Sissy?"

"Of course I am!" Annie turned and stalked off to the bedroom where she buried the letter, along with Sissy's first letter, under the stack of undergarments.

The next morning, Annie could hardly wait for Luke to leave the house so she could have privacy to write another letter. After she fed Daniel and Sarah their breakfast, she went to the desk to get her writing materials. Pushing aside the dirty dishes on the kitchen table, she laid Sissy's last letter out in front of her. She didn't want to miss answering any of her questions.

Daniel climbed onto a chair and leaned over the table. "What are you doing, Mama?"

"I'm writing a letter to my sister." Annie wagged a playful finger at her son. "And you don't need to announce this to your father. I'll tell him myself."

She turned back to her paper and began to write.

August 29

Dear Sissy,

Yesterday, I was feeling down in the dumps, but when I found your letter in the mailbox, I immediately felt happy. I'm still trying to get used to the idea that my long-lost sister has found me. It's like God performed a miracle!

You sound like a very smart person. I'm afraid I might feel stupid compared to you. I don't have much education because Amish people only go to school through the eighth grade. I can't imagine what it would be like to go to college or graduate school. I don't even know what graduate school is.

When we were little girls at Seffie's house, I always looked up to you. You were so good, and you always did the right thing. Even though you were only five, you seemed like a grownup to me.

I was jealous because I knew you were Seffie's favorite. I don't think she wanted me like she wanted you. But I'm not going to talk about that anymore, because it makes me sad. It means so much to know that you loved me back then. I'll never forget how kind you were to me.

You gave me a compliment when you said you were sure that I'm beautiful. Amish women aren't allowed to doll themselves up like English women do. But people tell me I'm pretty. I still have blonde hair and blue eyes. My hair is still long, but now I wear it in a bun.

I'm still short, not quite five feet tall. I'm pretty slim, except of course when I'm carrying a child.

Tell me what you look like. I'm curious. I wonder if we resemble each other.

Sissy, nobody has ever asked me the questions you asked me. It means a lot that you're interested in me. I really don't have any hobbies. Some Amish women like to sew or do needlework, but I don't enjoy that kind of thing. I like being around lots of people, just visiting and laughing and having a good time. I enjoy playing with my children and going for walks.

My favorite color is red. Amish women aren't allowed to wear red, but if I could, I'd wear it all the time!

Most Amish women are good cooks, and everyone likes to eat Amish cooking. But you know what I like better than chicken and ham and potatoes and noodles and all that stuff? I like sitting in a restaurant and eating hamburgers and French fries.

I don't know what to say about the music. I feel guilty telling you this, but I don't care much for Amish hymns. They're really slow and boring. I'm not allowed to listen to any other kind of music. I wish I could. One time many years ago, I listened to rock and roll, and I liked it. (Please don't ever tell anyone I said that!)

Now it's your turn to answer all those questions.

Before I close, I have to ask you something. Who is Stella? I remember Shaney when she was a baby, and when she was two, she stayed at our house for a week. But I've never heard of Stella. Is she another one of our sisters?

Love forever,
Starly

Annie knew she'd been too bold in some of the things she'd written. But before she could change her mind about anything, she sealed the letter in an envelope and addressed it to her sister. On the walk down the lane to the mailbox, she pulled Sarah in her little wooden wagon. Daniel skipped along at her side, happy to be part of his mother's good feelings.

Three days later, Annie heard a vehicle driving up the lane. She peered out the window and saw a florist delivery van parked in the driveway. When she opened the door, the delivery man handed her a large bouquet wrapped in green tissue paper.

Never in her life had anyone sent Annie flowers, and her heart pounded with excitement. She tore off the tissue paper to find a vase filled with a dozen red roses accented by greens and white baby's breath.

"Oh, my!" she said, overwhelmed by their beauty.

She read the card that accompanied the bouquet. *To my beloved sister Starly. Please enjoy these roses in your favorite color. Yours always, Sissy.*

Carefully, Annie set the vase of flowers in the center of the kitchen table, and then stepped back to enjoy the view. The splendor of the red roses lit up the entire room.

When Luke walked into the kitchen later that day, he stopped short when he saw the flowers. "Where did these come from?"

"My sister sent them to me." Annie was too happy to be apologetic.

"Why?"

"Because she loves me."

Annie didn't look at Luke. Absorbed in her own happiness, she didn't want to see the inevitable expression of concern on her husband's face.

Chapter 9

"Look, Mama, there's a hole in it." Daniel held up the towel he was using to dry the dishes Annie was washing.

"Well, don't stick your finger through it. You'll just make the hole bigger." Annie snatched the frayed towel from her son and took a look at it. "I think it's time to make a rag out of this. Mama will need to get some new dish towels out of her cedar chest."

As Daniel ran off to play, Annie went to her bedroom and opened the cedar chest sitting at the foot of her bed. She rifled through stacks of towels before choosing a set hand-embroidered with a floral design, a wedding gift she'd received six years ago. Inspired by the bouquet of red roses sitting on the table, she decided the colorful dish towels might help liven up her plain kitchen.

She placed her hand on the lid to close it, but then thought of something that had been buried at the bottom of the chest for ten years, something she shouldn't have kept. She closed the bedroom door so her children wouldn't see what she was doing. Then she dug through stacks of bath towels, blankets, quilts, and tablecloths until she found what she was looking for: the pair of blue jeans and the pink striped shirt she'd worn on her date with Olan Amstutz.

She unfolded the jeans and laid them out on the bed, then laid the pink shirt above the trousers to make it look as if someone was wearing the outfit. The garments had never been washed, and she noticed a small ketchup stain on the front of the shirt.

As she stared at the English clothing, she tried to remember what it felt like on her body. On impulse, she pulled up her skirt and sat down on the edge of the bed. She slipped one foot and then the other into the legs of the jeans, and stood to pull them up.

When she discovered she couldn't pull the jeans past her hips, she first giggled and then burst into tears. Suddenly, she wished she were anything but a young Amish women growing heavy with pregnancy. She sat down on the bed again, holding her skirt up, staring at her blue jean-clad legs.

Then she heard a clatter in the living room followed by Sarah's ear-piercing screams, and she knew her child had fallen off something. Quickly, she pulled the jeans off her legs, then wadded them up along with the pink shirt and slid them under the bed. *I'll put them away later,* she told herself as she rushed out of the room to rescue her wailing two-year-old.

That Sunday, the preaching service was held at the home of Willard and Sadie Amstutz. Annie wasn't feeling well. The baby in her womb seemed to be growing daily, and while she tried sitting and lying down in different positions, nothing eased her discomfort. So the hour-long sit on the hard church bench was nothing less than torturous, and the hot, stuffy environment in the Amstutz home made her nauseous.

The only way to escape from her physical misery was to wander off in her mind to thoughts of her sister. She tried to imagine the day when she'd meet Sissy. *Would the two of them resemble each other? Would they act alike, or talk alike? Would Sissy be tall or short, thin or heavy? What kind of English clothing would she be wearing?* Her thoughts then drifted to Shaney and Stella. She couldn't begin to imagine what they'd be like.

At the noon meal, Annie sat next to Luke at a long table with other church members. Daniel sat on the other side of his father so Luke could tend to his needs during the meal. Luke held Sarah on his lap, trying in vain to coax her to eat. But she was restless and slid down, and then begged for Annie to hold her.

Because of her swollen abdomen, there was scarcely any room on Annie's lap for a two-year-old. Sarah couldn't get comfortable, and she whined and fretted.

"Why don't you go see your grandma?" Annie suggested, pointing to Martha sitting at a neighboring table.

"Grandma!" Sarah chortled. She took off running in Martha's direction.

Annie sighed with relief, glad to have a break from Sarah's constant bid for her attention. She picked at her food, but her stomach was so upset she had little appetite.   Once again, her mind drifted off to thoughts of her sisters.

"Annie, you need to eat!" Esther Graber scolded from across the table. "You're eating for two now. I don't think you've put on enough weight with this pregnancy. You need to give that baby lots of good nutrition."

Mind your own business, Annie thought. But she forced a smile. "I'm not feeling well," she said. She pushed aside her plate of meat, potatoes, and vegetables, and reached for her piece of pie, hoping something sweet would be more agreeable to her stomach.

"Where's Sarah?" Luke asked suddenly.

The question jolted Annie to alertness. "Didn't she go sit with her grandma?"

"She's not with your mother," Luke said, irritation in his voice. "Annie, I thought you were watching her. Do I have to take care of everything?"

Feeling ashamed of her negligence, Annie jumped to her feet. *I'm just a burden to him,* she thought. *He'd be better off without me. He'd do fine taking care of the children on his own.*

"I'll go find her," she said, determined to do something right.

She walked up and down the rows of tables, looking for her daughter, but Sarah was nowhere in the crowd, nowhere in the front yard. Annie began to panic. She hurried around the side of the Amstutz house, moving as fast as her increased bulk would allow her.

"Sarah, Sarah," she called.

Sarah was not to be found in the back yard. Frantic, Annie headed toward the barn, picturing the worst: *little Sarah drowned in the cows' watering trough, or trampled underfoot in the horses' stalls.*

She circled around behind the barn. "Sarah, Sarah!"

"She's over there." The familiar voice startled Annie. She looked around and saw Olan Amstutz sitting on a bale of hay, smoking a cigarette.

"Where?" she gasped.

"Over there, with the kittens." With the hand holding the cigarette, Olan gestured toward the back door of the barn. "She's okay. I've been keeping an eye on her."

Annie rushed over to where her daughter was squatting on the ground petting a trio of kittens. "Sarah!" she exclaimed. "You scared your mama half to death, running off like this!" She took her by the hand and attempted to lead her away, but Sarah squealed in protest.

"Let her play for awhile," Olan said. "Sit down and talk with me. Your daughter's okay."

Annie hesitated, remembering her mother's stern admonition to avoid any contact with Olan Amstutz.

"Don't worry, I won't bite you," Olan said, amusement in his voice. "I won't even touch you. Have a seat." He gestured toward the bale of hay next to his.

It won't hurt to sit here for a few minutes, Annie told herself, thankful for the opportunity to get off her aching legs.

As she seated herself on the bale, she glanced sideways at her companion. Olan was still clean shaven, as he wasn't yet married, and the absence of a beard made him appear younger than other Amish men his age. Annie noticed his hair was cut differently than the last time she'd seen him, no longer in the Amish bowl cut.

He must've had it cut in an English barbershop, she thought. She was struck by how handsome he looked with his new hairstyle.

"I haven't talked to you for awhile," Olan said. "You've been steering clear of me, haven't you?"

"I . . . I'm a married woman," Annie stammered.

Olan laughed. "I know that, although I kind of wish you weren't."

Annie looked down, feeling guilty for enjoying Olan's attention, biting her lip to keep from blurting out something inappropriate.

"There's a rumor going around that you're planning to meet an English sister of yours," Olan said. "It's funny. All that time we were teenagers, I never knew you were adopted. But now that I know it, it doesn't surprise me. You've always been livelier than most Amish girls. I like that. It must be the English blood in you."

Tears welled in Annie's eyes. "You're the only one who likes it, Olan. It seems like I can't do anything right for anybody these days. I'm always upsetting someone. People don't really think I'm lively. They just think I'm stupid and bad and crazy." She felt a tear slide down her cheek, and she wiped it with her sleeve.

"It doesn't matter what they think," Olan said. "Just be yourself, don't take their criticism to heart. That's what I do. You know what people say about me. I never let it bother me."

He took a long draw from his cigarette. "Do you ever think about that evening we had together?"

"Of course," Annie said. "I still have those blue jeans." Immediately, she felt guilty for revealing her wicked secret.

Olan shot her a lecherous grin, but made no comment.

Suddenly, Annie blurted out, "Olan, have you ever thought about going English? It seems like something you might want to do."

Olan chuckled. "I've had plenty of thoughts about going English. As you might suspect, I've spent lots of time in the English world. I know the English ways, I know the Amish ways. I've got a foot in both worlds, and you know what? That's not a bad place to be. I like my life the way it is."

He leaned down and stubbed out his cigarette on the ground, leaving the butt in the dirt. Annie wondered if Willard Amstutz would be angry when he found the telltale sign of his son's smoking habit.

"How about you?" Olan asked. "Have you ever thought about going English?"

Annie squeezed her eyes shut, feeling dreadfully ashamed to admit to her fantasy. "Yes," she whispered.

"I bet you've been thinking this English sister of yours could set you up in the English way of life."

Annie's eyes popped wide open. "How did you know that? It's like you read my mind!"

"I didn't read your mind," Olan said, laughing. "But you and I are a lot alike, and it's not hard for me to imagine what I'd be thinking if I were in your shoes." He shifted his position on the bale, turning to face her. "So why do you want to be English, Annie?"

"Maybe because I was born English," she said. "I'm not good enough to be Amish."

Annie and her mother are spending the afternoon at the home of Miriam Hershberger. Martha and Miriam are in the kitchen making juice from fresh grapes, to be used for communion at next Sunday's preaching service.

Six-year-old Annie and Miriam's seven-year-old daughter Katie have grown bored with playing in Katie's bedroom. Katie takes Annie by the hand, and together they run, barefooted in their long dresses, to the barn to play in the hay loft.

The girls climb on the bales of hay, jumping and giggling and then climbing higher. Annie climbs to the point where the bales are stacked the highest and prances around like the queen of her castle. She begins to sing and do the dance that Sissy taught her when they stayed at Seffie's house.

"You put your right foot in, you take your right foot out, you put your right foot in and you shake it all about. You do the Hokey Pokey and you turn yourself about."

Annie sings loudly, hiking up her skirt, shaking her body with abandon, her blond braids flying.

"What are you doing?" Katie asks, horrified.

"I'm dancing, I'm dancing!" Annie calls out. "You put your right hip in, you take your right hip out."

She wiggles her hips seductively.

"You're not supposed to be doing that," Katie warns. "That's a sin. Amish people aren't supposed to dance."

"I'll tell you a secret," Annie says as she scrambles down to where Katie is sitting. She cups her hands around her mouth and whispers loudly in Katie's ear, "I'm not really Amish, I'm English."

"That's a lie," Katie says sternly. "You're not supposed to tell lies, Annie."

"I'll tell you another secret," Annie says. She whispers in Katie's ear, "My name isn't Annie, it's Starly."

"You're lying!" Katie points an accusing finger at her playmate. "I'm telling on you!" Hurriedly, she climbs down the ladder from the hay loft and runs to the house to inform Martha Bontrager of her daughter's errant behavior.

Unconcerned, Annie goes on singing her English song as she jumps from one bale of hay to another.

"Olan, what would you think about the idea of me going English?" Annie asked.

"Oh, I don't know," Olan said. "It probably wouldn't be that hard for you to adjust to English life. You'd learn to fit in quickly." Then his face took on a serious expression. "But you need to know it's not all it's cracked up to be. You need to know that before you make a decision."

He gazed around his father's farmyard. "Me, I get bored with being Amish, and I cross the line for a little while into the English world. Then I start feeling the need for some good home-grown security, and I come back to the Amish world. For some reason, I keep coming back to these God-awful preaching services and the scrumptious potluck meals. Having a foot in both worlds is just the way I like my life."

He looked at her pointedly. "But it wouldn't be that easy for a woman to live that way."

Annie was ready to question Olan as to why a woman couldn't live in both worlds when she noticed Sarah wandering away from the kittens. She made a move to get up.

"Just sit," Olan said. "I'll get her." He took several long strides and scooped up the toddler with a laugh, tickling her to make her giggle.

"You're good with her," Annie observed.

"Before you came, I was making friends with her." He kissed the top of Sarah's head and set her down on the bale of hay next to Annie. "She's a pretty little thing. She looks just like you."

Annie stared at Olan, surprised at his tenderness with her child. "I didn't know you liked children."

"I'm not as bad as everyone thinks I am," Olan said. "Maybe someday, I'll find myself a high-spirited Amish girl like you, and I'll settle down and raise a brood of my own youngsters." He winked at Annie.

Annie felt a rush of warmth toward Olan. *This man understands me,* she thought. *He's like Sissy, he understands me.*

"I've got to get back to my husband," she said, worried that if she stayed with Olan one minute longer, she'd do something impulsive like throwing herself into his arms.

"Of course you do," Olan said. "Luke's a good guy. Don't forget that, Annie. You'd never find an English man up to Luke's caliber."

Annie stood up and took Sarah by the hand. "Thanks for looking after my daughter," she said.

Then she turned and walked back around the barn toward the house, a mixture of emotions churning inside her. She felt both relieved and disappointed that Olan hadn't encouraged her to go English. In her mind's eye, she pictured herself and Olan holding hands, venturing together into the world of the English. But the vision vanished as quickly as it came.

With Sarah's hand in hers, Annie walked back into the front yard of the Amstutz home. Spotting her husband in the milling crowd of people preparing to go home, she walked up to him and slipped her arm through his.

"So you found Sarah," Luke said with relief.

"Yes. She was behind the barn playing with some kittens."

"Good thing you found her. It could be dangerous out there."

"I know," Annie said. She was glad Luke didn't know about all the dangers lurking behind the barn.

Chapter 10

Another letter from Sissy arrived in the mail the next day, and Annie was surprised to see how thick it was. Taking a break from dusting furniture, she sat on the sofa with a glass of iced tea to relax and enjoy her sister's correspondence.

When she opened the envelope and unfolded the letter, she discovered a small stack of photographs tucked inside. She set the letter aside for the moment, in order to look at the pictures.

The photo on the top of the stack was of a slender woman wearing a pair of white shorts and a blue tank top, standing in front of a two-story brick house that appeared to be newly constructed. Standing beside the woman was a stocky man wearing shorts and a polo shirt. The figures were very small next to the large house, and Annie had difficulty making out their features. She thought the man was bald, but couldn't tell for sure.

She turned the photo over to see if any identifying information was written on the back. Sure enough, Sissy had written, *This is my husband and me in front of our house last summer.* Annie marveled at what a big fancy home her sister lived in.

The second photo was of Sissy and her husband again, but this one was a close-up shot. They were wearing the same outfits, and Annie assumed the two photos were taken on the same day. Sissy and Stephen were sitting outdoors on lawn furniture. Sissy was smiling widely, her bright blue eyes sparkling in her tanned face. Her auburn hair was pulled back into a ponytail.

The close-up shot of Stephen confirmed that he was balding and heavy-set. Annie wondered why someone as beautiful as her sister hadn't chosen to marry a better-looking man. *Luke is more handsome than Stephen,* she thought, scoring a point in a competition with the sister who seemed to be a winner in every aspect of her life.

She turned the photo over for identifying information. *This is Stephen and me sitting on our patio in the back yard. We were having friends over for a barbeque.* Annie imagined Sissy had all sorts of inter-

esting friends who did worldly things like drinking beer, smoking cigarettes, and watching movies.

She turned the photograph back over to stare into Sissy's smiling
eyes. *I wonder if I'd look like her if I wore the same clothing.*

"She's so pretty!" she said aloud.

"Who?" Daniel asked, looking up from the barn he was building with
a set of toy logs. He scrambled up to see what his mother was doing.

"Who's that?" he asked as he snuggled up to Annie on the sofa.

"That's my sister," Annie explained, "the one who writes me the nice
letters. She's your Aunt Sissy."

Daniel scrutinized the photograph, then looked at his mother in confusion. "She's English."

"Yes," Annie said. "Your Aunt Sissy is English."

She slipped the pictures of Sissy and her husband to the back of the
stack, and then studied the next photo. Sissy, wearing a gray knee-
length skirt with a matching jacket and white blouse, was standing next
to the front door of an office building. Her wavy shoulder-length hair
framed her pretty face.

She looks important, Annie thought, *and very smart.*

Sissy was wearing high-heeled pumps, and Annie wondered how her
sister could manage to walk in such shoes. Annie had never even
slipped her foot into a high-heeled shoe. The only shoes she'd ever
worn were flat and sturdy.

She flipped the photo over to read the words on the back. "This is
my sister standing in front of the office where she works," Annie informed her son.

"Ladies don't go to work," Daniel objected, more confused than ever. "They stay home and take care of the children while the dads go to
work."

"Well, some ladies go to work, Daniel. English ladies go to work."

"Oh." He wrinkled his forehead, perplexed.

The next photo showed a well-dressed elderly couple sitting on a sofa. The short, stocky man had a full head of snow-white hair and was
wearing a dark suit. The woman, who appeared to be taller than her
husband, wore a pastel dress accented by a pearl necklace. Her short

gray hair was impeccably styled.

The objects appearing in the photograph suggested the couple's house was beautifully decorated. Annie flipped the picture over. *These are my parents, Leonard and Eileen Hartman. I took this picture several weeks ago. They'd just gotten home from church.*

"Who's this?" Daniel asked.

"These are Aunt Sissy's parents."

Now Daniel was completely confused. "But my uncles have the same mom and dad you have. Why does Aunt Sissy have different parents?"

Annie realized she'd been drawn deeper into the subject of her birth family relationships than she'd intended to go. "Daniel, my sister and I were both adopted."

"What's adopted?"

"Aunt Sissy and I were born to the same mother. But she couldn't take care of us. So your Aunt Sissy went to live with somebody else, and I came to live with your grandpa and grandma, Jonas and Martha. Grandpa and Grandma aren't my real parents. They adopted me. That means they took me into their home and raised me just like one of their own children."

"Am I adopted?"

Annie wrapped her arms around her son, pressing her cheek against his. "No, Daniel, you're my own precious son. You grew in my tummy, just like this baby's growing in my tummy."

She released her embrace and took his face in her hands. "But you see, I didn't grow in Grandma's tummy. I grew in another mother's tummy, the same mother that Aunt Sissy was born to."

She wasn't sure Daniel fully understood what she was saying, but he asked no further questions.

She moved on to the last photo, which almost took her breath away. It was Sissy as a child, and the picture made Annie's memories of her sister so vivid, she could hardly bear it. Sissy was wearing the fanciest little pink dress Annie had ever seen, with a lacey collar and puff sleeves. The skirt was constructed of several tiers of delicate fabric that floated away from Sissy's body. She was wearing shiny black shoes with buckles and little white socks trimmed with lace. Her curly hair was drawn up into two ponytails tied with pink ribbons.

The back of the photo said, *This is me on the day of my adoption. My parents threw a party to celebrate the occasion.*

"Who's that little girl?" Daniel asked.

"That's your Aunt Sissy when she was a child."

"She's pretty!"

Sarah toddled over to see what had captured her brother's interest. "Oh, pretty!" she echoed, trying to take the photo from Annie's hand.

Annie imagined what Sarah would look like wearing a fancy pink dress and ribbons in her hair. She knew her daughter would never have that experience, and the thought made her sad.

"That's all the pictures," she said to the children. "Now go run and play while Mama reads the letter from Aunt Sissy."

September 3

Dear Starly,

Did you receive the roses I sent? I hope they arrived okay. I tried to imagine the look on your face when you got them.

I decided that instead of trying to describe how I look, I'd send you photographs. Do you think we look alike? I sent the picture of me as a child to let you know this is really me, Sissy, not someone playing a trick on you.

Thanks for telling me more about yourself. You don't need to worry about me telling anyone else what you say. What we write is confidential between the two of us. So, dear sister, tell me anything, and it will go no further.

I understand that with your growing up Amish and my growing up English, our lives have been very different. That's okay with me. In fact, it makes you more interesting to me. There's so much I can learn from you. I hope someday I can come to your farm so you and Luke can show me everything you do.

Starly, please don't ever think of yourself as stupid. Education doesn't mean everything. So don't apologize or put yourself down. I'm sure you're every bit as smart as I am. In fact, I'm sure you're smarter than me in some ways.

Red is one of my favorite colors, too. My job is stressful, dealing with people's problems all day long. So when I have the time, I like to go sit somewhere alone and read. I guess reading is the hobby I enjoy most.

I don't know anything about growing a vegetable garden, so that's something I can learn from you. I don't blame you for not liking sewing or needlework. I don't think I'd enjoy that, either. It sounds like you're still the same outgoing, fun-loving, life-of-the-party Starly I knew when we were little!

There's something I need to tell you. I didn't want to bring it up in my first two letters, but I think it's time you knew. Our birth mother, Seferina Dickerson, has passed away. She died more than seventeen years ago, when we were still little girls. You may wonder how I learned about this. A friend of mine looked up some things for me on the computer and found that information. I don't know the cause of her death.

Annie stopped reading. Her body felt heavy, and suddenly it hurt to breathe. She wasn't sure how she felt about her birth mother's death, but the news was shocking just the same. *She died just a few years after I last saw her,* she thought. She was surprised to feel a tear trickling down her cheek.

"Come on, girls, we're goin' to the gas station," Seffie says. "I gotta get cigarettes."

Sissy and Starly look up from their play, bewildered. Seffie doesn't often take them anywhere.

"Hurry up!" Seffie says. "I'm gettin' cranky. I need my smokes. If you girls are good, I'll let you get some candy."

Seffie picks up baby Shaney and walks out the door of the mobile home. "Hurry up, slowpokes!" she calls to Sissy and Starly, and they scramble up to follow her. She puts Shaney in the battered baby stroller that sits in the middle of the clutter in the front yard.

She pushes the stroller along the street of the mobile home park, with Sissy and Starly trailing behind her. Sissy walks, while Starly prances and skips. Then she runs out ahead of Seffie.

"I'm warnin' you, Starly!" Seffie yells. "If you do that again, you ain't gettin' no candy. Now get back there and walk with Sissy. Sissy, hang onto your sister's hand."

Sissy obediently reaches over and takes Starly's hand. Starly becomes restless and tries to run ahead again, but Sissy holds her back.

When they walk into the gas station, Seffie points to the candy counter. "Okay, girls, pick out what you want. Only one thing, now. Sissy, keep an eye on your sister. Don't let her get into stuff."

Starly quickly grabs a bag of M & M's, while Sissy stands in quiet contemplation of her various options. "Get this, Sissy, its good!" Starly says, waving her candy in front of her sister's face. Sissy shrugs and gives into Starly's persuasion.

Seffie asks the clerk for a carton of cigarettes. "Put your candy up on the counter, girls," she says. Sissy puts her bag of M & M's on the counter next to the cigarettes. Starly can't reach the counter top, so Sissy takes her M & M's and places them next to her own.

"You've got the cutest little girls I've ever seen," the clerk says as she hands Seffie her change. "I don't think I've seen the one with the blonde braids. Is she yours, too?"

"Yup, she is." Seffie's voice is uncharacteristically gentle. "Her name's Starly. Right now, I keep her just half the time, but pretty soon she's going to be stayin' with me all the time."

"Well, that'll be nice," the clerk says. "She's adorable. She looks like a little sweetheart."

"Yup, she is!" Seffie says.

Surprised by Seffie's sudden tenderness, Starly looks up and sees her mother smiling down at her. On impulse, she puts her hand in Seffie's, and Seffie holds it for a moment before letting go.

"Come on, girls," she says. "Let's go. Now don't be gettin' into that candy before we get home. Starly, give your candy to Sissy and let her carry it."

Annie wiped the tear from her cheek, and then continued reading the letter.

I hope this news isn't too shocking for you. When we get together, maybe we can talk more about it. I think it's important for us to find out the cause of our birth mother's death, in case it involved any hereditary health problems. Maybe Shaney and Stella will have answers for us.

You asked me about Stella. When I thought about it, I realized you'd already left Seffie's home when Stella was born. I don't know if you're aware of this, but I lived with Seffie two different times. The first time, it was Shaney, you, and me. The second time, it was Shaney, Stella, and me. Stella was just a baby when I left the second time, and I never got to know her like I did you and Shaney.

When my friend found the information about Seffie's death, he also found out where Shaney and Stella live. They were never adopted. Apparently, they were raised by their father Jimmy McDaniel. They're currently living with him in Belmont.

I wrote them a letter on August 26, but I haven't heard anything back from them. I'm disappointed, but I guess it's still too soon to assume they won't be answering my letter. If I don't get a response in a couple of weeks, I'm going to try another approach to make contact with them. I would've called them, but evidently they don't have a phone. There's no James McDaniel listed in the phone book, and no Shaney or Stella McDaniel, either.

I know I say this in every letter, but I can't wait to meet you again! I think we should get together soon, because I know it won't be long before your baby comes, and it might be too difficult after it's born. I'd like to start making plans. Let me know how you feel about this idea. I'll keep you updated on my search for Shaney and Stella.
Your loving sister,
Sissy

True to his nature, Daniel couldn't hold back from reporting on the events of the day at the supper table.

"Papa, did you know our Aunt Sissy is . . . what's that word, Mama?"

Daniel, Daniel, Daniel, Annie thought. *You're going to keep on getting me in trouble with your father.*

Aloud, she said, "Adopted. The word is adopted."

"And Mama's adopted too. But she says I'm not."

Luke put down his fork and glared at Annie, his eyes asking, *What have you done now?*

"We'll talk about this after supper," he said.

Annie picked nervously at her food, dreading the confrontation that was soon to come.

After the children finished eating, Luke told Daniel to take Sarah upstairs to play. "Your mother and I need to have a talk," he said. Daniel shot Annie a worried look as he left the room, as if sensing something was amiss.

"So she's Aunt Sissy now?" Luke's voice was filled with undisguised contempt. "And you told Daniel about you being adopted. Don't you think you and I should discuss such things before bringing them up with the children? Daniel's too young to understand. You've only caused him confusion."

"I didn't mean to do it," Annie protested, cowering like a frightened child. "It just happened."

"How could such a thing just happen?"

"I was looking at pictures Sissy sent me in a letter today. Daniel saw them and started asking questions. I ended up having to explain what adoption means."

"Couldn't you have looked at those pictures in private?"

"I guess so."

Annie met Luke's gaze until she could no longer bear the displeasure in his eyes. "Do you want to see the pictures?" she asked timidly.

"No, quite frankly, I don't."

As much as she wanted to jump up from the table and run to the safety of her bedroom, Annie knew she had to broach one more topic with her husband.

"Luke, Sissy wants us to get together soon, before the baby's born."

"Well, this can't all happen on her timing. Just because she wants it doesn't mean it's going to be that way."

"Are you saying I can't go?"

"No, I'm not saying that." Luke's voice was bitter. "I know you won't give me any peace if I forbid you to go. But if you're going to do it, don't wait until the very end of your pregnancy. I don't want you traveling and putting yourself or the baby at risk."

"I understand," Annie said, hanging her head.

Luke got up abruptly. "I'm going back to the barn." When the door closed behind him, Annie breathed a sigh of relief.

Chapter 11

"Shirley Price is driving Moses Graber into Plymouth this morning," Luke informed Annie at the breakfast table. "I thought I'd ride along. I need to buy a new shovel and some nails. Do you want me to pick up any groceries?"

"Yes, we're running low on a few things." Annie got up from the table and rummaged through her pantry, making a list of items for Luke to buy at the grocery store.

He kissed her cheek before he went outside to wait for Shirley's van. Annie was glad her husband was back in his usual good spirits. *Maybe the worst is over,* she thought. *Maybe he's accepting my relationship with Sissy.*

Luke came home shortly before noon, just as Annie was preparing lunch. She peered out the window, watching him unload his supplies from the van. He set the bags of groceries aside, and then carried his shovel to the barn.

"Are you ready to eat?" she asked when he walked into the house with the groceries a few minutes later.

"Let me change my shirt first," he said. "I got it dirty when I was trying out the new shovel in the horse stalls."

Annie had just put sandwiches and coleslaw on the table, and was pouring glasses of milk for the children when she heard an angry bellow from the bedroom. "Annie, come in here!"

Alarmed, she rushed to see what her husband wanted. She found him standing in the middle of the room, his face like a thundercloud. He held the pair of blue jeans in front of him at arm's length, as if they were toxic waste.

Annie felt all the strength drain from her body. *Oh, no, no, no,* she thought. *I forgot to put them back into the cedar chest.* She sank down on the bed in despair.

"I dropped some coins on the floor when I was putting my money away." Luke's voice was a low hiss. "A quarter rolled under the bed. When I got down to look for it, I found these."

Glaring at Annie, he dropped the blue jeans on the floor, as if he could no longer stand to hold the despicable garment. "Explain to me how this pair of English trousers found their way under our bed. I want a direct answer, please."

Annie buried her face in her hands. "They were in my cedar chest. I found them when I was taking out some dish towels."

"Annie, I can hardly hear you. Hold your head up and speak to me clearly. Tell me why these trousers were in your cedar chest."

Slowly, Annie raised her head. The only way she could cope with Luke's angry stare was to muster a defiant attitude.

"When I was a teenager, I went on a date with Olan Amstutz. He wanted us to pretend we were English. He gave me that pair of blue jeans and a shirt to wear."

"Olan Amstutz? You went on a date with that swine?"

"Luke, it was ten years ago, before I started dating you. I was only sixteen. I went out with him one time, and my parents wouldn't let me see him anymore."

"Well, that was good thinking on their part. So where's the shirt?"

"It's under the bed."

"Get it for me."

Annie got down on her hands and knees, but her bulky abdomen made it impossible to look under the bed.

"Never mind," Luke said. "I'll get it." He lay flat on his stomach, reached one arm under the bed, and fished out the pink shirt. He stood up, inspected the shirt, and then tossed it on the floor with the blue jeans.

"I'm not done with the questions, Annie. Why have you kept this garbage all these years?"

"I couldn't bear to part with them."

"Why? Do you still have feelings for Olan Amstutz?"

Annie shook her head vigorously, knowing she was lying a little bit.

"Because you hoped some day you could wear them again?"

Annie dropped her gaze, unable to formulate a response.

"That's true, isn't it, Annie? You were thinking about wearing them again. Tell me why you pulled these filthy garments out of the cedar chest at this point in time. Does this have anything to do with your English sister?"

"No, no!" Annie protested. "It has nothing to do with Sissy. I just happened to think about them when I took the towels out of the chest. I was trying on the pants when Sarah fell off the sofa and started crying. I had to rush out of the room to take care of her, so I just shoved them under the bed. I was going to put them away again, but I forgot."

Suddenly, Luke laughed. "Annie, did you think these trousers would fit you now, with that big belly?"

Annie knew her husband was mocking her. Tears of humiliation stung her eyes and rolled down her face. She lowered her head again.

"Well, this trash isn't going back into your cedar chest. It is going out to the burn barrel where it belongs."

Please don't burn them, Annie thought. But she knew she had no grounds for protesting.

Luke bent over to pick up the despised clothing. "Stop crying and look at me, Annie. Your tears make me think you have an attachment to these things, and that disturbs me deeply. I'm telling you, I've tolerated a lot of nonsense from you these past few weeks. But you've crossed a line now, and I won't tolerate any more. This business with your English sister is over. You may write one more letter and tell her you can't meet her. And that's the last communication you'll have with her."

"No, Luke, no!" Annie pleaded. "Go ahead and burn the clothes. I don't care. Just don't forbid me to see Sissy. Please, Luke!"

"I've made up my mind," Luke said as he headed toward the door. "If you're going to weep, then stay in here. I don't want you carrying on in front of the children. They don't need to be drawn into this mess."

Annie lay down on the bed, facing away from Luke. She could hear him close the door behind him as he left the room.

Then she heard Daniel say, "What are you doing, Papa?"

"I'm going to burn some trash," Luke responded gruffly.

Not wanting to engender any more of her husband's wrath, Annie held the pillow over her face to muffle her sobs. Never before had she longed to die, but at that moment, she no longer felt the will to live.

The unborn child within her heaved and turned, as if sharing her emotional turmoil.

Sissy, Sissy, she screamed inside her head. *I need you, Sissy. Don't let them take you away from me again, Sissy.*

Mindy Barnes has just brought Annie back to the Bontrager home after a four-day stay with Seffie. The family is sitting down for supper. Jonas lifts Annie onto the thick catalog on her chair, which serves to boost her up so she can reach the table.

Annie slides off the catalog, and it falls to the floor. "No!" *she shouts. She doesn't know what she's protesting. Intense frustration is coursing through her tiny body, and she must discharge it somehow.*

Jonas places the catalog back on the chair and firmly plants Annie's bottom on it. She slides off again.

"Maybe she'll sit on my lap," *Martha says.* "Do you want to sit on my lap, Annie?"

Annie nods. She scrambles onto Martha's lap and buries her face in her mother's bosom.

"Annie, if you want to sit on my lap, you'll need to turn around and eat," *Martha says.*

Annie wriggles around to face the table. "Feed me," *she demands.*

Martha hesitates, searching for an appropriate response.

"Mom, why do you baby her so much?" *sixteen-year-old Eli asks.* "She'll never learn to grow up and act normal if you keep letting her be a baby."

This is the trigger Annie needs to fully unleash her rage. "I'm not a baby!" *she screams. She begins crying at the top of her lungs.*

"Martha, why don't you put her in our bedroom until she settles down?" *Jonas suggests.* "The rest of us need to eat our meal in peace."

Martha carries Annie to the bedroom and lays her on the bed. "You need to stay here until you stop crying," *she says.* "Then you can come out and eat your supper."

"Don't leave," *Annie wails.*

Martha hesitates, but tells herself its best not to give in to Annie's manipulation. She leaves the room and closes the door behind her.

The rest of the family finishes their meal accompanied by the pitiful cries from the bedroom. "Sissy, Sissy, I want Sissy!"

"For someone that small," Eli says, "she sure can make a lot of noise."

Sissy, Sissy, come to me. I need you. In the depths of her despair, Annie prayed that somehow her sister would sense her distress. *They can't take you away from me. Don't let them, Sissy. I need you.*

Suddenly, a feeling of peace washed over her. She imagined she felt what she'd been longing for, the gentle pat, pat, pat of Sissy's hand on her back. Her sister's love enveloped her, soothed her.

I'm coming to you, Sissy. Whatever it takes, I'm coming to you.

In her altered state of mind, Annie pictured herself leaving Daniel and Sarah in their father's care. She knew Luke would never allow her to carry the children into the English world with her. *But the unborn child belongs to me,* she reasoned. She envisioned herself living with Sissy and her husband. They had a big house. Surely, there would be plenty of room for her and the baby. She and Sissy would raise the baby together, one big happy English family.

Worn out from her crying and calmed by her fantasy, Annie fell into a deep sleep.

She awoke to the sound of Luke opening the bedroom door. The light in the room was dimming, as the sun was setting. Luke stood by the bed, looking down on her. When she saw the contemptuous expression on his face, the memories of the afternoon's events came flooding back.

"Get up, Annie," he commanded. "I'm taking you to your parents' house. You and I need some space between us tonight. Pack up your things so we can go."

"What about the children?" Annie asked groggily.

"They'll stay here with me."

While Annie packed her nightclothes, Luke and the children waited in the buggy. Luke didn't speak to her during the three mile drive to her parents' house.

"What are we doing, Daddy?" Daniel's voice was filled with fear.

"We're taking your mama to stay at Grandpa and Grandma's house."

"Why?"

"Because that's what's best."

When they arrived at the Bontrager home, Luke told Annie to stay in the buggy. "Let me talk to your parents first."

"What are you going to tell them?" she asked.

"Not much. It's up to you to confess what you've done."

Luke stayed in the house for only a few minutes before he came back to help Annie out of the buggy. "They're waiting for you," he said.

"When are you coming back for me?"

"I don't know."

He climbed back into the buggy, turned the horses around, and drove away. Annie walked alone in the dark down the long driveway to her parents' front door.

"Did you have supper, Annie?" Martha's voice sounded weary.

"No. But I'm not hungry."

"How about a cup of chamomile tea, then?"

"That would be good."

Martha sat down at the table while her daughter sipped the tea. "What happened, Annie?"

"Luke said I can't see my sister. He's ordered me to end all contact with her."

"Why did he do that? There must've been a good reason. Luke has always been a reasonable man."

Annie averted her gaze. "Mama, I'm too ashamed to tell you."

"All right, then." Martha told herself she really didn't want to hear the latest account of her daughter's misbehavior.

"Can he do that, Mama? Can he forbid me to see my sister?"

"Yes, he can, Annie. The Bible teaches us that a husband is the head of his household. A good wife doesn't go against her husband's decisions. You must do as he says." Martha sighed. "Annie, I'm very tired. I must go to bed. Do you need any help getting up the stairs?"

Stung by her mother's lack of sympathy, Annie shook her head. "No, I can manage."

They're running out of patience with me, she thought as she lay in her childhood bed. *I've ruined things with Luke, and I'm ruining things with my parents.* Her mind could identify only one solution to her problems: a life with Sissy.

I'll get to her, somehow.

Chapter 12

Martha fully expected her son-in-law to show up after breakfast the next morning, but he didn't come. She tried to hide her concern from Annie, as she was too weary to discuss the matter with her. She went about her usual routine of household chores, and Annie helped her with the breakfast dishes.

It seemed to Martha as if time had rolled back six years and Annie had never left home, that she was still her mother's unmarried daughter. Martha secretly wished this was true. Although she couldn't possibly resent the existence of Daniel and Sarah, it would be so much easier to help Annie manage her life without the complications of husband and children.

As Annie worked beside her mother, she wondered about the chores at her own home. *How had Luke fared with fixing breakfast for the children? Were Daniel and Sarah missing her? Had they cried for her last night? How would Luke manage to keep an eye on Sarah while he did his chores in the barn?*

Yet she too enjoyed the simplicity of just being Martha's daughter, without the challenges of being a wife and mother.

When the afternoon rolled around and there was still no sign of Luke, Annie began to fret aloud. "What if he never comes to get me?"

"Annie, don't be foolish," Martha admonished. "Luke will come when he's ready. You must allow him the time he needs to work through what's troubling him."

"What if he wants to divorce me?"

"You know better than that, Annie. Amish men don't divorce their wives. Luke knows the godly thing to do is to reconcile with you."

"I know, I know. But what would happen if he really didn't want me anymore? What would I do? Where would I live?"

"Well, I suppose you'd stay here with your father and me."

Both Martha and Annie harbored unspoken thoughts during this interchange. Martha couldn't be entirely certain Jonas would agree to the idea of Annie living with them. She knew that when it came to putting up with Annie's unstable ways, her patience extended farther than that of anyone else. She was quite aware that her own patience was wearing thin, and it was likely that Jonas's had already worn out.

And while Annie plied her mother with questions and expressed the insecurity typical of her nature, she knew full well that she didn't intend to fall back on the option of living with her parents. The plan to merge her life with Sissy's played unceasingly in the back of her mind, fleshing itself out, becoming more detailed. She felt confident that her backup plan was intact and ready to activate in the event that Luke wanted to end the marriage.

Suppertime came, and Annie shared a quiet meal with her parents. Jonas didn't broach the subject of why Annie was staying with them. Before going upstairs to her bedroom the second night, Annie said to Martha, "Luke will come, won't he?"

"Of course he will," Martha responded. But she was beginning doubt.

Early the next morning, Martha answered a knock on the front door, and when she saw her son-in-law standing there, her relief was so great she nearly collapsed. Luke looked like he hadn't slept the two nights his wife had been away from home. He was holding Sarah, and worried little Daniel stood at his side.

"How are you, Luke?" Martha asked.

Luke sighed wearily. "I'm not sure how to answer that question." He gazed vacantly around the room. "Is my wife still here?"

Martha reached out to take Sarah from his arms. "Yes, Annie's still upstairs in bed."

Luke stared at the floor, hands clasped behind his back. "Would it be okay if I went upstairs to talk with her?"

"That would be fine," Martha said. "But let me tell her you're com-ing."

"Whatever you think is best."

Martha laid her sleeping granddaughter on the sofa, then climbed the stairs and tapped on Annie's bedroom door.

"Yes?" Annie called out, sounding only half-awake.

Martha opened the door and stepped inside. "Annie, your husband is here."

Annie sat bolt upright. "Did he come to take me home?"

"I don't know his intentions. All I know is that he asked to talk with
you."

"Should I go downstairs?"

"No, Luke will come up to you. The two of you need to talk in private. The children are downstairs. I'll fix them a bite to eat while the
two of you talk."

Martha started to leave the room, then paused with her hand on the
door knob. "Annie, this is a time when you need to be very thoughtful.
It's a time to bite your tongue and hold your emotions in check. This
may be a critical moment for you and Luke. Please listen to what I'm
saying to you."

Annie nodded, her eyes large and frightened.

Martha turned and walked down the stairs. "She's ready for you,"
she said to Luke.

As Annie listened to her husband's footsteps on the stairs, her heart
pounded wildly. *How do I feel about him?* she wondered. *Am I angry
with him, or am I glad he's here? Will he be angry or loving with me?*
Suddenly, she felt overwhelmingly guilty for the escape plan she'd been
spinning, her fantasy foray into Sissy's English world. She hoped her
husband wouldn't sense it.

Then Luke appeared in her open doorway, shoulders slumped, a picture of dejection. When Annie saw him, her desire was so intense, her
heart wanted to burst out of her chest and fly over to meet his. She
sent a quick thought message to her sister. *Sissy, I want to be with you,
but unless Luke sends me away, there's no way on earth I can part with
him. I love this man. I really do.*

The two of them held each other in a silent gaze. Then Luke walked
over and sat down on the bed.

"Annie," he said, and then stopped. It seemed to her he was trying
to plan what he wanted to say, but instead he blurted out, "I miss you,
and I want you to come home."

"Oh, I want to come home, Luke," Annie moaned. "Please take me home with you."

"First, I have things I need to say to you." Luke dropped his head, staring at the pattern on the colorful quilt. "I know I was very angry with you when I found the English clothing, so angry that I had terrible thoughts about ending our marriage. I'm sorry for taking so long to come for you. But I needed time to think about the problems between us, and to take them to the Lord in prayer. And I believe He's spoken to me."

He looked up, his weary eyes searching her face. "I'm asking your forgiveness for judging you too harshly. I failed to take into consideration some of the factors I was well aware of when I married you. I knew about those things, and I wanted to marry you anyway. You were born English, which has probably endowed you with a livelier temperament than that of most Amish woman. I loved your high-spirited ways when I married you."

He reached out and brushed the wisps of hair from Annie's face. "And I still love them. How dull my life would be without you! You bring such light into our home."

Choking back a sob, Annie grabbed Luke's hand and kissed his palm.

He smiled at her, his eyes tender. "I know that when you were a child, you were forced to go back to your English mother for a time. No doubt, that has inflicted wounds on your soul that have never healed. I think I understand the reason you're so intent on meeting your sister. It has something to do with healing those wounds. Who am I to stand in the way of that? What right do I have to forbid you, just because it complicates my life?

"So, Annie, I've changed my mind about the meeting with your sister. You have my blessing to go. I trust you. But I have one request of you."

"What, Luke?" Annie whispered.

"If you have any ideas about going English, I'm asking you to put them out of your mind. Don't tell me about them. Just put them out of your mind, forever. Please don't do anything that would upset our family life. Promise me this, Annie?"

He drew her into his arms. "Because my life with you and the children means everything to me. I couldn't bear to lose that."

Annie nestled into the bliss of her husband's embrace. "I promise, Luke, I promise." In her mind's eye, the vivid details of her escape plan began to blur, then evaporated into a mist. She knew she'd never bring up that plan again. She'd never speak of it to anyone. Not even to Sissy.

Part III

SHANEY & STELLA

Chapter 1

"Ain't you one of Seffie Dickerson's girls?" The old man peered intently at Shaney as he laid two twenty-dollar bills on the counter.

Shaney nodded curtly as she handed him his change and a carton of
Marlboros.

"My Gawd, if you ain't the spittin' image of her! What's your
name?"

"Shaney. Shaney McDaniel." She said her last name with emphasis.
Not that she was proud of her father's side of the family, but claiming
her McDaniel heritage was far better than being identified as a Dickerson. She wished the old man would go away and leave her alone.

The old man guffawed. "Shaney! Who ever heard tell of a name like
Shaney! But then Seffie ain't no kind of a name, neither." He opened a
pack of cigarettes and shoved one into the side of his mouth. "That
Seffie, she was some gal! She sure knew how to . . ." His words were
lost as he shuffled out the door of the Speedway station into the hot
September afternoon.

Shaney glanced around the empty convenience store, jaw clenched,
arms folded defiantly over her chest. The conversation with her customer had riled her, and she needed to do something to burn off the
energy. Angrily, she stalked up and down the aisles, straightening dis-
plays of merchandize.

She snatched a pack of Big Red chewing gum that some careless customer had tossed into the Juicy Fruit carton. "Stupid idiots," she hissed
as she returned it to its rightful place. She grabbed a stick of beef jerky
that had been knocked to the floor and hung it up with the rest of the
display. "I don't know why we bother to sell this crap to the losers in
this town," she muttered as she pulled a damaged bag of potato chips
from the shelf.

She worked quickly, trying to focus on her task of tidying the store,
but she couldn't get the old man's words out of her mind: *If you ain't
the spittin' image of her.*

Angry tears stung her eyes. *I'm so sick of hearing that,* she thought. *I just wish everybody would shut up about that.*

From the time she was a small child, Shaney had known her mother was a local legend, and she was tired of living with that fact. Throughout her twenty-two years of living in the small town of Belmont, Seffie's story had become all too familiar to her. Jimmy and Big Stella often lapsed into bitter reminiscing, and it seemed like everyone in town over the age of forty had a tale to tell about Seferina Dickerson.

From her mother, Shaney had inherited the willowy figure that turned men's heads even when she was wearing her usual outfit of blue jeans and a tee shirt. She had the same finely chiseled features, the same fair complexion with a sprinkling of freckles across her nose, and the same light brown hair. Her bright blue, almond-shaped eyes were a dead giveaway to the fact that she was Seffie Dickerson's daughter. And she shared Seffie's mannerisms, the quick movements and restless energy.

Of course, there were differences. Shaney's five feet, ten inch height came from the McDaniel side. And while Seffie's long hair had hung in straight curtains on each side of her face, Shaney had inherited her father's thick, unruly curls. But her physical presentation was so strikingly similar to that of her mother, those who'd known Seffie would do a double-take when meeting her third daughter. Then they'd inevitably launch into a story about Seffie's live-on-the-edge, devil-may-care lifestyle that had both shocked and amused the community.

If life in Belmont ever seemed boring, the Dickerson clan could be counted on to raise an entertaining ruckus. If every small town needs a family that others can look down on in order to feel better about themselves, the Dickersons served that purpose in Belmont. Jimmy loved to pass idle hours telling stories about the Dickersons, shaking his head and counting himself fortunate to be a McDaniel.

Seffie was the seventh of nine children born to Ernie and Wanda Dickerson. According to Jimmy, Ernie was a worthless drunk and Wanda was a whore. Ernie did his drinking in the living room of his squalid home, sitting in a stupor in his filthy recliner in front of a flickering television set he never actually watched. Wanda's drinking took a different direction, sending her running to every bar in town. While Ernie was a sluggish drunk, alcohol made Wanda belligerent, and she picked fights with other brazen women who accused her of stealing their men.

No doubt there was some truth to these accusations, as more than half of the Dickerson children, particularly the younger ones, bore no resemblance to Ernie. Furthermore, as his alcoholism progressed, no one could imagine Ernie rousing himself enough to partake in any activity that would produce progeny. But the paternity question was never raised, and the Dickerson kids were simply the Dickerson kids.

No one ever accused Ernie and Wanda of abusing their children. Their parenting problem was neglect. They were simply oblivious to their children's needs, if not to their existence. The only time Wanda seemed to pay attention to her offspring was at their birth, when she named them. And how she named them! Elegant, regal names so out of place in the nasty reality of Dickerson life: Francesca, Glorianna, Angelita, Jennalia and Seferina for the girls, and Gabriel, Augustus, Orion and Tristan for the boys.

Welfare workers, briefcases in hand, were frequently seen standing on the Dickerson doorstep in a state of confusion, seemingly unable to comprehend the fact that this tiny shack reeking of sin and bodily waste was actually inhabited by eleven human beings.

Because of her father's determination to keep his daughters away from the corrupting influence of the Dickerson side of the family, Shaney had never known her maternal grandparents. When she was ten, Jimmy had pointed out Ernie's obituary in the newspaper, offering his commentary on her grandfather's utter worthlessness as a human being.

When she was nineteen, Shaney had overheard a conversation in the Speedway store about Wanda Dickerson being placed in a nursing home in Plymouth. Out of curiosity, she'd made a secret trip to Oakwood Manor. She'd found her grandmother, a skeletal figure misshapen by arthritis, lying on her side in a hospital bed, one bony hand clutching the bed railing. The poor creature periodically emitted a soul-piercing howl that sounded like the word *help*. Shaney had stared, transfixed by horror, then had turned and bolted from the room. She'd never returned to see Wanda Dickerson, and had never spoken of her experience to anyone.

Half of Wanda and Ernie's children were mentally slow individuals with colorless personalities, having spent the first nine months of their existence in an alcohol-saturated womb and a childhood in an environment devoid of positive stimulation. They failed miserably but quietly in school, dropping out at the earliest opportunity. As adults, they relied heavily on government assistance and the benevolence of local charities. While they were a drain on the community, they caused little disturbance, as the nature of their dysfunction was so passive, it was easily contained within the four walls of their rundown homes.

But the other half of the Dickerson kids showed a livelier disposition, and since their energy received no appropriate channeling, it had nowhere to go but headlong into trouble. These were the children through whom Wanda Dickerson's reputation lived on. These were the Dickerson's whose collective police record occupied two feet of space in the files of the Marshall County Sheriff's department. Their charges included DUIs, disorderly conduct, assault and battery, drug dealing, burglary, and even one attempted homicide. The deputies would groan in despair each time they received a domestic violence call involving a Dickerson. Sometimes they slogged through the motions of investigating the problem, but knowing the futility of any intervention, they often found reason to ignore the call altogether.

Seffie had been known as the most tightly wound of all the high-strung Dickerson children. Her schoolmates, now in their forties, still smirked as they recounted tales of her outrageous behavior. In first grade, she'd created a reputation for herself, and each year she grew more defiant, more daring, and more dangerous. Well-meaning teachers wracked their brains to find ways to reach this underprivileged child, but she scoffed at their efforts.

When Seffie was a fifteen-year-old freshman, the principal encountered her in the hallway and inquired as to why she wasn't in class. She responded with a swift punch to his abdomen. At that point, it was determined that her violent tendencies, coupled with the physical education teacher's suspicion that the girl was pregnant, created a greater risk than the school was willing to contend with. Seffie was told to leave and not come back.

Freed from school, she ran the streets, looking for the excitement she craved and all too frequently finding it. She never stayed long in one place, moving back and forth among the homes of her shiftless parents, her ne'er-do-well friends, and even unsuspecting strangers.

Seffie was far from stupid, and she knew how to play people to get what she wanted. When it served her purpose, she presented herself as needy and vulnerable, and her pregnancy helped the cause. Well-meaning folks, who believed all Seffie needed to become an upstanding citizen was a bit of love and attention, would feed her, buy her maternity clothing, take her to the doctor, and loan her money. But several weeks later, she'd disappear from their lives, along with some of their household belongings.

Using similar tactics, she managed to obtain a steady stream of boyfriends. Seffie was a pretty girl, and in spite of her wild ways, she possessed an elusive sensuality that deprived men of their reason. Some of her boyfriends were young and naïve, while others were ten or fifteen years her senior. Some were even married.

But none of them were the father of her unborn child. If Seffie knew the identity of her baby's father, she certainly wasn't telling anyone. Rumors abounded, but she side-stepped anyone who tried to pin her down to get the truth.

Right up to the end of her pregnancy, Seffie had men begging for the opportunity to love her and support her child. With an air of sweetness and gratitude, Seffie would take these fellows up on their offers. But the relationships were always short-lived, as Seffie's true snarling self would soon emerge and send the poor man running.

In July 1981, Seffie gave birth to a baby girl whom she named Sissy. With baby in tow, she resumed her former lifestyle. By the time Sissy was four months old, Seffie was pregnant again.

Marshall County Child Protective Services began receiving calls alleging that Seffie was exposing her baby to dangerous environments. Because of its experience with the previous generation of Dickersons, the department began watching her carefully.

Determined to beat Marshall County at its game, Seffie slithered across the south county line into Fulton County. However, Fulton County Child Protective Services also began receiving calls, and within several weeks, little Sissy was in foster care.

Now Seffie had a mission, not so much to regain custody of her child, but to win the war with Fulton County. She employed a range of battle tactics. From time to time, she'd burst into the Protective Services office, screaming, swearing and threatening the caseworkers with bodily harm. On other days, she'd weep pitifully, promising to reform her life and comply with the terms of her case plan.

Three weeks before her second child was born, Seffie wandered back into Marshall County and moved in with Wanda and Ernie. In August 1982, she gave birth to another baby girl, whom she named Starly.

Once again, Seffie resumed a life on the streets, sinking deeper into substance abuse and petty crime. She took little interest in Starly, and frequently left her home in the care of an inebriated Ernie. One day when Child Protective Services investigated a frantic call from the Dickersons' neighbor, they found Ernie passed out on the floor. Lying next to him was a screaming, emaciated two-month-old in a filthy diaper. Little Starly was immediately taken into foster care.

That night, there was quite a row at the Dickerson residence when Seffie returned home and discovered her baby was gone. Never before had Belmont seen such a deranged side of her. Seffie was not given to fighting with her parents, as they never hindered her from doing what she wanted. But that night, she assaulted Ernie and almost beat the old drunkard to a pulp. Her shrieking obscenities brought out all the neighbors and eventually the sheriff's department. She spent a few days cooling off in the county jail.

After her release, Seffie disappeared from the area for a year. It was rumored she'd gone north to Walkerton or North Liberty in St. Joseph County. But in November 1983, she resurfaced at the Fulton County Child Protective Services office and announced her intention to regain custody of two-year-old Sissy. Reluctantly, the CPS office provided her with a case plan for reunification with her child.

This time, Seffie appeared quite focused on demonstrating her acceptability as a parent. She began attending a church in Rochester, presenting herself in a way that tugged on the heartstrings of the pastor and his wife. They became enamored with the possibility of bringing out the good and the beautiful in Seffie, and within several weeks of meeting her, they invited the indigent girl to move into their home.

For four months, Seffie played the role of born-again church girl. She obtained a job at a fast food restaurant and enrolled in GED classes at Rochester High School. The pastor and his wife praised the Lord for Seffie's progress and accompanied her to the CPS office to vouch for her exemplary behavior. They expressed their commitment to provide long-term housing for Seffie and her child, leaving CPS with no choice but to return Sissy to Seffie's care.

For two blissful weeks, the pastor and his wife helped Seffie take care of her daughter. As each day passed, their attachment to the beautiful, blue-eyed toddler grew stronger. Then one morning, they awoke to discover that Seffie and Sissy had disappeared, along with money from the pastor's wallet and some of his wife's jewelry.

Shaney had heard this story from an elderly customer who'd attended the pastor's church. The old woman had actually wept when she described how Seffie's departure had devastated the pastor and his wife. "They gave so much to your mother," she told Shaney. "I just pray you won't follow in her footsteps." Shaney had been so outraged she could barely keep from chasing the old woman out of the store.

After leaving the pastor's house, Seffie had evaded Fulton County by migrating north into Elkhart County and settling in the small town of Nappanee. There, she applied for public assistance and rented a trailer in a seedy mobile home park.

It didn't take long for neighbors to notice a trail of suspicious-looking men passing in and out of Seffie's residence. In September 1984, she was arrested for dealing drugs and was sentenced to a year in the state prison in Indianapolis. Elkhart County Child Protective Services placed three-year-old Sissy in foster care.

After her release from prison, the undaunted Seffie was determined to regain custody of both her daughters. She approached Elkhart County regarding reunification with Sissy and Marshall County regarding Starly.

But in early 1986, she became pregnant with her third child. The father was James McDaniel, a tall, heavy-set, easy-going young man from a stable blue-collar family in Belmont, and Seffie surprised everyone when she decided to settle down with him. Jimmy was working steadily at the time, and was able to provide her with financial support. People often said that Seffie never loved him, that the only reason she lived with him was to impress Child Protective Services. Even Jimmy knew Seffie was using him.

But he had loved her. In spite of her rages, her drunken sprees, her infidelities, her cruel words that pierced his heart like daggers, in spite of the fact that she was a Dickerson, Jimmy's world had revolved around Seffie. He took care of her, cleaned up after her, and made excuses for her, hoping that someday she'd come to her senses and return his affection.

But within several years, he hated her as passionately as he'd once loved her.

Jimmy had sincerely supported Seffie's efforts to get her daughters back. He was confident that he'd love and care for Sissy and Starly as much as he would his own child. "I would've been happy to raise all four of you," he often told Shaney. "If your mother would've tried half as hard as I did, we could've done it."

Jimmy kept their rented mobile home reasonably clean and Seffie relatively subdued, and Elkhart Country Child Protective Services began to eye the situation favorably. Marshall County, with its knowledge of the Dickerson legacy, was not as easily impressed.

Shaney had often been told how her birth in August 1986 temporarily changed Seffie. Jimmy liked to boast that it was the birth of his child that finally triggered Seffie's maternal instincts. Maybe at the age of twenty-one, she was old enough to have some grasp on motherhood. In any case, she ran around less and stayed home more, taking care of baby Shaney while Jimmy worked to support the little family.

Elkhart County CPS was so impressed with Jimmy and Seffie's stability that they sent Sissy home in September 1986. Several months later,

Marshall County grudgingly allowed Starly to visit on weekends.

Jimmy always described Sissy as a quiet, well-behaved child. "She was a pleasure to have around," he'd say. "She never gave Seffie any trouble."

But when he talked about Starly, he'd shake his big head sorrowfully. "That little girl had a lot of problems. She was okay for me, but Seffie didn't have any patience with her. She'd fly off the handle. If you ask me, I'd say the two of them were too much alike. They butted heads.

"Seffie gave up way too easy on Starly. The way it looks to me, if she could've learned to handle that young'un, we could've made it as a family. She ended up signin' off on her. That's what she thought she wanted, but I could tell she didn't feel right about it."

According to Jimmy, one day in April 1987, he came home from work to find Seffie gone. "Starly was screamin' her lungs out. And Sissy was tryin' to give you the bottle. She was doin' a good job of it, too, even though she was only five."

He'd been so angry about Seffie's negligence, he kicked her out of the house, and for the next three days, he took care of the girls on his own. But then Seffie came home, teary-eyed and pleading, and his outrage was subdued when she announced she was pregnant again.

Jimmy had been afraid this baby wasn't his, given the fact that Seffie generally snarled and hissed when he tried to demonstrate his affection. In fact, no one in Belmont believed the baby was Jimmy's, and bets were placed regarding the identity of the father. Still, Jimmy plodded on, trying his best to hold the family together.

In spite of Jimmy's valiant efforts to help, Seffie was so unnerved by Starly's visits, her fragile thread of patience frequently gave way to bursts of rage. One day in July 1987, she stalked out of the house in a fit of temper, leaving the three little girls alone again.

This time, Jimmy didn't get home before the sheriff's department arrived on the scene. He pulled up just as Sissy and Starly were being helped into the deputy's car. He wept as his own child was strapped into an infant's car seat. Sissy and Starly were returned to their former foster homes, and eleven-month-old Shaney was also placed in foster care.

At this point, Marshall County Child Protective Services decided that Starly could never be successfully reunited with her mother, and they pressured Seffie to terminate her parental rights. She fumed and threatened, but eventually signed the papers voluntarily.

Jimmy did his best to cooperate with Child Protective Services, and after a month, they returned Shaney to his care. They emphasized that she was now in his custody, not Seffie's, and that if anything happened to Shaney while in Seffie's care, he would be held responsible. Recognizing the gravity of the situation, Jimmy enlisted the support of his widowed mother, Stella McDaniel, to check on Seffie and Shaney while he was at work, and to take over if Seffie needed a break.

Seffie's fourth daughter was born in November 1987. When Jimmy first laid eyes on this infant, all his doubts about her paternity vanished. The three older girls bore a striking resemblance to Seffie, but this chubby little baby was a McDaniel through and through.

While Shaney had been Seffie's special baby, this one was Jimmy's. Both he and his mother developed an immediate affinity for the child. They doted on her, and if Jimmy wasn't home taking care of the baby, she'd be at his mother's house.

Before Seffie could name this daughter, Jimmy claimed the right. "I won't have you callin' her somethin' silly like you did the others," he told her. He named the baby Stella after his mother, and the two Stella's were thereafter known as Big Stella and Little Stella.

In January 1988, when Little Stella was two months old, six-year-old Sissy was returned to Seffie's care. For the next nine months, the household struggled along without any outside interference. Then one day in September, while Big Stella was taking care of the baby at her house, Seffie left Sissy and Shaney alone.

"Sissy's seven years old!" Seffie had screamed when she came home and found a CPS worker preparing to take her children. "She's half-grown! She's old enough to watch her baby sister." But CPS didn't agree with Seffie's line of reasoning, and once again, Sissy and Shaney were placed in foster care.

"I'll admit it, I screwed up," Jimmy had told Shaney. "I trusted your mother, and that was a stupid thing to do. When she left you alone again, I knew right then and there I had to make a choice between her and my girls. And I did what any good father would do."

He had pleaded with Marshall County CPS to let him have his daughter back. He told them he'd leave Seffie, promising that he and his mother would take good care of Shaney and Stella. To prove he was a man of his word, that very day he left the mobile home he shared with Seffie and moved in with Big Stella. After two weeks, Marshall County returned Shaney to his care, accompanied by a stern warning to never leave his children alone with Seffie.

And Jimmy toed the line. In fact, he was more cautious than CPS dictated, in that he refused to allow Seffie anywhere near his daughters. From time to time over the next two-and-a-half years, Seffie pounded on Jimmy and Big Stella's door, demanding to see her children. But Jimmy never relented.

One night in the spring of 1991, Seffie showed up for the last time, shouting in the darkness that she was pregnant again. She taunted Jimmy with the news that the baby was a boy, the son he always wanted. But that baby was never born. One week later, Seffie was dead.

Shaney tried not to think of the day she'd heard the news of her mother's death. She'd become quite skilled in focusing her mind on something else if memories of that dreadful event ever crossed her mind. While Jimmy frequently indulged in bitter reminiscing about Seffie's life, no one in the family ever talked about how she died.

One day when she was twelve, Shaney had moved a stack of magazines in her father's room and had found an old newspaper clipping. The awful headline caught her attention, and as she read the story, icy fingers of horror grabbed and twisted her insides. She ran to the bathroom to vomit, then wadded the clipping into a tight little ball and flushed it down the toilet along with the contents of her stomach. Jimmy never asked about the missing story.

Even after her death, Seffie had remained the focal point of Jimmy's life. If Seffie was a local legend, then Jimmy was a giant monument to the pain and suffering she inflicted upon the lives of others. A large man to begin with, his weight ballooned to over four hundred pounds after her death. Now forty-seven, he'd been medically disabled with a bad back for the past fifteen years.

Jimmy blamed his disability on Seffie, just as he blamed her for all other misfortunes in his life. He frequently recounted the story of how Seffie had whacked him across the back with a cast-iron skillet during one of her rages.

Shaney's only conscious memory of Seffie was an angry voice shouting in the darkness outside Big Stella's mobile home. She couldn't remember her mother's face. But throughout her years of being raised by Jimmy and Big Stella, not a day had gone by when Seffie's presence wasn't felt in their home.

In fact, it sometimes felt like she, Shaney McDaniel, became Seferina Dickerson in her father's eyes. Whenever she did something to displease him, his face took on the same tortured expression he wore when reminiscing about his miserable years with Seffie. He didn't need to say anything. The look said it all: *You're just like your mother.*

Maybe he's right, Shaney thought in a moment of self-loathing. *Maybe I'm no better than she is.* As she scrubbed the fingerprints off the glass of the pastry case, she recalled her own unruly behavior as a child. It seemed she'd been in trouble, either at home or at school, on a daily basis. When she was twelve, she'd started running with boys, and her peers had called her ugly names, the same names people had called Seffie. At sixteen, she'd gotten pregnant with Cody and had dropped out of school. Contemplating the parallels between her life and her mother's life filled her with shame.

But I'm different now, she told herself. *I'm not going to end up like her.* She forced herself to focus on the differences. While she'd experimented with alcohol and marijuana in her early teens, she'd given up those habits for good when she realized she was going to be a mother.

She'd never lived on the streets like Seffie had. While she'd incurred Jimmy's wrath by briefly living with Cody's father, Juan, she'd moved back in with Jimmy and Big Stella when Juan moved back to Mexico.

Like her mother, Shaney had never lacked for attention from the opposite sex. But after a series of painful relationships, she'd sworn off men and had refused to date anyone for the past year.

And I also work, she thought. Thinking about her employment record eased her mind. While Seffie had been a stranger to paid employment, Shaney had gone to work shortly after Cody's birth, and had never been without a job since then. She'd worked for Scott King at the Speedway station for the past three years.

The front door beeped, signaling that someone was entering the store. Shaney looked up from her work, glad for the distraction from her troubled thoughts. She smiled as Scott limped in, followed by his children, Blake and Miranda. His face lit up at the sight of Shaney hard at work.

"Thatta girl, Shaney," he said. "Keep busy!"

Chapter 2

Scott limped up and down the aisles of the store, straightening the already-straightened rows of chips, cookies, cereal, and canned goods. Then he moved to the booths by the front windows, checking for stickiness and crumbs.

Shaney smiled, knowing this was Scott's routine every time he came into the store. It drove some of the other workers crazy, but Shaney understood her employer's ways. She could forgive his pickiness because she shared his perfectionist tendencies. And Scott rarely found anything to complain about when she was on duty.

While their father inspected the store, Blake and Miranda busied themselves with choosing items from the candy display. They spoke in soft little chirps as they compared the merits of the various treats. After a few minutes, they brought their candy to the counter, and Scott handed Shaney several dollar bills. Even though the money eventually ended up in his own pocket, he always paid for his children's treats when they came to the store.

"By the way," he said, "Mona called in sick, so my mom will be helping out during the busy part of the evening."

"Okay," Shaney said, glad for the news. She didn't enjoy working with nervous little Mona. She much preferred the robust personality of Scott's mother, Dorothy King.

Scott limped to the back room and turned on his computer. Blake and Miranda sat in the front booth, chatting quietly while they ate their candy. Shaney marveled at how well-behaved Scott's children were. She wished she could say the same about Cody.

Feeling restless, she looked around for something else to clean. When she noticed smudges on the front door, she reached into the cupboard behind the counter for the bottle of glass cleaner. The small panes above the door were beyond her reach, and she tried to think of something she could stand on.

Suddenly, she remembered Jimmy's chair. She went to the back room and scooted it out of the corner, where it was usually tucked out of sight. The chair's sturdy metal frame was dented and scratched, and the dark green vinyl seat, split in several places under Jimmy's tremendous weight, had been patched with silver duct tape. An identical heavy-duty chair sat in the kitchen in the McDaniels' mobile home.

Scott frowned when he saw what Shaney was carrying. "Do you have to keep that ugly thing in here?"

Shaney winced. She hated displeasing Scott. "But my dad comes in almost every night, and he's too big to sit in a booth."

Scott sighed. "I know, I know. I don't want this business turned into a local hangout. But since it's your family . . . ."

"Thanks, Scott." Shaney didn't like Jimmy sitting in the store, either, but she knew there'd be hell to pay if she ever tried to stop him.

Scott straightened the items on his desk, and then got up to make a perfunctory check of the back room. When he was satisfied that all was in order, he called, "Okay, kids, let's go." Blake and Miranda slid out of the booth and followed their father to the door.

"See you later, Shaney," Scott called as he left the store. "You're working tomorrow night, right?"

"Yes, I am."

Shaney watched out the window as Scott and his children walked to his car. She saw him struggle to keep his balance when his bad foot hit an uneven spot on the pavement.

She always cringed when she watched Scott walk. Fifteen years ago, Scott King had been the golden boy of Plymouth High School. Powerfully built and quick as lightening, he'd distinguished himself in several sports. As quarterback for the football team in 1993, he'd set a school record for total yards thrown in one season. And of course, he'd been popular with the girls, all of whom craved the attention of a superstar.

But six years ago, Belmont's most tragic event of the decade occurred when Scott and his wife Pam were hit by a semi-truck whose driver had fallen asleep at the wheel. Pam had been killed instantly. Scott's left leg had been mangled and only narrowly saved from amputation.

Scott had won a lawsuit against the trucking company, and had used the settlement money to buy the Speedway station. The store had proven to be a profitable investment for him, as he managed the business with the same shrewdness and determination that had served him well on the football field. It also allowed him the flexibility to spend most of his time with his children, who were now seven and eight years old.

From the right side, Scott's profile was as handsome as ever, with his aquiline nose, strong jaw-line, and thick, blonde, carefully groomed hair. But from the left side, his good looks were marred by a wicked scar running across his cheek from ear to chin. Scott still worked out, and the muscles in his upper body were strong and sculpted. But when he walked, his left shoulder dipped so that his once graceful body appeared ungainly.

The front door beeped as a man came in to pay for his gas. Shaney glanced at her watch and saw that it was 3:45 PM. Belmont's first-shift factory workers were now on their way home, and traffic in the store would be heavy for awhile.

At 4:00 PM, Dorothy King bustled in. "Hi, honey," she called in a voice made husky by years of smoking. "Guess you're stuck with me for the evening." She tucked her handbag into the cupboard behind the counter and opened the second cash register.

Being around Scott's mother always lifted Shaney's spirits. Dorothy, known to everyone as Dort, was a strong-willed, outspoken woman in her late fifties with a short, stout build. Shaney always felt safe when Dort was around. She admired the way Dort handled difficult customers without getting flustered, using her *I'm in charge* attitude. But while Dort wasn't easily conned, she was the first to respond when a situation called for sympathy.

Whenever Scott had a staffing problem at the store, Dort would show up to cover the bases. Each time she worked, Scott would offer to pay her, but she'd refuse his money, saying, "I'm just glad I can help out, Scotty." Shaney sensed Dort had never gotten over the tragedy of her only child's accident.

True to the typical weekday pattern, Shaney and Dort served a steady stream of customers between the hours of 4:00 and 6:00 PM.

Then traffic began to taper off.   When the store finally emptied, Shaney sighed, deeply exhausted.   She wondered how she'd get through the three hours left on her shift.

"Uh oh!"   Dort gestured toward the window behind the counter. "Here comes trouble!"

Shaney peered out the window and saw a semi-truck pulled along-side the diesel pump on the south side of the station. The door beeped, and she turned to see a tall man in a western hat swagger in. She'd seen the man in the store several times in the past month, but had nev-er been the one to wait on him.

"Hey there, Dort!" the man called, his voice low and smooth.

"Hi, Terence, whatcha up to?" Dort responded.

Terence was a broad-shouldered man who appeared to be ap-proaching middle-age. He wore a western shirt and blue jeans slung low on narrow hips. Had it not been for the beginning of a potbelly, he would have been a fine figure of a man.

He paid Dort for his gas, and then walked the length of the counter, thumbs hooked in his belt-loops, the heels of his cowboy boots clicking on the floor. Stopping in front of Shaney's register, he took off his hat and laid it on the counter. His dark brown hair, graying at the temples, was swept back on the sides and hung slightly over his collar in the back. While his rugged facial features were not quite handsome, there was still something alluring about him.

Shaney caught her breath as he rested his folded arms on the coun-ter and leaned toward her. She could smell the strong scent of his co-logne mixed with the odor of cigarette smoke.

"Well, well, who do we have here?" he crooned.

Shaney felt her face flush, and she lowered her gaze.

Terence cocked his head to one side. "What's your name, darlin'?"

She glanced up and met his intrusive gaze, then looked down again. "It's Shaney."

"Shaney! What a purty name! It suits you." He leaned closer, grin-ning lasciviously. "I've seen you in here before. You probably thought ol' Terence didn't notice you, but you better believe I did. Good-lookin' as you are, a man couldn't help but notice you."

Shaney's face grew hotter, and she shifted her weight uneasily. Terence smiled broadly at her discomfort, showing tobacco-stained teeth.

"Am I embarrassin' you, darlin'?" Chuckling, he stepped back and scrutinized her figure, his gaze lingering on her breasts before moving up to her face. "You know what, darlin'? You remind me of somebody."

A bolt of anger shot through Shaney. She knew what was coming next. Terence knew very well who she was. She didn't know how he knew, but he knew, just like everyone else knew. The man was toying with her.

The door beeped again, and a woman came in to pay for gas. "I'm busy, I don't have time to talk," Shaney snapped at Terence. Then she called to the new customer, "I can help you over here." As the woman approached her register, Terence was forced to step aside.

"Hey, I didn't mean to upset you, Shaney." His voice had changed, sounding almost sincere.

Ignoring him, Shaney focused her attention on her customer. Terence shrugged and walked away.

"Well, who does he think he is?" Shaney fumed after Terence left the store.

Dort grinned. "That's Terence Buckwalter. He's a local boy. He was gone for a few years, and just moved back several months ago. He drives truck for Royer Foods in Plymouth." She shook her head, chuckling. "The old snake! He thinks he's God's gift, if you know what I mean. You handled him well, Shaney. I'm proud of you."

Dort decided to stay on until the end of the shift. Shaney was glad, as she was still unnerved by her encounter with Terence Buckwalter.

The local-yokel traffic, as Dort called it, was fairly heavy that evening. Soon after Terence left, Roger Whalen came in for his usual evening coffee.

Roger was the second-shift foreman at the Belmont wiring harness plant, and on work nights, he took his evening break at the Speedway station. He was a tall man in his late-twenties, six feet four inches and pencil thin. No one knew much about him, except where he worked and the fact that he'd been divorced for several years. Roger was utterly predictable, always showing up at the store at the same time, always dressed in blue jeans and a white tee shirt.

"You could set your clock by that man," Dort would often say.

Shaney never saw Roger without a feed cap pulled low over his face, obscuring his intense brown eyes. He always requested his deli order with succinct politeness, and would then sit in the back booth with his food and coffee for the next forty-five minutes. He rarely spoke, but often smiled at the action going on around him.

Shaney watched Roger walk to his usual seat, carefully balancing his coffee. After the disturbing incident with Terence Buckwalter, the sight of this familiar figure comforted her. She noticed how long his legs were.

"Did you ever see such long, skinny jeans?" she whispered to Dort when Roger was out of earshot.

Dort chuckled. "Can't say that I have. He probably orders them out of one of those tall men's catalogs."

Ten minutes later, the Robertson brothers pulled up in their battered pickup truck. Clarence and Clifton, identical twins in their late-forties, were simply known as *the twins* by residents of Belmont. Neither of them had ever married. They lived together north of town in the house they'd been raised in, and farmed the land inherited from their parents.

The twins reminded Shaney of Pillsbury Dough Boys, with their short pudgy forms, their silly smiles, and their eyes crinkled into slits of perpetual amusement. Both were bald, with the same fringe of graying hair encircling the shiny domes of their heads. The twins never appeared in public as individuals, and one was never seen without the other. The only way Shaney could tell them apart was that Clarence had a mole on one cheek.

She could hear the twins approaching as they walked from the north parking lot around the front of the store toward the door. Their mouths were in constant motion, yakking away about nonsense, joking with anyone they encountered. They seemed to spark each other, laughing hilariously over each other's tall tales.

The twins were notoriously foul-mouthed, with the town's largest repertoire of dirty jokes. But Shaney knew that under all their vulgar talk, they were harmless as kittens. She actually enjoyed the high energy they brought into the store when they stopped by several evenings a week, as long as they didn't overstay their welcome.

The twins greeted Dort and Shaney boisterously, and then took their coffee to the back booth to join Roger. Clarence sat down across from him, while Clifton elbowed Roger in the ribs and slid into the seat beside him. Shaney could hear bits and pieces of their smutty stories, frequently broken up with raucous laughter. She heard Clifton say, ". . . and ol' Roger here wouldn't know what to do with it if he got some." He nudged Roger again, and his twin pounded the table and howled with laughter.

Shaney jumped when she heard a clatter in the parking lot. Dort peered out the door. "It's just Petey," she said. "He dropped his bicycle."

The door opened, and Petey shuffled in. He was a diminutive man, hunched over with seventy years of age. His dark, greasy face, crisscrossed with a roadmap of wrinkles, sported a week's growth of stubbly white whiskers. One watery blue eye stared straight ahead while the other was cocked off to the side. In spite of the September heat, he was wearing a filthy winter coat and stocking cap.

He shuffled past the counter, mumbling under his breath. The sound reminded Shaney of a buzzing insect. A foul odor followed him, and she held her breath for a few seconds.

"Hope you didn't hurt yourself, Petey," Dort said.

Petey let out a sharp cackle, exposing his few remaining half-rotted teeth. Resuming his buzzing, he turned and shuffled past the booths to the dairy case, where he stood for several minutes cackling at the cartons of milk and orange juice.

Scott reluctantly put up with most of the people who hung out in the store, but Petey was more than he could tolerate. The old man spent his days wandering around town, and he drifted into the store two or three times a day. It wasn't actually Petey that Scott objected to; it was his stench that permeated the store, lingering long after he left. Scott had given his workers specific instructions for handling Petey.

"Time to go now, Petey," Shaney said. Petey turned obligingly and shuffled out the door, buzzing and cackling.

"See you later, Petey," Dort called after him. "You be careful, now."

When Petey was gone, Dort reached into the cupboard and brought out a bottle of Lysol. With brisk steps, she circled the store, spraying the disinfectant into the air.

"Stinkin' little son-of-a-bitch, ain't he," Clarence chortled, waving his hand in front of his nose.

"Little fart ain't playin' with a full deck," observed Clifton.

As the evening passed, Shaney began to think Jimmy wasn't going to make his daily visit to the Speedway station. She was glad for the relief from the tension she usually felt around 7:00 PM when Jimmy waddled in and parked his huge bottom on the green chair.

Shady Acres Mobile Home Park, where Shaney lived with Jimmy, Little Stella, and Cody, was diagonally across Main Street from the Speedway station. As the McDaniels' mobile home was close to the front of the park, Shaney could walk to work in two minutes.

But the disadvantage of living close to work was that Jimmy also had easy access to the station, even though the short trek took him ten minutes. It had been years since Jimmy had been able to squeeze behind the wheel of a car, and Little Stella had never bothered to get her driver's license. So if Shaney wasn't available to chauffeur him in his old Buick, Jimmy's mobility was limited to the short distance he could walk.

For several years, Jimmy had depended on the Speedway station for his supply of soda, chips and cigarettes, and trips to the store were the high point of his day. His social life was limited to the hours he spent sitting on his green chair, visiting with the customers in the booths.

Shaney's heart sank when the door beeped and Jimmy's massive frame, clad in enormous bibbed overalls, filled the doorway. Little Stella's sullen face peered over her father's shoulder. Then, quick as lightening, Shaney's skinny, dark-haired son squeezed through the narrow space between Jimmy's leg and the door frame, bursting into the store ahead of his aunt and grandfather.

"Cody!" Shaney exclaimed. She thought she'd made it clear to Little Stella that her son wasn't allowed in the store during her work hours.

"Hi, Mommy, Mommy, Mommy!" Cody chanted, bouncing up and down in front of her cash register. "Gimme some pop, gimme some pop, gimme some pop."

"Wait a minute," Shaney said. "You have to sit down and be quiet first."

"No!" Cody shouted. "I want it now!" He began dashing up and down the aisles, making screeching tire sounds as he rounded the corners.

"Where's my chair, Shaney?" Jimmy asked, breathing hard from the exertion of his walk. "Bring it back here. I'm gonna sit here with my buddies."

Shaney obligingly scooted the green chair out of the back room and around the counter. Jimmy grabbed it and pushed it to his favorite spot alongside the back booth. Hiking up his pant legs, he eased himself down on the chair, grunting with relief.

"Hey, Jimmy, how's it goin'?" Clifton called. Clarence lifted a hand in greeting.

Little Stella helped herself to a large Coke from the soft drink machine, plopped a few coins on the counter, and squeezed into the second booth. She sat with her back against the wall, one hefty leg extended the length of the bench.

Old Floyd Everingham entered the store, bought coffee and a jelly donut, then settled into the front booth. His toothless gums mashed down on the pastry, and Shaney stifled a giggle when she noticed how his nose and chin nearly touched as he chewed.

Cody rounded the corner by the booths with an ear-piercing screech. The twins laughed and grabbed at him playfully. Encouraged by their attention, Cody increased his speed and volume.

"Whoa there, buddy, you need to slow down!" Dort scolded.

"Come here, son," Jimmy called. Jimmy always called Cody *son*, a habit that annoyed Shaney.

Cody ran to his grandpa, arms outstretched. Jimmy smiled and extended his arms to catch him. But at the last minute, Cody rammed his fists into Jimmy's abdomen, his little arms sinking up to his elbows in the folds of flesh.

"Blubber belly!" he shouted. Then he dashed up and down the aisles, chanting at the top of his lungs, "Blubber belly, blubber belly, Grandpa's a blubber belly!"

Jimmy's face darkened and his mouth hung open, as if trying to form words he couldn't bring to mind.

Roger looked uncomfortable. Glancing at his watch, he mumbled something about getting back to work. Clifton stood up to let him out of the booth, and Roger was out the door in several long strides.

The twins were no longer laughing. "Cut it out, kid!" Clarence shouted.

Jimmy attempted to restrain his grandson as he ran by, but Cody giggled and slipped out of his grasp.

"Boy, if I'd acted up like that when I was a kid, my old man woulda taken the razor strap and whipped the tar outa me," Floyd Everingham drawled. "It's that Dickerson blood comin' out in him."

Jimmy's expression changed, and Shaney saw relief on his face. *Now you have an explanation for Cody's behavior,* she thought bitterly. *Go ahead, Jimmy, blame Seffie again. Make it her fault. Never mind how much you spoil my son. Never mind how you go against me when I discipline him. Just chalk it up to Seffie's bad blood.*

"You're probably right, Floyd." Jimmy's voice had taken on the familiar high-pitched whine he used when enumerating the miseries of his life with Seffie. He and the old man lapsed into exchanging unfavorable opinions about the Dickersons.

Shaney's face burned with embarrassment and rage. She clenched her fists and bit her lower lip to keep from screaming at the two men.

"Take it easy, honey," Dort cautioned.

Shaney brushed past Dort and stalked angrily to the second booth, where Little Stella slurped the last of her drink, impassive to the uproar around her.

"Take Cody home!" Shaney voice shook with fury. Little Stella looked up, lifting one eyebrow in an attitude of defiance.

"Take him home now!" Shaney repeated. Then she felt Dort's reassuring hand on her back, and she stepped aside to let the older woman take charge.

"Stella, you need to take Cody home." Dort's voice was calm, but firm. "We have a business to run here."

Stella shot Shaney an ugly look as she slid out of the booth. "You're just lucky I even babysit your brat," she snarled. Grabbing Cody with one arm, she carried the kicking, screaming child out of the store.

Chapter 3

"How'd it go last night?" Scott asked Shaney when he came into the store Saturday afternoon. "Any problems?"

"It was okay," Shaney lied. "Petey came in, but we got him to leave after a few minutes, and then we used the Lysol." She hoped Dort wouldn't tell Scott about the problem with Cody.

"Good job," Scott said. "By the way, Mona called this morning and said she's quitting. So I guess my mom will be helping out until I get someone else hired."

"Okay." Shaney turned back to her work, smiling at the prospect of spending more time with Dort.

Little Stella came into the store late that afternoon, carrying a bag of food from McDonalds. She was wearing her usual ratty gray sweat pants, oversized tee shirt, and flip-flops. After helping herself to a Coke, she flopped down in the first booth and pulled an order of fries out of her bag.

"Little Stella, we serve food in here," Shaney called from behind her cash register. "Don't you know it's rude to bring in food from some-where else?"

"I like McDonalds fries," Little Stella said, as if her preference in fried food excused everything.

"Then why don't you eat them at McDonalds?"

"Because I get the family discount on my Cokes here, dumb-ass."

The name-calling riled Shaney, and she felt like tearing into her sister. "You don't need to be eating fries anywhere," she said through gritted teeth. "The rate you're putting on weight, you're going to catch up with Dad soon."

Little Stella's eyes clouded with pain, but she quickly assumed an arrogant smirk. "What's good about bein' skinny? You just get your butt kicked more often."

She popped a French fry into her mouth and chewed as if she had all the time in the world. Then she said under her breath, "At least I'm not a slut like somebody I know."

Shaney was ready to come back with another insult, but told herself it wasn't worth it. Glancing at Dort, she rolled her eyes and mouthed, "She's hopeless." She would've gladly given up the ten percent discount Scott gave employees and their families just to keep Little Stella out of the store.

She turned her attention to a customer and rang up his gas, cigarettes and groceries. After he left, she turned to her sister again.

"Where's Cody?"

Little Stella chewed a French fry with deliberation, while Shaney waited impatiently for her answer. "With Dad," she finally said.

Shaney's temper flared again. It was her sister's responsibility to watch Cody while she worked. Little Stella showed no interest in getting a real job, and Jimmy liked having her at home to keep him company. It was an unspoken assumption in the family that Little Stella would live with Jimmy for the duration of his life, doing for him what his bad back and tremendous weight kept him from doing for himself. So it worked out well for Little Stella to keep an eye on Cody, and Shaney paid her enough to keep her in spending money.

"You know I don't want you to leave Cody alone with Dad," Shaney snapped. "He can't move fast enough to stop Cody if he gets into something."

"He'll be alright," Little Stella said indifferently.

Shaney sighed. It wasn't worth it to pursue the matter. Little Stella would just threaten to stop babysitting, like she always did if Shaney confronted her about her care of Cody. At least she hadn't brought him into the store again.

Little Stella continued to lounge in the booth, watching her older sister serve a string of customers, her large, plump hand moving in a slow rhythm between the bag of fries and her mouth.

People who knew the McDaniel sisters often commented on how unfair it was that Shaney got all the good looks. They would have been surprised to know how much she envied her little sister. Shaney envied Little Stella because there was not one thing about her that could remind Jimmy, or anyone else, of Seferina Dickerson.

Little Stella was unmistakably a McDaniel, a tall, big-boned girl who'd grown steadily heavier throughout the twenty years of her life. She had her father's broad face, deep-set hazel eyes, and curly brown hair, which she pulled back into a frizzy ponytail. Little Stella had been born with a lethargic disposition, and was seldom stirred up about anything. She'd managed to mosey her way through high school, but since graduation, she'd shown no sign of planning for her future.

"If Little Stella has a comfortable chair, a bag of chips, and a working television set, she's happy," Dort had once told Shaney. "She's different from you. You want more out of life." Dort's comment had sent Shaney deep into thought.

Little Stella finished her fries and slid out of the booth, leaving behind her empty cup and crumpled bag. Then she ambled over to the display of snack foods and deliberated a few moments before selecting a bag of flavored corn chips. She slapped two dollars on the counter, and Shaney handed her the change.

Little Stella stood unmoving at the cash register. "You haven't paid me for babysitting this week," she said.

"The week's not over," Shaney snapped. "I'll pay you when I get home tonight."

"I need the money now."

"What for?"

"None of your business."

"Little Stella, now's not the time. I've got customers coming in. Get out of the way so I can do my work."

Little Stella didn't budge. She stared stubbornly at Shaney, and Shaney knew the look: *If you want me to watch your kid, you'll do what I say.*

"Oh, for Heaven's sake, Little Stella!" Shaney reached for her handbag and pulled out several twenty dollar bills. "Now get out of here and leave me alone."

"Shaney, why are you so mean to your sister?" Dort asked as the door closed behind Little Stella. "You need to cut her some slack."

"I can't believe you're taking her side," Shaney retorted. "She's a lazy slob, and she makes me sick."

"She is who she is," Dort said, "and you're not going to change her. You've got a lot more on the ball than she does. Just be thankful for that."

Shaney turned away from Dort, rolling her eyes. She felt ashamed of the way she'd treated Little Stella. But she knew her misdeed hadn't begun to avenge what she'd suffered over the years, all those years her sister had basked in the role of Jimmy and Big Stella's favorite while she'd taken the never-ending punishment that belonged to Seferina Dickerson.

At Dort's urging, Shaney took a mid-evening break. She sat in the back booth sipping a Coke, allowing relaxation to creep through her tired body. But when Terence Buckwalter walked through the door, she tensed up again. She watched warily as he paid for his gas and bought a cup of coffee.

As he stood looking around the store, Shaney slunk down in her seat, wishing she could make herself invisible. But he spotted her and flashed a smile. As he walked toward the booth to join her, she noticed the previous night's swagger was gone.

"Still mad at me?" Terence grinned sheepishly as he slid into the booth across from her.

"Should I be?" Shaney's voice was cold.

Terence leaned toward her, his expression sincere. "I'm sorry about last night. Sometimes I get carried away and act like a jerk. You had a right to put me in my place. You're really pretty, but you're tougher than you look. I can tell you don't let anybody mess with you."

Shaney stared at Terence for a few seconds. "Apology accepted." Then she leaned back, sighing wearily.

"Tired?" he asked. "I bet your day gets pretty long, being on your feet all the time and dealing with crazy customers like me."

Shaney smiled against her will. "You got that right."

"I do some pretty long days, too," Terence said. "I start out at 6:30 in the morning, run into Plymouth, pick up my load, run to Indianapolis, unload. You can see how late it is by the time I get back."

"What exactly do you do?" Shaney asked.

Terence launched into a colorful description of his truck-driving job with Royer Foods. His way of talking was spellbinding, and Shaney found herself being drawn into his story. She interrupted him from time to time to ask questions.

"Yes, it can be stressful," he concluded. "But all in all, it's a pretty good deal for me. I'm not a person who likes to stay in one place, and this job lets me roam. I run into some interesting people. And I make some damn good money."

"Wow!" Shaney said. Terence made his job seem so exciting compared to hers.

"You ever have a day off?" he asked. "Why don't you make a run with me sometime? I take friends with me every now and then. I enjoy the company."

Shaney felt a surge of excitement, but then looked down, embarrassed. "I'll think about it," she said.

"Okay, let me know." Terence gave her hand an affectionate squeeze as he slid out of the booth. "I enjoyed talking with you. You're a nice kid. See you around."

After Terence left, Shaney joined Dort behind the counter again. She felt giddy, and could hardly stop herself from giggling. Suddenly, she became aware of Dort's stony silence, and she turned to meet her coworker's stern gaze.

"What?" Shaney asked, annoyed.

"Be careful," Dort said.

"What are you talking about?"

"Terence. Don't mess with him. Steer clear of that man."

"Why? He seems like a nice guy. He's interesting to talk to."

Dort folded her arms, shaking her head. "Shaney, don't you see what he's doing? He struck out with you last night, playing Mr. Macho. So now he's trying a different tactic, being the nice guy. Terence doesn't give up easily."

"So what if he likes hanging out with me?"

"Okay, honey," Dort said, "I'm going to be blunt with you. I know Terence, and I know what he's capable of. Sure, he can be charming, the nicest guy you could ever know. And he's interesting all right! But he goes through women like a box of tissues. I bet he's had kids by half a dozen girls, and the weasel slides right out of taking care of them."

Shaney shrugged and turned away, but Dort caught her arm. "And he drinks, honey. I've seen him drunk. He's nasty. Terence can look like the best of the best, but believe me, he's the worst of the worst!"

Shaney shook Dort's hand off her arm. "Okay, okay!" she said testily.

Dort sighed. "Honey, I give you advice because I care about you, and I don't want to see you get hurt. But you can take it or leave it. It's your life."

Tears stung Shaney's eyes. She couldn't bear to be to be angry with the woman who felt more like a mother than anyone else she'd ever known. It hurt to have hard feelings between them.

"I'm sorry I was rude," she whispered as she wiped a tear off her cheek.

"It's okay, sweetie," Dort said. "I still love you."

"Are you working tomorrow?" Dort asked Shaney as they were leaving the store at the end of the shift.

Shaney made a face. "No, it's my day off. You know what happens when Scott gives me a Sunday off? I have to take Jimmy and Little Stella to see my grandma in the nursing home. Believe me, I'd rather work."

"Now, Shaney!" Dort said in mock reproach.

"Oh, Dort, I almost forgot. Can I ask you a favor?"

"Depends on what it is."

"Could you watch Cody for a few hours tomorrow afternoon? I've tried taking him to the nursing home, but he's just too much to handle."

"Sure!" Dort said. "Cody's my little man, God love 'im. He's always an angel for me. Sure! Bring him over tomorrow."

When Shaney arrived home that night, she was greeted by a familiar bittersweet odor that permeated the mobile home. Little Stella was sitting on the couch watching TV, her feet propped up on the cluttered coffee table.

"Little Stella, have you been smoking weed in here?" Shaney barked.

Little Stella shrugged indifferently.

"You better not have smoked in front of Cody. Because if you did, your ass is mine!"

"I know better than that, stupid!" Little Stella retorted. "I waited until he went to bed."

Shaney shook her head, incredulous. "You used your babysitting money to buy pot, didn't you? Couldn't you have used it for something better? Like some decent clothes or something for the house? I'm busting my butt to earn that money, and you go and smoke it up!"

"It's my money," Little Stella said. "I can do anything I want with it. I don't know why you're being such a hypocrite. You used to smoke weed."

"That was six years ago. I was a kid then. And Dad threw a fit about it. I don't know why he lets you get away with it."

Little Stella grinned evilly. "He smokes some himself, every now and then. It settles him down when he gets worked up."

"My God, Little Stella! That's what rednecks do, lay around and smoke weed all the time."

"Well, who do you think we are, Miss High-and-Mighty? The last time I checked, we were all rednecks. Might as well be proud of it."

The familiar rage welled inside Shaney. She wanted to burst into Little Stella's room, rifle through her drawers, and flush her stash down the toilet. But she checked herself. She knew such action would do nothing but inflame her sister and her father.

"The two of you just go ahead and smoke then," she muttered. "It'll just make you both fatter and lazier." She raised her voice. "But if either of you do it in front of Cody, there'll be hell to pay. I mean it! There'll be so much hell to pay!"

Chapter 4

The morning sun peeked through the gaps in the broken window blind, sending shafts of light into the tiny bedroom. Shaney lay awake in the top bunk, while below her Cody snored softly. She stared at the water-stain pattern on a ceiling tile, savoring the peace and quiet, one of the rare moments she had just for herself.

For the past five years, Shaney had shared this room with her son. They'd started out with his crib alongside her twin bed. By the time Cody was three, he was too big for the crib, so Shaney had saved up money and bought the bunk beds.

The McDaniels' mobile home had been one of the largest models on the market when Big Stella and her late husband Albert had purchased it twenty-five years ago. Albert had died a year after they moved in, and Big Stella didn't like living alone. So she'd welcomed the company of Jimmy and her grandchildren when they needed to leave the home they shared with Seffie.

Now the mobile home seemed cramped and shabby. It consisted of three bedrooms, one bath, a kitchen, and a living room. As long as Shaney could remember, Jimmy and his king-sized bed had occupied the master bedroom. Prior to Big Stella's move to the nursing home four years ago, she and Little Stella had shared a double bed in the larger of the two small bedrooms.

Shaney had always occupied the smallest room. When Cody outgrew his crib, she had tried to convince Little Stella that they needed to switch rooms. But Little Stella had refused to budge. "It's not my fault you got pregnant and had a brat," she said. So Shaney gave up and bought the bunk beds.

A musty odor permeated the trailer, the result of several decades of neglectful housekeeping. The cheap paneling was chipped and scratched, tiles were loose on the kitchen floor, and the areas of the living room carpet visible under the piles of clutter were soiled and matted. One set of curtains in the living room was missing, and Little Stella had tacked up an old blanket over the window to prevent the afternoon sun from glaring on the TV screen.

The living room was roughly organized around Jimmy's needs, as he spent most of his day resting on the sagging couch. A small table at one end of the couch held a perpetually overflowing ashtray, empty soda cans, coffee cups, and rumpled bags of salty snacks. The coffee table was littered with more of the same, along with old magazines and newspapers. The television set was positioned directly opposite the couch, and the remote control could usually be found buried under the mess on the coffee table. Jimmy had Little Stella bring food and cigarettes to him on the couch, so occasional trips to the bathroom were the only times he left his seat.

Little Stella's dingy recliner was positioned on the other side of the small table, so she, too, had an unobstructed view of the TV screen. Her video game system lay in a tangle on the floor in front of the television. She'd taught Cody how to play video games, and most of her babysitting hours were spent with the two of them sitting on the floor, controls in hand, staring bug-eyed at the screen.

The condition of the rest of the home was no better than that of the living room. Little Stella had never been inclined toward housework, and Jimmy was too immobile to accomplish much of anything. Since Big Stella had left, it had been only Shaney's efforts that had kept the residence from becoming completely overrun by filth. She would set about cleaning when the home became too repulsive to live in.

But the one room in the trailer that Shaney kept spotless was the bedroom she shared with Cody. This tiny room was her haven within the home. A dresser stood against the wall opposite the bunk beds. Shaney's neatly folded pajamas, socks, and underwear occupied the top two drawers, while Cody's clothing was kept in the bottom two. Cody's toy box sat on the floor next to the dresser. The closet had long ago lost its sliding door, but Shaney's shirts and jeans were neatly hung, and the few pairs of shoes she owned were carefully arranged on the floor.

Each evening before she climbed into the top bunk, Shaney tidied up the room, as she couldn't relax and fall asleep if things were out of place. If anything belonging to Little Stella or Jimmy wandered into the room, she simply tossed it into the hallway. As long as her personal space was in order, she felt as if she had a measure of control over her life.

Shaney thought about the upcoming trip to the nursing home, wishing she could go to work instead. Sighing, she slipped down from her bunk. She had to get herself ready before Jimmy got up. He always took a bath on Sunday mornings before going to the nursing home, a process which tied up the bathroom for several hours.

Cody had been up late the night before, and was still in a deep sleep. Little Stella allowed him to stay up as late as he wanted when she babysat him, and he was often still awake when Shaney came home from work. He'd just started kindergarten, and Shaney had arranged for him to attend the afternoon class. That way, they could both sleep late into the morning. She knew she'd need to get her son on an early bedtime schedule before he started first grade next year.

One of Cody's skinny brown legs was sticking out from under his tangle of covers. The little boy had inherited the shiny black hair and dark complexion of his Mexican father, but like his mother, he was slender and long-limbed. He'd been chubby as an infant, weighing nearly ten pounds at birth. His size had amused Jimmy and Little Stella, who dubbed him *Buffalo Baby*. Shaney had been horrified, fearing that she'd given birth to another McDaniel destined for obesity. But once Cody began to crawl, he thinned out quickly.

As Shaney gazed at her sleeping son, her heart welled with sadness. She wouldn't have traded Cody for anything in the world. But he'd come along too soon, before she'd had a chance to get her own life on track. In many ways, Cody was living the same kind of life she'd lived as a child, and she knew it was hurting him just as it had hurt her.

It pained her deeply that she couldn't do more for her child. She felt as if she'd spent her whole life at the bottom of a deep pit, trying to scale the slippery walls. Now, climbing up had become even harder, as she had to carry Cody along with her.

Early that afternoon, Shaney sat waiting in the driver's seat of Jimmy's rusty old Buick. Impatiently, she drummed the heel of her hand against the steering wheel, while Cody bounced in the back seat.

"I can't wait to see Aunt Dort," he chortled. "She's got cool toys at her house."

The door of the mobile home opened, and Jimmy lumbered down the steps, leaning heavily on the iron railing. Little Stella followed.

"Hurry up, Grandpa, you slowpoke!" Cody shouted out the open car window.

"Hush up, Cody," Shaney warned.

Jimmy eased himself into the front seat next to Shaney, and she felt the right side of the car sag under his tremendous weight. Little Stella got into the back with Cody.

The car sputtered and stalled twice before Shaney succeeded in starting it. "Goddamn it, Shaney, when are you gonna learn how to drive this car?" Jimmy whined.

"Goddamn it, Shaney," Cody echoed. Shaney knew she should correct his disrespectful behavior, but she couldn't muster the will to do it.

As she backed out of the driveway, she glanced sideways and saw Jimmy's face beaming with excitement. Car trips were a major event in his life.

"Let's have a little music," he said. He reached over and tuned the radio to the Plymouth station, and the twang of country music blasted through the car. Little Stella began singing along, and Jimmy joined in with his high-pitched monotone.

God, we're pathetic, Shaney thought as she drove down Main Street to the nursing home on the south side of town.

The music stopped for a political announcement. Marshall County Sheriff Herb Wilcox was running for office again. In his nasal southern drawl, he invited all county residents to a hog roast at Plymouth's Centennial Park. Tickets cost only five dollars, with children under the age of twelve admitted free. He identified grocery stores and gas stations where tickets could be purchased.

"Why, I believe I'd like to go to that hog roast," Jimmy said. "Five bucks ain't too bad, and Cody can eat for free. Shaney, you can get us some tickets at the Speedway Station."

Shaney groaned inwardly. When Jimmy set his mind on something, there was no talking him out of it.

Shaney held the door as Jimmy, followed by Little Stella, waddled into the front lobby of the Woodlands nursing home. She waited while Jimmy checked in at the reception desk. Then, eager to get the ordeal over with, she headed down the long hallway.

Breathing shallowly to avoid inhaling too much of the rancid air, she looked straight ahead toward her destination, Room 118 at the end of the hall. She didn't want to see the old folks slumped in their geriatric chairs, muttering to themselves and fidgeting with their clothing. She refused to look at the pitiful bodies under the bedcovers, who, mistaking her for a nurse, called out for her assistance.

Suddenly, she realized how fast she was walking, and she stopped to wait until her father and sister caught up with her. Jimmy, already winded, was clutching Little Stella's arm.

The drab beige walls in Room 118 were stained and in need of painting. A curtain divider was pulled through the center of the room to separate Big Stella's space from that of her roommate, who occupied the bed nearest the door. Several of the roommate's children were visiting, fawning over their frail mother.

On the other side of the curtain, Big Stella's massive girth filled the width of her hospital bed. She was lying on her back with her head elevated, wearing a cotton floral housecoat. The thin flannel blanket covering the lower half of her body was askew on one side, revealing a blotchy purple leg and a swollen foot in a pink terrycloth slipper. She reached out her left hand to her guests, while her stroke-damaged right hand lay lifeless on the bed.

"Oh, oh, oh, I'm so glad you're here," she whimpered. "I was afraid you weren't gonna come."

"How are you, Mama?" Jimmy asked as he waddled around to the right side of the bed. "They treatin' you okay in here?" With great effort, he leaned down and kissed his mother's flaccid cheek. Then he settled himself on a chair, relieved to be off his feet.

"Hi, Grandma!" Little Stella's voice was cheerful and childlike. She went to the left side of the bed, and wrapping her arms around Big Stella's shoulders, she gave her a noisy kiss.

Big Stella reached up with her good hand to caress her grand-daughter's face. "How's my baby girl?" she crooned.

Little Stella lowered the bedrail, pulled a chair alongside the bed, then sat holding her grandmother's hand.

Shaney stood by the window, feeling separate from the others, a skinny alien who'd mistakenly landed on a planet inhabited by beings of a different order. She shoved her hands into her jeans pockets and nervously jangled her car keys.

Big Stella's eyes leaked self-pitying tears while she complained about her loneliness and the poor care she received in the nursing home. "Why don't you come see me more often? I was expecting you all last Sunday."

"Grandma, you know we have to wait for Shaney to get a day off," Little Stella soothed as she handed her a tissue.

Big Stella's gaze drifted over to the window, and her eyes focused on Shaney for the first time.

"Shaney, don't you think your boss would give you more Sundays off if you asked him?"

"I don't know," Shaney mumbled, her eyes downcast. "We're pretty busy."

"You still workin' at that gas station?"

Shaney nodded, cringing.

Big Stella shook her head, clucking her tongue. "It's a shame. You were always such a smart girl. If it wouldn't have been for that mother of yours, you could've made somethin' of yourself." She moaned, her good hand moving to her chest. "Lord help us, that woman . . . ."

The sudden pounding on the door startles four-year-old Shaney as she sits playing on the living room floor. A shrill voice shouts from the darkness outside the trailer.

"Open this goddamn door, Jimmy McDaniel! You let me in right now, you son-of-a-bitch. I wanna see my kids. You got no right to keep'em from me. Open up, or I'm gonna break your fuckin' door down."

Jimmy swears and heaves himself off the couch. He goes back to his bedroom and rummages around in the closet. The shouting and pound-

ing continue. Shaney scrambles up on the couch, pulls aside the curtain, and peers out into the darkness. She sees shadowy forms moving under the window.

"Mommy?" she whispers.

Jimmy comes out of the bedroom carrying a shotgun. As he passes the couch, he swats Shaney on the bottom. "You get down from there!"

Then he flings open the door and shoots into the darkness. Shaney hears more swearing and the sound of someone running.

"Mommy?" she whispers again.

Big Stella clutches Little Stella to her breast, tears streaming down her fat cheeks. She rocks in her distress, blubbering, "That woman. Lord help us, that woman . . . that woman . . ."

"Well, Shaney girl, don't be a stranger," Big Stella said. "Come give Grandma a kiss."

Shaney shook herself out of her reverie. Smiling bleakly, she walked to the bed and dutifully planted a kiss on Big Stella's cheek. "It's good to see you, Grandma," she said. Then she retreated to her spot by the window, hoping to be left alone.

But Big Stella wasn't finished with her. "Where's that little boy of yours? Didn't he wanna come see his great-grandma?"

Shaney knew she needed to choose her words carefully. "I left him with a babysitter," she said. "Last time we came, he acted up in the hallway and disturbed the residents."

The explanation was partly true. After they'd left Big Stella's room, Cody had run wildly up and down the hallway, until Shaney finally caught him and carried him out of the building. But the real reason Shaney hadn't brought Cody again was because of his reaction when she got him back to the car. He'd cried and said he was scared of the weird-looking people. Shaney had remembered her reaction to old Wanda Dickerson, and had decided the nursing home was no place to bring a child.

"Shaney, Shaney, you're gonna have to get a handle on that little one." Big Stella's voice was reproachful. "If you don't, you're gonna be awful sorry later on."

Anger rumbled in the pit of Shaney's stomach. She knew there was truth in Big Stella's words. But she also knew how systematically her family worked against her efforts to discipline Cody. If he threw a fit when he didn't get his way, Jimmy and Little Stella gave in to him just to shut him up. If Shaney attempted to put restrictions on him, they'd say, "Don't be so hard on him, he's just a little boy." But the minute Cody would really get out of hand, they're response would change to, "He's your kid, do something with him."

After exhausting the topics of Big Stella's lunch and the fact that the nurse had been rude when she gave her a shower that morning, the conversation lulled. Jimmy mentioned Sheriff Wilcox's hog roast, a subject that provided five minutes of idle chit-chat.

Then Little Stella grabbed the remote control and flicked on the television set mounted on the wall across from Big Stella's bed. Pushing her chair as close to the bed as possible, she linked her arm through Big Stella's good arm and leaned her head against her grandmother's shoulder, her eyes half-closed, her face childlike.

Suddenly, Shaney understood something about her sister. Except for the fact that Little Stella had made her entrance into the world through Seferina Dickerson's birth canal, her biological mother had absolutely nothing to do with her life. Big Stella was the only mother figure Little Stella had ever known. Her grandmother's love enveloped her like a warm blanket, and even though Big Stella had moved to the nursing home across town, an invisible cord bound the two kindred spirits together.

Shaney had never been loved like that by anyone. While she worked relentlessly to prove her worth, her sister had already become everything she needed to be. Little Stella's sole purpose on earth was to be the object of Jimmy's and Big Stella's affection. They asked nothing more from her, and she wanted nothing more for herself.

Once again, Shaney envied her sister.

Chapter 5

The puny maple tree in the front yard didn't offer Little Stella much protection from the hot afternoon sunshine. She'd been sitting out-doors for an hour, and the movement of the sun had shifted the small shadow cast by the tree.

"Damn it!" she muttered as she hoisted her body out of the lawn chair. She repositioned the chair in the shade, and moved her bag of chips and pack of cigarettes alongside it. Then she seated herself again, lit a fresh cigarette, and sat back to watch the trailer park traffic pass by.

A familiar pickup truck slowed down and parked on the street in front of the McDaniels' mobile home. Uncle Art, Jimmy's older brother, swung himself down from the driver's seat.

Art McDaniel weighed in excess of three hundred pounds, although next to Jimmy, he appeared slim. Like the other McDaniel men, he was tall and massively built. His enormous flannel shirt, with the sleeves cut out for relief from the heat, hung like a tent over his protruding belly, and his blue jeans sagged precariously off his hips. A feed cap covered his curly gray hair.

Uncle Art looked like he was on a mission, and Little Stella watched curiously as he headed toward the front door. Then he spotted her, and his face broke into a broad grin. Changing his course, he walked over to where she was sitting under the tree.

"Hey there, Stella!" he said, playfully bumping his fist against her upper arm. "You ain't been workin' too hard, have ya?"

Little Stella grinned and smacked his hand away.

"Where's that little guy you look after?"

"Cody's in school now."

"You gotta be kiddin' me! I had no idea Shaney's boy was that old."

"Yup, he just started kindergarten two weeks ago."

"Well, ain't that somethin'." Uncle Art looked enviously at Little Stella's Coke. "Got anything for your old uncle to drink?"

"There's stuff in the fridge. Coke and beer both."

"Is your dad home?"

"Yup, he's inside."

Uncle Art grabbed the waistband of his sagging jeans and hiked his pants up a few inches. "I need to talk to him."

"Just go on in."

Uncle Art headed toward the door, and Little Stella turned to watch him climb the steps. On impulse, she got up and followed him into the house.

When she walked through the door, Uncle Art was already sitting in her recliner. Seating herself cross-legged on the floor in front of the TV screen, she picked up the controls to her video game system. She turned the volume off so she could hear what her uncle had to say.

"Whatcha been up to, Jim?" Uncle Art asked.

"Nothin' much. Went to see Mom yesterday."

"I've been meanin' to get out there myself. How's she doin'?"

"Good as can be expected, I guess."

The two men sat in silence for a few minutes. Then Uncle Art said, "You're purty good at that game, Little Stella. They didn't have nothin' like that when we were kids."

Little Stella looked over her shoulder and grinned at her uncle, then turned back to her game, waiting for the real conversation to begin.

"Well, Jim." Uncle Art's voice sounded serious. "I need to talk to you about somethin'."

"What's that, Art?"

"I got a mighty strange phone call last night."

"Oh, yeah?"

"Some woman called me. She sounded kinda high-falutin'. I forget what she said her name was. I wrote it down." Uncle Art pulled a folded piece of paper from his shirt pocket. "Cecily Hartman-Gray. She said she was lookin' for James McDaniel."

Jimmy's eyes widened with interest. "She was lookin' for me? Did she say what she wanted?"

"Nope, she didn't. I asked her, but she gave me the run-around. First off, she asked me if I knew James McDaniel, and I said, 'Yes, I do, he's my kid brother.' Then she asked me if you had a phone, and I told her you didn't have a home phone, you only had a cell phone. And then she asked me for your number."

"What did ya tell 'er?" Jimmy asked.

"Well, I told her I wasn't gonna give out that information without your permission, especially since she wouldn't say why she wanted to get hold of you. You know there's a lot of weirdoes out there these days. She got kinda pushy with me, and I finally said, 'Let me ask Jim, and if he says it's okay, I'll give you his number.' Then she told me she'd call me back in a few days."

"Well, I'll be goddamned." Jimmy sat with his brow furrowed, eyes narrowed to slits as he contemplated the mystery of the phone call. After a few moments, he said, "Go ahead and give 'er my number."

"You sure that's okay?" Art asked.

"Yup, I'm sure. If there's a problem, I can handle it."

"Okay, then." Uncle Art hoisted his massive body out of the chair. He gave Little Stella's ponytail a playful tug before he ambled out the door.

"Uncle Art came over today," Little Stella told Shaney when she came home from work that night.

Shaney was tired, and her sister's irrelevant announcement annoyed her. "So what's the big deal about that?"

"He said some woman called him and was lookin' for Dad."

"That's none of my business," Shaney snapped.

"Well, excuse me for livin'!" Little Stella snapped back. "I just thought you might wanna know."

Chapter 6

Wednesday, Shaney had the day off work, and she hadn't the slightest idea what she wanted to do with her time other than catch up on laundry. She slept late into the morning, waking just an hour before her son needed to be at kindergarten.

After walking Cody the three blocks to his school, she decided the day was too beautiful to head straight home. The previous night's rain had washed away the sticky heat, leaving behind a crystal blue sky and a hint of fall in the air. As she walked along the familiar streets of her hometown, she wondered if she'd end up living there the rest of her life. The thought depressed her.

"Where would I go if I left Belmont?" she asked aloud.

She gazed into the endless dome of the sky, contemplating the fact that the same sky covered other towns, other states, even other countries. Suddenly, she felt a rush of hope. *There may be something waiting for me that I can't even imagine.* Smiling, she tucked the thought into the back of her mind for safekeeping.

When she got home, she piled her dirty clothing, along with Cody's, into two laundry baskets. She carried them to the building that housed laundry facilities for the park residents, only to discover that all the machines were in use.

"Damn it!" she muttered as she lugged the baskets back to the mobile home. She'd counted on having the laundry done before Cody came home from school.

"Can I borrow the car?" she asked Jimmy. "I need to go into town to do my laundry."

"If you do a load of mine," he whined.

Shaney gritted her teeth. "Okay, but you have to give me some money."

"Bring me my wallet," Jimmy called to Little Stella. When she laid it in his outstretched hand, he opened it and pulled out a five dollar bill.

"This is the last of my cash," he told her. "How about goin' to the bank to get me another forty or fifty bucks? Shaney can drop you off on her way to the Laundromat."

"You can walk," Shaney snapped at Little Stella. "The bank's only a block and a half away."

"Shaney, you don't need to be so goddamn rude," Jimmy scolded. "It won't hurt you to do your sister a favor. Why do you always treat her like she's dirt?"

After Shaney deposited four loads of dirty clothing into washing machines, she sat on a bench in the Laundromat, rifling through the out-of-date magazines on the table next to her. When none of them held her interest, she decided to splurge on an unusual treat. She counted the cash in her wallet, then crossed the street to the drug store and purchased a paperback romance novel. She passed the rest of her time in the Laundromat engrossed in the glamorous life of the novel's heroine.

That evening, Shaney isolated herself in her bedroom, sitting cross-legged on the top bunk immersed in her novel. Jimmy and Little Stella were watching TV in the living room, while Cody played with his collection of miniature cars. Shaney could hear him imitating the sounds of engines and squealing tires. Occasionally, his aunt or grandfather would bark at him to quiet down.

She was so engrossed in her story, she was only vaguely aware of the fact that Jimmy's cell phone was ringing.

Little Stella fished the phone from under a pile of papers on the coffee table and handed it to her father.

"Hello," he said. "Yes, this is James McDaniel. What? Who did you say this is? Oh, my God! I never woulda thought I'd hear from you in a million years!"

The tone of her father's voice alarmed Little Stella, and she glanced over at his face, which had grown pale. The hand holding the phone to his ear was shaking. "I'm fine, just fine, thank you," he said. "Yes, they do, they sure do. Sure you can, hold on just a minute."

He handed the phone to Little Stella. "I think you better take this to Shaney," he whispered.

"Who is it?" Little Stella whispered back.

Jimmy didn't answer. Tears spilled from his eyes, and his entire body began to tremble.

Little Stella shrugged, then ambled down the hallway to Shaney's room and knocked on her door. "The phone's for you," she called.

Reluctantly, Shaney slid off the bunk, opened the door and took the phone from Little Stella's hand. "Hello," she said.

"Is this Shaney or Stella?" asked the female voice on the other end of the line.

"This is Shaney."

"Shaney! Oh my God, I can't believe I actually found you!"

Shaney couldn't tell whether the caller was laughing or crying. "Who is this?" she asked, bewildered.

"I'm sorry," the caller said. "I know I'm catching you off guard. This is your older sister, Sissy."

"Huh?" Shaney was dumbfounded.

"This is Sissy," the caller repeated. "Your older sister. Actually, your half-sister. Do you remember me? Maybe you don't, because you were really little when I lived with you."

The unexpected announcement jolted Shaney so hard, she felt weak and dizzy. She sank down onto the bottom bunk, her mind careening into the past.

Two-year-old Shaney sits naked on the battered coffee table. An open package of Oreos lies beside her. Her mouth is crammed full of cookies, her face covered with chocolate crumbs. A bottle of Pepsi sits in front of her, encircled by her tiny legs.

She smashes a cookie and pokes crumbs into the narrow opening of the bottle. Then she tilts the bottle up for a drink, and the sticky fluid dribbles down her chin onto her bare chest and tummy.

She hears the school bus rumble to a stop on the street outside the mobile home. Her eyes brighten with excitement.

"Sissy's home," Seffie calls from her seat on the couch.

Shaney scrambles off the table and runs to the door, overturning the bottle of Pepsi in the process.

"Shaney, you little brat!" Seffie yells as the bottle rolls off the table and spills its contents onto the already soiled carpet. "Look what you did!"

Sticky naked little Shaney bounces up and down in front of the door until it opens, and then jumps excitedly into the arms of her seven-year-old sister.

"Hello, my sweet Baby Shaney," Sissy croons.

Shaney panicked as the seconds ticked by. *What am I supposed to say to her?* "I remember you a little bit," she finally blurted out. "I don't remember much. But my dad's told me a lot about you."

"Did you and Stella get my letter?" Sissy asked.

"No, I don't think so. I don't remember any letter."

"I sent it three weeks ago, to Shady Acres Mobile Home Park, Lot 17, in Belmont. Is that your correct address?"

"Yes, it is. I don't know why we didn't get it. I'll have to check with Little Stella to see if she knows anything about it."

"Little Stella?"

Shaney felt embarrassed. "That's what we call my sister. She's named after our grandmother. We call Grandma *Big Stella* and my sister *Little Stella*."

"Oh, I see," Sissy said. "I was confused for a minute."

An awkward silence passed before Sissy spoke again.

"There's a reason I'm calling. I explained it all in the letter I sent you. It must've gotten lost in the mail. But I'll just tell you now. A few months ago, I had a very strong feeling that I needed to find my sisters. I'm sure your dad has told you stories about when we all lived with him and our mother Seffie."

Shaney cringed at the sound of her mother's name. "Yes, he has. He's talked about it a lot."

"You know about me and Starly being adopted?"

"Yes."

"Well, I was able to find Starly. It was hard, but I finally did it. I thought it would be easy to locate you and Stella, but when I didn't get a response to my letter, I started worrying. I couldn't find your names in the phone book."

"No, we aren't in the phone book. We only have a cell phone."

"I started calling all the McDaniels listed in the phone book," Sissy continued, "to see if I could locate a relative. And I finally found your father's older brother, Arthur McDaniel."

Oh my God, Shaney thought as the meaning of Uncle Art's recent visit became clear to her.

Another awkward silence ensued. Then Sissy said, "Shaney, is it okay that I called? When I didn't get an answer to my letter, I was afraid you didn't want any contact with me. Some people don't want their lives disturbed by someone from their past. But something in me said I had to give it another try."

"Oh, I'm glad you called," Shaney said, hoping she sounded convincing.

"In my letter, I talked about the idea of all four of us girls getting together again. Do you think you'd be interested in that?"

"I'll have to think about it."

"I understand." Sissy sounded disappointed.

"I don't mean to be rude," Shaney said. "I'm really glad you called. But I have to get used to the idea. I'm pretty sure I'll be interested. I just need some time."

"Of course," Sissy said. "I don't mean to rush you. What about Stella? Do you think she'll be interested?"

I doubt it, Shaney thought. But aloud, she said, "I really can't speak for her."

"Is Stella there? Can I talk to her?"

"Let me check." Shaney poked her head out her bedroom door. "Dad, is Little Stella here?"

"No," Jimmy said. "She went to the store a few minutes ago."

"She's not here," Shaney informed Sissy.

"That's okay," Sissy said. "I should let you go. This is probably enough excitement for you for one night."

"It's all right."

"Can I call you again? Or should I write you another letter? You can call me, too, if you want to. Let me give you my phone number."

"I have it," Shaney said. "It's on the caller ID. Where do you live, anyway?"

"South Bend. Not very far from you, actually." Sissy paused, and when Shaney didn't respond, she said, "Well, it was lovely talking with you, Shaney. You have no idea what this means to me. We'll talk again soon. Call me any time you want. And tell Stella I'm sorry I missed her."

After hanging up, Shaney stalked out to the living room and confronted her father. "Did we get a letter from Sissy? She said she sent one. Did you see it?"

"I haven't seen any letters." Jimmy still looked dazed from the shock of hearing from his stepdaughter. "Little Stella brings in the mail. She usually puts it there on the kitchen counter."

Shaney rushed to the kitchen and rifled through the pile of bills and junk mail lying on the sticky, cluttered countertop. There was no letter from Sissy.

Just then, Little Stella walked in the door with a six-pack of Coke and a bag of groceries from the Speedway station.

"Little Stella, what've you been doing with the mail?" Shaney barked. "We were supposed to get a letter from Sissy, and we didn't. I've looked through this mess several times, and it's not here." She flipped her hand through the stack of mail, making her point. Several envelopes fell to the floor, and one slid down into the narrow space between the cabinet and the stove.

Suddenly, Shaney knew exactly what had happened to Sissy's letter. She got down on her knees and peered into the dark crevice where the envelope had fallen. Sure enough, four or five pieces of mail had fallen into the space at some point in time.

"Bring me the broom, Little Stella," she demanded. Turning the broom upside down, she poked the handle into the small opening, dragging out the filth-covered mail. She picked up a grease-stained envelope addressed to Shaney and Stella McDaniel. The return address indicated the letter was from C. Hartman-Gray, South Bend, Indiana.

"Damn it, Little Stella, can't you keep track of anything?" she yelled. She took the letter into her bedroom and slammed the door.

August 26

Dear Shaney and Stella,

You must be very surprised to receive this letter. I am your older half-sister, Sissy. Many years ago, we all lived together with our mother, Seferina Dickerson. Shaney, you were two years old when I last saw you. Stella, you were just a baby, so you wouldn't remember me at all. We also have another sister, Starly. As I'm sure you know, Starly and I were both adopted. My adoptive parents changed my name to Cecily.

Several months ago, I started thinking about the times I shared with my sisters when we were little girls, and I just couldn't get you off my mind. I had a strong feeling that I wanted to find all of you.

So I began to do some research. I was able to find Starly. We've been corresponding, but we haven't met in person. I found your address through the internet.

I really hope we can get to know each other again. I've been talking with Starly about the possibility of all of us getting together in the near future. What do the two of you think about that?

Let me tell you a little bit about myself. I was raised by Leonard and Eileen Hartman in South Bend, and they've been wonderful parents to me. I was their only child. I've been married for four years to Stephen Gray. We don't have any children. Stephen is a chemist and a part-time professor at Notre Dame. I work at South Bend Community Mental Health Center as a therapist.

Please write back and tell me something about yourselves. And let me know how you feel about a meeting. I can't wait to hear from you!
With much love,
Cecily Hartman-Gray (Sissy)

Shaney sat motionless on the bottom bunk, staring at the letter. Never before in her life had she received news of this magnitude. Learning that she was pregnant with Cody had been quite a jolt. Big Stella's stroke and her subsequent move to a nursing home had also been life-changing. But hearing from a sister she barely remembered, someone she hadn't seen in twenty years, was an event that spun her world into a state of confusion.

She told herself she should be happy to hear from Sissy. But any excitement she might have felt was drowned out by bitterness. She could tell from the letter that Sissy had led a far more fortunate life than she had, that Sissy was lucky to have been adopted.

"Who does she think she is, barging into my life and throwing this up in my face?" she muttered.

She continued staring at the letter, trying to muster kind feelings toward her sister. *Maybe something good will come from this,* she thought. *Who knows?*

It suddenly dawned on her that the letter wasn't hers alone. It had been addressed to Little Stella as well. She carried the letter to the living room, where Little Stella was sitting in her recliner.

"You need to read this." Shaney handed her the letter.

Little Stella silently perused the letter, then handed it back to Shaney.

"Well?" Shaney said. "What do you think?"

Little Stella shrugged. "She's nothin' to me. I wasn't raised with 'er."

At that moment, Shaney felt caught in a nebulous space between the worlds of her sisters: an older sister gifted with a life far out of her reach, and a younger sister indifferent to anything but a mundane existence.

I'm not high and mighty, she thought, *but I'm not a lazy slob, either. Where do I fit in?*

Chapter 7

Most nights, Shaney could put aside the problems of the day and fall asleep within minutes of laying her head on the pillow. But that night, she lay wide awake, watching the patterns of light on the ceiling made by the headlights of passing traffic shining through her bedroom window. She felt spooked and jittery, teased by vague memories just out of reach of her conscious mind. She startled at each sudden noise in the trailer park, the slam of a car door or the loud voice of a neighbor.

In the early hours of the morning, she finally drifted off into a restless sleep, but around 7:00 AM, she was rudely awakened by a blow to her head with a pillow.

"Wake up, Mommy!" Cody shouted, rested and playful after his lengthy slumber. He scrambled onto the top bunk, crawled under the covers with her, and began tickling her in the ribs.

"Leave me alone, Cody," Shaney protested. But she knew there would be no more sleep. Groaning, she got up to start her day.

When she arrived at work that afternoon, Shaney was exhausted, distracted, and on the verge of tears. She forced herself to go through the motions of her job, but even the simplest tasks required extraordinary effort on her part. When the store was empty during the slow hours of the early afternoon, she sat down in the front booth and rested her aching head on her folded arms.

When Scott came by to check on the store, he was surprised to find his most ambitious employee in that position. "What are you doing, Shaney?" he asked.

Shaney startled and lifted her head. "Sorry, Scott." She quickly got up and began stocking the shelves behind the counter with cartons of cigarettes.

When Dort bustled in with her usual cheerful greeting, she found a subdued coworker, and her efforts at initiating conversation were met with half-hearted responses.

Scott came out of the back room to observe Shaney for a few

minutes. He'd been privy to her emotional ups and downs, but he'd never seen her like this before. Her distracted manner and slow, awkward movements were so unlike her usual energetic ways.

He watched a customer inform Shaney that she'd given him the wrong change. She mumbled an apology, and with shaking hands, corrected her error. After the man left the store, she turned away from the register, face in her hands, her shoulders heaving with sobs.

Scott usually made a point of staying out of his employees' personal problems. But Shaney's emotional distress was interfering with her work, and he decided to take action. He walked over to his bewildered mother and engaged her in a hushed conversation, then took Dort's place behind the cash register while she led the weeping Shaney to the back room.

"Honey, what on earth is going on?" Dort asked. She pulled a tissue from the box on Scott's desk and pressed it into Shaney's hand.

Shaney blew her nose. "I'm just tired," she sniffled. "I didn't get much sleep last night."

"Why not?"

"I don't know how to explain it."

"Take your time, sweetie. I'm listening."

"Well, I got a weird phone call last night."

"What do you mean? An obscene caller?"

Shaney shook her head. "No, it was from my sister. My older sister."

Dort looked puzzled. "I didn't know you had an older sister."

"Actually, I have two older sisters," Shaney said. "They're half-sisters. My mother's first two daughters. They weren't by my dad."

"Oh, yes," Dort said. "Now I remember. I hadn't thought about those girls in years. They were taken from your mother when they were just little tykes. I don't think people around here remember them."

"I barely remember Sissy, the oldest one," Shaney said. "But I don't remember Starly at all."

"So which one called you?" Dort asked.

"Sissy." Shaney's face twisted with pain.

"But that's wonderful, isn't it? Hearing from a long-lost sister?"

Shaney burst into tears again. "I don't know, I don't know," she sobbed. "I don't know why I feel this way."

Dort reached up and put her arms around Shaney, allowing the girl to weep on her shoulder. "I know this came as a shock to you, honey," she said. "It sure did stir up your feelings. But it'll be all right. It'll be all right."

Shaney's sobs subsided, and she pulled away from Dort's embrace. "Oh, shit," she said. "I probably look like a wreck now. Is my mascara smeared?"

Dort pulled several more tissues from the box and dabbed at the black smudges under Shaney's eyes. Shaney took a tissue and blew her nose again.

"What did Sissy want, anyway?" Dort asked when it seemed like Shaney was ready to talk again.

"She's been looking for me and Little Stella. She wants to get to know us. She wants all four of us sisters to get together some time soon."

"Wow!" Dort began to grasp the importance of the situation. She'd watched television shows about family members reuniting with long-lost loved ones, but she'd never been this close to such a story. "Shaney, this is exciting! This could change your life!"

Shaney's face clouded up again, but she forced herself to smile. She decided not to tell Dort about her resentful feelings toward Sissy. "Of course! It's stupid to be crying like this."

"Honey," Dort said, "you're all done in from the shock of this. Why don't you take the rest of the evening off? Go home and get some rest. Scotty and I can manage."

"No," Shaney said. "I'll be all right. If I go home early, Jimmy and Little Stella will be asking questions. I don't want them to know I got upset."

She ran her fingers through her hair and straightened her clothing, then marched out of the back room to finish her shift.

Two days later when Shaney came home from work, Little Stella said, "You got another letter from that girl in South Bend."

"You mean our sister," Shaney corrected her.

Little Stella shrugged. "Whatever."

"My God, Little Stella," Shaney muttered under her breath as she walked into the kitchen. She saw that Little Stella had flung the mail on the kitchen table instead of the counter. Apparently, she'd learned something from the episode of the lost letter. Shaney rifled through the pile and found the letter from Sissy, then sat down at the table to read it.

September 17

Dear Shaney and Stella,

I hope this letter finds both of you doing well. Shaney, I enjoyed talking with you last night. Stella, I'm so sorry I didn't get the chance to speak with you. Hopefully, we can talk soon.

I think it's been twenty years since I lived with the two of you. But you, my dear sisters, have been in my heart all that time. I often wondered who ended up raising you, and how your life turned out. I'm so glad to know you were able to stay with your father.

Since you didn't get the last letter I wrote, I thought I'd write another one, telling you a little bit more about myself. I was adopted when I was seven, by Leonard and Eileen Hartman. I'd been in and out of their home as a foster child for about four years, and when our mother lost her parental rights to me, I became legally theirs. I was raised as an only child. My adoptive parents are truly wonderful people. They've done so much for me.

But being adopted is complicated, and sometimes it's lonely. I always feel like I'm caught between two worlds. I love my adopted parents dearly, but I miss the family I was born into. And that's why it's so important to me to get to know my sisters. Nobody else can take your place in my heart.

I've been married to Stephen Gray for four years. He's a chemist, and he also teaches at Notre Dame. He's been a wonderful husband to me. We don't have children, although we're thinking about starting a family soon.

About four years ago, I started my career as a psychotherapist at

South Bend Community Mental Health Center. My specialty is family therapy. Ever since I was a little girl, I've wanted to dedicate my life to helping families. I'm sure that's because our family had so many problems when we were little.

I think that's all I'll say for now. I'll save the rest for later. I've been thinking about a time when the four of us can get together. I know that I'm entering your life uninvited. But I do hope you'll consider my invitation for a reunion. Please write back and let me know if you're interested. Also, tell me something about yourselves. You're still total strangers to me!

I'm going to write to Starly and let her know that I've made contact with you. She'll be as excited as I am!
Lots of Love,
Sissy
P.S. Please give your father my greetings. There was a time in my life when Jimmy was a father to me, also. He took good care of us girls, and I have warm feelings for him.

"Shit!" Shaney hissed as she angrily stuffed Sissy's letter back into the envelope. Once again, her resentment flared. *Compared to Sissy's life, my life is crap. Why does she think she needs to keep flaunting all her lucky breaks in my face?*

She sat staring into space, trying to regain her composure, trying to believe that her sister's arrival in her life could be a good thing. Then she got up from the table and went to the living room, where Little Stella was watching TV.

"This letter's for you, too," she said, tossing the envelope into her lap.

Little Stella tossed the letter back at her. "I'm not interested."

"Why not?" Shaney asked.

"I told you, she's nothin' to me. I wasn't raised with her."

Little Stella doesn't care about anything, Shaney thought. *No feelings, no imagination, no dreams.* She decided to test her.

"What about me?" she asked. "Am I something to you?"

Little Stella didn't respond. Her attention was back on the program she was watching.

Shaney planted herself in her sister's line of vision, obstructing her view of the television. "What about me?" she repeated. "I was raised with you. Am I something to you?"

"Leave me alone, Shaney," Little Stella barked.

"Answer my question," Shaney demanded.

"Leave me alone!" Little Stella picked up an empty Coke can from the end table and threw it at Shaney.

"Ouch!" Shaney yelled when the can struck her arm.

"What are you girls fussin' about?" Jimmy called from his bedroom. "Quiet down, I'm tryin' to sleep."

Shaney picked up the letter and carried it to her father's bedroom. "We got another letter from Sissy," she said. "You wanna read it?"

"Sure," Jimmy said. "Turn on the light, would you?"

With great effort, he pulled himself to a sitting position, and then reached for the letter. He read it slowly, silently forming the words with his mouth, his multiple chins aquiver. When he reached the end, Shaney saw a tear trickle down his cheek.

"Well, well, well." Jimmy's voice was soft and husky. "Ain't this just somethin'! I never expected to hear from that little girl again. Ain't this somethin'!"

He fell silent and began reading the letter again. This time his eyes crinkled with laughter. "Who'd ever imagine that our little Sissy would become somethin' as high falutin' as a therapist? A family therapist! We needed a family therapist back in those days, we surely did. And here Sissy goes off to college and becomes one! A little too late to do us any good, though."

The irony of the situation seemed to amuse him, and his huge body heaved with laughter. "A family therapist! Tee-hee-hee, a family therapist!"

Bewildered by her father's reaction, Shaney retrieved the letter and backed out of the room.

Seven-year-old Shaney sits in the chilly beige office of Mrs. Titus, the school social worker. The vinyl of the chair is cold and clammy against her bare legs. Her eyes are wide and scared, and she nervously twists a lock of her curly hair. Jimmy and Big Stella sit on the couch facing Mrs. Titus, two huge mounds of silent anger.

In her prissy voice, Mrs. Titus is listing her concerns related to Shaney's behavior in the second grade classroom. Shaney doesn't follow instructions. She can't seem to stay in her seat. She bothers other children while they're trying to work. She talks back to the teacher.

Shaney curls into a ball of shame and huddles in the corner of her chair.

"I think you should have her checked out by her pediatrician," Mrs. Titus says. "And I'm also suggesting that you try family counseling." She writes on a piece of paper and hands it to Jimmy. "You can call this number for an appointment."

No one says a word to Shaney in the car. When they get home, she tries to run and hide in her room. But Jimmy grabs her up in his massive hands and plunks her bottom down on the kitchen counter. He brings his face, dark and contorted with rage, nose to nose with hers.

"You listen to me, little girl," he snarls, his breath hot and stinking, his voice low and ominous. "Don't you even think you're gonna pull the same shit your mother pulled. I've had enough of the Welfare Department and those damn social workers to last me a lifetime. You're not bringin' them people back into our lives again, you hear me? Now knock off the crap at school, or you're gonna wish you had!"

Jimmy never hears from Mrs. Titus again. Shaney always begs her not to call.

Shaney went to work the next day with more than her usual level of energy. During the slow hours of the day, she cleaned, polished and straightened everything in sight. Dort was happy that her coworker had recovered from the shock that had slowed her down several days earlier, but little did she know Shaney's energy was fueled by anger.

"Have you heard from your sister again?" she asked late in the evening, when it appeared Shaney's frenetic activity was slowing down.

Shaney turned and fixed her with a cold stare. "Yes, I did!" She spat out the words.

"And . . . ?"

Shaney reached into her pocket, pulled out the letter, and slapped it into Dort's hand. "Read it yourself!"

Dort perused the letter and then looked up, not sure what reaction Shaney wanted from her. "What did Stella think of this?" she asked.

"She didn't read it. She said she wasn't interested. You know how Little Stella is."

"Are you going to write Sissy back?"

Shaney snatched the letter and shoved it back into her pocket. "Just what do I have to say to her?" Her words spewed out like hot lava from a volcano. "What am I supposed to say to someone who brags about all the lucky breaks she's had in her life? That I'm so proud I got knocked up when I was sixteen? That I'm raising a kid I can barely support? That I never finished high school, and will probably work at a gas station all my life? That I still live with my daddy in a rundown trailer park? That I come from the number one white trash family in town? That I'm just so thrilled her life is so perfect?"

She turned and stomped off to wipe down the booths one more time. Dort followed her.

"Shaney, hon, listen to me."

Shaney gave no indication that she heard Dort's words. Dort took her by the shoulders and turned her around.

"Listen to me, Shaney. You know I love you like the daughter I never had. You know I don't give you advice just for the sake of hearing myself talk. I'm giving you advice because I care about you. You can take it or leave it.

"I know you're not happy with your life, and I can see why your sister's letter got you all riled up. But honey, she means well. Her love for you is all through that letter. I don't think you should give up this chance to meet her. If it turns out that you don't like her and you don't want to see her anymore, well, you don't have to. But you'll never know if you don't try."

She gazed into Shaney's stony face. "Shaney, I have the feeling that something good could come of this for you. Don't turn your back on your sister just because you're not happy with yourself. But you have nothing to be ashamed of. Nothing. And what you said about white trash, that's not true. You're not white trash, you're far from it. And it doesn't make sense, because Sissy came from the same family you came from."

Dort's last statement elicited a bitter chuckle from Shaney, but she offered no other response.

"Think about it, Shaney," Dort insisted. "At least think about it."

"Okay, okay!" Shaney shrugged Dort's hands from her arms and turned back to her cleaning.

Suddenly she stopped and looked at Dort, her eyes filled with pain. "I just don't want . . . I just don't want to dig up all that stuff from back then."

"What stuff, honey?" Dort asked, bewildered.

Shaney didn't answer, and Dort decided it was best to let the matter drop.

But Shaney did give Dort's advice some consideration. By the end of her shift, the heat of her anger had dissipated, and she began contemplating the idea of including another sister in her life. Little bursts of excitement shot through her body, alternating with surges of resentment.

Within the next couple of days, word got around town that one of Seffie Dickerson's older daughters had resurfaced and was trying to re-unify with the McDaniel girls. Shaney would have preferred to keep the news to herself, at least until she figured out what she was going to do about it.

However, she knew that privacy in a little town like Belmont was impossible. Dort had undoubtedly told the story to a few of her friends, and the day after reading Sissy's second letter, Jimmy had strutted into the store, eager to share the big news with his cronies.

But what made the situation especially irritating to Shaney was that the story came back to her in distorted forms. When the Robertson twins stopped by the store one afternoon, Clifton said, "We heard your older sister's moving back to town."

Shaney sighed and rolled her eyes. "No, she's not moving back here. She just wrote me a couple of letters. That's all."

But the twins preferred their version of the story. They left the store laughing and elbowing each other in the ribs, speculating on what they'd like to do to Shaney's sister when they met her.

Shaney stared at them, shaking her head. "Idiots!" she said to Dort. "I just hate it when things like this happen."

After Roger Whalen paid Shaney for his coffee that evening, he hesitated at the register. "I heard you got a letter from a sister you haven't seen in years," he said. "Somebody told me she wants you to move to where she lives."

"Oh, no, no, no!" Shaney laughed. "She just wants us to get together, just to talk and get to know each other."

"Oh, okay." Roger seemed relieved.

When Petey came into the store that evening, his buzzing and muttering seemed more purposeful than usual. He focused his good eye on Shaney, raised his voice, and aimed a lively stream of gibberish in her direction. He punctuated his monologue with three sharp cackles, then turned and left the store.

"Now even Petey knows my business," Shaney sighed as she sprayed Lysol into the air.

Chapter 8

Sheriff Wilcox's hog roast was scheduled for the last Saturday in September, and Scott had granted Shaney's request for another day off.

"Damn it, Dort, I wish he would've said no," Shaney grumbled as she stuffed the tickets she'd purchased into her handbag. "I don't wanna take my dad and Little Stella to that stupid pig roast!"

Dort looked puzzled. "Then why did you ask for the day off? You could've just told your dad you had to work."

"You don't understand how things go in my family," Shaney said. "If I don't take them, I'll never hear the end of it. My dad will carry on for weeks."

Saturday turned out to be an unusually hot day for late September. Shaney swore loudly as she wrestled Jimmy's chair into the trunk of the old Buick. Then she tied the trunk lid down with a piece of the twine Jimmy kept around for such occasions.

Already wound up from the can of soda Little Stella had given him, Cody ran in excited circles around the car. Shaney could hear Jimmy moving heavily about inside the trailer, fussing like an old woman as he made preparations for the outing.

"Shaney, what did you do with that John Deere cap the twins gave me?" he shouted out the door. "Gotta have somethin' to keep the sun outa my eyes."

"I didn't do anything with that stupid cap," Shaney shouted back. "I haven't even seen it."

She leaned against the car, waiting on her father and sister, knowing she might as well be patient. Finally, the trailer door opened and Jimmy lumbered out, John Deere cap on his head. In spite of his morning bath, beads of sweat stood out on his face, and the armpits of his tee shirt were already soaked. Little Stella followed, carrying an old blanket.

A now familiar thought flitted through Shaney's mind: *what would Sissy think of this?* All week long, she'd been trying to picture her life through her older sister's eyes. *What would Sissy think of this old junk heap of a car? This nasty trailer? What would Sissy think of big fat Jimmy? Of frumpy Little Stella? Of unruly Cody?*

She looked down at her cheap tank top and denim shorts. *What would Sissy think about the way she dressed? What would Sissy think about her, period?* She wondered if Sissy would be less interested in a reunion if she knew what kind of lives her sisters lived.

"Open up the trunk," Little Stella grunted, gesturing that she wanted to put the blanket in with the chair.

"No," Shaney snapped. "I just got it tied down. Take the blanket in the back seat with you."

Little Stella stood glaring at her sister, refusing to budge.

"Good God, Little Stella," Shaney grumbled as she undid the knot on the twine.

"Hurry up, there, Shaney," Jimmy huffed as he approached the car. "We got a long drive ahead of us."

Shaney had counted on a forty-minute drive to Plymouth, but they made the trip in twenty-five. When they arrived at Centennial Park half an hour before the event was to start, hardly anyone else was there.

A large tent had been erected next to the empty bandstand, and four hogs were roasting in huge drums over coals. Six charcoal grills were loaded with ears of corn roasting in their husks. A few men bustled about, checking the corn, turning the drums of meat, and tending pots of beans inside the tent. The heavy aroma of baked beans and roasting pork wafted through the open car windows.

"Why don't we wait in the car for awhile?" Shaney suggested as Jimmy opened his door and began to heave himself out. "We're early."

"Hell, no!" Jimmy retorted. "I'm gonna get me a good seat."

"I wanna get out and play!" Cody shouted as soon as he spotted a swing set and slide. He bolted out of the car and ran to the playground before Shaney could stop him.

Shaney followed reluctantly as Jimmy and Little Stella slowly made their way toward the tent. Little Stella carried the chair while Jimmy had the blanket draped over one arm. Jimmy stopped directly in front of the bandstand.

"I'm gonna sit here," he announced. "I heard the sheriff's brother Ronnie and his band are gonna do some live entertainment, and I wanna see it."

He took the chair from Little Stella and paced around until he found a level spot on the ground. Then he settled himself onto the chair, happily waiting for the festivities to begin. Little Stella spread the blanket on the ground and lay down on her side, watching the activity in the tent.

Embarrassed by the spectacle Jimmy and Little Stella were creating, Shaney sat down at a picnic table under a tree twenty yards away.

"Come on over here, Shaney," Jimmy called. "You can get a good view of the band." He grinned broadly when one of the men in the tent waved at him.

"I have to sit where I can keep an eye on Cody." Shaney was glad for the excuse to keep her distance from her father and sister.

What would Sissy think of this hog roast? She couldn't imagine her sophisticated sister in such an environment. She tried to picture Sissy in her mind, imagining her as beautiful and slender in elegant clothing. But she hoped her picture was wrong. *Maybe Sissy's fat and plain like Little Stella. Maybe I can at least outdo her in the looks department.* The thought comforted Shaney.

"Why, look there!" Jimmy pointed toward a uniformed man inside the tent. "I do believe that's Sheriff Wilcox. I know him from his picture in the paper." His eyes shone with excitement as he followed the sheriff's movements. Little Stella sat up to get a better view.

More people began arriving at the park. Families with swarms of children filled up picnic tables, unfolded lawn chairs, and spread blankets on the grass. Shaney surveyed the crowd from her isolated spot under the tree. She didn't see anyone she knew, and she suspected that most of the people had come from Plymouth.

"God, I wish I wasn't here," she muttered.

Before long, Sheriff Wilcox came out of the tent to mingle with the crowd. He walked over to Jimmy and extended his hand.

"Hello," he said in a jovial voice. "I'm Herb Wilcox."

Jimmy's mouth hung open in amazement. He grabbed the Sheriff's big hand and pumped it enthusiastically. "I'm Jim McDaniel, from Belmont."

"From Belmont, huh?" the sheriff said. "Glad you came out. I'd appreciate your support on election day."

"You bet, Sheriff Wilcox!" Jimmy said, still pumping vigorously. Then he nodded toward Little Stella. "This here's my daughter, Stella. She'll be votin' for you, too."

The Sheriff extricated his hand from Jimmy's grasp and extended it to Little Stella. "Pleased to meet you, Stella," he said. She smiled and gave his hand a limp shake.

Sheriff Wilcox ambled away to greet others in the crowd. Jimmy sat grinning from ear to ear. *You'd think he just shook the hand of the Queen of England,* Shaney thought. She felt relieved that Jimmy hadn't pointed her out as his other daughter, but also hurt that he hadn't thought to do so.

Several men came out of the tent and began carving meat from the hogs. Another man shouted to the crowd that the food was ready. Shaney went to the playground and rounded up a resistant Cody. She managed to get him through the food line with a minimum of disturbance to the people around them, and guided him back to their picnic table with a plate full of food.

Cody took a mouthful of beans, talking excitedly about what some boy on the playground had done. He nibbled on his ear of corn. "Yuck!" he said, throwing it on the ground.

"Try some of the meat," Shaney urged. "This is a hog roast. This is special meat."

Cody poked at the meat with a dirty finger. "It's gross!" He took a long drink of his fruit punch. "I'm not hungry," he said, looking comical with his pink mustache stain. "I wanna play."

"Okay," Shaney sighed. Quick as a flash, Cody was off to the playground again. Shaney retrieved his ear of corn and threw it into a trash can. Then she sat down and began to pick at the remains of his food. She found she wasn't hungry, either.

Little Stella came out of the tent with two plates piled high. She handed one to Jimmy and set the other one down on the blanket. Then she went back into the tent and re-emerged with two paper cups filled with fruit punch.

For years, Shaney had witnessed the unpleasant spectacle of Jimmy and Little Stella's voracious eating. But that afternoon, she watched from a new perspective, through Sissy's eyes. Little Stella sat cross-legged on the quilt, head bent low over the plate on her lap. She shoveled large bites into her mouth, chewing mechanically, not pausing to look around. The pace of her eating remained unchanged until her plate was empty.

Jimmy tore ravenously into his meat, his jowls shiny with pork grease. Bringing his plate close to his mouth, he spooned in the beans, dribbling juice down the front of his tee shirt. Then he tackled his ear of corn, chomping noisily down one row after the other.

When he finished, he set his plate on the grass beside him and wiped his greasy hands on the legs of his overalls. He belched loudly, then turned to Little Stella and said, "I believe I'll have some more of them beans." Little Stella picked up both empty plates and disappeared into the food tent again.

"Good Lord, what would Sissy think?" Shaney muttered under her breath. She suddenly felt nauseated. She got up and tossed the rest of her food into the trash can. Then, with one hand shading her eyes, she scanned the crowd of children on the playground. She spotted Cody darting around in the group. *He's okay for now,* she thought. She sat back down at her picnic table, waiting for the miserable afternoon to come to an end.

Then she saw Terence Buckwalter sauntering toward her, wearing his jaunty cowboy hat. Shaney hadn't seen him in the store for a week. She'd almost forgotten about him, as she'd been preoccupied with thoughts about Sissy.

"Hey there, good lookin'," he called. He sat down on the bench next to her, and putting one arm around her shoulders, he gave her a friendly squeeze. "I saw you sittin' over here all by your lonesome, and I thought I oughta pay you a visit."

"Hi, Terence." Shaney's voice was flat.

"Whatsamatter, little darlin'?" he crooned. "You're lookin' all down in the dumps. What's on your mind? Come on, talk to Terence. He's got some broad shoulders for you to cry on." He gave Shaney another squeeze and brushed her cheek with a kiss.

The kiss burned on Shaney's face, and she wanted to reach up and touch the spot. Her mind raced wildly. She remembered the evening she and Terence sat talking in the booth at the Speedway Station, and she felt warm and happy. Then she recalled Dort's advice, and suddenly felt frightened. A question flitted through her mind: *What would Sissy think about Terence?* She was quite sure the answer wouldn't be positive.

But Terence cares, she said to herself. *See the way he is now? He understands how I feel. He's a good friend. Dort's wrong about him, and I don't give a damn what Sissy would think.*

She took a deep breath and began to talk. "You're right. I do have a lot on my mind. You just wouldn't believe what happened to me about a week and a half ago. I got a phone call from a strange woman who said she was my sister. I've never met her. Well, I guess I did when I was really little, but I haven't seen her since I was two. Anyway, I barely remember her."

She glanced sideways at Terence. His arm had slid off her shoulders, and his eyes looked vacant and bored. He startled when he realized she was looking at him. "Go on," he said, "I'm listening."

"Well," Shaney continued, "she said she'd been looking for me and my other two sisters, and she wants us all to get together. I feel so mixed up. I don't know what to do."

She glanced at Terence again. His eyes were riveted on a group of people at the edge of the crowd. "Uh oh," he said. "There's Jeff Richards. I need to talk to him. Son-of-a-bitch owes me fifty bucks. Sorry, darlin', I'll catch you later." He rested his hand on Shaney's bare thigh, and then got up and walked away.

Tears stung Shaney's eyes as she watched Terence's broad back moving away from her. He'd taken on his arrogant swagger, and was now waving and calling loudly to the group at the edge of the crowd. *Dort's right,* she thought. *What a snake!*

Terence's group of friends consisted of half a dozen men and women who appeared to be in their twenties. They were drinking from soda cans, and seemed to getting rowdier by the minute. Several of them were undoubtedly drunk. Shaney knew that alcoholic beverages weren't allowed in the park, but she suspected Terence's friends had sneaked in their drinks in other containers. She knew the trick. She'd done that sort of thing as a young teenager.

When Terence reached the group, a young man pulled a Mountain Dew can out of a cooler and offered it to him. Terence accepted the drink, laughing loudly. Shaney wondered why someone as old as Terence was hanging out with such a young crowd. Then she remembered that just a few minutes earlier, he'd been hanging out with another young person, herself. It occurred to her that Terence had never matured beyond that stage, and probably never would.

She watched him fondle the bare midriff of a young woman in a halter top. He whispered something in her ear, then kissed her cheek. Shaney felt like throwing up. "God, can this day get any worse?" she muttered to herself.

The twang of a banjo rose above the noise of the crowd. Glad for the diversion, she turned her attention toward the bandstand, where several men were setting up speakers and tuning their instruments. Then the sheriff's brother, Ronnie Wilcox, stepped forward and introduced his bluegrass band, *The Rocky Top Boys*. The band launched into their theme song, followed by *Blue Moon of Kentucky* and *Fox on the Run*.

A couple of scruffy men began a silly dance in front of the bandstand, stomping and swinging each other hoedown style. The crowd hooted and whistled.

The lively music lifted Shaney's spirits, and she found herself tapping her foot and clapping with the rest of the crowd. But then Ronnie began crooning *Blue Eyes Cryin' in the Rain* in his mournful nasal voice, and her melancholy mood returned.

Suddenly, she heard a piercing cry from the direction of the playground. She realized it had been awhile since she'd checked on Cody. She sprinted over to the playground, where she found her son and another little boy thrashing around in a heated fight. Cody had a fist full of the other child's hair, and the little boy was screaming hysterically.

"Stop it, Cody!" Shaney shouted. She grabbed her son and squeezed his hand until he released the hair. Cody continued to kick out at the other child while Shaney dragged him away.

"What's going on?" she demanded to know.

Cody stopped raging and began to sob. "He . . . called me . . . a . . . nigger boy! I'm . . . not . . . a . . . nigger boy!"

Shaney shuddered. Now and then, dark-skinned Cody became the object of racial slurs, and the names he was called chilled her to the bone.

"No, of course you're not a nigger boy." Shaney hugged her son tightly. "It's time you come sit with me." She took Cody's hand and coaxed him to walk beside her. "Come on. We can listen to the music together."

"Don't wanna sit with you."

"Okay, then. You can sit with Grandpa." Shaney led her scowling child to where Jimmy and Little Stella were sitting. "Keep an eye on him, will you?"

"Come here, son." Jimmy smiled and reached toward Cody. "Come sit here with Grandpa." Cody obediently sat down on the quilt next to Jimmy's chair. He looked tired, and Shaney hoped he would fall asleep.

She headed back toward her picnic table under the tree, but saw that someone else had claimed it in her absence. So she stood at the edge of the crowd in front of the bandstand, watching the dancers.

The group of dancers had grown to a dozen couples, who entertained the crowd with their ridiculous gyrations. A man in a black tee shirt with a bandana tied over his long hair held his hand out toward Shaney, inviting her to dance. She shook her head, shrinking away from him.

Then she heard a familiar voice calling. "Hey Seffie! I mean Shaney! Hey Shaney!"

Jolted by the sound of the two names, she turned and saw Terence pushing his way toward her through the crowd. He was staggering slightly, slurring his words. "Shaney! You better not dance with that asshole! Come dance with me!"

Shaney froze, not knowing what to do. But at that moment, she heard a child's cry and instantly knew it was Cody. She glanced toward Jimmy and Little Stella. Both were mesmerized by the entertainment, oblivious to the fact that Cody was not with them.

The cry sounded again. Shaney turned and bolted toward the playground. She knew Terence would think she was running from him, and that he'd be angry. She had an excuse. She had to get to her son. But she was also running away from Terence Buckwalter as fast as she could, as if her life depended on it. His awful words echoed in her mind: *Hey Seffie . . . I mean Shaney.*

Cody and the little boy were fighting again. Shaney grabbed her screaming son and headed back toward the crowd. He kicked her shins and pounded on her chest, and it was all she could do to keep her hold on him. She made her way toward Jimmy, who turned when he heard Cody's screams. She mouthed the words, "We've got to go!" Jimmy frowned and shook his head.

"We've got to go!" Shaney shouted. "Now!"

By the time she got Cody to the car, he'd stopped struggling, and his shrieks had given way to heart-wrenching sobs. She sat him down in the front passenger seat, where he curled up and popped his thumb into his mouth. Then she slid into the driver's seat and leaned her head against the half-open window, allowing tears to stream from her own eyes. The rhythm of her sobs soon matched those of her child.

When she heard the crunch of heavy feet on the gravel, she raised her head and wiped her eyes with the back of her hand, then got out of the car and loaded Jimmy's chair into the trunk. She scooped Cody out of the front seat, holding him tightly for a moment before depositing him on the back seat beside Little Stella.

"I was enjoyin' myself," Jimmy grumbled as he eased himself into the car. "Don't know why we can't go nowhere without havin' problems."

Chapter 9

"Have you written to your sister yet?" Dort asked Shaney at work the next day.

"No," Shaney snapped. "I'm still thinking about it."

Dort decided it was best not to ask any more questions.

After a week of obsessing about Sissy, Shaney realized she hadn't even begun to contemplate the idea of her other sister. She had enough information about Sissy to form a mental picture of her, but Starly remained a total mystery.

The mail came early on Tuesday, and Shaney brought it in before she left for work. When she tossed it on the kitchen table, she saw an envelope addressed to Shaney and Stella McDaniel, in large, rounded handwriting. The return address told her the letter came from Annie Kauffman in Bremen, Indiana.

"What on earth!" Shaney exclaimed. "Who the hell is Annie Kauffman?" She sat down at the table and tore open the envelope.

September 25

Dear Shaney and Stella,

You're probably very surprised to receive this letter. I'm your sister Starly. Sissy wrote to me last week to tell me the wonderful news that she found you. I was so happy! She gave me your address because she thought I should write to you and tell you something about myself.

God has blessed me with a wonderful life. I was adopted by Jonas and Martha Bontrager. They've been very good to me, and they've helped me through a lot of difficulties. We are of the Amish faith.

I have six older brothers, but the only sisters I have are the two of you and Sissy!

I'm married to Luke Kauffman, and we have two children. Daniel is five and Sarah is two. I'm now carrying our third child. It is due to be born in six weeks. We live on a farm, just a few miles from my parents' home.

Even though I love my parents very much, I've always wondered about my sisters from my birth family. It seems like God has worked a miracle in bringing us together after so many years of being apart. Every day in my prayers, I thank God for Sissy, Shaney, and Stella.

Shaney, you were a baby when I stayed in Seffie's home. But my mother reminded me of something I'd almost forgotten. When you were two, you were a foster child in our home for a week. Do you remember that?

Stella, I didn't even know you existed until Sissy told me about you. You weren't born yet when I was at Seffie's house.

I can't tell you how much I'm looking forward to meeting you! There are so many things we can talk about. I hope the day of our visit will arrive soon. If not, I might burst with excitement!

Love,

Your sister Annie (Starly)

P.S. You may be puzzled about my name. Our birth mother named me Starly Ann. The name Starly isn't right for an Amish person, so my parents called me by my middle name and raised me as Annie. But I'd like my sisters to call me Starly.

Shaney stared openmouthed at the letter in front of her. "Oh my God!" she exclaimed. "I can't believe it! Starly is Amish!"

She felt dazed and a little weak. All her life, she'd seen Amish buggies on the road, and once in a while when she went to Plymouth, she'd see Amish people in the stores. She'd never thought much about them.

But now she had an Amish sister. More than that, she herself had stayed with an Amish family when she was a child. Try as she might, she couldn't wrap her mind around that idea.

Two-year-old Shaney lies sleepily in the crook of Martha Bontrager's arm. She's just come out of a warm bath, and her damp curls are sticking to her forehead. She's wearing a long flannel nightgown and a soft cloth diaper.

Martha tucks a quilt around Shaney's tiny body and begins to rock and sing. Shaney's thumb moves to her mouth. Her eyelids droop. She snuggles against Martha's warm breast, and her breathing becomes slow and deep.

The room is completely still except for the creak of the rocker and the sound of Martha's strange, sweet song. Then Shaney hears soft footsteps approaching, and feels a small hand caress the top of her head.

"Say goodnight to your baby sister, Annie," Martha says.

Shaney feels a kiss on her forehead, and her eyes flutter open. "Goodnight, Baby Shaney," Annie whispers. Then the footsteps move away.

Little Shaney closes her eyes and sleeps soundly.

Rousing herself from her reverie, Shaney glanced at her watch. It was a few minutes past two o'clock. She was late for work. She shoved the letter into the pocket of her jeans, then dashed out the door and sprinted all the way to the Speedway station.

That afternoon, Shaney floated dreamily through her work. Nothing upset her. Ornery customers hassled and teased her, but instead of responding with her usual sharp retorts, she smiled sweetly.

Dort had been privy to Shaney's erratic moods the past week, but this behavior was new to her. "What kind of high are you on, girl?" she teased.

Little Stella came in for a Coke, and Shaney was almost happy to see her. She walked over to the booth where her sister was sitting. "Guess what?"

Little Stella looked up at Shaney suspiciously. "What?"

"We got another letter."

Little Stella shrugged. "So?"

Shaney took Starly's letter from her pocket and laid it on the table. "Seriously, you gotta read this one." She walked back to her place behind the counter, where she watched Little Stella's face. She knew she'd get a reaction this time.

Dort reached over and put her hand on Shaney's forehead, as if checking for a fever. "You feeling okay? You were almost nice to your sister!"

Little Stella read the letter, and then looked up at Shaney, her eyes wide with amazement. "Wow!" she exclaimed.

Shaney chuckled at her sister's shocked expression.

"She's really got a thing about God, doesn't she?" Little Stella said. Then her eyes crinkled in amusement. "Shaney, you're partly Amish! You were raised partly Amish!"

"Don't be ridiculous!" Shaney shot back. "I only stayed there a week."

"What on earth are you girls talking about?" Dort asked.

"It's a letter from our other sister, Starly," Shaney explained.

Little Stella handed Dort the letter, and then continued to tease her sister. "Shaney Rose! Shaney's not a good name for an Amish girl. Maybe we should start callin' you Rosie."

"Knock it off, Little Stella." Shaney's protest was mild. She hated her middle name, and Little Stella knew that. But she didn't want to spoil her good mood by arguing with her sister.

Dort finished the letter. "Well, I'll be! You girls have an Amish sister! I wouldn't have imagined that in a million years!" She handed the letter back to Shaney. "Do you know anything about the Amish?"

"I've seen them all my life," Shaney said. "I know they ride in buggies."

"I've seen Amish people in stores," Little Stella added. "Those Amish women wear long dresses and big black bonnets." She grinned. "Wonder what you'd look like in one of them bonnets, Shaney."

Dort laughed heartily. "I'd love to see that!"

The door opened, and Scott limped in.

"You just missed some big news, Scotty," Dort said. "Remember me telling you about Shaney and Stella's sisters? Well, they just found out one of them is Amish."

"You're kidding me!" Scott exclaimed. "There's no way that's true!"

"It is true," Dort said. "They got a letter from their Amish sister today."

"Hey Scott," Little Stella said, still in her playful mood. "Can you imagine Shaney all dressed up like an Amish woman, with that black bonnet and all?"

Scott turned to look at Shaney, and her face reddened under his gaze. "Yes, I can picture that," he said. "And she still looks beautiful."

"So, have you decided what you're going to do about those sisters of yours?" Dort asked Shaney when they were alone again.

Shaney smiled broadly. "I'm going to that meeting! This is too much to miss, one sister all high and mighty and the other one Amish. I gotta see that."

"That's my girl!" Dort wrapped her arms around Shaney and gave her an affectionate squeeze.

That evening, Shaney showed her father the letter from Starly. "Why didn't you tell me Starly lived with an Amish family?" she asked.

Jimmy frowned and scratched his head. "Well, to tell you the truth, I never thought much about it. I just didn't think to tell you."

"Did you ever meet Starly's family?"

"Matter of fact, I did. That week you were stayin' there, I went to visit you a couple of times. Them Amish folks were real good about me comin' over. One time, they asked me to stay for supper. Real nice people, they were. Took real good care of you."

Jimmy appeared deep in thought. Shaney stood up to leave the room, but stopped when he spoke again.

"You know, I felt real bad when them older girls got taken away. But when they took you, my own flesh and blood, it purty near broke my heart. Yep, I went over there to see you, 'cause I didn't want you to forget I was your daddy."

A sob rose from Shaney's stomach. As it escaped her throat, she turned it into a cough. She coughed several more times, turning away from her father so he couldn't see the tears in her eyes.

Chapter 10

Once Shaney made up her mind to cooperate with Sissy's reunion plans, she saw no reason to delay her response. She woke up Thursday morning determined to write a letter to her sister.

Now, how do I do this? she asked herself. No one in the McDaniel household owned a computer, so the letter would have to be handwritten. She rummaged around in the messy kitchen drawers and found a few sheets of unlined paper, but they were dirty and crumpled. She remembered that Cody had some wide-lined paper in his schoolbag, but that wouldn't do, either.

I guess I'll have to buy some, she thought. Then she called to Cody, "Wanna go to the store with Mommy?"

Ten minutes later, Shaney stood in front of the stationary display at the drugstore, considering her options. She wasn't sure what she wanted, but she knew she didn't want her letter to look tacky. Cody began to whine impatiently, so she made a quick selection, a box of note cards with a scenic picture on the front.

Back at home, she sat down at the kitchen table to re-read her sisters' letters before beginning her response. She couldn't remember the last time she'd written a letter to anyone. She decided to write her first draft on scrap paper, so as not to ruin one of the note cards if she made a mistake.

October 1

Dear Sissy,

I'm sorry it took me so long to write back to you. I had to think awhile before I could answer your letter.

You already know that when all of us girls got taken away from our mother, my dad got to keep Stella and me. We've always lived here in Belmont. I have a son named Cody, and he's five years old. He just started kindergarten this year.

Shaney thought about following her sisters' leads in praising their parents. *Should I tell them Jimmy was a good dad?* She wasn't entirely sure that was true, so she decided not to say anything about the nature of her upbringing. She decided not to write anything about her job, either, as she didn't think working at a gas station sounded impressive.

She looked at Sissy and Starly's letters again, and realized she needed to say how she felt about meeting her long-lost sisters. Taking a deep breath, she began to write again.

I have decided to come to the meeting you're planning. I'm looking forward to meeting you and Starly. It will be nice to get to know sisters I haven't seen for so many years.

I need to say whether or not Little Stella is coming, she thought. *Sissy expects both of us to be there.* She knew what Little Stella's answer would be, but she got up and walked to the open door of her sister's room, where she was still lounging in bed.

"Little Stella?" she called. "I'm writing a letter to Sissy to let her know I'll be going to the meeting she's planning. She needs to have an answer from you, too."

Yawning sleepily, Little Stella rolled from her side onto her back. "I already told you," she said. "Those girls are nothin' to me. Now stop buggin' me about it."

Shaney went back to the kitchen table and wrote:

But I don't think Stella will be coming. Just let me know when you're going to have this meeting so I can make sure to get the day off work.
Sincerely,
Shaney McDaniel

Shaney perused what she'd written and decided it would do. She copied the letter onto one of her note cards. As she sealed the envelope, anxiety fluttered in her stomach. She hurried to the post office to mail the letter before she could change her mind.

"I did it!" Shaney told Dort that afternoon at work. "I wrote a letter to Sissy telling her I'd go to the meeting."

Dort smiled. "Look out, world, here comes Shaney!"

Shaney looked puzzled. "Why did you say that?"

"This whole thing could change your life, honey. I just have that feeling about it. You're not going to be the same person."

The store was unusually busy that evening, and the booths were filled with a noisy crowd of local customers. Scott had work to do in the store, and he'd brought his children with him. Since Blake and Miranda had no place to sit, they wandered in and out of the back room, and it seemed like Dort, Shaney, Scott, and the children were constantly bumping into each other. In spite of the aggravation, Shaney felt light-hearted.

But her mood changed abruptly when Terence Buckwalter sauntered through the door. "Oh shit, oh shit," she hissed, wishing she could duck down behind the counter. She had known she'd have to face Terence sooner or later, but she'd tried to block that unpleasant thought from her mind.

"What's wrong?" Dort asked.

"It's Terence!" Shaney whispered.

Dort looked at her, bewildered. Shaney hadn't told her what had transpired between her and Terence at the hog roast.

Terence was wearing his usual broad, toothy smile, but there was something sinister about his manner that evening. He strolled over to Shaney's register and leaned in close to her. She recoiled when she detected the sour odor of whiskey on his breath. Her right hand was resting on the counter, and Terence covered it with his left hand.

"So you thought you could run away from me the other day." He grinned evilly. "Let me tell you a little secret, darlin'. It's not that easy to get away from Terence Buckwalter."

Inside, Shaney felt like a scared little girl, but she faced Terence with a cold stare. "Leave me alone, Terence. I'm not interested in you." She tried to free the hand he was holding captive.

But his big hand clamped down hard. "So you think you're too good for me, huh? Well, let me tell you somethin', sweetheart. If your mother wasn't too good for me, then neither are you, girlie, neither are you."

Terence's words hit Shaney with the force of a hammer blow, and she reeled backward. Her stomach churned, and her chest felt so tight she struggled to breathe. She tried to jerk her hand away, but Terence gripped it like a vise.

"Let go of me!" she screamed. She jerked her hand again and finally pulled it free. But one of Terence's heavy rings gouged a furrow in the thin flesh on the back of her hand. "Oh, no!" she cried when she saw the blood.

Pandemonium broke loose in the store. Dort grabbed a napkin from the holder on top of the deli case and pressed it on Shaney's hand to stop the bleeding. Scott and his two children came running from the back room. Little Miranda clung to her father and cried. The local customers scrambled out of their seats to see what was happening.

"Hey, what's goin' on there?" yelled one of the twins.

Roger took several long strides toward the counter. "You okay?" he called to Shaney.

Scott thrust the weeping Miranda into Dort's arms and rounded the corner of the counter, his limp exaggerated by his haste. He stood glaring up at the much taller Terence. "Get out!" he ordered.

"Hey, I didn't mean any harm," Terence protested.

"Get out!" Scott ordered again. "And don't bother to come back. You can take your business elsewhere."

Terence flashed Shaney a hateful look, then turned and stalked out of the store.

The hubbub of voices died down. All eyes in the store focused on Scott, who stood by the door, shaking with anger. "I'm trying to run a respectable business here," he said, "not some damn saloon."

Then he looked at Shaney, his eyes cold and hard. "If you have to carry on with people like that, then do it somewhere else and on your own time."

White-faced and trembling with fear and shame, Shaney held the crumpled napkin to her hand and leaned against the counter to keep from collapsing.

"Take her to the restroom and fix up her hand," Scott snapped at Dort. "There's a first-aid kit in the cupboard."

Dort handed her sobbing granddaughter back to Scott, then put an arm around Shaney's waist and guided her to the ladies' room.

"What was going on out there?" Dort asked as she dabbed ointment on Shaney's wound. "Was Terence threatening you?"

Shaney nodded. "He's mad at me. I saw him at the hog roast. We talked for a little bit, and then he went to hang out with his friends. Later he came back, and he was drunk and he wanted me to dance with him. He made a mistake and . . . and . . . he called me Seffie. I was so upset, I ran away from him."

"Oh, honey, that's awful! I'm so sorry. He's such a jerk." Dort pressed the bandage into place on the back of Shaney's hand. "What did he say to you tonight?"

Shaney opened her mouth to respond, but a lump of sickness swelled in her stomach and rose to her throat. She leaned over the commode and vomited repeatedly. When she was done, she rinsed her face in the sink, and then slumped wearily against the wall. Dort looked at her questioningly.

"He said . . . ." Shaney covered her face with her hands and slid down against the wall until she was in a crouching position. Dort got down on her knees next to her so she could hear her muffled words.

"He told me that if my mother wasn't too good for him, then I wasn't either. He screwed my mother, and now he wants to do me. Oh, God, Dort, I want to die. I just want to die."

"That son-of-a-bitch!" Dort exclaimed. "That sick, perverted son-of-a-bitch!"

"Don't say it," Shaney said. "Don't say I told you so."

Tears of sympathy welled in Dort's eyes. "Honey, all of us women get played for a fool sometimes. Even the best of us get taken in."

She gathered Shaney into her arms and held her. "I hate that man for what he did to you. I'm never going to speak to him again, except to give him a piece of my mind."

"Scott thinks it was my fault," Shaney sniffled. "He must have a pretty low opinion of me."

Dort released her embrace. "Oh, that Scotty! He was too rough on you out there. I'll have a talk with him later. He doesn't think badly of you, honey. He thinks the world of you. Don't you know how he feels?"

"What are you talking about?" Shaney asked, bewildered.

"Scotty probably thought you and Terence had something going on, and he was jealous. He was just covering up his feelings when he was gruff with you."

Shaney stared at Dort, incredulous.

"Oh, honey, haven't you seen the way Scotty looks at you? You mean you never knew?"

"Are you saying Scott has feelings for me?"

"Of course he does! I know my only son better than I know myself, and I can see plain as day how he feels about you. He's too scared to approach you, beautiful young girl that you are, what with his leg the way it is."

"Oh, Dort, I just never thought of Scott in that way."

"Hush," Dort said. "I'm not suggesting anything. I'm just trying to explain things. I know that bum leg puts a lot of women off. Anyway, Scotty needs someone older, someone to be a mother to those children. You wouldn't have any business trying to mother them. You've got your hands full with Cody."

Shaney buried her face in her hands again. "This is all too much! I can't take it."

"Do you want to go home early?" Dort asked. "I'm sure Scotty will let you."

Shaney slowly stood up and inspected her appearance in the mirror. "No," she said. "I'll get it together."

Dort must have had a few words with her son, because later that evening, Scott came to Shaney to apologize. "I'm sorry about what I said earlier this evening. I was out of line. What happened wasn't your fault. Terence Buckwalter is a jerk, always has been a jerk, and always will be a jerk. If he comes in again, don't hesitate. Call the police."

Chapter 11

After mailing her letter, Shaney expected a quick response from her sister. But when a week passed with no letter from Sissy, she began to wonder if her sister had changed her mind about arranging a meeting.

Maybe this will all blow over, she thought. *Maybe all this fuss won't amount to anything.* The idea brought a sense of relief, but also a pang of disappointment.

The awaited response finally came on the ninth day. This time, the envelope was addressed to Shaney only. She took the letter to her bedroom and sat on the bottom bunk to read it.

When she opened the envelope, a small photograph fell out. She stared at it, knowing that the pretty woman with the sleek auburn hair was her sister. The serious blue eyes seemed familiar.

I think we look a little bit alike, Shaney thought. Sighing, she ran her fingers through her unruly curls. *Well, so much for hoping that Sissy won't be good-looking. Damn it, she's gorgeous!*

She unfolded the letter and began to read.

October 10

Dear Shaney,

I'm absolutely ecstatic that you said yes to a reunion! My dream is coming true! Now if we could only persuade Stella to come, everything would be perfect.

I'm sorry I didn't get back to you right away. I had to touch base with Starly in order to make the plans. It may sound like I'm rushing things, but I hope we can meet two weeks from today, which will be Saturday, October 24.

There's a reason for my urgency. Starly is a month away from delivering her baby. If we wait any longer, it will be too risky for her to travel, and after her baby is born, it will be very difficult for her to get away.

I'm going to suggest a plan, and I'll count on you to let me know if it suits you. I want to treat my sisters to lunch at a lovely restaurant. Our reunion will be such a special event, and I want everything to be just right. The place I have in mind is a restaurant in South Bend called Madison Gardens. It's a historical landmark, a beautiful, romantic spot that should be perfect for our grand occasion.

Starly informed me she could get a driver to bring her to the restaurant. I hope you won't have any problem driving to South Bend. I don't know how well you know the city, so I'm enclosing a map and some directions.

I'd like to meet for lunch at 2:00 PM. That way, we should miss the noon crowd, and should have plenty of space and privacy for talking. I'll be there early, waiting for you in the lobby. I've enclosed a picture so you can recognize me.

So, shall we do it? Lunch at Madison Gardens, 2:00 PM on Saturday, October 24? Don't worry about anything, the treat is on me. Please call me as soon as possible to confirm the plan. As soon as I hear a yes from you, I'll make reservations for three. If Stella changes her mind, let me know right away, and I'll make reservations for four.

I can hardly wait until the day we meet!
Much love,
Sissy

As Shaney stared at the letter, she felt strangely numb. She knew a storm of feelings would hit her later, but for now she was calm. *There's not that much time,* she thought. *Only eleven days. What do I need to do first? Call Sissy and let her know I can come? No, I need to make sure I can get the day off.*

Little Stella had just gotten out of bed, and was banging around in the kitchen looking for something to eat. Shaney decided not to say anything about the letter. Bringing up the subject of the reunion would just put her sister in an ugly mood.

And Shaney had to admit to herself that she was glad Little Stella wasn't going with her. *I'll have a hard enough time handling this myself,* she thought as anxiety began pushing its way through her composure. *Little Stella wouldn't be able to pull it off. That girl in some fancy restaurant? Ha!*

Shaney waited impatiently for Scott to come into the store that afternoon. She knew she'd be pushing the limits by requesting another Saturday off. Scott had difficulty getting good weekend help, and he and Shaney had made an agreement: she would work all weekends with one Sunday off per month, and he would pay her an additional dollar per hour for that time.

He came in with Dort around 4:00 PM. "How's it going, Shaney?" he asked.

He's in a good mood, Shaney thought. *Now's the time to ask.* She took a deep breath. "Scott, I've got a favor to ask you. Can I have the day off on Saturday, the twenty-fourth?"

Scott raised his eyebrows. "I thought we had a deal about weekends. I just gave you a day off several weeks ago."

"What's this about?" Dort asked. She looked at Shaney's anxious face. "Is the twenty-fourth the big day?"

Shaney nodded.

"Oh, let her go, Scotty!" Dort's sweet, but forceful, command left her son with no option but to consent to Shaney's request. "She's going to meet her sisters! This is a once in a lifetime opportunity for her!"

"Okay, go ahead," Scott said grudgingly.

Once Scott agreed to her request, the anxiety Shaney had been warding off hit her full force. A jagged pain shot through her abdomen, and she almost doubled over in agony.

"Oh my God, Dort!" she wailed when Scott was out of earshot. "I don't think I can do this!"

"Sure you can," Dort said. "What's the plan?"

Shaney pulled Sissy's latest letter from her pocket.

"Wow!" Dort exclaimed as she read the letter. "Madison Gardens! I've never been there myself, but my sister and her husband went there for their anniversary last year. They said it was something else. Really, really nice!"

"Dort," Shaney whimpered, "I've never been to a fancy restaurant in my entire life!"

Dort chuckled. "Well, honey, it's time you broaden your horizons. You'll love it."

"Oh my God, Dort!" Shaney wailed again. "What am I going to wear? What do people wear when they go to places like that? I don't have anything but jeans!"

"Tell you what, hon. We'll solve that problem. I'll take you shopping."

"With what? I don't have money to spend on fancy clothes."

"We can go to a discount store and get something nice."

"I bet Sissy doesn't shop at discount stores!"

"Okay then, we'll go to a department store and see what we can find on sale, something nice enough for when you meet that prissy sister of yours." Dort chuckled. "Anyway, you silly girl, have you thought about what Starly will be wearing? You could wear anything in your closet, and you wouldn't look as out of place as your Amish sister."

"Oh," Shaney said. "I didn't even think about that."

"Can I borrow your cell phone?" Shaney asked Dort when she was ready to take her evening break. "I need to call Sissy to tell her I'll be there. It'll be too late to call by the time I get home."

"Oh, absolutely!" Dort dug into her purse to find her phone.

Shaney stepped outside the store and nervously dialed her sister's number. She waited as the phone rang four times. Just as she was ready to hang up, she heard an answering machine click on. A pleasant male voice said, "You have reached the Hartman-Gray residence. We're unable to come to the phone. Please leave a message."

Unnerved by the unexpected voice, Shaney was speechless for a few seconds. Then she realized she was running out of time, and she began speaking in a breathless rush. "Sissy, this is Shaney. I'm calling to let you know that I got the day off and I'll see you next Saturday at 2:00 o'clock at the restaurant. Thanks. Bye!"

The answering machine clicked off, and Shaney hung up feeling stupid, wishing she could erase her message and start over again. But she was relieved that at least she'd been spared the anxiety of talking to a live person.

That Friday morning, Dort drove Shaney to Plymouth for their shopping expedition. After browsing through racks of clothing and trying on half a dozen outfits, Shaney emerged from the store's dressing room wearing a short black skirt, a low-cut top, and high-heeled sandals.

"That's it!" Dort exclaimed as she scrutinized Shaney from head to toe. "That outfit's perfect on you. It really sets off those gorgeous long legs. God, I'd kill for legs like that!"

Shaney cringed as she handed the sales clerk her money, knowing what a bite the purchase was taking out of her budget.

The following week was a quiet one for Shaney. Her thoughts about the upcoming reunion absorbed her so completely, she appeared withdrawn. Dort sensed that Shaney needed space, and wisely left her alone.

On Wednesday evening, Shaney realized she hadn't talked with her father about borrowing the car. Standing in the doorway of his bedroom late that night, she asked, "Can I take the car on Saturday, Dad? I'm planning to go to South Bend to meet Sissy and Starly."

Jimmy slowly sat up in his king-size bed, his eyes filled with a hundred questions. "So you made plans then? Goin' to South Bend, huh? That's quite a ways to take that old Buick. Whatcha gonna do when you get there?"

"Sissy wants to treat us to lunch at Madison Gardens. She says it's a really nice restaurant."

Jimmy shook his head in amazement. "Never heard of such a place." Then the heavy folds of his face sagged. "Never been to any fancy restaurant myself. But here you are, gettin' the chance."

He sighed as he rummaged around on his cluttered bedside stand for a cigarette. "Your little sister ain't wantin' to go with you, is she?"

"Nope, Little Stella said she's not interested."

"Oh." Jimmy lit his cigarette. "Probably just as well."

"Why'd you say that?"

"Little Stella's the type of girl that's better off stickin' close to home."

He's right, Shaney thought. *He's not holding it against me for not taking her along. He knows she'd be out of place.* She suddenly felt sorry for her ungainly sister.

"So can I take the car then?" Shaney forced herself to be patient. She knew her father didn't like to be pushed.

Jimmy sucked deeply on his cigarette. "You ain't never driven in South Bend, have ya? Ain't like drivin' in Plymouth, you know. I remember takin' my mother to a doctor's appointment up there ten, twelve years ago. They got them one way streets with four lanes runnin' through town. You never know which one you're supposed to be in. Purty near had myself a nervous breakdown drivin' in South Bend."

"I've got a map." Shaney tried to sound confident. "Sissy sent me directions. I can do it."

Jimmy took another drag on his cigarette. "Well, go ahead then. I ain't gonna be the one to stop you, if you got your heart set on goin'."

"Thanks." Shaney turned to leave the room.

"That Buick's been leakin' oil," Jimmy called after her. "Be sure to put a quart in before you go."

Friday night, after a long evening at work with a silent, grim-faced Shaney, Dort decided it was time to venture a question. "Are you scared about tomorrow?"

Shaney nodded. She knew if she spoke about her feelings, she'd fall apart.

"Come over to my house in the morning," Dort said. "I'll help you with your hair and makeup. We'll get you all dolled up for your big day."

Chapter 12

Early Saturday morning, Shaney awoke with a start. *Oh my God,* she thought, *this is the day!*

It was still dark outside, and she knew it was too early to get up. But the longer she lay in bed, the more terrifying her thoughts became. She finally slipped out of her bunk and wrapped a blanket around her shoulders to ward off the morning chill. Settling herself into Little Stella's recliner, she flipped through the television channels, but could find nothing interesting enough to distract her racing mind.

Unable to sit still, she went to the kitchen, where she ran water into the sink and threw herself into the task of washing a mountain of dishes. When she finished scrubbing down the table and countertops, she looked at the clock. It was 8:00 AM, time to start getting ready.

She wrinkled her nose in disgust as she stepped gingerly into the grungy bathtub and pulled the moldy shower curtain closed. Standing under the feeble stream of water, she vigorously scrubbed her hair and body until she felt the hot water turn cold. As she stepped out of the tub, she tried not to touch any surface in the dirty bathroom for fear of sabotaging her efforts to make herself presentable.

She moved quietly around her bedroom so as not to wake her sleeping son. She searched through her dresser drawer to find a pair of panties and a bra that weren't totally ratty. *No one will know the difference,* she told herself. But it seemed that wearing her best underwear was part of putting her best foot forward.

She slipped on a pair of blue jeans and a tee shirt, then gathered up her new skirt, top, and shoes. As she picked up her stained canvas handbag, she realized it didn't go with her outfit. *Oh, well, it'll have to do.*

She was glad no one else in the trailer was up. With her nerves on edge, she was in no mood to deal with nosey questions or irritating comments. Carrying her load of new clothing, she slipped out the front door of the trailer and drove to Dort's home six miles west of town.

"You're early," Dort said when she answered her front door still wearing her nightgown and robe. "It's not going to take that long to get you gorgeous."

"Sorry," Shaney said. "I was too nervous to stay home." As she glanced around the living room of Dort's immaculate house, she felt a twinge of shame. *I'm glad she's never seen where I live.*

"We can use my bedroom," Dort said. "I told my husband he had to stay out of the way."

She led the way to her room and gestured for Shaney to sit on the chair positioned in front of the large dresser mirror. Shaney was dismayed by the array of cosmetics Dort had laid out. "Are we going to use all these?" she asked.

Dort smiled. "Probably not. Anyway, we're going to do your hair first." She ran her fingers through Shaney's curls. "How about if I cut some layers in it? That would make it more manageable."

"Whatever," Shaney said. "I trust you know what you're doing."

"Don't worry," Dort said. "I used to do hair. Matter of fact, I had a salon here in the house."

She draped a cape around Shaney's shoulders, wet her hair down with a spray bottle, then picked up a pair of scissors and began snipping.

"Do you want to wear it curly or sleek?" she asked when she was finished. "Either way would be pretty."

"You mean you could make it sleek?" Shaney asked, incredulous. "I didn't think it could be anything but curly."

"Sure, I can smooth it out," Dort said. "I can blow it dry using a large styling brush.

"Go for it." Shaney watched in amazement as Dort applied a styling product and deftly smoothed out her hair with the blow dryer. *It looks as good as Sissy's,* she thought.

"Now for the makeup," Dort said. "I don't think you need much foundation with that flawless complexion of yours."

She studied Shaney's face, choosing colors that suited her skin tone, and then coached her through the process of applying eye shadow, liner, mascara, lipstick, and hint of blush on her cheekbones.

"There!" she said. "How do you like it?"

"Wow!" Shaney said. "It doesn't even look like me." The face in the mirror, framed by the sleek hair, belonged to a stranger, a sultry glamour girl. She giggled. "I look kinda hot!"

Dort laughed. "That's what I wanted to hear!" She handed Shaney the tube of lipstick. "Put this in your purse for touchups." As an afterthought, she handed her the mascara. "Better take this, too. Sometimes family reunions get a little weepy."

She stepped back, a sly smile on her face. "Now honey, I've got something for you. You get dressed while I go get it."

Shaney stood teetering on her stiletto heels when Dort returned to the bedroom and handed her a small box. She opened it to find a pair of large hoop earrings.

"They're beautiful!" she exclaimed. "Dort, you didn't need to do this!"

"Just a little good luck gift, honey," Dort said. "It's not every day a girl goes off to meet her long-lost sisters. I thought they'd go with your outfit."

After Shaney put on the earrings, Dort stood back and surveyed her from head to toe. "Now if you aren't a feast for sore eyes! Absolutely stunning!"

Shaney's eyes welled with tears.

"Don't cry now, for Heaven's sake!" Dort scolded. "You'll ruin your makeup!"

"I don't know if I can do this, Dort," Shaney whimpered.

Dort shook her head. "Shaney girl, you've got a problem with the way you view yourself. You're always thinking you can't do something, that you're not good enough. That's not true, and it doesn't do any good to think that way. You'll do fine, I promise."

"You're really sure?"

"Absolutely! And I'll tell you one thing for certain. You've got to be the prettiest one out of all the sisters. It's not possible for either of them to be any better looking than you. Now don't be hanging your head like that. You've got nothing to be ashamed of. No matter what happens, keep your chin up!"

Shaney swallowed hard and managed to smile.

"Do you have enough money?" Dort asked.

"I've got ten bucks," Shaney said. "I already filled the car with gas, and Sissy said lunch was on her."

"I think you'd better take more, just in case. You never know what'll happen. I can loan you twenty dollars."

Shaney shook her head. "No, you don't need to do that. "I'll go pick up my paycheck at the store." She glanced at her watch. "I better get going. I need to cash my check before the bank closes at noon."

She looked at Dort, and her eyes welled with tears again. "Thanks so much. I don't know what I would've done without your help."

"Hey, don't be getting mushy on me." Dort escorted Shaney to the front door and stood on the steps as Shaney walked gingerly to the car on her stiletto heels.

"Keep your chin up, girl!" she called as Shaney backed the car out of the driveway.

As Shaney drove into town, she desperately hoped the Speedway store would be empty. No one she knew had ever seen her dressed like this, and she wanted to avoid a scene. Her heart sank when she pulled into the lot on the north side of the station and saw half a dozen vehicles parked there.

As she walked toward the store, the door opened and Roger Whalen stepped out. It was the first time Shaney had seen him without his cap, and she noticed that his black hair was thick and wavy. He was wearing tan slacks and a cotton shirt in a dark pattern. She realized she'd never seen Roger on a weekend, out of his workday garb, and was surprised at how handsome he looked.

"Hi, Roger," she said. "I almost didn't recognize you without your cap.

He stopped and stared at her. "Shaney! I didn't recognize you. You look really pretty."

"Thanks," Shaney said, blushing.

"Is it some special occasion?"

"Actually, it is. I'm on my way to South Bend to meet my two older sisters for the first time."

"Wow! That is quite an occasion!" Roger smiled shyly. "I hope you have a nice time."

"Thanks, Roger."

He glanced toward where his pickup truck was parked and clicked his remote control key to unlock the door. Then he looked at Shaney again. "How's your hand?"

She held out her hand so Roger could see the faint red streak left from where she'd been gouged by Terence's ring. "It's healed up."

"Is Mr. Buckwalter still bothering you?"

"No, I haven't even seen him since he came into the store that night. I hope I never lay eyes on that jerk again."

Roger looked down at his feet. "Let me know if he does bother you. Let me know if you have any problems with him, okay?"

"Okay, I will," Shaney said, taken aback by Roger's concern. "Thanks."

Roger suddenly looked nervous. "Well, I've gotta get going. I've got stuff to do."

"Have a good day," Shaney called after him as he walked toward his truck.

"You too," Roger called back. "Have a good time with your sisters."

Before Shaney opened the door to enter the store, she turned to watch Roger pull out of the parking lot. As she lifted her hand to wave, she wondered about the uncharacteristic warm feeling in her heart. Roger smiled and waved back.

But the warm feeling vanished the minute she stepped into the store. The twins and three of their cronies were sitting in the two front booths. They immediately assaulted her with a cacophony of whistles and ribald comments.

"Whee! Look at them purty legs!"

"Was ol' Roger out there hittin' on you, sweetheart? I'm gonna have a talk with that guy."

"Boy, don't she clean up nice!"

"Where you goin', honey? Can I come with you?"

Refusing to look at the leering men, Shaney headed straight for the back room where Scott sat at his computer.

"What are you doing here, Shaney?" he asked, looking up from his work.

"I came to get my paycheck. I need to cash it before the bank closes."

Scott rifled through his desk drawer, then handed her an envelope. "You look nice," he said.

Red-faced, Shaney snatched the check and rushed out of the store, almost tripping as she caught her heel on the doormat.

"Be careful on them high heels, honey," one of the men called.

At ten minutes to twelve, Shaney pulled the Buick alongside the drive-through window of Belmont's First National Bank. She signed the back of her check, and then stuffed the money the teller handed her into her handbag. Then she circled around the bank and pulled into the northbound traffic on Main Street.

"Here we go," she said aloud. She glanced down at the front of her blouse and thought she saw the thin fabric pulsating with the wild pounding of her heart.

Part IV

REUNION

"What do you think about this outfit, Stephen? Do you think it's okay for meeting my sisters?" Cecily stood in the doorway of her husband's home office, wearing open-toed pumps and a flowered dress with a fitted waist and full skirt.

Stephen glanced up from his computer screen. "It's fine. You look lovely."

"Do you think it might be too flashy?"

"Well, maybe. You might want to tone it down a little bit."

"You're right. I don't want to overdo it on our first meeting."

A few minutes later, she stood in the doorway again, this time wearing dark slacks and a light blue sweater. Her hand resting on the door frame trembled visibly. "I'm scared, Stephen. I'm more nervous than I've ever been in my entire life."

"Why?" he asked. "This is what you've been wanting for months. Why should you be nervous?"

"I don't know, I just am. Well, I'm ready to go."

"Come give me a kiss," Stephen said. "You'll do fine, honey. You always do."

Before she turned her key in the ignition, Cecily checked her watch. She had plenty of time to make the ten-minute drive to Madison Gardens, to get there early enough to be prepared and waiting when her sisters arrived. As she drove, she practiced deep breathing exercises, trying to relax. *Everything's going to be just fine,* she told herself.

But as she approached the railroad tracks crossing Ironwood Drive, she noticed the traffic was slowing down. She strained to see what was ahead, and saw a train inching along at a snail's pace.

"It's okay, Cecily," she said aloud as the traffic in front of her came to a stop. "Don't panic. You still have plenty of time."

And then the trained stopped.

"Oh God, no!" she cried. *This can't be happening! Starly and Shaney will get there, and I won't be waiting for them like I promised. What if they think I've stood them up? What if they don't wait for me and go home? Oh God, don't let this fall apart!*

"This brings back old memories, doesn't it?" Shirley Price said to Annie as she drove her van north on S. R. 331 toward South Bend.

"What do you mean?" Annie asked.

"When you were a little girl, I'd pick you up at your parents' house and drive you to meet your birth mother and sisters. Remember that? Martha would ride along with us. We'd meet Seffie at some halfway point, usually McDonalds. Then Seffie would take you back to her house. That was more than twenty years ago, wasn't it?"

"Yes, it was." Annie turned her face to look out the window. The memory made her feel blue, and she didn't want to spoil her excitement.

"You'd be fussing and fretting all the way to McDonalds, telling your mother you didn't want to go, demanding to know why she was making you go. But once you got there, you'd be okay. Seffie would usually bring the other two girls with her. You'd stop crying the minute you'd see your older sister. You'd jump out of the van and run up to give her a hug."

Annie smiled, her excitement returning at the thought of seeing Sissy again.

"What was that name they called you? It was so unusual."

"Starly. They called me Starly. That's my real name, you know."

Shirley focused on her driving, trying to remember where she needed to turn. Then she said, "I was so glad when those visits were over and done with. Letting you go was so hard on Martha. You'd be crying on the way there, and she'd be crying on the way back home. I was worried about you, too. You were hardly more than a baby, so young to be put through something like that."

"Yes." Annie wished Shirley would get off the subject.

"Anyway," Shirley said, "who would've guessed that all these years later I'd be driving you to see your sisters again?"

"That's something, isn't it?" Annie said. Then she winced and placed her hand on her abdomen.

"How's the baby doing?" Shirley asked. "Is everything all right?"

"It's fine. It moves around a lot, and it kicks so hard it wears me out."

"I can imagine. You're such a little thing to be carrying such a big load. When's the baby due?"

"In about two weeks. Luke was afraid to let me come. He thought it was too close to my due date, but I told him I'd be all right. I just couldn't miss this day."

"Yes! This is a big day! Are you nervous, Annie?"

Annie buried her face in her hands. "Oh, Shirley, I'm very nervous! I'm so excited, but I'm nervous, too."

"Why?"

"Can't you imagine, Shirley? My sisters are English, and I'm Amish. I'm afraid I'll feel out of place. I'll look so different from them. What if they're embarrassed to be seen with me? And I know I'll say something wrong. When I'm nervous, I say stupid things."

"Annie, I think you're worrying for nothing. Living in this community, your sisters are used to being around Amish people." Shirley pulled into Madison Gardens' parking lot. "Well, here we are. Should I let you out at the front door?"

Annie stared at the massive building, taking in the grandeur of the architecture and the picture-perfect landscaping. Enormous mounds of chrysanthemums and asters added splashes of fall color to the magnificent scene. She turned to Shirley, her face stricken with terror. "Shirley, I don't know what to do! I've never been to a place like this before!"

"You'll do okay, Annie. Let me help you out. I don't want you to fall." Shirley got out of the driver's seat, walked around the van, and steadied Annie as she stepped down.

Annie clutched her arm. "I don't know what to do, Shirley," she repeated.

Shirley put her arm around Annie's shoulders. "Just go in the front door. We're a little early. If your sisters aren't there, just sit down on one of the benches in the lobby and wait. Do you know what your sisters look like?"

"Sissy sent me a picture. I'll recognize her. But I don't know what Shaney looks like."

"Annie, I was going to do some shopping, but I've changed my mind.

I'm going to stick around. I brought a book with me, and I'll park over there under that tree." Shirley pointed to a large shade tree overhanging the far end of the parking lot. "If you need me, I'll be right there."

"Thank you, Shirley. I think I'll be alright."

Shirley watched Annie's back as she laboriously climbed the flight of steps to the restaurant entrance. The diminutive figure in the long blue dress and black bonnet looked vulnerable and lonely.

"God, let her be okay," Shirley murmured.

The stubborn train refused to budge, indifferent to Cecily's sense of urgency. "Stay calm, Cecily," she said aloud. "Think, don't panic." *What do I do now? I'll call someone. I can't call Starly, she doesn't have a phone. Shaney. I'll call Shaney and tell her I'm running late.* She reached into her handbag for her cell phone. Her fingers shook as she dialed Shaney's number.

"Hello." The voice was Jimmy's.

"Hello, Jimmy. This is Cecily Hartman-Gray. Is Shaney available by any chance?"

"No, she's not. She left the house this morning before I got up. I imagine she's on her way to South Bend about now."

Of course she's on her way, Cecily thought, her heart sinking. "Do you have any way of reaching her?" she asked.

"Nope, I don't. We only have the one phone."

"Okay. Thanks, Jimmy."

"You girls have a good time."

"We will, I'm sure." Cecily ended the call and stared forlornly at the unmoving train. Then she dialed her home phone number.

"Stephen!" she wailed when he answered. "There's a train stopped on the tracks here at the Ironwood crossing! I can't get through! I'm going to be late! I tried calling Shaney, but she's already on her way, and she left her phone with her dad."

"Relax," Stephen said. "The train's got to move eventually."

"We have a reservation for two o'clock. Starly and Shaney will be there, and I won't be there to meet them like I promised. They'll think I let them down."

"They'll be okay," Stephen said. "They're adults. They'll figure it out."

"Stephen, I'm scared this is all going to fall apart!" Cecily's anxiety mounted as she waited for a response from her husband.

After a lengthy pause, Stephen said, "Why don't you call the restaurant? Let the hostess know you'll be running late. Have her tell your sisters."

"Thanks, Stephen, that's a wonderful idea. Can you get the number for me?"

"Sure, hang on." A minute later, he read Madison Gardens' number from the phone book. Cecily jotted it down, then dialed. The phone rang six times before a breathless hostess answered.

"We're really busy," she said after Cecily informed her of her plight. "I don't have time to be delivering messages. I can't promise you anything. And I can't hold your table indefinitely. If you're not here in twenty minutes, I'll have to give it to someone else."

"Oh, please don't!" Cecily pleaded. But the hostess had already hung up the phone.

Shaney glanced at her watch as she hurried up the steps leading to Madison Gardens' main entrance. It was three minutes before two o'clock.

"Good," she whispered to herself. "I'm right on time." She paused as she clutched the ornate handle of the massive door, wondering what would transpire when she walked inside. She felt as if she were about to enter a portal into an entirely different dimension.

The lobby was packed with people, some sitting on benches, others standing in impatient clusters, waiting to be seated at their tables. She scanned the crowd, looking for the face in the photo her sister had sent her.

A man seated to Shaney's right glanced up and down her body, then smiled at her. Shaney averted her gaze, feeling conspicuous in her short skirt. She continued to scan the crowd for signs of Sissy. No one looked remotely like her picture.

Am I in the right restaurant? Shaney asked herself. *Did I come on the right day?* She wished she'd brought Sissy's last letter with her, so she could double-check the date and location.

Her attention was drawn to her left when a baby began to cry. The baby's parents had two other small children in tow, and were busy trying to corral the restless youngsters. At the end of the family's bench, a fourth child sat, angled away from Shaney, wearing a dark dress and bonnet.

They must be having a Halloween party here, she thought. *She's dressed like a little pioneer girl.*

As if aware of being watched, the girl shifted in her seat, turning slightly, her eyes meeting Shaney's. Shaney saw she was not a little girl, but a young woman, whose bulging abdomen overpowered her tiny frame. *Oh my God, it's a pregnant Amish woman! It's got to be Starly!*

Shaney smiled, and the Amish woman smiled back. Shaney willed herself to walk over to her, but her feet seemed to be glued to the floor. The Amish woman studied Shaney's face curiously, and then opened her mouth to speak. Shaney couldn't hear what she was saying over the din of the crowd, so she was forced to muster the courage to move closer. As she towered over the tiny woman on the bench, she felt as if she were seven feet tall.

"Are you Starly?" she asked, her voice sounding hoarse in her own ears.

"Yes, I'm Starly." The young woman continued to gaze curiously at Shaney's face. "Are you Sissy?"

"No, I'm Shaney."

"Oh!" Starly laughed. "I didn't think you looked quite like the picture Sissy sent me. But you do look a little bit like her."

Shaney's legs felt like jelly, and she was afraid she might teeter off her high heels. "Is Sissy here?" she asked.

"I don't think so," Starly said. "I've been waiting here for awhile, and I haven't seen her. I was beginning to think I made a mistake and came on the wrong day. I'm so glad you're here."

The hostess called the family with the three young children, and they vacated the bench where Starly was sitting.

"Sit here with me." Starly patted the seat next to her.

Shaney obligingly sat down next to Starly, tugging on her skirt to cover as much of her thighs as possible. The two young women shared an awkward silence that seemed to go on forever.

Suddenly Starly turned to Shaney and reached out her arms for a hug. "My baby sister Shaney!" she chortled. Then she began to giggle, covering her face with her hands. The giggles turned into sobs.

"Are you okay?" Shaney asked, bewildered by Starly's emotional outburst.

"I'm sorry," Starly said. "I'm so nervous and excited that I don't know what to do with myself." She hugged Shaney again, subsiding into more giggles. Shaney started to relax and giggled along with her.

Starly released her embrace and gazed up at Shaney's face. "Baby sister, you are so pretty! So tall and so pretty! You look like a lady in a magazine!" She reached up and caressed Shaney's cheek.

Shaney was not accustomed to such a gesture, and the sweetness of it brought tears to her eyes. As Starly lowered her hand, Shaney caught it in her own. A surge of energy pulsed through Starly's tiny hand into hers, and Shaney felt a sense of kinship she'd never known before.

Starly smiled up at Shaney, her blue eyes sparkling. "How did you get to be so tall, Shaney? I'm so short, and you're so tall. I envy tall people. They see things I can't see, and they can reach everything."

"My dad's tall," Shaney said. "Do you remember my father Jimmy?"

"Yes, I remember Jimmy," Starly said. "He was nice."

"I guess he's pretty nice." Shaney decided the moment called for a focus on Jimmy's best attributes.

"My dad was short like me," Starly said. "I took after him." She scooted closer to Shaney and linked her arm through hers. "My beautiful tall sister!" She giggled again.

"Well, if you need anything from a high shelf while we're here, I'll reach it for you," Shaney said playfully.

"I wonder where Sissy is," Starly said a few minutes later. She was suddenly gripped by fear. "What if something happened to her?"

"This is weird," Shaney said. "She told me she'd be waiting for us."

"What time is it?" Starly asked.

Shaney glanced at her watch. "It's 2:20."

"Oh my!" Starly said. "She's really late." She looked up at Shaney. "What should we do? Do you think we should keep waiting?" She thought about Shirley in the parking lot, and was glad her driver hadn't left.

"How about if we wait until 2:30? If she's not here by then, it probably means she's not coming."

Tears welled in Starly's eyes. "I'll be so disappointed if I don't get to see Sissy. But at least I got to see you. Maybe today, it's just you and me."

"Nothing wrong with that," Shaney said.

Starly leaned back to survey Shaney's body from head to toe, trying to take in the entirety of her sister. *I wonder how I would look in clothes like that,* she thought. On impulse, she laid her hand on Shaney's bare thigh. "You have such lovely legs."

Shaney blushed, and Starly quickly withdrew her hand. "I'm sorry. Sometimes I do things before I think. That's the way I am."

Shaney covered her mouth, stifling a laugh. Then she leaned over and whispered in Starly's ear. "You're not the only one who thinks I have nice legs. That guy over there by the door has been staring at them ever since I came in. I shouldn't have worn such a short skirt."

Starly laughed, then put her arm around Shaney's neck and pulled her down so she could reach her ear. "I should've brought you a dress like mine. That would've covered your legs just fine."

Shaney clutched her stomach and doubled over with laughter. "Starly, you're a hoot! I had no idea. I thought Amish people would be more serious."

Starly cocked her head coyly. "Well, I've got news for you. I'm not very good at being Amish. Ask anyone, they'll tell you that."

After the two of them indulged in another paroxysm of giggles, Shaney laid her hand on Starly's belly. "How's your baby doing?" She gently caressed her sister's abdomen, surprisingly comfortable with the intimate gesture. "Is it a boy or girl?"

"I don't know," Starly said. "It will be a surprise."

"Oh, I felt it kick!"

"It's so happy to meet its Aunt Shaney."

"You're so much fun, Starly." Shaney thought her heart would burst with the affection she felt for her sister, the sister who lived worlds apart from her, yet seemed so close.

Sissy dashed up the front steps of the restaurant, out of breath and feeling off-kilter. *I'm a mess,* she thought as she entered the lobby. She was dismayed to find the restaurant packed with patrons. She ran her fingers through her hair and straightened her sweater, then surveyed the lobby for her sisters.

And then she saw a tall girl with long legs barely covered by a mini-skirt, her left arm resting along the back of the bench she was sitting on, loosely encircling the shoulders of a tiny woman in a long dark dress. The tall girl's right hand was resting on her companion's bulging abdomen. The two of them appeared to be engaged in a lighthearted conversation, punctuated by giggles.

Starly and Shaney! Sissy suddenly felt lightheaded and thought she was going to swoon. As she watched them, she felt profoundly relieved that they were there waiting for her, that they hadn't left, that they'd found each other. But at the same time, she felt disappointed. She'd pictured herself arriving early at the restaurant, poised and ready to greet her sisters, to make introductions, to take charge.

Her sisters were still unaware of her presence. *They've started the party without me,* she thought. *They don't even need me.* Taking a deep breath, she took several steps toward them. "Starly? Shaney?" she called.

"Shaney, there's Sissy!" Starly squealed. "Oh, isn't she beautiful!" She stood up as quickly as her pregnant body would allow and ran straight into Sissy's arms. The two sisters held each other tightly, neither making the move to let go.

"Oh, sweetie!" Sissy murmured into Starly's ear. "I'm so glad to see you."

Starly's body heaved with sobs. When she finally released her embrace and looked up at Sissy, she saw tears running down her sister's cheeks.

Sissy took Starly's face in her hands and kissed her on the forehead. "Starly, honey, you're an adorable doll. You look just like I remembered you. You haven't changed a bit."

Shaney's heart sank as she watched the affectionate interchange between her sisters. Only a minute ago, she'd had Starly's full attention, and had basked in the role of the adored sister. Now it looked like nothing existed for Starly except Sissy.

Shaney stared at her slender, auburn-haired sister, who looked poised and elegant in her tailored slacks and expensive sweater. *I look like a slut,* she thought as she compared her short skirt and low-cut top to Sissy's tasteful outfit. It struck her as odd that she felt more self-conscious about her appearance with Sissy than she had with Starly. As she stood up, she once again tugged her skirt down over her bare legs.

Suddenly, she realized Sissy's attention was on her. Sissy held out her arms for a hug, and Shaney bent down to receive her sister's embrace. Sissy took both of Shaney's hands in hers and stood back to gaze at her.

"Baby Shaney!" she exclaimed. "I never imagined you'd grow up to be so tall and so beautiful!"

Shaney forced a self-conscious smile. "It's nice to see you, Sissy."

"I'm so sorry for being late," Sissy said. "I didn't want it to be this way. I got held up by a train that stalled on the tracks."

"It's okay," Starly said. "We're just glad you're here now."

"No problem," Shaney added. "We found each other, and we were doing fine."

The hostess approached the group of waiting patrons. "Hartman-Gray party of three?" she called. "Are you ready to be seated?"

Sissy held up her hand. "We're here," she said. "We're ready."

What on earth was I thinking, bringing them here on our first meeting? Sissy asked herself after they were seated. She sensed her sisters' discomfort in the elegant setting. Shaney's eyes were downcast, while Starly stared around the room, taking in the ornate woodwork, the massive paintings, the fine tapestries, the fancy table setting.

"This place is a mansion," Starly said. "I've never been anywhere like this before."

Shaney glanced up. "Neither have I."

"Sissy, do you come here often?" Starly asked.

They think I'm above them, Sissy thought, kicking herself for her poor judgment. *I didn't mean for this to happen.* Aloud, she said, "Oh, no! I've only been here a few times, on very special occasions. I thought our reunion was special enough to be held here."

The waitress came with the menus, looking curiously at the trio of women in their contrasting outfits.

Starly giggled. "She doesn't know what to think about us." She looked up at the waitress, her eyes twinkling with humor. "We're sisters," she explained.

"That's nice," the waitress said, looking even more puzzled. "I'll be back in a few minutes to take your orders."

Shaney opened her menu, wincing when she saw the prices of the entrees. "Order anything you like," Sissy said. "It's on me."

"Are you sure?" Starly asked as she looked at her own menu. "These prices are so high! That's a lot of money!"

"I brought money," Shaney said, trying to sound confidant. "I can pay for my own." She began scanning the menu for the cheapest entree, knowing what a bite this would take out of her paycheck.

"No, really, it's on me," Sissy insisted. "I'll just put it on my credit card."

Shaney glanced at Starly, then shrugged. "Okay," she said to Sissy. *God, she and her husband must have a lot of money. She acts like this is no big deal.* The old bitterness welled in her again.

"I don't know what to order," Starly said, turning the multiple pages of the elaborate menu. "I don't know where to begin."

"What kind of dishes do you like?" Sissy asked. "Beef? Poultry?"

"Something with chicken, I think. Nothing too spicy." Starly patted her abdomen. "My stomach is a little sensitive these days."

"How about this?" Sissy pointed to an entrée listed under the poultry section of the menu. "It's really tasty, and not too spicy."

"Okay, thanks."

Sissy turned to Shaney. "Do you know what you want?"

"I think I'll have what Starly's getting," Shaney said, not wanting to reveal her own awkwardness with the menu.

"You know what?" Sissy said. "I think I'll order that, too. It sounds really good to me."

Shaney looked down to hide her smile. *She's trying really hard to make this go right,* she thought. Knowing that Sissy was also feeling uncomfortable made her seem less intimidating.

The waitress returned to take their orders, raising her eyebrows when the three of them requested the same entre.

"We're triplets," Starly said. "We do everything the same." She burst into giggles at the confounded look on the waitress's face.

"Starly!" Shaney playfully slapped her sister's arm. "You're such a nut!"

"We really are sisters," Starly said to the waitress. "Half-sisters. We all have the same mother." She pointed to Sissy, then to herself. "The two of us were adopted out." She pointed to Shaney. "She was raised by her father. We haven't seen each other for more than twenty years. We just found each other again. Can you imagine that? This is our grand reunion!"

"Seriously?" the waitress said. "You mean to tell me this is the first time in twenty years you've seen each other? My God, you ought to be on TV!"

"Well, there goes my mouth again!" Starly said after the waitress had gone. She clamped her hand over her mouth, as if to restrain herself from speaking.

"You were okay," Sissy said. "You didn't do anything wrong."

"I told Shaney out in the lobby that I have a problem. When I'm nervous or excited, things just pop out of my mouth before I can think."

"That just makes you fun," Shaney said.

Sissy began to panic when her sisters fell silent. *Now what do we talk about? I feel like I need a script, or something. I should've planned this better.*

She saw Starly place a hand on her abdomen and wince. "How are you feeling, Starly?" she asked. "Is everything okay with the baby?"

"Oh, it's just fine. This one is so active. I thought Daniel and Sarah were active, but this one has them beat. It kicks up a storm."

"Cody was really active, too," Shaney said. "And he's still active. I can't keep up with him."

Sissy listened as Shaney and Starly launched into a lively discussion about their children's mischievous ways. "You'll have to bring Cody over to play with Daniel and Sarah," Starly said. "Daniel would love showing Cody around the farm."

"How will you manage after the baby comes?" Shaney asked. "I can't imagine taking care of three!"

"Oh, my mother will help," Starly said. "And the ladies in my church will bring in meals until I'm back on my feet. And Luke is so good. He already does so much to help. I'm not worried." She looked at Sissy. "Do you wish you had children?"

Sissy felt her face redden. "I hope to have children someday. Maybe sometime soon."

"How many children do you think you'll have, Starly?" Shaney asked.

"Oh, probably lots!" Starly caressed the curve of her abdomen. "Luke and I can't seem to leave each other alone."

Shaney burst into laughter. "I can't believe you just said that, Starly!"

Sissy smiled at Starly's humor. *This is a different turn of events,* she thought. *I didn't expect Starly and Shaney to have this kind of connection with each other. They don't even need me.* Refusing to succumb to that negative thought, she straightened her slumped shoulders and willed herself to rejoin the interaction.

"I have something in common with each of you," Starly said when she and Shaney stopped laughing. "Sissy and I are both married, and Shaney and I both have children."

"Is Cody's father anywhere in the picture?" Sissy asked Shaney.

"No, not at all," Shaney said. "Our relationship didn't last long. He moved back to Mexico after he found out I was pregnant. He's never seen Cody."

"A Mexican man?" Starly's eyes widened with interest. "You were with a Mexican man? This is like a fairy tale. Did you love him? Were you heartbroken when he left? Tell us all about it."

"There's not much to tell," Shaney said. "I was upset for awhile. But I don't think I was ever really in love with him."

"Is there anyone special in your life now?" Sissy asked.

"No," Shaney said.

"That can't be true," Starly protested. "You're so beautiful. Men probably line up to take you on a date."

"I'm sure you could have your choice of men," Sissy added.

Shaney smiled, basking in her sisters' attention. "It's not that they don't ask. But a year ago, I took a vow."

"What kind of a vow?" Sissy asked.

"I swore off men for a year. I was having so many problems with them, I said to heck with it."

"But the year's up," Starly pointed out.

"Is there anyone you're interested in dating?" Sissy asked. She and Starly looked at Shaney expectantly.

"No, I don't think so."

"Oh, come on now," Sissy said, smiling coyly. "You're holding out on us. Are you sure there isn't somebody?"

Shaney looked down, embarrassed. "Well, maybe. But it's too soon to tell."

The waitress brought their triplicate order, and for a few minutes, the conversation centered on the delectable food.

Then Starly said, "You two look quite a bit alike. Same eyes, almost the same hair."

Smiling, Sissy laid her hand on Shaney's arm. "It's a compliment to say I look like this gorgeous girl."

Shaney ran her fingers through her sleek hair. "I don't usually look like this. My hair's actually curly. My friend straightened it for me this morning."

"We're tall, medium, and short," Starly said, pointing to Shaney, Sissy, and then herself. "I'm short like my dad, and Shaney's tall like her dad. How about you, Sissy? What size is your dad?"

Sissy felt her chest tightening with pain. "I don't know what size my dad is," she said, staring down at her half-empty plate. "I've never seen my biological father. I don't even know his name."

Shaney's eyes widened. "You really don't know anything about him?"

"No, I don't know anything. Nothing at all." Sissy looked intently at her. "Do you know something?"

Shaney averted her gaze. "Not really. I only know what people say."

Cecily gripped the arms of her chair, excitement and apprehension coursing through her body. "What do people say about my father? Please tell me, Shaney."

Shaney took a deep breath. "My dad told me this, and I've heard other people say it, too. When our mom was fifteen, she crashed a frat party at Notre Dame. They say some college student got her pregnant. They say both of them were drunk, and that our mom didn't even know who he was."

Sissy felt the energy drain from her body, and the room began to spin around her. Leaning her elbows on the table, she buried her face in her hands. It seemed like her sisters were far away, and she was alone in the world of Shaney's shocking revelation.

My father was a college student, she thought. *He must've been fairly intelligent if he was attending Notre Dame. Wow, he certainly had a lapse of judgment when he slept with my mother! But then I'm glad he did, because I wouldn't be me if he hadn't. I wonder what he looked like. What was he interested in? What was he good at? What was his major? Oh my God, Evan would want to know this! I wish I could tell him. He said I must've had an intelligent father.*

The thought of her former friend and confidant filled her with sadness, adding to her emotional turmoil.

She felt Starly's gentle hand on her arm.

"I'm so sorry," Shaney said. "I shouldn't have said anything."

Sissy raised her head. "Don't be sorry, Shaney. I've wondered about my biological father my entire life. Now at least I know a little bit about him. Thanks." She took a deep breath, trying to orient herself again. "I'm sorry I got so upset. I feel kind of out of it right now."

"Sissy, you don't need to be perfect for us." Starly's voice chimed strong and clear, like an oracle proclaiming a profound truth. She reached out and took Sissy's hand in hers. Shaney took her other hand.

Sissy felt the warmth from her sisters' hands running up through her arms, all the way to her heart. Tears trickled from her eyes, but she didn't extricate her hands to wipe them.

Triggered by Sissy's emotion, Starly sobbed into her cloth dinner napkin. As Shaney watched, she dabbed at her own eyes with a tissue from her handbag. She was surprised at the tenderness she felt toward Sissy. *She's not so high and mighty after all. She needed my help. We're all the same now.*

"Speaking of fathers," Sissy said after the trio had regained their composure, "how's Jimmy doing?"

"He's doing okay." Shaney felt strangely openhearted toward her father. "He's on disability. He's got a bad back, and he doesn't get around very well."

"He was a nice man," Starly said. "He was good to us."

"Yes, he was," Sissy added. "I always felt safe when Jimmy was around. He treated Starly and me like we were his own children."

"My dad's talked a lot about the two of you," Shaney said. "He gets down on himself because he wasn't able to raise all of us together. He thinks he screwed up."

She saw Starly and Sissy exchange glances, and imagined they were both glad they hadn't been raised by Jimmy. She wished she hadn't revealed her father's regrets.

"Bless his heart," Sissy murmured. "Tell him we don't hold it against him."

Starly looked thoughtful. "I believe everything turned out exactly the way it was meant to be."

"You're probably right," Shaney said. "The two of you were better off where you were." She looked down at her hands clenched on her lap. *I'm not saying anything more about this. I'm not telling them how awful it was, how awful it still is.*

"How's Stella?" Sissy asked, breaking the awkward silence that had fallen over the three of them. "We don't know anything about Stella, do we Starly?"

"Little Stella spends most of her time looking after Dad," Shaney said. "It works out well that way." She knew she was sugar-coating the situation, but she felt uncharacteristically protective of her younger sister. "And she watches Cody when I go to work."

"What does Little Stella look like?" Starly asked. "Does she look like you?"

"She's tall like me," Shaney said, "but she's kind of heavyset, like my dad. She favors the McDaniel side of the family. She's got curly hair and hazel eyes."

"I'm sure she's pretty in her own way," Starly said.

"I suppose so." Shaney considered the possibility for the first time.

The waitress appeared and began clearing dishes from the table. "Take your time," she said to the sisters. "There's no rush. I'm sure you have lots to talk about."

"Here's something I don't know about the two of you," Starly said after the waitress had gone. "I don't know your middle names. I'm Starly Ann. What about you two?"

"I'm Shaney Rose," Shaney said.

"Shaney Rose!" Starly exclaimed. "How lovely! Like a beautiful flower. It suits you perfectly."

"It sounds like the name of a singer or a movie star," Sissy added. "Someone exotic."

Shaney had never in her life felt like she was anything better than ordinary, but at that moment, she felt exquisite. The feeling was so foreign, it made her uncomfortable. "So what's your middle name, Sissy?" she asked, trying to divert attention away from herself.

"My adoptive parents named me Cecily Dawn," Sissy responded. "Our birth mother didn't give me a middle name. The only name that ended up on my birth certificate was Sissy. I guess back then, Seffie didn't have it together enough to give me a proper name."

"She never did get it together," Shaney blurted out.

"That's what I was afraid of," Sissy said. "I was hoping it would be different."

The three sisters looked at each other sadly. "We've been sitting here talking for over an hour, but we still haven't talked about our birth mother," Sissy observed.

"I don't know what to say about her," Starly said. "I never knew Seffie very well. When I was little, I refused to believe she was my birth mother. I thought she was lying when she told me that. Nobody could convince me that Martha Bontrager wasn't my real mother."

Sissy chuckled. "I remember you arguing with Seffie about that."

"We didn't get along very well," Starly admitted. "I acted like a brat. I didn't like Seffie at all. I'd tell my adoptive mother I hated Seffie, and she'd tell me not to say that. Now I feel bad about it. I wish I could've had a chance to see her one more time, just to tell her I'm sorry for being so ornery."

"You know," Sissy said, "I feel the same way. When I was little, I knew she wanted to be my mother, but I didn't want her. There was no way she could measure up to my adoptive mother. When I got older, I was afraid Seffie felt rejected by me. I wish I could've made it up to her."

"Tell us what you remember about her," Starly said.

"She was so young, not grown up at all. Compared to Eileen Hartman, she was a child who didn't know the first thing about being a mother. Eileen took care of me so well, and I was used to that. I think I grew up a lot when I stayed with Seffie, because I had to learn to fend for myself."

"I remember her as hot-tempered," Starly said. "She didn't have patience for anything. My adoptive mother would talk to me when I misbehaved. Seffie would hit me."

"I remember that," Sissy said. "That would make me so sad." She held Starly's gaze, the two of them remembering the time when a distraught Starly's only comfort was her big sister.

Then Sissy turned to Shaney. "You probably remember more than we do."

"Not really," Shaney said. "I was only two the last time I saw her. When both of you were taken away, my dad and I and Little Stella went to live with my grandmother. But for a couple of years after that, our mother would come around our trailer every now and then, mostly at night, cussing and screaming at my dad to let her see us. I don't remember her face, but I remember how she sounded."

"Did you want to see her?" Starly asked.

"Sort of, but not really." Shaney shuddered, remembering her mother's shrill, angry voice. "The way she carried on scared me to half to death."

Her sisters stared at her wide-eyed, waiting for more information. She took a deep breath and continued. "In a way, it seems like I knew her, because I've heard so many stories about her. For some reason, people in Belmont like to talk about her. I guess the way she acted gave people a lot to talk about."

"Shaney, I feel awkward bringing this up," Sissy said. "But I know we need to talk about it at some point. Starly and I don't know how Seffie died. Do you know?"

Shaney suddenly felt heavy, and a dark mood crept over her. *Oh my God,* she thought, *why did this have to come up today?*

"Yes," she mumbled, "I do."

Four-year-old Shaney is awakened by the sound of insistent knocking on the trailer door. She hears Jimmy's heavy footsteps as he goes to answer it. Sitting up in bed, she listens intently to the sound of muffled conversation. Then she hears the door close.

She scrambles out of bed and peers out her bedroom window. She sees two men in dark uniforms walking toward the police car parked at the curb.

"Oh, no!" she hears Jimmy cry out. She runs to the living room, where her father sits on the sofa, head in his hands, weeping in big,

noisy gulps.

Big Stella sits in the recliner, sniffling, dabbing at her tears with a tissue. "You know I never cared for the woman," she says to Jimmy, "but I wouldn't wish this on my worst enemy."

Three days later, Jimmy, Big Stella, Shaney, and Little Stella sit in their car in the parking lot of Jordan's Funeral Home, watching people walk into the building. "Do you really think we should be here?" Big Stella asks. "It makes me nervous bein' around all these Dickersons."

"It's my obligation to make a showin', seein' as I'm the father of her children," Jimmy says. He's wearing a crisp plaid shirt he bought from Wal-Mart the day before. He gets out of the car and helps his daughters out of the back seat. Big Stella carries Little Stella into the building, while Jimmy leads Shaney by the hand.

As they approach the closed casket, Jimmy lifts Shaney and holds her in the crook of his arm. He points to the casket. "Your momma's in there."

Shaney stares at the big brown box, then turns to her father, puzzled. "Why?"

"Because she's dead."

"Why?" she asks again.

"Because somebody hurt her real bad."

Seized by a feeling of desolation, Shaney wraps her arms around her father's bulky frame and hides her face against his shoulder. He pats her little back.

"It's okay," he says, "it's okay."

Shaney was suddenly aware that she'd been silent for several minutes. She raised her head and saw both of her sisters gazing at her, concern on their faces. She opened her mouth to speak, but couldn't form the words.

Sissy laid a hand on her arm. "Shaney, you don't need to tell us if it's too hard."

Shaney excelled forcefully. "No, I might as well tell you now. It was homicide. She was murdered." She saw the horrified looks on her sisters' faces, and then covered her own face with her hands.

"Oh my God," Sissy whispered. "How?"

"Stabbed," Shaney said from behind her hands. Her voice sounded mechanical in her own ears, and she realized this was the first time she'd ever spoken of that dreadful event. "Stabbed eleven times, to be exact. It had to do with drugs. She was running a meth lab."

Starly pressed her napkin to her mouth. For a moment, she thought she was going to lose her lunch.

"Starly, are you okay?" Sissy asked.

Starly clutched her abdomen. "I think I'm going to be sick. I'd better go to the ladies' room." She stood up, but her legs shook so badly, she sank into her chair again.

"I'm sorry, I'm so sorry," Shaney said. "I shouldn't have told you."

Sissy scooted her chair next to Starly's, laying her hand on her sister's back. "Breathe, honey. Take some deep breaths."

Everything around Starly seemed blurry, and she teetered on the verge of passing out. But after several minutes of Sissy gently rubbing her back, her dizziness subsided.

"It's my fault," she whispered when she could speak again. "It's all my fault."

"How on earth could this be your fault?" Sissy asked.

Tears began pouring from Starly's eyes. "I was such a bad kid. I drove her crazy. If I hadn't been so bad, maybe we could've all stayed together, and she wouldn't have gotten into that kind of life. It feels like I killed her."

Sissy placed her hand on Starly's cheek, gently turning her face so they were looking into each other's eyes. "Listen to me, Starly. It's important to me that you believe what I say. It's not your fault that Seffie died. Not even a little bit. None of what she did was your fault. The way she treated you wasn't your fault. All those times she yelled at you and hit you weren't your fault. You were just a little kid. She was the adult. Promise me you won't ever think that way again."

Starly smiled bleakly at her sister. "I'll try not to."

Sissy scooted her chair back to her own place at the table. She'd been so busy consoling Starly that she hadn't fully absorbed Shaney's shocking news. As sorrow washed over her, she recalled the moment Evan had informed her of Seffie's death. *I guess I shouldn't have been surprised. I should've known that if she died at twenty-six, it wouldn't be of natural causes.*

"Wow," she said to her sisters. "This is so heavy. I can't even wrap my mind around it."

"She never had a chance to live a full life," Starly said. "That's so sad."

"I wonder whether she could've learned to live better if she'd lived longer," Cecily mused. "Before I knew she'd died, I had a fantasy about finding her grown up and settled down and living a decent life. She'd be forty-three now, I think."

"She was pregnant. When she died, she was eight months pregnant. It was a boy." As soon as the words popped out of her mouth, Shaney wondered why she'd introduced yet another painful topic.

Sissy drew a sharp breath. "Oh my God! We would've had a brother!" She gestured toward the empty chair at the table. "We could've had a brother sitting here with us."

"We do have a brother," Starly said, her tears flowing again. "We'll meet him in Heaven. I'm sure of that."

Shaney suddenly became aware of how exhausted she felt. She could tell by her sisters' faces that they were as emotionally drained as she was.

"But you know what?" Sissy said. "We've survived all this mess. That says something about us."

Smiling through her tears, Starly pumped her fist into the air. "We're strong!"

"I guess we are," Shaney said. "I guess it takes something special to survive being the daughter of Seferina Dickerson."

Then Sissy's eyes took on a far-away look. "Do either of you have dreams about Seffie? When I began my search for you, I started having strange dreams about her."

Starly's eyes widened with interest. "I had one."

"In my dreams, Seffie's always saying she's sorry," Sissy said, "in one way or another."

Starly's face turned pale. "It was the same in mine! She looked so sad, and she told me she was sorry. Oh, this is so weird, it gives me goose bumps!"

"I've never had any dreams about her," Shaney said.

"I can't believe this!" Sissy suddenly exclaimed. "Look what's coming!"

Their waitress, followed by the manager and several other restaurant employees, approached their table carrying a small, beautifully decorated cake.

"I know it's not anybody's birthday," the waitress said, "but we wanted to do something for the three of you on this special occasion." She set the cake in the center of the table.

The manager stepped forward with a camera. "May I take your picture? We have a wall where we hang pictures of celebrities who come here."

"We're not celebrities," Sissy protested.

"But this is a rare occasion, to have family members reuniting after years of being apart. We feel pretty special that you chose Madison Gardens for the reunion."

Sissy looked at her sisters. "What do you think? Starly, are you allowed . . . ?"

Starly waved her hand dismissively. "It's not a problem. Amish people aren't supposed to get their pictures taken, but I'm sure God will forgive me this one time."

Sissy pulled a camera from her handbag. "Will you take some shots with mine, too?" she asked the manager.

The manager took several shots of the sisters sitting at the table with the cake, and then had them pose for standing shots. "Let's have the tall girl in the middle. The other two squeeze in close, please."

The sisters wrapped their arms around each other's waists, giggling.

"We'll leave you alone to enjoy your cake," the manager said after the picture-taking session was over. "We hope you'll come back to

Madison Gardens for your next reunion."

"We won't be having another reunion," Starly said.

"Oh?" The manager looked taken aback.

"Because we're not going to be separated again," Starly explained. "We're going to be together forever."

The sisters looked at each other and smiled.

"That's absolutely right!" Sissy said.

"Together forever!" Shaney added.

"I didn't know you were home, Cecily," Stephen said as he walked into the living room. "I was downstairs and didn't hear you come in."

Cecily was curled up on the sofa, covered by a blanket. "Hi," she said. Her voice sounded weak.

Stephen sat down on the other end of the sofa. "You okay, honey?"

Cecily pushed the blanket aside and slowly sat up. "Yes, I'm fine. Just tired. Really, really tired."

"How did your meeting go? Did you get there on time?"

"I was a little late. But everything was wonderful."

"Everything you hoped for?"

"Well, it was different than what I expected. But it went really well. It was perfect, actually. I learned a lot of new things about my birth family, and I was just lying here trying to make sense of everything. My mind feels like it's been blown to pieces."

Stephen looked at her questioningly. "This was a big deal for you, wasn't it?"

"Yes!" Cecily said. "It was a huge deal! I spent months thinking about it, fretting about it. And it finally happened. I can hardly believe it. It seems unreal. We had a marvelous time, but now I'm so tired, like all the energy has been drained out of my body. And I feel kind of . . . lost."

"So was it all worth it, then?"

"Absolutely, Stephen. Absolutely!"

"Are you and your sisters going to see each other again?"

"Oh, yes, of course we will. We plan to keep in touch by letters, maybe phone calls now and then. I'm sure we'll visit, too. I'll have to figure it out. I mean, we'll have to figure it out."

Stephen caught the nuance of what his wife was saying. "This isn't all on you any more, is it?"

Cecily sighed deeply. "No, it's not. I don't have to do it all. My sisters are capable people, and they can make plans, too."

Stephen scooted close to Cecily, encircling her with his arm. She leaned her head against his shoulder.

"Honey," he said, "I want you to know I'm proud of you. While you were gone this afternoon, I started thinking about what an amazing thing you did. I didn't pay much attention to you while you were working on finding your sisters. At best, I was indifferent, and at the worst, I was a jerk. I'm not a very sentimental person, and until today, I didn't understand what you were doing. I wasn't any help to you, but that didn't stop you. You had a dream, and you followed it."

Cecily nodded. "Yes, I did."

"You wanted this thing so much," Stephen continued, "and you made it happen. Not many people have the courage to do that. I know I wouldn't even have the guts to take the first step. You're one of the strongest people I know, Cecily." He squeezed her shoulders and brushed her cheek with a kiss.

"I don't feel strong, Stephen. Right now, I feel exhausted. My thoughts are spinning, and I don't know what to do next."

"For right now," Stephen said, "you need to rest. I'm sure you'll know what to do when you're rested up."

"You're right," Cecily sighed. "I know you're right."

Stephen got up and tucked the blanket around her as she stretched out on the sofa again. "Just rest while I fix dinner," he said. "Are you hungry? Knowing you, you were too wound up to eat much for lunch."

Cecily smiled fondly at her husband. "Actually, I'm ravenous. I feel like I could eat and eat and eat, then sleep for a week."

"You've been so quiet, Annie," Shirley said as she turned the van onto the gravel road leading to Luke and Annie's farm. "Are you okay?"

Annie stared out the window. "Yes, I'm okay," she mumbled.

"You don't seem very happy. Did something go wrong between you and your sisters?"

Annie turned to look at Shirley. "Oh, no, everything was wonderful. It's just that . . . ." A sob escaped her throat. "It's just that . . . ."

"What is it, Annie?"

Annie's tears began to flow. "I want two things at the same time," she wailed. "I want my sisters. I enjoyed them so much, I could hardly say goodbye to them. It broke my heart to leave them. I almost felt like I was English, just like them. I didn't feel out of place at all."

"Oh?"

"But it was too much for me, and I can't wait to get home to be with Luke and the children. Really, most of me doesn't want to be English. How can I want both things? I feel like I'm losing my mind!"

"Annie, I don't see the problem. Why can't you have both things? Why can't you be Amish and stay with Luke, and still keep the relationship with your sisters? You can visit them just like you did today, and then go back home."

Annie looked thoughtful. "I guess you're right. But it jars me to go from one thing to another. This afternoon, I got so comfortable with my English sisters that I almost forgot I was Amish. Now I'm going home to my Amish family, and I have to switch back to that way of life. I think Olan Amstutz was right."

"Olan Amstutz? Who's he?"

"He's a friend. He goes back and forth from being Amish to being English. But he told me it wouldn't be that easy for me. He's right. It's hard."

"Annie," Shirley said, "it'll get easier with time. Each time you visit your sisters, you'll adjust easier as you go from one world to the other. Remember how you did it when you were a little girl?"

Annie smiled. "It wasn't easy, but I managed it. I'm an adult now, and I'll do okay." Suddenly, she doubled over in pain. "Ouch!"

Shirley shot her a concerned look. "You're in labor, aren't you? I'm glad we're almost home."

Five minutes later, Shirley's van pulled into Luke and Annie's long driveway. Luke stepped out the front door to greet them, followed by Daniel and Sarah. Shirley rolled down her window.

"Luke," she called. "I think you'll need to help Annie out of the van. She's having contractions."

"Oh, no," Luke said, "I was afraid this would happen if she traveled."

"Is the baby coming early?"

"Just by a few weeks. Nothing to worry about."

As Luke opened the van door, Annie doubled over with another contraction. Luke allowed her to sit until the wave of pain passed. Then he gathered her in his arms and lifted her from the van.

She looked up at him, both smiling and teary-eyed. "Don't worry, Luke, I'm not going anywhere."

"What do you mean, you're not going anywhere?" Luke chuckled. "You're going into the house. Shirley, could you give the midwife a call and tell her Annie's in labor? And would you please stop by her mother's house on your way home and give her the news?"

Annie put her hand on Luke's cheek as he carried her into the house. "I mean I'm staying here with you and the children."

Luke laughed. "Where else would you go, silly?"

Little Stella looked up from her magazine as Shaney walked through the front door. "God, Shaney, you look like a slut in that outfit."

"Whatever!" Shaney waved her hand dismissively. "Where's Cody?"

"He's playing at Ryan's."

Shaney grimaced. She'd paid Little Stella to watch Cody, not to send him to a friend's house. But she decided not to make a big deal out of it. She wasn't going to let her sister burst the bubble of her good mood.

After her foray into another world, Shaney felt disoriented in her old surroundings. She glanced around the living room, taking in the array of newspapers, food wrappers, and soda cans. Then she looked at the kitchen to her right, already messy after she'd cleaned it that morning. Turning to her left, she saw the litter of dirty clothing and shoes in the hallway.

The scene didn't induce its usual response of shame and despair. She had a feeling that all of this was going to change for her, very soon.

She felt the urge to tell someone about her afternoon's adventure. Little Stella wouldn't be the audience she needed. She spotted Jimmy's cell phone on the coffee table and took it to the kitchen, where she dialed Dort's number. No one answered, and when the machine kicked on, she ended the call instead of leaving a message. *I'll talk to her tomorrow at work,* she thought.

"Is that you, Shaney?" Jimmy called from his bedroom. "Come on back here and tell me about your meeting."

Shaney found her father lying in bed, still sleepy-eyed from his nap. He heaved himself into a sitting position.

"Did you have a good time?" he asked.

Shaney sat down on the foot of his bed. "Yes, I had a really nice time."

"How are them little girls?" Jimmy's eyes looked soft.

"They're good." Shaney hesitated, unsure whether she wanted to share the details her father longed to hear. But suddenly they spilled from her.

"Sissy isn't like what I thought she'd be. She's not uppity, she's really nice. She's kind of quiet. She's pretty, but not all that fancy. She's loving and caring."

"The same as when you were little girls," Jimmy said. "Sissy was always tryin' to be helpful, wantin' everybody to be happy."

"She's kind of medium height, shorter than me," Shaney continued. "We look a little bit alike. But Starly's really short, very tiny. She's like a little Amish doll with a big belly. She's pregnant, you know. She's going to have her baby soon."

"Really? Is this her first one?"

"No, her third. She's got a boy Cody's age, and a two-year-old girl. Someday, I'll take Cody to visit his little cousins."

"Now wouldn't that be somethin', seein' Cody runnin' and playin' with them little Amish kids!"

"Starly's really funny." Shaney chuckled. "You never know what's gonna pop out of her mouth. It's surprising, coming from an Amish girl."

Jimmy laughed heartily. "Then I guess she hasn't changed, either. That young'un was a character, she was. Always up to somethin'."

"I like her. I like Sissy, too. I like both of them more than I thought I would."

"I'm glad," Jimmy said. "I was afraid this meetin' wouldn't go well, that you'd get your feelin's hurt, or somethin'. I didn't wanna say nothin' to spoil it for you. But I'm glad it turned out good."

Shaney suddenly felt vulnerable to the tenderness in her father's voice, and she lowered her head to avoid meeting his gaze. "Dad," she said, "they asked questions, and I had to tell them."

"About what?"

"About our mother, how she died."

"Oh." Jimmy's body sagged. He closed his eyes, shaking his head slowly. "I was hopin' that wouldn't come up. But then it was their mother, and they'd wanna know."

"Starly got really upset and blamed herself."

"I know how that feels," Jimmy said, his voice shaking. "I blamed myself, too. For so many years, I kept tellin' myself that if I woulda stayed with Seffie, maybe I coulda kept her in line. But then I woulda lost you girls. There was just no way a situation like that coulda turned out good."

Shaney nodded, wiping a tear from her eye with the back of her hand. "I know."

"I just feel so bad," Jimmy said. "I feel so bad for all you girls."

Shaney felt an urge to reach over and take her father's hand, but the thought embarrassed her. With her hands clenched together in her lap, she said, "Sissy and Starly talked about you. They said they want to visit you sometime."

Jimmy looked startled. "Oh, I wouldn't want them to see me like this," he mumbled. "Not like this, not in this trailer."

Shaney averted her eyes, not knowing how to respond to her father's insecurity.

"Well, maybe I could sit and have coffee with them somewhere," he said. "We could meet at the station. You might wanna show them where you work."

"That might be okay," Shaney said. "We can think about it."

When she stood up and turned to leave her father's bedroom, she was surprised to see Little Stella standing in the doorway, a look of interest disrupting the usual placid lines of her face.

EPILOGUE

November 7

Dear Starly and Shaney,

My mind keeps going back over the wonderful time we had at Madison Gardens two weeks ago. I'm enclosing copies of the photos that were taken of us. They turned out really well, don't you think? I have a hard time believing that this really happened, that I actually found my sisters. I have to look at the photos to convince myself that my dream came true.

Starly, I keep wondering whether you've had your baby yet. Tell us everything about your little bundle of joy!

What's new in your life, Shaney? How's Cody?

I have some wonderful news to tell you. I'm finally going to be a mother! Stephen and I are so happy! Our baby is due next June. I think I'm ready, but I'm scared. I'm going to count on my little sisters for advice about taking care of a baby.

Stephen says it's time for me to take a break from my job. I know he's right. I'm exhausted. So I'll work for just a few more months. Then I'll take time off to be with my child, may a year or two, maybe more.

I miss both of you, and I can't wait to see you again.

Love always,

Sissy

November 12

Dear Sissy and Shaney,

I'm so excited to tell you about my baby girl! She was actually born the day of our reunion. Isn't that amazing? I started having labor pains on the way home, and she was born that night, just a few minutes before midnight. So the date October 24 is special to me for two reasons.

I wanted my daughter to have part of each of us in her. So I named her Rosanna Dawn: Rose for Shaney Rose, Anna for Starly Ann, and Dawn for Cecily Dawn. She's beautiful and healthy, and she has blue eyes like the three of us. Daniel and Sarah love her, and Luke is so proud. We're all doing well.

Sissy, I was happy to receive the photos you sent. I was afraid to let anyone see them, because I thought they might disapprove. But in the end, I just had to show them to my mother. She wasn't upset with me. She said all three of us favor each other.

My mother wants to have you and your families over for a home-cooked meal sometime. She'll be so tickled to meet you.

Congratulations on your pregnancy, Sissy! You shouldn't worry. You'll be a wonderful mother. Daniel, Sarah, and Roseanna Dawn have lots of adoptive cousins on my side of the family, but now they have blood cousins.

Shaney, are you ready to tell us about that special man in your life? I just know you have somebody!

I'm looking forward to seeing both of you again. Let's not wait too long! You may not recognize me without my big belly. I'll soon be thin as a rail, running after my three children.
Love to both of you,
Starly

November 30
Dear Sissy and Starly,

I've been thinking a lot about you. Thanks for the pictures, Sissy. My dad was so happy to see them. He wanted one of them, so I bought a frame for it, and now he has it sitting on his nightstand. He says that in his heart, the two of you are part of his family.

Congratulations, Starly, on your baby girl! That's so cool that Roseanna Dawn has all three of our names. She's our reunion baby!

Sissy, I think it's wonderful that you're pregnant. I've been talking to Cody about his cousins. He doesn't understand what a cousin is, because he's never had one before. Now he has three, going on four.

Okay, Starly, you're right. I do have a special man in my life. I've been dating Roger for over a month. He's shy, but he's really a nice guy. He's so different from the other guys I've dated. He's got a good job, and he treats me like a queen. And he's good with my son. He doesn't have any children of his own, so he likes spending time with Cody.

Somehow, he can get Cody to settle down and listen, without even yelling at him. Cody already wants to call him Daddy. I tell him it's too soon, that he should just call him Roger. But I really think Roger is going to be around for a long time. We're good together.

Here's another good thing in my life. In January, I'll start classes to get my GED. Maybe I'll go to college after that, who knows? Roger tells me I'm smart enough to do it.

Remember when the two of you talked about your dreams about our mother? Well, two nights ago, I had a dream that freaked me out! The three of us were sitting around the table at Madison Gardens. All of a sudden, Seffie walked into the room and sat down in the empty chair. I don't remember how she looked in real life, but in the dream, I knew it was her. She had a beautiful smile on her face. She kept looking at us and smiling, and then she said, "My sweet daughters, I'm so proud of you." Then she disappeared. The dream seemed so real, it gave me the shivers.

Little Stella said the next time we get together, she wants to come along. That totally shocked me, because the last time she wasn't a bit interested. But she stared at the pictures of us at the restaurant for a long time. Maybe something clicked in her brain to make her change her mind.

We definitely need to get together again soon. We shouldn't waste any more time staying apart.

Love forever,
Shaney